SILAS DEER BURDEN HOUSE

1 ROOM OF MR. AND MRS. TORREY'S SITY
2 CHAMBER
3 MISS TORREY'S ROOM
4 GUEST CHAMBER
5 GUEST CHAMBER WHERE MRS. BURDEN'S BODY WAS FOUND
6 MISS BURDEN'S ROOM
7 MISS TORREY'S BEDCHAMBER

THE MURDERER'S MAID

A Lizzie Borden Novel
By Erika Mailman

bonhomie ◯ press

THE
MURDERER'S
MAID

ISBN: 978-0-9970664-4-9

Library of Congress Cataloging-in-Publication data available upon request.

Printed in Hong Kong.

Interior design by Rose Wright.
Cover design by Andy Carpenter.

This book has been set in Bembo regular.

10 9 8 7 6 5 4 3 2 1

Published by Bonhomie Press, an imprint of Yellow Pear Press, LLC.
yellowpearpress.com

Distributed by Publishers Group West

To Christa,
for all the love and support.

CHAPTER 1

Bridget

AUGUST 4, 1892

Bridget Sullivan would later learn that the mundane paths her feet took that day were important, worthy of mapping, as if she were a queen whose bannered progress changed the fates of kingdoms. Yet she was just a servant in a dour household, dipping her rag into the vile spice of vinegar to ruin her hands.

She'd spent the morning trotting back and forth to the barn to refresh the pail of water as it blackened, cleaning the windows of the grit that clung to the glass. Fall River, Massachusetts, was a mill town, its air a smoke-infused vapor that clogged the lungs and smudged the panes.

Her trips to the barn would later be seen as a counterdance to the interior goings-on. Although the windows were high, and she used a brush affixed to a long pole, she also used a ladder. Had she been able to peer into *this* window, what would she have been able to see just before ten o'clock in the morning? At *that* window, would she have affected movements inside? Had she already moved to the north side of the home by the time blood was itinerantly spreading in the upstairs guestroom?

By ten-thirty, she was back inside, washing the other side of the glass. She heard her employer, Andrew Borden, trying to enter through the side screen door as usual, but for some reason the hook and eye had been engaged and, although she rushed to help, he'd already given up and gone to the front door, ringing the bell.

She ran to the front door and worked at the locks. There were no fewer than three to manipulate on this single door. She couldn't understand why today they were giving her trouble. Easy enough to unlock a door from the inside, wasn't it? On the front stoop outside, Mr. Borden would be impatiently awaiting entrance into his own home.

This family was fervent in its use of iron and latch to keep out the intruders of the world. Even interior doors were locked, as if kin feared kin.

"Oh, pshaw!" she said, angry now. From behind her, she heard a peal of laughter.

An inexplicable sound that doubled in its merriment as Bridget turned to glance at Miss Lizzie, stationed on the stairs. The middle-aged woman, her face broad and only a few shades short of handsome, thick-necked and somewhat jowly, yet with lovely auburn hair, stood about four steps down from the top. What was so comical about a door refusing to open?

The key finally turned, and Bridget pulled the door wide, stepping back to let Mr. Borden pass. He entered, his face an atlas of discontent. Predictably, he said nothing, not a scold nor a joke, as he brushed by her to enter the parlor with his newspaper. He wore his usual black double-breasted Prince Albert frock coat, even in summer, a prideful choice of warm garment to display his wealth. At sixty-nine, he showed his age with his snow-white hair and chinstrap beard, and deeply hooded dark eyes. The thinness of his downturned mouth seemed to hint at the parsimony for which he was known throughout town.

After the distraction of his passage, Bridget turned again. Lizzie walked past her, having descended, following her father into the sitting room.

Bridget was to forever remember the heartless bout of laughter on the stair, tossing at night thinking of the soul that could offer up such unholy gaiety when, had Miss Lizzie only turned her gaze, she would have been at eye level with the shape on the floor of the second-floor bedroom. It was the face-down body of Abigail Borden, the stepmother despised as any in a fairy tale, her head bearing vicious gashes from a hatchet.

Mrs. Borden had been crawling, her body partially under the bed, trying to protect her head. Anyone looking into the room halfway down the stairs would see her heaving her way toward the door, extinguished of life.

Had Lizzie been laughing at the sight of her devilish handiwork, her victory over the stepmother who had plagued her into seething odium? Or had she been laughing at the idea that the house with its faulty locks was preventing her father from entering, giving him temporary respite from an identical fate?

If Bridget had paid attention, she might've prevented the second death. If she had mounted the stairs or gone to fetch the dirty linens, she would've found the body. Instead, Mrs. Borden lay silent and lifeless, her ear to the floor as if listening to her husband, a level below, who, while dozing after reading the *Providence Journal,* accepted the same hatchet blows.

Perhaps it had been the washing of windows that saved *Bridget's* life. If her task had been the sweeping of floors, would she be another body savagely attacked and left to cool in a bath of her own blood? Was it the luck of her pastime to not be in the house as an intruder prowled through its rooms, as she fecklessly washed and rinsed glass on the other side? Or was it more than luck—did someone know her routes and movements and plan the dual crimes on a day and at times when the master and mistress were left unattended by even the mildest of possible assistance?

She would never forget the sights of that day: Mr. Borden recumbent upon his sofa, his body politely slumped in a way that kept his Congress boots off the furniture, his face an unidentifiable festival of shattered bone, cartilage, and brain.

At Miss Lizzie's request, Bridget had raised the alarm, running to fetch the doctor across the street, and thus the whole charade of an investigation began. Bridget was sent upstairs to get a sheet to cover Mr. Borden's body—finding the second corpse as she climbed, which had been easily visible to Miss Lizzie when her laughter had chimed at the same spot where Bridget then quailed.

CHAPTER 2

Bridget

NOVEMBER 9, 1889

Her interview with Mrs. Borden three years earlier had been a brisk, smileless affair. "The Remingtons have good words for you," Mrs. Borden had said, referring to the family with whom Bridget had last been employed. Bridget had left, thanks to the roving gaze of Mr. Remington, and before that, had left attorney Charles Reed for the same licentious fault. Smoldering looks led to wandering hands, so she was always quick to move on. She'd lived in three different states since coming to America three years earlier. Bridget was relieved Mrs. Remington had given her a good character, unaware of her husband's furtive appearances in the kitchen. Hopefully, working for this family, with Mr. Borden already so old, would put an end to the mischief.

Mrs. Borden, in her early sixties, was the kind of woman one could tell had never had a heyday. Her face and lips had a froggish appearance, her hair thin, yet her expression conveyed the kindness of the humble. She wore a fawn-colored gown of cotton with a blue sprig, and her obese body was surprisingly active; she moved in and out of chairs with, if not grace, at least energy.

"We expect good, solid fare. The grocery budget is standard, and we appreciate well-cooked meats and a variety of dishes on the table. Nothing too fancy or expensive. We do like sweets."

"Of course, ma'am," murmured Bridget. She wasn't certain if she was meant to reply.

"We have washing on Monday, ironing on Tuesday," Mrs. Borden ticked off the list. "We dress ourselves."

Bridget's eyes widened. This was fortunate. One less job in the morning and evening—and avoidance of the uncomfortable intimacy of buttons and sashes, of seeing no-longer-slender bodies in their chemises.

"Besides Mr. Borden and myself, Emma and Lizzie live here in the house. They're my stepdaughters, although I think of them as mine. I've been their mother since Emma was fourteen and Lizzie five. I'm not sure Lizzie even remembers her mother; she was only two when she died."

Bridget nodded. She'd heard a dozen such sad stories if she'd heard one. Women so often succumbed to the interior battles that made their wombs a grave. Headstones were frequently carved in tandem, for mother and child, named and often nameless. The Borden daughters had survived their mother and found their way through the thickets of childhood without the calming maternal fingers that could strip thorns from branches.

"You'll need only gather up their clothing and sundries for laundering," continued Mrs. Borden. "They do their own chamber work."

"Truly!" Bridget blurted out in confusion. So few duties! Did this household not understand the typical obligations of a maid?

"It's how we do it," said Mrs. Borden stiffly.

"And it's fine luck for any maid," Bridget quickly said.

"I'll show you the house." Mrs. Borden stood up from the kitchen table, pushed her chair in, and led Bridget into the dining room.

The next rooms—the sitting room and the parlor—were unremarkable, the furnishings simple. Bridget noted the old-fashioned florid wallpaper and paintings tilting off their piano wire. She was used to opulent interiors. Her two former Fall River employers lived in the Highlands neighborhood, where homes were built to impress and interiors suggested affection for expensive things: lamps with frosted glass hoods, vases shipped from the Orient sitting atop lacquered tables. Although Mr. Borden was rumored to be quite affluent, as the president of one bank, director of two others, and the owner of three textile mills in town, his house suggested a frugality that might not have been requisite.

Bridget was hired on a winter day, so the blinds were open, and the rooms filled with a cold light that seemed acceptable if not cheerful. It wasn't until months later that summer forced those same blinds down and curtains covered the hot glass, so the house grew somber as the world grew brighter. The rooms were darkened as if the family was leaving for the season, furniture now looming, corners in shadow. Bridget then loved the tasks that brought her outside. The hanging of wet laundry on the line, the gathering of kitchen herbs, could be stretched out, and she could wander over to the fence and talk to the Kellys' girl, Mary Doolan, who told her the history of the strained relations in that house, the sounds of arguing that often drifted out over the small lawns.

Bridget and Mrs. Borden now climbed the staircase to the second story and paused before a closed door at the top. "This is our spare room," said Mrs. Borden. She pushed it open and entered.

Inside, two women in their middle years sat in chairs near the bed, sewing. The room was large and airy, and Bridget noticed a sewing machine in the corner. The women looked up, aggrieved.

"Mrs. Borden," said the younger, with tightly-curled auburn hair and eyes so pale they appeared taken from a pewter version of her.

"I've asked you many times to knock before entering."

Bridget waited, askance, for Mrs. Borden's reaction. Who might speak to Mrs. Borden this way in her own home?

"I'm bringing the new maid around," said Mrs. Borden, ignoring the bold reprimand. "This is Miss Bridget Sullivan."

Bridget glanced at Mrs. Borden in disbelief. How could she pay no heed to such an affront? She looked back at the two women, who instantly returned to their work as if no one was in the room with them, heads bent, needles moving. Could these possibly be Miss Emma and Miss Lizzie—the women Mrs. Borden thought of as her daughters? But the younger had just referred to her as "Mrs. Borden"!

They were both plump, fastened in their chairs with nary an inch between them and the sides. The elder was slightly less so, perhaps considered more attractive, although she had the kind of misshaped eyes that made her look perpetually surprised. They both had nicely dressed hair, curls oiled into subservience, with straight parts. It was all Bridget could truly judge of them at this vantage point, with their heads bowed.

Before she realized it, Mrs. Borden had exited, leaving Bridget still staring. Miss Lizzie lifted her head, and Bridget was fixed by her contemptuous gaze. A slow wave of disquiet went up her arms, causing all the hairs to rise.

"She's gone on," said Lizzie coolly.

Without thinking about it, Bridget dropped a quick curtsy and spun out of the room. Behind her, there was only silence: no muffled laughter, no murmurs of amusement. She should've walked out right then and there, she'd think to herself later. Should've listened to her heart and stayed at a boardinghouse until another position became open, or even perhaps taken her place at the foot of a loom, bandying the shuttle back and forth like any other mill girl.

There was not a whit of welcome in that house.

She found Mrs. Borden in the next room, a small chamber with a bare dresser. A quilt made of plain scraps covered the bed. This family was wealthy—why weren't there silks and velvets in the pieced-together display of the heritage of worn-out gowns? Bridget looked again at Mrs. Borden's dress; it looked shabbier than she'd first noticed.

"This is Emma's room," said Mrs. Borden, and then, "through here is Lizzie's."

Surprisingly, Lizzie's room was an annex to Emma's with only the one door. It was even smaller. What penury this family lived in.

"We have to go back downstairs to view the other rooms on this floor," said Mrs. Borden. "They can't be accessed from this staircase."

On their way to the staircase, Mrs. Borden pointed to a door at the end of the landing, saying, "That's the clothes press."

As they began descending, Bridget glanced back at the spare room, whose door she had left ajar as she hastily left. The sisters were visible, quietly sewing, but by the time Bridget and Mrs. Borden reached the bottom, Bridget heard the door close above them.

They returned to the first floor and passed through to the kitchen in the back of the home, and to the side door entry, where Mrs. Borden mounted a second staircase. Bridget muffled a gasp. The master and mistress of the home used the servant's stairs to reach their rooms?

Mrs. Borden showed her the master bedroom and the side dressing room, then they ascended to the third floor, and the room that would be Bridget's. Up under the eaves, the room was tiny, the bed lodged beneath the slanted ceiling, but Bridget made only a cursory examination before nodding her approval—she wanted to return downstairs where it was slightly less oppressive.

They went outside where Mrs. Borden showed her the tools and the water pump in the barn. There was a kitchen garden plot now dormant for winter and a small yard. The entirety of her world now. Pinched and cramped and dim.

"And that's the lot," Mrs. Borden said, concluding. "I believe there's nothing more to show."

Bridget felt overwhelmed. "It's all in order," she said respectfully.

"That it is." For a moment, Bridget saw on the older woman's face something that she wished to say, perhaps something reassuring. After all, no one could have lived this way for years . . . surely, there was a time in Mrs. Borden's life when she'd been carefree and laughed like a girl. A time when the sullen women upstairs had also laughed, and she had been their mother in deed *and* name.

CHAPTER 3

Bridget

NOVEMBER 10, 1889

Bridget came back the next day by hack with her trunk. There was considerable traffic on Second Street, and the driver, a man in his mid-twenties like Bridget, had to wait a bit for it to clear to pull over in front of the house.

While they sat, Bridget took a good look at the clapboard facade of the Greek Revival home. While nothing grand like the residences on the hill, the Bordens' house boasted an off-center entry with two slim columns flanking the inset door. The inset was hardly enough to shake out an umbrella but gave the house a scant bit of style. A few stone steps led up to the door, while heavy shutters framed each window. A pitched roof, set aside by crossbeams as a triangle atop the house, supported several chimneys of varying heights. A neat, well-kept picket fence enclosed the pretense of a front yard.

The driver wedged the hack in between the two trees that shaded the front. Bridget climbed out, holding his hand, and wondered how to proceed. He removed her trunk and followed her to the side door.

Luckily, Andrew Borden emerged from that door to greet her. He looked to be in his seventies, with pure white hair and a gaunt frame.

"Welcome, Miss Sullivan. I'll take that up," said Mr. Borden cheerlessly.

Bridget looked quickly at the driver. Mr. Borden didn't seem up to the task due to his elderly build, and the driver was already protesting. "It's the burden of a moment, sir, and I'll spare your back," he said.

"It's unnecessary."

The driver, not a bad-looking man, with dark coloring and ruddy cheeks above the scruff of black beard, shrugged. "So be it." His services had been paid at the other end by her previous employers, and all that remained was to thank him.

She opened her mouth to do so, and he winked at her. She pressed her lips together and gave him her back. She knew what happened to maids who accepted winks.

Mr. Borden had already entered the slim entry hall with her trunk and started up the steps. She stepped inside, pulling the door closed behind her firmly.

Mr. Borden's passage on the stairs was slow. Bridget regretted his laboring, but her trunk wasn't heavy—no harp from Tara's halls, she reflected, nor plate, nor silver. She wondered why he hadn't let the driver take it for him, but as they approached the second floor, she suspected why: the strange layout of the home. The door they now paused in front of was Mr. Borden's own chamber. Whether a stranger would know this to be the case, it may have made the older gentleman feel vulnerable.

Mr. Borden stopped to catch his breath, his back still turned to her. As she waited, she examined the stairwell. No windows brightened its narrow, steep pitch. Mr. Borden—a millionaire if the scuttlebutt around town was correct—lived like a tradesman in a tenement. No generously proportioned, cambered flight did he climb at night with his lamp, a statue posted at the landing to remind him of the glories of Rome. No thick carpeting to muffle his tread, soften his passage as he climbed. Just a threadbare rug covered the stairs to his chamber, and stark wooden boards for the remaining steps up to hers.

Bridget reflected that even the main staircase in the home's front entry, the one that led to the sisters' rooms, was unadorned and graceless. She hung her head, waiting for Mr. Borden to resume. Why didn't the man make his lodgings more comfortable? He didn't have to cut his meat with golden cutlery, but it was beneath him to live like this.

"We have some odd arrangements in this house, and I'll welcome your keeping quiet on our personal matters," he said quietly.

"Of course." Bridget allowed a note of horror to creep into her voice. She'd been raised for a life of service, and her mother back in Allihies, County Cork, had instructed her that discretion was as important as a strong hand with the broom.

"Maggie, our previous maid . . . she was a bit too eager to share the doings of our household with her friends, and word came back to me," said Mr. Borden. He did then turn and regard Bridget with a serious, but not unkind, visage. "We'll reward your stilled tongue with continued employment. Avoid the gossips of Fall River, and we'll have a long and fruitful association."

"Yes, sir. I surely will," she said.

"Good."

At that, he hoisted up her trunk and resumed the climb to the third floor. In her chamber, he stooped to tuck it under the ceiling's half slant.

"It's nice our side of the home doesn't convey the noise of traffic from Second Street," he said, gesturing to the window. She pulled aside the lace to see the backyard and the stable.

To the side, the southern neighbor's maid beat a rug on the line, a flume of smoke arising like she was mistress of her own small factory. Bridget smiled, about to posit this fancy to Mr. Borden, an actual factory proprietor, but he had soundlessly exited.

She went to the open door and watched him plod down to the story below. She wondered what she was to do. There was no need to unpack, although she did take out her two dresses and hang them from the hooks to avoid wrinkling.

She went again to the window. Was this the maid Maggie had gossiped with, to her detriment? Bridget determined that she would be careful.

It was Mary Doolan, creating factory smoke out of domestic grit, and Bridget would indeed listen to her friend's idle chitchat despite her resolve, but that would not be the cause of her service ending. Would that it had been, and she merely disgraced, while Mr. and Mrs. Borden continued their safe, if not wholly happy, lives.

Downstairs, she acquainted herself with the kitchen. She raked the ashes in the stove and fed in a log. She opened drawers and cupboards until she'd formed a mental inventory of the dismally small collection of knives, spoons, serving platters. She descended to the cellar to tally the root vegetables stored there and the twine-wrapped meats hanging from the rafters.

She'd eaten quite well at the Remingtons', but she'd merely make do here. The larder held slender fare, but her lot was not to complain. She'd begin with dinner. She could prepare a stew of the mutton she'd seen upstairs with a few carrots, potatoes, and onions. She'd get it started now, to hopefully soften the meat by the time they ate hours later. For supper, perhaps, turnips and gravy, with biscuits.

As Bridget set herself to peeling potatoes, Miss Lizzie came into the kitchen. Bridget hadn't realized, seeing her seated the day before, how imposing the older woman's stature was. She cut a nearly manly figure, with her sharp posture and broad chest and shoulders. She wore a calico day dress of sprigged maroon and walked with assurance. Going straight to the white bowl on the sideboard, Lizzie plucked out an apple. She polished the fruit on her dress as she turned and surveyed Bridget.

"Good morning," said Bridget. Something in her years of training stretched her face into a smile. It was not returned.

"You weren't able to make it here early enough to serve our breakfast," said Lizzie.

"No, I served a final time for the Remingtons."

"We scraped by for ourselves, as we've done now since Maggie left," said Lizzie. "Will you be sure to make doughnuts for tomorrow?"

"Certainly, miss, if you wish."

Lizzie took her first bite of the apple, standing so as to block the light from the window, creating her own batch of shadow in the close kitchen. Bridget wondered if it would be rude to lower her head and apply her knife to the potato again.

"I attend the same church as your former employers," said Lizzie.

"Is that so?" asked Bridget, surprised. The church was far from Second Street.

"Yes, I've found the First Congregational Church to be fusty and old-fashioned in its views."

Bridget had no answer for that. She began to wish Lizzie would step aside so she could see the potato's pockmarked surface better as she skinned it.

"The house was grand, I'm sure," said Lizzie.

"I'm sorry?"

"The Remington home."

Bridget couldn't help a small sound of disbelief. Did she expect

Bridget to sit here and tell the tales of that house, recite the value of each object, gleefully recount the lush fabrics used in the linens, the carpets, the curtains? Was she meant to catalog its splendors for this prying chit who would never set foot in the drawing room Bridget had dusted?

Bridget immediately saw the error of her response. Lizzie threw the rest of her apple into the dry sink with a certain amount of vehemence. "I've wanted to entertain here," said Lizzie stiffly. "There's no reason why I can't return the favors of so many lovely dinners I've had out at the homes of friends. But my father can't stomach the idea."

Bridget tried not to frown. Did she wish Bridget to support her in this idea? But no servant would ever willingly ask for more work, and besides, what sort of clout could she ever hold with Mr. Borden?

"You may think you've come down in the world, to work in this house," said Lizzie.

"Not at all. I'm grateful for the chance."

"You're not grateful. You took one look at this miserable place and shuddered. We're two doors down from a grocery, of all humbling conditions!"

"There's no shame in a grocery," said Bridget quietly.

"It's not indicative of our standing. We could have the finest house on the hill! Instead we live like drudges, five steps from the street."

"The house is quite nice," said Bridget.

"Our home isn't even connected to the gas main, while our *Irish* neighbors freely avail themselves of that costly convenience."

Bridget startled at the slight to her own kind, but Miss Lizzie interpreted it as shock for her father's refusal to use gas. "That's right; we are still using kerosene lamps, smoking and spluttering. And my father . . . sometimes he'll sit in darkness to not waste fuel. That's the man who holds the wallet and won't open it up to save his own eyes as he reads."

"How sad for his vision." Bridget didn't know how to hold this conversation. All her life, she'd witnessed people working extraordinarily hard to purchase the very barest of needs. A middle-aged woman bragging about the excess of money—while ranting about her lack of access to it—was a strange circumstance.

"I've begged him."

"He'll come to want to save his sight," said Bridget, focusing on the one thing she could remark upon. How did one discuss a man's miserliness without getting oneself fired? She was not unaware he was likely somewhere in the house. And she had been specifically *warned* against rumormongering.

"Oh, he won't," said Lizzie. "He'll go blind to save a dime."

Bridget stiffened. This was simply too much. She stood up, setting the half-peeled potato and paring knife on the table. She crossed to the stove and moved the kettle from one side of the hob to the other, then lifted up the eye to add a small piece of wood.

"Good day to you, Maggie," said Miss Lizzie behind her.

Bridget whirled around, catching the smirk on Lizzie's face. "Maggie" wasn't just the former maid; it was a deprecating way to address any Irish servant whose actual name didn't matter.

"It's Bridget, miss," she said.

"So it is, and I apologize!"

Lizzie moved closer, and Bridget couldn't help but be drawn in and repulsed at the same time by the pale argent eyes. It seemed the coins Lizzie's father couldn't spend had landed in his daughter's gaze. Bridget had been punished, she knew, for daring to stand up and walk away from Lizzie, casting tacit judgment on the cruel words spoken about Mr. Borden.

"Miss Lizzie, I must return to my work," said Bridget softly.

"Indeed, you should. I'll not stop you."

Lizzie took a second apple from the bowl and walked away

polishing it on her breast. Bridget listened until she heard the creak of Lizzie ascending the front steps to resume peeling the potato, its pale skinned flesh now browned from sitting in the air.

CHAPTER 4

Bridget

NOVEMBER 10,1889

That night, Bridget blew out her lamp and went to the window. There was comfort in the closeness of the homes: the Churchills, unseen, to the north and, visible now, the lights of the Kellys, an Irish family that had somehow clambered up to respectability. She got into bed and closed her eyes.

But they opened.

She peered through the gloom. It was unsettling knowing that outside her door was the attic, open for the entire footprint of the house. Besides one small bedroom, a counterpart to her own, the enormous space was uncontrolled by walls. She didn't like the thought of the asymmetric towers of crates and discarded, hulking furniture, the mice that made their nests there, the unknowingness.

Directly below her were Mr. and Mrs. Borden, and she could hear them readying for bed, the wife's labored steps across the floor, the bed creaking as she sat to take off her shoes. The low murmur of husband and wife surprised her; after the stillness between Abby and her stepdaughters it almost seemed extraordinary that these two spoke to each other.

Bridget craned her head to catch a glimpse of the moon as she lay inhaling the cheap soap scent on her pillowslip, everything unfamiliar. She permitted her mind to drift back to her mother, surely awake now whatever her hour, bracing herself against the stiff wind off Ballydonegan Bay as she walked, skirts flapping, to old Mrs. Twomey's for a packet of currants for her soda bread. It had been years since Bridget had seen her mother, and she begged God nightly to keep her well until she could see her again . . . yet the loss felt suddenly so raw that Bridget succumbed to tears.

There was no warmth, no hearth, no tales. No lingering by the fire of an evening, as the knitting needles clicked out friendly accompaniment to accounts told of the day. This family ate in shifts to not be with each other. Bridget served and cleared, served and cleared. She witnessed the contempt that had taken up residence in the eyes, there so long that it was a permanent lodger.

She pitied Lizzie and Emma the death of their mother, especially Lizzie's having been so young and helpless. She imagined the young toddler might not have even been readied to use the chamber pot yet, and how Mr. Borden might have shrank from the womanly chores demanded of a widower. Emma must have taken on those duties, and herself a child, too. Perhaps these women's coldness arose, Bridget thought, from this long-ago grief. Young Lizzie's understanding of the world had been that all good things may be snapped out of one's hands with an instant's notice.

But knowing the route a character took in forming itself didn't absolve it of its faults. How unfair that she who loved her mother so deeply must find an ocean between them, while in the same household people who cared not a grain for each other walked and ate in troubled circuits. Bridget wiped her tears on the sleeve on her nightgown, which still smelled of the lavender soap the Remingtons used in their laundering; she might never wash it again.

In Bridget's trunk was a bit of blue copper from the mines her da worked. She wasn't sure he was supposed to take it, but he'd never be caught for it now, the evidence of his crime having sailed all the way to America. The mine had closed two years before she'd sailed to the States, her father's loss of livelihood a strong signal that she needed to help the family pay its bills. As one of thirteen children, two of whom had died young, she was simply another mouth to feed. So she'd shipped off. She could hide her father's spiriting away of the copper. She could keep a closed mouth, as any good servant.

She was the girl who could listen to gossip but never donate any.

CHAPTER 5

Bridget

NOVEMBER 11, 1889

The next morning, she made the acquaintance of the Kelly maid who'd beaten the rug while she watched out the window. The woman hailed Bridget as she stepped outside to cool her face after hovering over frying onions. And so Bridget walked to her across the hardened, and in places icy, yard. The maid stood standing on the other side of a short picket fence.

"Hello and welcome!" she said. "I'm Mary Doolan."

"I'm Bridget Sullivan." The two women shook hands over the fence. There was frank curiosity on the other maid's face.

"And how are you getting on?" she asked.

"It's all very new, but as time will tell, it should be satisfactory."

"Isn't that a mouthful for a red-haired lass! *It should be very satisfactory*, says the mistress of the house."

"Ah, don't mock me!" said Bridget, but without offense.

"How can I not, when you put coal in your mouth and talk around it?"

Bridget laughed.

"There now, that's better!" said Mary. "Is the family treating you all right?"

"I can't complain on the second day," said Bridget carefully. "All is well."

"You *can* complain on the second day, and the third and fourth too! Fill my ears."

Bridget bristled. Would no one on Second Street keep their unpleasantness to themselves? "I'll keep my own counsel."

Mary burst into laughter. "You'll have to! But there's aught to tell; I see it in your eyes. And I know it, too. Your family holds themselves so very high. They won't even talk to the family I serve."

"Whyever not?"

"Stupid girl, you know why. Their name's Kelly! They're as Irish as you and me."

"And the Bordens won't speak to them on that account?"

"Aye. And Mr. Kelly a doctor, even!"

Bridget looked down at her own hobnailed boots, her hem that needed a good cleaning of mud and dust. If the Bordens refused to acknowledge the existence of the Kellys, decent homeowning citizens on an equal economic par, what did they think of Bridget, sleeping under their roof with nothing to her name but the items that fit in a trunk?

"Makes you feel low, don't it?" observed Mary. "But they aren't much themselves. The missus weighs the same as a pony, I'll wager—"

"Oh, hush!" said Bridget in a panic, looking to be sure they weren't overheard.

"And him an old man; he must be seventy if he's a day. The whole city knows he's a miser who loves his money too dearly to ever spend it. Lizzie and Emma are spinsters that none's touched despite all that lovely family money—now, why do you think *that* is?"

"You're like to get me sacked, and I've been employed all of one day!" said Bridget.

"They'll do nothing to you," said Mary.

"Mr. Borden told me himself that Maggie, the girl afore me, lost her post for telling tales."

"That's not what Maggie said."

"And what did she say?"

"She left of her own accord. She said she was scared."

"Whatever of?"

"The people in that house."

Relieved, Bridget laughed.

"Ye can laugh at that?" Mary asked.

"Foolish Maggie, and her loss is my gain."

"Well, aren't you the cat that swallowed the cream," said Mary with some disappointment. It was clear she'd hoped for some more dramatic reaction from Bridget.

"Bitter cream, but yes," said Bridget, and Mary indulged in peals of laughter.

"I think we'll get along famously. Might you join me of a Saturday night at Nancy Spain's Pub for a *ceilidh*? They do it once a month and open the doors for the women."

Bridget's eyes widened. "I would!"

"You'll be crying at the sound of the uilleann pipes again, as if the green turf were under your feet again. You are from County Cork; are ye not?"

"Aye, from Allihies."

Mary nodded. "I'm from Mitchelstown. This whole neighborhood's been transplanted from Cork, it seems. The Bordens better watch themselves if they don't like our sort encroaching!"

Bridget eyed the other woman and made a point of turning around to survey the windows of the Borden household. "Sound travels," she observed.

"That it does," agreed Mary. "And instructs, even. Now then, miss, I'll collect you out front at half four on Saturday."

"We'll walk?"

"Aye, 'tis only five blocks this way," said Mary, pointing toward Main Street.

Bridget clasped Mary's hand in sudden emotion. To hear the ballads again! To dance to the rhythms of pipe, fiddle and *bodhran* and leave behind, for an evening, the oppressive nature of the Borden home. She longed to hear in full force a roomful of the lilting language she grew up with, the tones soft even in anger, what the world called a brogue, for some reason attaching a soft untanned shoe to the glory of the dulcet.

"I'm beholden to ye," she told Mary. "Truly so."

CHAPTER 6

Brooke

JULY 6, 2016

She has one rolling suitcase and a Rubbermaid tub, which holds all her possessions.

And here's her new apartment. She always rents them furnished; she moves so often, it isn't possible to haul furniture along with her. She has culled her property to the spare kernel of necessity, because the very word *belongings* intimates something she can never do: *belong*.

The apartment's not bad. She called from Tucson and rented it unseen. In the Boston outskirts, it's perhaps a little too close to where she grew up, but they always seem to find her, so it hardly matters.

She walks the small hall to inspect the sole bedroom with the dated mirror slider for the closet and the cheap carpet with pet stains. The bathroom is relatively clean, but she'll reserve judgment until she runs the shower the first time to see if it drains well.

Back in the kitchen, with its flimsy cupboards and scratched linoleum, white gauze curtains lift in the breeze, bringing in a sweet, earthy smell from outside. Brooke has always loved this household drama, wind writ large, but knows it isn't for her. Other people can relax in semitransparency, aware their shapes are visible to those in the darkness beyond . . . without caring. Others don't mind that their voices carry into the yard beyond.

But this is not the case for her. She takes one last breath of the outdoors before closing and locking the window. She pulls her black-out curtains from her suitcase and swiftly threads them through the curtain rod, pulling them across the window as the gauze presses to the other side until completely superceded.

She inhales the blessed darkness of privacy. She can relax enough to unpack her small, curated collection of possessions.

Tomorrow, she'll start her new job at the coffeehouse. The wages she earns being paid under the table are enough to keep her going. She did get a fairly decent insurance payout when her mother was murdered and converted it to traveler's checks that she cashes only every now and then. She's learned how to live with very little, studio apartments usually, with cinder-block walls. No cable, no wifi other than what she can catch through her neighbor's walls. She shops at thrift stores on their 50-percent-off days. She does her own nails.

She always gets a library card and reads for free, and that is the key to her happiness. Brooke reads voraciously in the true crime genre. She takes strange comfort in these devastating tales, because when the killers come for her, it won't be that bad. They didn't torture her mother, and her death must have been fairly quick. It's unsettling, though, that they taunted Brooke with the dinner plates, and that they now amuse themselves with a cat-and-mouse game. She hates that playfulness, the long stretch of years in which they've denied themselves closure. Because if they know where she is, why haven't they already killed her?

They let her move from town to town, reinventing herself, taking a new name. Each time, she thinks maybe she's gotten away, but then they eventually give her some sign, some indication that they've found her.

She's learned to live with this slow chase, feeling temporary re-lief—like now—when she's in a new city. She reads true crime to understand the motives, the thinking behind the pursuit . . . because maybe when they come for her for real, she'll know what to say.

So she studies up, has read every Ann Rule book. She knows details of strangers' murders with an encyclopedic memory, probably better than their own family members, loath to hear about and thus visualize their loved ones' last moments on Earth.

She had started reading at the group home as a way to distract herself from the pain of her mother's murder, a death so much less gruesome than those in these horrible pages. Her beautiful mom had been pushed off the road by a car that didn't linger and which no one caught the plates of. A drunk driver, the police had concluded, but she knew better. Instead of murder, it had been called *manslaughter.* She hated that word. As a girl who grew up speaking both English and Spanish, she found it very strange. Slaughter was how animals became meat, and her mother was not even close to being a man.

In her mind's eye, she could see the drivers as they'd looked four years ago, furious brothers who had to tick off the years until the eldest could get a driver's license and exact revenge.

She worked hard to avoid thinking about her mother during her final moments and instead burrowed into other people's tragedies: the abductions, tortures, the gut-based screams unheard by potential saviors—and sometimes heard but disregarded.

When she's done unpacking, she opens her laptop and pulls up her Facebook account. Her profile picture is the default egg, but once inside her page, the cover photo is one of her and her mother, arms slung around each other, standing at the shores of Lake Havasu. Just the two of them, none of the spring break hordes.

Her mother, Magdalena, had been able to afford a week only in the off-season— their rental, though, still reeked of beer, tequila, and the dim but unmistakable scent of vomit. "A good cleaning could get rid of that smell," her mother had said, and with a smile at Brooke, shrugged. The maid on vacation doesn't clean.

Brooke's thirteen years old in the photo, wearing a bikini whose flimsy top pieces meet with a large silver ring. "A keyhole," the cashier had said when she rang it up. All that summer, Brooke had struggled with whether she invited the mental image of exactly what key might fit that hole. It was a summer that felt like sex still lingered on the beach, discarded by the spring break kids for any teenager to pick up like a sand dollar.

She'd looked critically at her mother's figure in her own bikini that summer, a sky blue color that made her skin glow. Her Mexican skin was pre-tanned by God, Brooke had thought . . . and therefore so was hers—although one shade lighter. Her mother's body was slim, muscular, curvy, all at once and in the right places. With perfect posture and a graceful stride, her mother walked the distance from their beach towels to the waves over and over. That summer, Brooke had looked at bodies hungrily, surveyingly, trying to understand her own place in the hierarchy of physiology.

As she looks below the photo, she sees a message waiting on her wall for her. Miguel had typed, *"How's the new place?"*

Miguel's profile picture's a joke, a detail of a large mural painted on a taqueria wall. It shows an Aztec warrior spiriting off a woman, breasts spilling out of her animal-skin dress. Miguel had chosen the warrior's face to represent his own.

It's okay, Brooke comments in the thread he's started. *I just kind of wish it had a soul.*

You don't want a place with soul, mija. That's how you get a hotel like in The Shining.

So he's online, or at least ready to jump on in response to his phone's alert.

True. I'll dial back my expectations.

Wish you didn't have to keep moving.

I know. She pauses. Miguel understands; she had told him the story all those years ago when the two of them were co-prisoners at the GHAC, the "group home for abandoned children"—their nickname designed to find humor in their own scarred existences.

It'd be cool if someday you end up moving right into my city.

She starts to type something snarky, but her fingers stall on the keyboard. She's wished this many times, that she was the sort of person who was free to live a normal life, who could renew an acquaintance with an old friend from her troubled teen years. She remembers all those hushed conversations on the back porch of the group home, her fingernails pulling paint shreds off the peeling floorboards and making a little pile of the results as they shared war stories in the battle of growing up. Who isn't a survivor from the wreckage of childhood?

She types, *Someday, I'll do it.*

I'll put out the red carpet, baby.

No paparazzi, please, she types. *You must know all the media attention is painful to me.*

You just want to live your life, right?!

She snorts, and writes, *Gotta log off now. Need some sleep.*

Night, mija.

She closes Facebook and sits thinking. A joke about media attention, but she's always felt the unwanted attention focused on her, keen and intent.

Furious, even.

When Brooke first met Miguel, she was fourteen, bewildered at the loss of her mother and the apparent dearth of relatives to take her in. She'd known her mom had come from a large family in Mexico, but her physical move to the United States had also been an emotional one. As far back as Brooke could remember, there were no phone calls, no packages, no sign that her mother had family she cared about. Brooke's father had been a fling, and she hadn't been permitted to know his name. The birth certificate, she saw when she had first studied it, reported his name as "Dirtbag"; someone had crosshatched it out but she could still discern it.

Brooke became a ward of the state and entered the foster care system, awaiting adoption along with Miguel. Some of the kids were orphans like her, while others—like Miguel—had parents, but worthless ones. Still a third group of residents was there for behavioral issues, rejected by their parents whether worthless or not.

It was hard not to think of the home as a sort of prison since they weren't allowed to come and go as they pleased. Brooke had been a latchkey kid pretty much all her life; it was startling to be denied the right to step out for a Popsicle on a warm summer evening.

And summers were the worst.

When school didn't dissolve a major portion of the day, the group home became a lame summer camp: the city pool twice a week, all day, so she was fried and sunblind by the end; stupid "matinees" on the smelly carpet of the home's living room, each kid with a coffee filter full of popcorn, watching oldies on the VCR, itself an archaic electronic that somehow wouldn't die and lay to rest its compatriot library of forgotten Hollywood goofs.

The upside, in her second year, was the arrival of Miguel. He'd been waiting for his parents to come home and make dinner, but they'd pulled to the side of the road for a fentanyl/heroin snack and overdosed. In the ambulance, the medical personnel found Miguel's school photo in his mom's wallet and dispatched police to ring the doorbell. His parents were alive but not going to be able to resume their parental duties for quite some time, so Miguel wound up sitting next to Brooke at his first dinner at the home, sticky spaghetti with mealy-textured meatballs.

"Is this really meat?" he'd cocked his head and asked her.

"It's brown and ball-shaped, and that's all I can say," she'd answered.

They'd been close friends since then, not just because of their good behavior in the midst of proto-juvenile delinquents, but also because of their Mexican heritage and the lilt in their voices that informed the world so.

"I'm trying to train myself out of it," she'd confided once when he caught her imitating the flat tones of the NBC anchor.

"Mija, never," he'd said. "Your voice is too pretty."

She and Miguel had aged out around the same time, she a few months earlier than him. They'd both taken the jobs and living situations offered them without thinking of refusing, he in Baltimore and she in Houston. College was never an option. Neither had the grades. With her mother's insurance payout, she could afford community college tuition, but knew she'd rather dole out the money over her work life rather than blowing it in a few years.

She hadn't wanted to follow in her mother's footsteps as a maid, so she was relieved when she was placed in a pop-up café as a low-wage barista, subsidized by a state grant.

The café got her for free in return for training her, and the grant paid her a meager salary, the idea being that when the grant ran out she'd move on to a genuine job with a gleaming entry on her résumé.

It was like her mother's death all over again to lose Miguel. As the years passed, she saw him now and then, saving up money to take separate rooms at a Motel 6 somewhere between their two cities. They'd shyly bring each other up to speed by the pool separated from the big rigs in the parking lot by a chain-link fence. By the roar of the idling diesels, they'd sum up their years apart. The blue paint on the bottom of the pool peeled like a sunburn.

Romance never happened for them. She figured they both knew their friendship was a vital brick that kept their walls upright. They didn't dare mess with the mortar. Life without each other wouldn't have been worth living. Friends fight—and they did—but only lovers take savage joy in ripping the other from their life.

Brooke had tried to kiss him once at one of these reunions, and he'd put his hands tenderly on her face as he pulled away.

"Mija, if this didn't work . . . ," he had said.

"I know. But we're never going to try?"

"To be honest, if a relationship failed, the friendship would, too. And that would kill me."

"It would kill me, too."

So they didn't risk it, and he resumed being the brother she'd never had. In their world untethered by parents, they provided stability to each other.

They really did best on Facebook, relaxed, joking, unselfconscious. Under their fake avatars, they were each other's only friend. They live-chatted pretty much daily, and her feed was a long row of funny and sweet things he'd said to her. He was her brick, her wall, her touchstone, her core.

The next day, Brooke shows up for her new job at the coffeehouse. She's adjusted her speech and her clothing to look like the illegal immigrant she's posing as, so she can be paid under the table. This is what she's had to do to avoid being tracked: she changes her name every few years, moves, and finds a job where an employer is happy to look the other direction in exchange for paying a pittance.

With her looks and fluency in Spanish, it's easy to pass as someone who doesn't have a legitimate Social Security number. She has long black hair with a bit of natural curl at the ends, dramatic eyebrows, high cheekbones, and caramel-colored skin. Her body is lean and strong, thanks to not being a fantastic cook and not eating many meals out. She's beautiful, but her understated way of dressing and behaving lets her easily be overlooked.

"Hi, Brooke!" her employer greets her. Jane is an older woman with gray hair braided into a Germanic-looking crown atop her head. She wears vests and approximately three huge silver rings per finger, an entire flea market table's display on two hands. Jane had explained at Brooke's interview how she felt sympathy for the plight of so many stranded Mexicans and she knew the government was wrong to impede immigration, so it was her own politically subversive act to therefore hire Mexicans even if they couldn't appropriately and honestly fill out the I-9 form. She said nothing about how this then released her from the burden of paying minimum wage; no, it was all about screwing "the man," not screwing the young woman in front of her.

"Going to be a busy day?" Brooke asks.

"It was . . . I had you come after the rush so it wasn't stressful. This is Maria, and I'll have her train you. You already know how the equipment works, but we have a few things we do differently from other places you might've worked."

Maria, in a low-plunging tank top that gives a view of what Brooke suspects to be only the top 30 percent of a cresting serpent tattoo, gives her a friendly tour of the workspace, interrupted a few times by customers. Maria stands back and lets Brooke wait on them, and Jane gives an approving smile after each interaction.

After Jane leaves, Maria says in Spanish, "You have to be careful not to make her mad. She threatens to call Immigration."

"Seriously?"

"Yeah. When you first meet her, she's all 'Oh, I love to help you; I know you had a hard life in Mexico,' but what she likes is the power of knowing you're illegal."

"I'm not, actually," says Brooke before she can help herself. *Way to go. Contradict the fiction that's keeping you safe.*

"Oh, really? You're working these shit wages because . . . ?"

"It's hard to explain."

"I bet. Anyway, don't cross her."

"Okay."

Maria looks to the glass café front and grins. "Here's our rush hour. Offices must be very difficult places to work; the workers stream out of them like their asses are on fire!"

Together they grind beans, scald milk, forge designs on the blank canvas of the latte foam. They press paninis and stock the sugars, ease a spatula into the pre-cut slices of a red velvet cake.

When the next shift arrives hours later, Maria leaves without saying goodbye to Brooke. It's better that way—Brooke doesn't want to get close to someone who will ask all the questions she's had to rehearse answers to. But there's still a pang at how their camaraderie had only been because they were on the clock together.

CHAPTER 7

Brooke

JULY 11, 2016

The days pass in a slow, loud way—the clatter of plates, the endless screech of the espresso machine. Brooke meets the other employees, their shifts spread so they are all just one hour under full-time so Jane won't have to pay benefits.

It's a rainy Monday when a guy comes in and shakes his umbrella in the doorway, creating a pool of water that Jane mutters will cause accidents and thus litigation.

"Go mop it up!" she says urgently to Brooke.

"Sorry," the guy says as Brooke approaches with a mop.

"It's okay."

He gives her a nice smile. He's in his early twenties like her, wearing a gray raincoat over black pants and nice shoes. His conservatively-cut hair is brown, and he's clean-shaven, his jawline looking a little raw. More than anything, he's handsome in a serious way; he looks like a male model in an eyeglasses ad. He's devoid of the rough edges that define her—the way a stranger can tell you once ate dinners constructed of saltines and peanut butter, and fielded playground queries about a missing, unnamed father.

Unexpectedly, he seizes the mop, cleaning up the puddle himself. "My mom taught me to clean up my own messes," he says.

She's speechless for a second.

"Next you'll be making your own latte," she says, and he laughs.

"No, I trust that to your expertise."

He hands her the mop and for the moment before she turns away, he holds her gaze. He *sees* her. She's never dated a white man before; they seem to order their espresso drinks without noticing the person on the other side of the counter. Either that, or the glance is purely sexual. His attention seems interested, curious.

"I haven't seen you here before," he says. "You're new?"

"I've only been here about a week."

He nods. "I was on a business trip when you started. I'm Anthony," he says, extending his hand.

It literally takes her a second to remember the name she's using here, and she nearly stutters on it. "Brooke. Nice to meet you. Let me put this away and get some coffee for you."

She turns and retreats to the counter, buzzing a little from the encounter. She returns the mop to the bucket and washes her hands at the small sink. The mop always emits a sour smell when wet, as if milk has formed the majority of its addressed spills.

Anthony has disappeared by the time she looks up to take his order, but a moment later the bathroom door at the rear of the café opens, and he comes out. He must've been disgusted by the mop, too, perhaps regretting his impetuous move to take it from her.

"What can I get started for you?" she asks.

"A large Americano."

"Sure."

By the time she's made his drink, there's a line behind him, so he takes it without anything more than a quick "Thank you" and goes to sit down. She's disappointed by the abrupt ending, but what did she expect? She looks over at him sitting near the windows, his profile outlined against the rain-battered glass.

Over the next few days, Anthony comes daily to get his Americano and sometimes an orange-cranberry scone. He greets her by name and always a few minutes of small talk, but nothing more arises.

She doesn't think their brief interactions are worthy of note, but the third time he walks away from the counter, her co-worker Maria crosses her arms and gives Brooke a secretive smile. "Girl, he's been coming here every day since I started working, and he never so much as looked at me. He must like girls who are more quiet."

Brooke smiles but doesn't meet her eyes. Maria's sexuality is as open as her eyes, mascara applied so heavily each lash operates independently. Her low-cut shirt offers up her breasts, pushed up for view by a bra whose cup tips are visible, supportive caves for the serpent tattoo.

"Go and talk to him," says Maria. "Take a rag and clean the table next to his."

Brooke shakes her head.

"You're crazy, chica!"

"No."

"Have you ever dated a white guy?"

"No."

"Well, it's *nice*. They're so like . . . If they don't see you as a domestic, then they're super nice because they're psyched to have someone with hot Latin blood."

Brooke rolls her eyes.

"Yeah, you laugh, but it's fun. I highly recommend it."

Across the café, Anthony lifts his head from his phone and looks straight at Brooke. He smiles, then looks back down.

"Oh, my God! He didn't hear us, did he?" breathes Brooke.

"No way. It's too noisy. Plus, what are the odds he knows Spanish?"

"He looked right at us."

"Correction; he looked at *you*. And it's because he's burning to drape your gorgeous raven locks on his pillow."

Brooke lets out a howl of laughter and sinks down behind the counter, out of view of the patrons.

"Don't you think so?" asks Maria.

Unfortunately, Anthony leaves forty minutes later with nothing more than a smile and a two-finger wave. Brooke looks over at Maria, and they both shrug.

The next day, the café's not too busy when Brooke arrives. She sees a few tables where moms sit chatting while their kids doze in the strollers parked next to them. A man types away on his laptop. A little girl sits by herself playing a game on an iPhone, and Brooke wonders why she's not in school.

Behind the counter, Maria's wearing a Beyoncé tour shirt with the sleeves and neckline scissor cut. She looks Brooke up and down in her cropped khakis and black V-neck. "You need some jewelry."

"Good morning to you, too," says Brooke.

"You've got to try a little harder."

"Thank you."

"You're actually very beautiful, chica, but no one would ever know it the way you carry yourself."

Brooke doesn't say anything, just sets her purse down and washes her hands.

"Like, that guy yesterday? If you just showed 1 percent of effort, he'd ask you out."

"Maybe I have someone already."

Maria's eyes widen. "Why didn't you say so?"

"Because I don't."

Maria mock hits her.

"But I don't need a matchmaker, and I don't want advice, okay?"

"No one ever wants my advice," Maria grumbles. "Oh, by the way, the bathroom needs cleaning."

"Oh." Brooke smiles to herself; Maria's friendship only goes so far. She saved the unpleasant job for Brooke. "I'll just wait for that kid's mother to come out of the bathroom." She points at the girl—maybe a ten-year-old?—glassily looking at the phone screen.

"She's mine," says Maria. "Babysitter bailed."

"You have a kid?"

"My pride and joy. Not too thrilled about how she came to me, but I'm sure glad she's here now."

She turns back around, effectively ending the conversation. Brooke grabs a pair of food service gloves and walks to the back. Maria's daughter has long, beautiful hair. She's a pretty girl, and her vacant expression reminds Brooke of herself at that age—back when her mom was still alive and she didn't know how good she had it. She'd fight to stay up late to watch movies, sulk when not allowed, resist doing homework, all with a sour face. A few years later, the walls of the world would blow up and she'd be willing to kneel in snow for a year to have her mother back and treat her right.

It's stupid to try to engage the trying-this-hard-to-be-disaffected, but as she walks past Maria's daughter, she can't resist giving it a shot.

"Great score," she says although she has no idea if it's a good or abysmal one. She's never played a game on a phone. Never truly used one, never swiped her index finger in that languid way that is oddly sexy.

The girl doesn't reply, which makes Brooke wonder if she heard. She's probably been told not to talk to strangers.

Brooke opens the bathroom door, winces at the vista inside. Toilet paper clogs the toilet and cloys the floor at its base. A puddle of brown water sits in the sink, which appears to be stopped, although it has no plug.

She closes the door so customers can't see her ministrations. She knows Maria's shift started an hour ago; so much for their friendship.

She snaps on the gloves—powdery condoms for the hands—and works on the sink first, moving the masses of clumped food until water begins to drain again. It looks like somebody tried to make multiple scones go down the drain. She sprays cleaner until the air is toxic in the small space.

She hadn't brought the mop and has to go back for it. "It's nasty in there," she says to Maria. She's learned after years of being the new girl that if she doesn't stick up for herself, she gets the worst tasks.

Maria doesn't answer, restocking napkins.

"Did you go in there?" Brooke presses.

"Just clean it. Don't make it a *Sixty Minutes* investigation."

"Next time, maybe you can take care of it when you see it."

"The employee of less than a week doesn't call the shots."

Brooke considers a few rude responses, but doesn't want Maria's daughter to hear. She goes into the bathroom with the mop and wheeled bucket, moving the gray water around until it's soaked up. She regards the toilet and gives it a flush, terrified it will overflow, mop at the ready. Thankfully, the mass disappears.

Brooke sprays down the commode and wipes it dry with paper towels. She never kneels to clean a toilet; it's always done from afar, standing. Unlike her mother, she'll never have to concentrate on a stranger's toilet, giving it her all. Her mother had made her promise she'd never work as a maid.

"Please tell me, mija, you'll only clean your own home. No one else's," she'd said. Her mom had wanted higher education for her, not foreseeing the lackluster grades her daughter would pull off in the land of fruit and plenty. She in fact had a quite specific job in mind for her: attorney.

"How proud I'll be to see you in your suit in the courthouse," her mother would say. "You will tell all those men how the law works, and they will listen to you."

Brooke checks herself in the bathroom mirror before opening the door. She looks pretty good for someone who has disappointed her mother and innocent defendants.

When she emerges, she sees that Anthony is at the counter. To her credit, Maria looks embarrassed on her behalf, as if she wished she had cleaned the bathroom after all. She gives Brooke an apologetic smile.

Nothing to do but walk toward them, pulling the clattering yellow mop bucket with her.

"Just can't seem to let go of that mop, can you?" jokes Anthony as she gets closer.

"At least no clowns are making puddles in the doorway today," she says with a smile.

"Ouch."

She puts the bucket away and notices that he's still standing there. "Were you not helped?" she asks.

"He forgot he wanted coffee," shoots Maria, and he blushes.

He blushes!

And, perhaps predictably, Brooke feels warmth spread across her cheeks, too.

"A large Americano?" she manages to ask.

"Yes, please."

"I'll bring it to you."

It's time to take a chance, she thinks. When she brings him his drink, she pulls out a chair and sits down at the table with him.

"I would ask if you want to get coffee sometime," she says. "But that would be silly."

A grin launches across his face, and she feels a resulting lurch in her heartbeat. "How about dinner?" he says.

"That sounds good."

"Tonight? When you get off work?"

"Yes."

"I'll come back a little after five for you."

"Okay, that's great. I'll see you then."

There's nothing more to say. They made their plan, and she should go back to the counter. She wishes she had started with some small talk before cutting to the chase, because now she has to get up and go. He bites his lip, apparently feeling the same awkwardness, and she stares at that row of white teeth indenting the soft flesh before he realizes she's looking and closes his mouth.

As soon as she rises, she feels guilt descend on a reverse trajectory. He's a good guy—a guy who *blushes*! And bites his lip. She shouldn't bring him into her weird underworld of evading people who want to kill her.

He's too sweet. She should take it back. Why did she ever sit down next to him? It was all because of Maria and her daughter and the bathroom.

She looks over at the girl now, immobile as a statue staring down at her phone. Poor thing.

CHAPTER 8

Brooke

JULY 4, 2002

That day the lake had sparkled with a blue Brooke had previously only seen in ads. Even the color of the water was affluent, different from the brackish blue-brown of the river that sidled through town.

The Carr family lawn ran lush and rolling down to meet the lake, except for two terraces built for a croquet court and a massing of wicker chaises with fat cushions—such decadence to have something soft outdoors that could be ruined by unexpected rain. Brooke's own backyard, spattered with patches of grass painful on bare feet, held only plastic versions of Adirondack chairs, easily tipped by wind.

"My dad's putting steak and shrimp on the barbecue for you," the elder Carr boy had informed her. "Because you never have it."

What a kindness, but she didn't understand the sneer that accompanied his words. So guileless she was, that his cruelty didn't penetrate.

"Your mom's not as pretty as our mom," said the younger one. She'd always remember his name, Ezekiel. Who named their child such a mouthful? But Biblical names often did require total commitment from tongue and teeth, her own mother's name being the same number of syllables yet somehow melodic rather than dire: Magdalena.

This cruelty Brooke understood. "Yes, she is," she said loyally.

Mrs. Carr was as short as her mother, but plump and buxom where Magdalena was slim. Mrs. Carr favored pink and cream to complement her frosted blond hair, and her pink manicured nails—hands and feet as Brooke noticed through the open-toed sandals—were soft and unused looking. Blue eyes just a shade too large, and a mouth clearly too thin, created a mom who passed muster in the PTA swift-glance gauntlet, but appeared to Brooke as lacking her own mother's true beauty. Magdalena's brown eyes, always alert and rimmed with mascara to emphasize her long lashes, seemed like a face much more worth looking at. Her brown skin, slim body, and rough hands looked like the epitome of womanhood to her daughter.

"Your mom's from Mexico," said Abraham, the elder brother, pronouncing the country as if he were talking about rat droppings in the kitchen.

The three of them were on the dock, but still wearing regular clothes instead of swimsuits. Brooke was told she had "the run of the house," the friendly Mrs. Carr saying so, but instead made her way to the water where she could survey the mansion from a comfortable distance. Cicadas added their laconic complaint to the heat of the day, and Brooke watched smoke rise in some alarm, but it was only the rose-clad Mrs. Carr moving coals on the outdoor grille.

"Yes, she's from Mexico, but she's American," replied Brooke. She wished the boys would go away and leave her alone. She liked squinting up at the house, sprawling white on the top of the rise, and pretending it was hers.

"No, she's not. My dad said she's illegal. He's just hiring her to be nice."

"Like today," added Ezekiel. "We have to spend the day with you guys just to be nice."

"She's not illegal!" Brooke stood up at this. "My mom is a citizen, and she has every right to be here!" She wanted to shove that boy into the lake. He was placidly sitting there, legs dangling, shoes nearly touching the water, unruffled.

"Maybe if she marries someone and gets her green card," he said.

She felt her cheeks flush. Always this aimed at her, and with no rejoinder she'd ever developed to pull out of her pocket and devastate inquirers. Where was her dad? And who was he?

"You just don't know!" she fired at them both, mildly smiling up at her. The calm of the empowered. "She's married! She's just . . . "

"She doesn't wear a ring," Ezekiel pointed out.

"My dad's a great guy, and he has so much more money than your dad!" she lied. "His house is like a huge mansion, and it's three stories high!"

"Then why's your mom a maid?"

"It's just a job," Brooke sputtered, before she turned and ran back up the hill, fragrant from a recent mowing, past the beds of lilies and irises, the weeping willow with a wrought iron bench beneath its natural curtains.

She was out of breath before she reached the house. She paused to wipe tears off her heated cheeks. There was something wrong with being a maid, she could tell by the boy's tone as he said the word. She hadn't known before that there was anything shameful to it. A maid, a cashier, a policewoman: what difference did it make?

Mrs. Carr was bent over, snapping a white linen tablecloth on the outdoor table, and didn't see Brooke pass her.

Brooke stepped into the kitchen where she'd last seen her mother. It was a huge shining affair, with cupboards lit from inside like museum cases, displaying blown-glass bowls and goblets. An island as large as Brooke's entire kitchen held dominion.

Her mother wasn't here. Brooke went into the living room with its lifeboat-sized sofas and built-in bookshelves. Ancestor portraits were here, the original Abraham and Ezekiel who had traded wampum with the Indians and promptly built fences on the land they purchased. Enormous picture windows gave onto the lake, where she saw the two boys still sat on the dock.

She padded along to the foot of the staircase, which curved in double lines like the one where Cinderella made her grand entrance at the ball. Brooke knew it was wrong to walk around someone else's house—but she liked the thrill. And after all, Mrs. Carr had said, "*Mi casa es su casa,*" and Brooke's mom had immediately congratulated her on her accent.

"I'm learning!" Mrs. Carr had said. "It's good to have you around. Maybe the boys will pick up some Spanish."

So Brooke didn't pause too long before climbing the stairs, gliding her hand up the fat, polished banister.

"I'm going up to bed," she pretended, banishing the boys from her head. She daydreamed that upstairs held only a bedroom with a canopy bed for her. Even Mrs. Carr, she decided reluctantly, would have to go, nice as she was. Brooke wanted her own mom in the master suite.

And handsome Mr. Carr?

Maybe he could stay.

After what seems like a slow workday, Anthony shows up at 5:06. Brooke ignores Maria's sly grin and gets her purse, thinking about how carelessly she'd shaved her legs in the shower that morning. Had she known, she would've taken more time.

Because, if she lets Anthony in, it'll be just for one night.

The woman who moves to a new city every half-year or so and adopts a new identity can't get deeply involved. Fielding questions, letting them get to know her: it can't happen. So she's made the decision in recent years to allow only one-night stands. If Anthony says the right things tonight, he'll get everything he wants from her, and then she'll throw him back like a fish, for his own good as well as hers.

"I was wondering if you like Thai food?" he says as they stand on the sidewalk outside the coffeehouse.

"It's not really my favorite," she reluctantly admits.

"How about a burger, like a good one?"

"That sounds perfect."

"There's a gourmet burger place a few blocks away that doesn't take itself too seriously. We can walk there." He gestures the way with his hand still in his trench coat pocket so he looks like a magician brandishing his cape.

They start out, and their paces match each other's. She's always been a fast walker, veering around people slowly meandering down the middle of the path.

"Well, you're not vegetarian; we've got one thing figured out," he says.

"No. But I'm sure if I went to see how the animals are treated, I would be."

He smiles. "A convenient ignorance always abets a carnivore."

She almost stops walking at that. He's out of her league, this guy who uses the word *abets* in casual conversation.

"What are you?" she blurts out.

"What do you mean?"

"Are you a . . . you look like a stockbroker."

"Thanks! I think. Assuming that's a good thing?"

She nods.

"You're close. I'm an attorney."

"Oh."

She thinks of the courtrooms she'd been in after her mother's death, close, windowless, low-ceilinged affairs in which advocates decided her fate while consulting the notes in their files. "Family court," it was called, and until she'd attended, she could only picture it as a dinner table, with a mom at the head wearing one of those British barrister wigs and wielding a gavel at the loud witnesses who wouldn't eat their vegetables.

"What kind of attorney?"

"I work in a criminal law firm." He coughs. "It doesn't really work to say I'm a criminal lawyer, because then it sounds like I'm the criminal."

He knows well the world she was thrust into, both with her mother's murder and then with the books she'd turned to for answers.

"What?" he says after too much time has passed.

"My mom wanted me to be an attorney."

"But you were not inspired?"

"I didn't have the . . . " *grades*, she's about to say, but it's more than that. It's that attending college and then law school would've required her to put down roots and become a stationary target. "I guess I wasn't on fire to do it."

"Yeah, you can't really be lukewarm."

"You always knew you wanted to be a lawyer?"

"Pretty much. People always told me I was a good arguer."

"It's nice you knew what you wanted."

"And you?"

"You mean, was it my life's goal to work in a coffeehouse?"

"Well, you're young," he says.

She doesn't respond.

"I have to take that back, because it implies that where you are isn't your final stop, and it may well be."

She laughs. "Don't worry, I'm not offended."

"Good."

But the moment does seem to have been a conversation killer, underscoring the fact that he's on an upward trajectory and she's not.

"You work with murderers?" she asks after they've walked a half block.

"Everyone deserves fair representation."

"No," she says firmly. "I don't think so. Some people are evil." She tucks her hair behind her ears, a nervous habit.

"The law provides that everyone is innocent until proven guilty."

"But what if it's clear as day that they're guilty? It's already proven? They've got blood dripping off their hands, standing over the victim, their bootprint in the victim's face: Why do they need a trial?"

They continue in silence as he formulates his answer, past a closed bakery still radiating a smell of sweetness out to the street, and a bodega where the shopkeeper wears headphones and winks salaciously at Brooke as they pass.

"In that—let me just say, graphic and awful—case, it's to ensure due process of the law and to decide sentencing for that clearly guilty individual."

"That's what I mean," says Brooke doggedly. "Due process of the law. They don't need it. They're guilty."

In a sudden rush, she dislikes him for his mouthful of multisyllabic words, for the way she knows he derives pleasure from saying them, especially in a courtroom faced with someone like her or, even worse, someone whose grasp of English might not be stellar. Those assholes in their expensive suits take great satisfaction in using words only other lawyers know, a parade of formal language to befuddle the poor soul on the witness stand.

It doesn't help Anthony's cause that he smiles, not at her, but privately. She is sure he's thinking she's stupid, doesn't "get" the beauty of his well-oiled law machine. And that she's a hot-headed Mexican who wants murderers to go straight to the chair. Thank goodness for cool-thinking intellectuals like him. He doles out *fair* treatment contemplated at hole 14, while some relative of the accused follows at his heels lugging the golf bag so he doesn't have to.

"If you were ever accused of a crime," he says, "you would want someone like me on your side. Sometimes the people who appear to be guilty aren't. Or there are extenuating circumstances, and we want to take them into consideration while sentencing."

"Extenuating circumstances." She wants to spit. "That example I thought of, someone straddling the victim, blood literally dripping off their elbows . . . I want to hear how you think that person should get off."

"Suppose the accused acted in self defense," he says mildly. "Maybe that dripping blood is her own."

"Okay, what if there's no sign of injury to the, the . . . "

"Accused. Well, then, let's say that there's been a long history of attacks on the accused, and she believes that another is about to rain down on her. She preemptively—"

"Then it's not self-defense."

"Perhaps not, but it would affect the court's leniency in determining how long this individual should be kept away from society. It's not like there's a chart somewhere that says, *strangle someone, you get thirty years*. Well, actually, there kind of is . . . but it's more that there's a span of time, *fifteen to thirty years*. And so the due process of the law might determine this wife has been beaten for years and so this time when her dirtbag of a husband brandishes his baseball bat, she goes after him. Do you think we'd want her to serve at the minimal or maximal end of the sentencing limit?"

She turns away to stare at the display in the store window. She can't even tell what she's looking at. All she can think of is his use of the word *dirtbag*. What her mother, Magdalena, had called her father on the birth certificate.

Tears don't come. They never do. She's never been a crier. How she hated the sobs in the group home. With the little kids, okay, but the teens should've been able to clamp it down. She has nothing to cry about anyway. She doesn't know if her father hit her mother. She doesn't know if he was in her mother's life, or a one-night stand, or a rapist. She has no idea what he was to her—which means he is a nonentity to Brooke.

"I read a lot of true crime," she says. "I know there are some people who walk this earth . . . well, let me ask you this. Have you ever been the victim of a crime?"

"No, other than having my swim goggles stolen out of my car once. What about you?"

She could kill herself for directing the conversation exactly where she didn't want it to go. This was the question she's spent years dancing around, maneuvering ways to not talk about her past. And she led him straight to it.

"No. I've been lucky."

"I'm glad to hear it. So, you were making a point?"

"I just . . . I've read so much. I've thought about it a lot."

"And?"

"It seems so clear that there are some people who can't be rehabilitated."

"I respectfully disagree," he says. "I just took over a case from one of the older attorneys in our firm. I worked hard with the client for his parole hearing, and it was invigorating to see what I could do for him. He was young and stupid when he committed his crime, and now he can rejoin society as a productive member."

She looks Anthony straight in the eyes and a wash of blackness pulls at her skull from inside. He's so nice. He's handsome. He's doing what he thinks is right. And she'd love to go home with him and feel his skin under her palms and his taste on her tongue, but it just isn't happening.

They're so close to the burger place she can smell the fries in their oil from the exhaust fan on the roof.

"I feel awful saying this, but I just got hit by the worst headache," she says.

She sees by his face that he gets it instantly. All that pressure, all that build-up, released in a second. There will be no dinner, no seduction. Her past has gotten in the way of enjoying things, once again. For him, their discussion was probably light and interesting; for her, it was like digging a nail into a paper cut.

His eyes search her face, and his shoulders slump almost infinitesimally.

"Let me walk you back," he says. "I don't want you to run into someone who'll make blood drip off your elbows."

CHAPTER 9

Lizzie

MAY 21, 1872

The new home on Second Street was a bit of a disappointment but at least it got the family away from Uncle Hiram, that rude and distasteful man. It was also farther from the fishy smells of Crab Pond and the loud, machinic bravado of the mills and the train, all just a few blocks away when they lived on Ferry Street.

Their moving day had been relatively easy, although Mother had fretted about furniture being chipped during the cart ride over. The new home was a little strange; everyone had to walk through Emma's bedroom to get to their own. Lizzie's room was very small, but she knew Emma deserved the larger chamber.

After only one night on Second Street, Emma had asked Lizzie to help her move her bed so it blocked the door into their parents' room. "Abby and Father can use the back stairs," Emma had said.

"But that's for the maid."

Emma had shrugged. "He chose to buy a house without a central hallway. He can use the servant's stairs, and she, too."

As she had at Ferry Street, Lizzie loved poking around in Emma's room, touching the ephemera left to her by their true mother: a cake of perfumed soap, a brooch Lizzie wanted desperately, but there was only one so it must go to the eldest. Emma cherished the Frozen Charlotte doll, undressable, molded in one immobile bisque unit with garish face painted on. Lizzie frequently asked if she might have it, since, at twenty years old, Emma was long past the age of playing with dolls, but she wouldn't even let Lizzie hold it, concerned she would break it. The doll reclined permanently in a cigar box, with a scrap of calico as her blanket.

Whenever Emma was away for any secure amount of time, Lizzie would take a quiet tour of her treasures as if the room were a forbidden museum open only to very particular collectors. She perused, she touched, she placed things back exactly as they had been, so the curator would not notice upon her return. She spent the most time with Margaret, Emma's name for the doll, but mostly, she was drawn to look at the photograph of her late mother, which was sequestered in Emma's bottom drawer. It was a framed image of her in a paisley gown and a severe hairdressing, holding infant Emma firm on her lap with a dark-gloved hand. Emma, in her off-shoulder dress with lace-daggered hem, had been scared of the photographer.

Lizzie traced the loop of the necklace around her sister's neck. Where had that ever ended up? She set the photograph up on the dresser top, and carefully balanced Margaret before it on her thick, flat feet, so she too could study the mother and daughter portrait.

Her father had often commented that Lizzie had her mother's eyes, which were large and looked rather fierce. In looking at the photograph, though, Lizzie could see that her mother was more handsome than her.

Lizzie took the doll in her hand and sat upon Emma's bed. They'd been in the new house only a month, and Lizzie liked exploring. The attic in particular was a vast and shadowy place.

"Emma's room is so much larger than mine," she said. "I have just this little closet, here. See?" she told the doll.

"She is the eldest," said Margaret loyally.

"But must she have everything? Why did not Mother give *me* such a doll as you?"

"Emma already told you. You weren't old enough for a bisque doll before she died. You had a soft rag doll, and where is she now?"

Lizzie gripped Margaret hard in her fist. She moved her thumb so it pressed against her mouth and nose, cutting off her breathing. She let the doll struggle for a bit before releasing her.

"You played too roughly with her," Margaret continued. "So you have not a thing to remember your mother with, you bad girl."

Although it was just a conversation she was having with herself, Lizzie found herself filled with longing and rage. Her mother was a black spot in her life around which everything else seemed to revolve. She couldn't remember the face that must've loomed over her cradle, the deft hands that took care of her diapers and soothed her. Maybe her mother sang her to sleep. Lizzie's small body must've slumped wearily against this woman's larger one, but she couldn't remember a moment of it.

As her mother lay dying, she had made Emma promise to take care of Lizzie. And so Emma was her lamp in the dark, and the other woman, whom she called Mother, was like a candle, far less important and prey to the wind's power.

It was horrible not knowing the very special thing that everyone else knew about. It made Lizzie an outsider. Even Abby, who had taken her mother's place, had been acquainted with her.

Lizzie spat on Margaret's face and then used her sleeve to dry her off. Spittle lingered in the caverns of the doll's eyes. She rose from the bed, readying to put Margaret back until their next secretive encounter. But her innate clumsiness made her lose her footing, and the doll sailed from her hand, crashing against the dresser front with a *plink* and then onto the carpeted floor with a thud.

"Oh, no! Dear Margaret, what have I done?" cried Lizzie, crawling to the pale white limbs separated from the torso. Margaret had lost both arms and one leg.

Breathing heavily, Lizzie positioned the limbs where the breaks were, trying to see if she might use glue to mend them, but Emma would see the hairline cracks. Lizzie would never hear the end of it; Emma enshrined that doll. In a panic, she gathered up the pieces and hurtled down the stairs.

The only thing she could think of was to get rid of the doll. Emma would miss it in the dresser drawer, but maybe not for a long while, and Lizzie could lie and say she knew nothing of its whereabouts. That was better than the doll being found with the spider lines of repair.

She went out the front door and clung to the side of the house, making her way to the barn. It was a crisp fall day, and pears were hanging pendant on the trees in the orchard. After she got rid of Margaret, she would come and eat some.

She opened the rough wood door to the privy and held her breath as she stepped inside. She dropped the smaller body parts first and watched them disappear into the murk.

She kissed Margaret on the lips. "I'm sorry I'm such a bad girl," she said, and then held the doll over the reeking pit. "She should've given me my own," she muttered and dropped her.

It was months before Emma missed the doll. On a December morning, racing downstairs into the sitting room, she confronted Lizzie, who denied any knowledge of the doll's location. Mr. Borden, overhearing, asked if Emma had seen the doll since the move from Ferry Street.

"I did, of course, Father," said Emma aloofly. "She is very valuable to me, and I would never have left her behind."

"I didn't mean to suggest you left her behind," he said. "Only that she may be misplaced."

"Lizzie has her."

"I do not!"

"You stole the most important thing that I have from our mother! You wretched, cruel girl!"

"I don't have it. I promise, Emma!"

Abby placed an arm around Lizzie's shoulder, which was promptly shrugged off. "I'm sure the doll is somewhere," she said. "We're all confused after the move. I haven't been able to find several of my own pieces of jewelry."

"Check Lizzie's dresser! Oh, you don't need to; I already did, looking for Margaret! She must have all the things she's stolen cached somewhere."

"This is a serious thing of which to accuse your sister," said Abby.

"She's been a thief since she was born," spat Emma. "But I didn't think she'd dare to take something so treasured."

"Emma!" said Abby in a cross tone.

"Don't you take up her part!" shouted Emma. "You're not my mother; you're not anyone's mother!"

"Emma, go upstairs! I won't have this," said Mr. Borden.

Emma shot one murderous look at her sister, another to Abby.

"You're too old to play with dolls," said Emma. "Why couldn't you just leave her alone? She's all I have to remember Mother."

"I didn't play with her," said Lizzie.

Emma was right, though; at twelve Lizzie should not have been making voices for a doll. In four more years, her dresses would be made to reach the floor like a woman's, and she'd start wearing her hair up.

"You're a liar and a thief," said Emma as she stormed out.

"I don't believe you did it," said Abby quietly with a kind smile.

Lizzie hung her head. It just proved what Emma had always said, that Abby didn't know them, wasn't truly part of the family. Abby couldn't tell a lie from a truth, but Emma could, because Emma had taken on their true mother's role.

Lizzie wanted badly to go upstairs and fling herself onto her bed, but in this new home's terrible layout, she couldn't do so without going through Emma's room first.

She didn't want to go to the kitchen, where the maid Oona gave only narrow sympathy for her boredom, and it was too cold to go outside. She was trapped in this small house. Even her father radiated fury as he sat down with his newspaper, rustling it loudly as if at her.

She moved toward the parlor, but at the doorway Abby called her back. "I just dusted in there."

Wordlessly, she ascended the staircase. She walked quietly so Emma wouldn't hear. Halfway up, she sat on the stairs, listening to the sobbing coming from Emma's room, and the tart words down below.

"She will never accept me," said Abby.

"She doesn't need to," he said. "You're my wife."

Lizzie sat back against the wall, waiting for the house to catch up to her mood. She stared idly across at the floor of the guest room, reserved for visitors who only rarely came, or for sewing. Why was she not given this chamber?

She was never treated well. Certainly not as she deserved.

It was an odd vantage point, at eye level with the floor like a mouse. She felt an odd propulsion to seep through the banister railings, formless as smoke, and crawl under the bed.

CHAPTER 10

Bridget

NOVEMBER 16, 1889

At half four on Saturday, Bridget stood waiting on the front stoop wearing her nut-brown serge dress with many pleats, fashioned by her mother all those many years ago and kept good by Bridget's careful laundering. She had emerged from the side door and made her way to the front steps, looking up at the sky between the twin fastenings of the oak trees, the "bride and groom" positioning to showcase the house.

As she waited for Mary Doolan, she watched her breath clouding in the crisp air and the carriage traffic on Second Street, the horses' hooves smelting the odorous piles they left, hay discernable in the thick masses. There were shops interspersed with the modest homes here. Kitty-corner from the Borden house, several women rapped on the door of the home with a small sign indicating it was the residence of a Dr. Bowen. Whatever the downturn in fortunes, this neighborhood boasted two doctors, which Bridget felt to be advantageous. She curiously watched as the door was opened to the women, but just then a cart began to pass, blocking her view.

She turned her head against the stink, and a male voice boomed, aimed at her, "Fancy a ride, lass?"

It was the same as winked at her a week ago when she arrived, trying to tote her trunk. "Ach," she said under her breath, willing him away.

"Been up and down this street on your behalf," he said. The hack had halted, and the horses tried to mark her past their blinders, wrestling against the bit. "Never caught a nick of your shadow."

Reluctantly, she looked at him perched above her, nearly touching distance due to the house's closeness to the very street. He was smiling, sure, but not insolent. He touched his cap as soon as he had her eye.

"Are ye getting on fair?" he asked.

"Aye," she said.

"And is there any place ye need a pleasant ride toward?" His dark eyes fastened on hers, and the smile left. He was serious, for whatever cause.

"No," she answered.

"You are in the custom of standing at the door for no call?"

"I'm waiting for a friend," she said.

"I could be one," he said, and she burst out laughing.

Just as his eyes lifted behind her, she heard the door open. She turned and saw Miss Lizzie, her eyebrows high in censure. Bridget found herself blushing though she'd done naught.

"Bridget, whatever are you doing?" asked Miss Lizzie, her silver gaze fixing on the man in the hack.

"I'm off for the evening," said Bridget.

"And you snuck out from the back? I've been in the sitting room this entire time. Does Father know you're out?"

Bridget felt her heart skip a bit. The accusation leveled against her was a bold one. She needed to address it, and quickly. "I found it just as easy to come down the stairs I was on, and there was no craft about it," she said. "It's my night off of the fortnight, and your Father does know that's my due."

"I fail to trust he'd approve of roadside discussions with men as they pass," said Miss Lizzie. "This is not a reputable practice."

"I was the driver who brought her here," said the man in the carriage. "I was only asking after her settling in." He looked uneasily at Bridget and broadcast a sort of apology with his eyes.

"From the seat of your carriage, calling out like a commoner," said Miss Lizzie. "This is the home of Andrew Borden. It is not a harlot's port."

"Miss Lizzie!" said Bridget, stepping back in horror and, in doing so, losing her balance on the uneven stone steps. She managed to catch herself before she fell to the ground, but her entire body felt the affront of the hard surface radiating up through her shoes, the jolt in her bones.

"I can see I'm causing more trouble than I'm helping, so I'll pass along," said the man. "I hope you are all right, miss."

Bridget didn't answer him, and only looked at her shoes. How could Miss Lizzie voice such an odious, preposterous idea in front of the man?

"Your place in this household requires a certain degree of respectability," said Miss Lizzie. "Come back inside at once."

Her jaw sore from the snapping of her teeth as she stumbled, Bridget walked back up the steps. Miss Lizzie opened the door, and she was just about to step inside when she heard Mary Doolan call out, "You're after going the wrong way!"

Bridget looked at Miss Lizzie's face, half-shadowed as she was inside the home now. She was a study of gloom and sunlight, her nose the silhouetted wall in the ombre garden of her face. Yet in that complex field, Bridget saw clearly the argent eyes and their message.

"I cannot go with you this time," said Bridget.

"But you must!" protested Mary. Fearlessly, she mounted the steps to stand with Bridget. "I couldn't help but overhear the exchange, Miss Lizzie. I can't vouch for the decorum of the driver, but Bridget's only after a bit of fun, clean and decent, at the Irish hall. 'Twas not her fault he called out to her."

"What mean you by 'a bit of fun?'"

"'Tis only dancing and the playing of our traditional tunes. Singing, too. I'll pledge her propriety and return her safely later tonight."

Miss Lizzie hadn't looked at Mary at all, only kept her eyes on Bridget. "You will need to mind yourself," she said. "You can't bring shame to this house."

"I will mind myself," Bridget said.

"I'll mind her, too!" said Mary gaily. "Now let's get along, or we'll miss the beginning."

Miss Lizzie's reply was the closing of the door between them. Wordlessly, the two Irish women went down the steps and onto the street again. Mary set a rapid pace so they were soon away from the house and able to speak freely.

"She's a case, ain't she?" asked Mary.

"I've no idea her problem. Did ye hear what she *said*? Implying me a harlot!"

"Calm your boilin' blood and don't let her spoil your one night out. She's just fashed no handsome lad ever calls out to her! You're pretty, and you're Irish, and she's dissatisfied with her own sad lot in life."

"I didn't hardly answer him," said Bridget.

Mary stopped and cast Bridget a look of exasperation. "You can't put any credence in what she suggested of your character."

"I put credence in it if it costs me my post!"

They walked on a bit until Mary, in a low voice, said, "I'm sorry,

Bridget, and I know my boldness isn't always welcome. I don't want you to get into trouble for my sake. But sheets and bloody linens, all you did was stand there a half moment waiting for me!"

"I ought to have gone out the front door and told where I was going. I think that's the root of her anger. She must've looked out the window and seen me talking with him."

"But then you'd earn it for daring to use the family door rather than the servants'! And must you account for all your comings and goings? Lord knows we only get one night a fortnight, and it's *ours* to do with as we wish."

"That has been the case with my previous employers," admitted Bridget. "But she has new rules for my conduct, and I'll obey them."

"She? Why she? Does she pay you? Or is it her father? It's none of her business what you're doing of a Friday night!"

"I know you are right, and yet I don't know what I'd do if I lost this position without a good character."

"There's always a better spot somewhere else."

"If I can get it," said Bridget. "I don't have your confidence."

"Well, if worse comes to worse, you can live in the barn until they discover you," Mary said. "And eat the pears off the trees, and I'll bring you table scraps."

"Good gracious! You sound as if you've thought of this before!"

"Your predecessor," said Mary.

"Truly?"

"Indeed. Oh, and now here we are! Can you hear the music from down the street?"

A thin thread of sound came from a public house, but as soon as Mary grasped the door and opened it, the music flooded out loud, strident, unapologetic: completely Irish. It was the "Hayman's Jig", and inside the sets were already there with knees flying and skirts flouncing. Instantly, Bridget wanted to be on the floor dancing, too.

The space was small and cramped with so many bodies. There was a long bar with many golden taps, and tables pushed to the edges to create the dance floor. A smell of sweat and sodden wool from the men's caps created a not-unpleasant whiff to the room, along with the overflowing glasses of hops and doctored tea.

"Hello, Miss Doolan!" greeted a man behind the bar, and Bridget was relieved he was addressing her friend formally.

"And good evening to you. This is my new friend, Miss Bridget Something or Other!"

"Sullivan," Bridget supplied.

"I'm Mr. Seamus Dorgan, and I welcome ye. Where might you hail from?"

"Allihies, sir."

"Indeed, and let's all drink to Allihies!"

A roar went up, and all the men took a swallow of their ales. For a second, Bridget saw the scene through Miss Lizzie's eyes: was this disreputable, men drinking so good-naturedly and loudly? Drinking to her village for her? Was it too rough?

Then Mary caught her arm and twirled her around, a makeshift jig that had Bridget's feet flying, and soon others gathered around them, forming the straight lines until they were threading the needle, their feet following the time-worn steps.

Each song melded into the next, the fiddlers at the back of the room wiping sweat off their brows whenever they could manage between notes, the pipers and *bodhran* player taking sips off their pints while the music momentarily faltered. It was grand and glorious, and if Bridget closed her eyes, as she did sometimes in the dizzying twirls as she swapped grasps with new partners, she could almost imagine herself in the barn back home, with nothing outside but a stretch of cold yet fertile land offering greening hillocks to the travelers who lifted a lantern to the sea.

At one point, Bridget's lungs could take it no more, and she stepped outside the set, giving a smile to Mary who kept dancing. She made her way to the table where meat pies and scones could be had for a few pennies. She bought a beef pie and a tea, and stood balancing both against the wall.

"I haven't seen ye here afore," said the woman standing next to her. She was tall and willowy, her red hair in a bun that was losing its formality from, presumably, her dancing.

"No, it's my first time. I came at the invitation of Mary Doolan."

"Ah, she's grand."

"It does my heart good to hear the tunes well presented, rather than my own deplorable whistling," said Bridget.

The other girl laughed. "I'm Maggie," she said.

"I'm Bridget. Pleased to make your acquaintance. Where do you hail from?"

"Kinsale on the coast."

"So lovely!" said Bridget. "I went once on a holiday."

"And you're from?"

"Allihies."

"I've heard of it. And when did ye make your way to these shores?"

"Five years ago," said Bridget.

"Broken heart?"

"Broken purse more like."

"Ah, those of broken purses tend to fill up the ships heading west across the Atlantic, do they not?"

"Aye. I'm sending a bit back home each month and hoping to keep myself out of rags as well."

"'Tis a noble aspiration, to keep all the body clothed," agreed Maggie with a grin.

"A lofty one indeed!"

The rhythmic beat of the *bodhran*, a tempered sort of drum, percussion with a lilt like all things Irish, fastened onto Bridget's mind and became the cadence of their conversation. Everywhere she looked, she saw smiling faces. Unfettered of the general mistrust of immigrants they faced on the street, the group blossomed into joy. They all remembered, in place of the brick mills and soot-darkened windows, the green expanses of their childhoods, the hills besmocked with mossed rocks, the willows bending to the water.

"'Tis gay," the other girl observed, and as if to underscore her point, a lad in a heather-colored wool cap pulled her off to join a set. Bridget laughed outright at her new friend's surprised expression.

"Go on and show him the lightning of your footwork!" she called, but too late to be heard.

Bridget ate her pie and drank her tea, lukewarm now. It was good fare, which she hadn't needed after the dinner she'd made for the Bordens and of which she'd eaten the leavings, but as they were plodding their way through the same tired roast of pork, she was glad to eat a second, more pleasing repast.

As soon as she'd finished and set down her cup and plate, a man appeared as if he'd been waiting. He was flush-cheeked with eyes blue as spatterware and smiled and indicated with a nod of his head that he'd like to squire her onto the floor. She nodded, gratified at the attention, and they joined into the mix. She couldn't stop grinning for she loved this song.

The row of dancers faced her, full of merriment, darkened hair at the brow where sweat gathered, and circles of dark cloth appearing under their arms. She cared not a whit.

She cocked her leg in front, then curled the other behind, drag-stepping to the right, everyone in accord although not all were graceful—but it didn't matter, it was only the doing of it that mattered, the shoes bouncing off the floor and returning lightly.

She danced twice more, then begged off with the speechless gentleman who only smiled his regret to lose her. She returned to the corner where Mary Doolan and the girl named Maggie were talking.

In contrast to the gaiety, they were talking quickly with their eyes intent on each other.

"Oh, so ye know each other," Bridget greeted them. "What's at odds?"

"Maggie's worried about you," said Mary.

"About me?" Bridget looked at Maggie, whose face indeed reported concern, her lips thinned and her dimples gone.

"It's not enough to leap out of the frying pan to save my skin," she said. "When another jumps in after me."

"Whatever do ye mean?"

"Maggie's the girl who worked for the Bordens afore ye," explained Mary.

"I worked up my courage to leave," said Maggie. "I didn't think about ever meeting the girl who took my place. And you're so nice . . . I can't not warn ye."

On the instant, Bridget felt her stomach unsettle. Had the meat from the pie gone bad? It had tasted fine, but maybe its thick juices masked the bad.

"What is it?" she asked.

"It's Miss Lizzie."

The two looked at Bridget, and she pressed her hands against her protesting stomach, suddenly cramping.

"I'll need the privy," said Bridget.

"We'll take you," said Mary. They walked through the crowd, receiving a few elbow blows from conversationalists deep in their cups, gesticulating to illustrate their stories. They walked past the musicians, red-faced with effort, heads nodding full-force as if snapping awake from a nap over and over.

Mary and Maggie led Bridget out the back door to the small courtyard with its double privies to handle the volume of the pub-turned-dance hall.

Bridget entered the small wooden privy, but her stomach wasn't upset after all. She looked at the moon through the moon cut into the door, a tacit pun that made her feel weary. She gave herself time while she listened to the murmur of the women talking and the muffled music from inside.

No, it wasn't the pie making her stomach feel off. It was what Maggie had said . . . or not yet said about Miss Lizzie.

"Are ye all right in there?" asked Mary, now close to the door.

"Aye, I'll be out in a trice."

The stench made it no place of respite. She stood, let her skirts to the floor and went back outside, gustily inhaling the fresh night air. She bent to the nearby bucket to wash her hands. A cake of soap exuded its own milk in a tin dish.

"Tell me then," she said.

"You've noticed she's . . . " began Maggie strongly, but then she trailed off.

"She's what?"

"It tests one to talk about sommat in your gut with no true reason behind it."

"But you left."

"I left, not even knowing the next place I'd land."

"And where did you?" asked Bridget.

"I'm renting a flat with five other girls. They're at the mill, and I take in laundry, sewing, odd jobs. I made the meat pie you just ate."

"So you can make a living just with that?"

"Close to it. I'll serve again if I can find another home without a character."

"Mr. Borden wouldn't give you one?"

Bridget straightened. So Maggie had been booted after all, in opposition to what Mary had told her in the backyard that day. And perhaps now she was casting Bridget against the family in revenge?

"I went to him with my fears, and he was angry."

"What were your fears?"

"I worry Miss Lizzie is dangerous."

Bridget responded with an exhale, crossing her arms. "And dangerous how, you say?"

"Have you not seen the rage that sits in her eyes?"

Bridget said nothing. Above their heads, the stars sprawled in their chosen arrangements. Some ancient peoples had looked at the mess up there and managed to see patterns. "Her eyes are a quite unnatural color," she said finally.

"Hers unnatural, and yours blind," said Maggie.

"What did you fear?"

"I feared harm." Maggie's voice took on a tone of defensiveness now rather than persuasion.

"You feared she would harm you?"

"Yes. I wished to end all association with her and leave the house forever. She isn't right, and if you don't see it yet, you will."

"Did she yell at you?"

"No, but worse. It's the quiet that scares me. I tried to talk to Mr. Borden about it, and he wouldn't hear it. So I tendered my resignation."

"You left good employment just because of a feeling?"

"I did, and you ought to as well."

"And who will serve the Bordens? Do you intend to dissuade every maid until there are none left in Fall River?" Bridget hated the words coming out of her mouth and didn't know why she was being cruel to a girl who was only saying the things she had already thought.

"I don't care who serves them! Let them stew their own mutton a hundred times over!"

"Persuade her better," said Mary. "Use that blarney. Tell her what you saw that makes you so wary."

"Well, that's the trouble, isn't it? I've naught to report other than a feeling deep in me gut that Miss Lizzie was the sort of trouble I wanted nothing to do with." She regarded Bridget in exasperation. "Did you never find yourself on a dark street and something amiss at your back? No one's there but you hasten your pace till you're flying."

"Aye," said Bridget.

"So that's how I felt with Miss Lizzie."

"And tell her about the way Lizzie stopped calling her stepmother Mother," said Mary.

"Two years ago, for love of nothing but money, Miss Lizzie suddenly stopped calling her Mother, which she had done since her father married her. She raised Miss Lizzie since she was a child, and suddenly she's Mrs. Borden to her."

"What happened?" asked Bridget.

"Mrs. Borden's half-sister—whom she helped raise—goodness, this lady has been mother to so many and yet none from her womb . . . her sister had been bandied about by her husband, not good with money or rents or those matters. So Mr. Borden provided her a house on Fourth Street, deeding it to Mrs. Borden. The girls were in an uproar about it."

"How so?" asked Bridget, amazed. "Family sticks together, and what uproar did they make of a kindness?"

"She's not blood to them," said Maggie. "Abby's not, and her half-sister even less so. So the house became a morgue of stillness with their darting looks and their prim faces until one morning it exploded in anger, and Mr. Borden gave them their own house."

"And it didn't placate them?"

"Not a bit; he might as well have given them a coal from the fire for all it pleased them."

"I wonder that they don't move into the other house," said Bridget.

"Not fit for them," said Maggie with her chin lifted and a haughty expression adopted on her face.

"You're just the picture of her!" breathed Mary Doolan.

"It's the house they once lived in with their true mother, and they didn't want to return! They're renting it out. And it's over that bundle of pettiness that they began calling her Mrs. Borden."

"The very greed of it," marveled Bridget.

"Yet they're unashamed. They lost a 'mother' for the sake of helping out a family member with a no-good husband and two young children to provide for."

A fellow came out then, bringing music and cheer with the opening of the door, and the stark silence of the stars as it swung shut behind him.

"Evening, ladies," he said. For the sake of his privacy, of one accord they nodded and moved back toward the dancehall.

"Well, I've done my job in warning you," said Maggie. "All the rest is up to you now."

They were swallowed by sound as they entered, and Bridget felt weary of the music that had previously invigorated her. She felt the other two were of the same mind, troubled by what they'd talked of. The grins on others' faces were no longer infectious and instead a reminder of the blankness in her gut.

"If ill befalls you, come to me," said Mary. "Throw stones at my window, and I'll let you in."

"I hope it won't come to that," said Bridget. "Oh, Mary, would you mind much if we left now?"

"I've gone and spoilt your evening," said Maggie.

"Thank you for your concern, truly," said Bridget. "I've not many options, though. I'm the breadwinner, and my family still in Ireland waiting on the odd coin I send."

"And isn't that the very brunt of it; it always comes down to money," said Mary.

"Watch yourself," said Maggie, "and you can always bunk with me if the times get rough."

"You're very kind," said Bridget. She stared at the other girl, who she knew not from Adam, but whose disquiet for Bridget had taken over the evening. "*Go raibh maith agat,*" she added in Irish.

"*Tá fáilte romhat,*" said Maggie. "You're welcome indeed."

On the walk home, Mary Doolan hummed the titular tune of the pub, a ballad about a headstrong lass who took a ring off a fellow and then crossed the ocean without him. They walked in companionable silence other than the droning strains, but Bridget soon realized she was dreading the return to the dark house. The pub had been too merry, but the home would be too low.

Soon enough, they were at the Kelly house, where Mary turned off with a flash of a grin and an immediately contrary somber face. "'Twas up and down tonight, weren't it?" she said.

"Aye," said Bridget with a rueful smile.

"I'll see you in the backyard then," said Mary, and with a nod she was gone.

Bridget continued on a few more paces until she reached the Borden home. She surveyed its simple, asymmetric face, the pitched roof. No curtain might twitch for her; the rooms that faced the street were only the sewing room and the clothes press. Would she work here until her serving days were over? Was this clapboard tenement to be her final stop?

She went to the side door and used her key. No lamp had been left for her, but it was easy enough to climb the stairs with the guidance of the brittle banister. She trod quietly, aware that her footfalls might awake Mr. and Mrs. Borden. She passed the landing where she could hear the breathing of her sleeping employers, long abed on a Saturday night. She carefully felt with her foot for the turn and the beginning of the next flight of stairs.

She began to climb, her eyes becoming accustomed to the dark. It was then she saw the shape ahead of her on the staircase, a silent immobile mass that she strained to see. A rook-colored pillar, fathom-less, black as carbon.

She stopped, hand clenching the banister.

The shape stirred a bit, arousing itself from the glut of darkness. It was a woman.

Bridget could detect her standing five steps above her, in full skirts that acquired the plum flush of belladonna, not black, as her eyes adjusted.

The woman pressed herself to the other side of the steps, against the wall, as if merely a cask one might need to step around. She was trying not to be seen.

It was Miss Lizzie.

Bridget discerned the silhouette now, the frizzed hairs, the stone-shaped head. She couldn't see Lizzie's face or her blankly savage eyes. Both women remained rooted in place.

Bridget's falter and stare must have surely alerted Miss Lizzie that she could see her, yet she said nothing. Bridget gripped the banister so tightly that her nails dug in. She knew she must move, but how? Retreat downstairs? Run to Mary Doolan across the moon-dappled yard?

Continue on climbing to the attic bedroom meant to be her sanc-tuary but now guarded by a Cerberus in human form?

She could not now, after this long silence, call out a greeting to Miss Lizzie and pretend all was well. The wait became interminable. Her heart took an immodest leap in her throat.

She quelled the impulse to turn and steeled herself to continue her way to her room. Miss Lizzie's stealth seemed intentional, and so she would preserve the pretense that she wasn't there.

She forced herself to continue climbing, no hitch in her step, as they drew even and Miss Lizzie's silver eyes caught hers.

The coldness of the gaze shocked Bridget. It was imperious, frig-id glance of someone who did not care. Miss Lizzie faced forward;

only her eyes had crept to the side to capture Bridget's. The whites took on a luster in the stairwell, and Bridget shuddered as she bolted the remaining steps. She resisted the urge to look back, feeling the skin on her neck crawling, cold despite the sweat from the warm evening's walk.

She grasped the doorknob, fumbling and nearly muttering an oath to herself at the panic she felt to put a door between her and the silent mistress.

Had Miss Lizzie been in Bridget's room? It was her house after all, and she had the right to enter any room, but what might she be after in Bridget's attic? Or had she not entered and only stood in the gloom, waiting for Bridget to return?

The door relented and Bridget pushed forward into the dark room. As she turned to close it behind her, she saw that Miss Lizzie had not moved, still facing forward, crushed to the side of the wall, perhaps in some illusion of invisibility.

Bridget closed the door and sank down against it. She waited in vain, weariness dogging her eyelids, for the swish of skirts to alert her that Miss Lizzie had left her strange post.

The darkness, implored for movement, laid bare no secrets. She bent to peer at the small strip where the door did not meet the floor, half expecting the silvery eye to regard her from the other side. It was too dark to see. She listened and wished her night to be essayed afresh: to not have gone out, but to have stayed safely in her quarters, each corner scrutinized by lamplight until the kerosene gave out, to not know of the figure monolithic on the stairs, and most of all unwitting of Maggie's accusations formed in this very chamber.

CHAPTER 11

Bridget

NOVEMBER 17, 1889

In the morning, Bridget rose to the lambent light. She went to the window. Mr. Borden was down in the backyard dumping his night soil, trousers pulled up under his linen nightshirt. The sky was stamped with rose-tinted clouds and the beginning grit from the factory chimneys stoking up at that hour.

She brushed her hair, long strokes through the brunette, as she circulated the small room, looking for evidence of Miss Lizzie's having entered. The nightstand with its Irish lace doily appeared untouched, and she opened her trunk to tally its humble contents. She pulled the curtains closed to wash and dress and then opened them again to catch the light.

The cedar waxwings chattered their high-pitched notes, and as Bridget pressed her hand to the glass to melt the frost that hovered by the bottom, she felt the events of the night before subside into a haze of unreality.

She opened her door and saw the stairwell undramatic, plagued by nothing more than dust that she'd do well to sweep out. She descended into the bowels of the house to fetch coal and wood for the kitchen stove and start its fire, the ashes spavined and ready for shoveling. That done, she pumped water, brought in the milk cans, and commenced slicing bread and boiling millet.

Mr. and Mrs. Borden came down first for their breakfast, ringing the bell for her. She served them, and they spoke quietly of their day's plans as she came in and out. When they finished, she cleared away the plates and bowls, their pattern a simple blue and white positioning of peacocks beneath a willow tree, all spreading their pride-filled spray. She used the brute of her hand to sweep away crumbs and set the table again.

The sisters arrived so promptly that she wondered if they had waited upstairs listening through the wall for the sounds of their elders resettling in their rooms or the front door closing behind them.

Miss Emma appeared in the doorway in a dress of blue lawn, a brooch at her neck, while Miss Lizzie came in behind in pink dimity with brown thorns, a glossy ornament pinned to her breast. Bridget stiffened at the sight of Miss Lizzie.

Her posture was firm and straight, yet her shoulders hunched a bit or perhaps her neck was short, providing her a distinctive profile, last seen as sable upon sable in the night stairway.

"Good morning," said Miss Emma as she took her place at the table.

"Good morning, Maggie," Miss Lizzie echoed carelessly, walking rapidly to her side of the table and sitting with no sense of polish. She bore a confidence that Bridget had never felt. The Borden girls basked in their father's money even if they could not freely spend it. In their dowdy clothes, they appeared to still feel the height of their station, like princesses kept in hiding by cunning regents.

"Good morning," replied Bridget.

"Millet," Miss Lizzie pronounced, looking at her bowl with distaste. "This is what I feed my pigeons."

"It's all right now and then, Maggie, but we don't prefer it," said Miss Emma. She tempered the correction with a smile, but all Bridget heard was the dismissiveness of calling her another servant's name.

"I'll remember," said Bridget. "Shall I take it away?"

"Not this time."

"The doughnuts you made previously are in keeping with our hopes," said Miss Lizzie. Her voice, low and flat-toned, had the hush of gentility that her graceless body lacked. She looked up, and their eyes caught. It was a fleeting moment, but Bridget thought she sensed the other woman's triumph at not being questioned for her odd behavior the night before. She knew she'd been seen, but that Bridget was powerless to do anything about it.

As Bridget stepped back into the kitchen, Emma asked her sister, "Could you not sleep last night? I heard you pass through and stay away quite some time."

Bridget waited on the other side of the doorway to hear the reply. "I sat downstairs and read," lied Miss Lizzie calmly.

Bridget fumbled with the plates, nearly dropping them. She bent over, capturing them against her apron, gaining a smear of slimy millet for her trouble. And of course, the stain fell in the middle of the blank field of the apron, glaringly visible and embarrassing in its placement, as if she'd lost control of her natural functionings. She'd have to change into another, and God help her if that became tinged for there were only two.

So the miss could baldly lie; could she? Sitting and reading, was it, rather than hovering outside garrets in the dark?

She blotted the apron quickly. As soon as she'd got the coffee made, should Mr. Borden want another round, she'd go upstairs for the other apron. She went back into the dining room for the other plates.

"I wonder at you, Lizzie," said her sister. "Why come all the way downstairs when you might simply read abed?"

"I was restless," said Miss Lizzie. "And it was close."

"The rooms do get stuffy upstairs," Miss Emma agreed. "I wonder how it is in the attic." The two Borden women looked at Bridget, but she was already on her way out, keeping her back turned to them to prevent their seeing the stain, so she threw Miss Emma a smile over her shoulder and continued on.

She quickly ground the coffee beans, rotating the wooden-balled handle while the aromatic beans gave way unto coarse grains. The smell filled the whole kitchen, and she opened the drawer at the bottom of the grinder to shake out the ground coffee into the pot, adding water and then putting it on the stove to boil.

She untied her apron and shrugged it off, going to the wash pail to work out the stain before it set. She used the flakes of detergent to make a weak lather to dab on the spot. She relaxed as she worked at it, for the day stretched ahead of her with not much to do in it.

She heard the rustle of skirts as someone came into the kitchen. Lifting her eyes, she saw Miss Lizzie there, waiting for her to acknowledge her.

"What sort of trouble did you invite last night?" asked Miss Lizzie.

Bridget made no answer, aware her jaw must be open. Her fingers tightened around the folds of the apron in her hands.

"Off with the Kelly girl, who is trouble no doubt," she added, and Bridget suddenly understood she meant trouble out on the town, not trouble in the back stairway of the home.

"'Twas only a night of merriment, and no harm done," said Bridget.

"Were there men in attendance?"

"Aye, but none I spoke with."

"And alcohol?"

"Not so much."

"I campaign for temperance," said Miss Lizzie. "So many lives have been destroyed because of its ruinous nature. I do not approve of alcohol."

"Nor do I, and there was hardly any there, just enough to moisten and soften the tongue."

"Did you drink an alcoholic beverage there, Maggie?"

Bridget stiffened at the false name. "I had tea."

"And the Kelly girl?"

"Tea as well, I suppose, if she had anything. I saw her take none."

"Was there dancing?"

"Aye."

"And the men had taken drink?"

"Not to the degree that you worry over, Miss Lizzie. The evening was a respectable one, and not the carousing I fear you envision."

Bridget tried to keep an even tone, but she felt a bit of Mary Doolan's ire. She could do as she wished on her nights out, so long as it cast no shadow on the Bordens' propriety.

"Well, I don't envy you dancing and sweating in such a hot milieu," said Miss Lizzie. "I've never understood the lower classes jumping around like crickets."

Bridget's dander was officially up like a post in the newest-plowed field, and so she made no reply. She pressed her lips tightly against each other to keep hot words from bursting out. She dropped her gaze and made herself busy as a whirlwind, tossing the apron aside and taking perverse pleasure in slamming down the mugs and crocks in their transport to another work surface, making enough noise to prevent Miss Lizzie from adding more egregious words to the ones already spoken.

She examined the smoking furnace of her feelings as she did so. Somehow Miss Lizzie had adjusted from an object of no small terror in the night, to the annoyance of bigotry and contrary opinions. Bridget hardly knew which was worse.

One was a subject she knew well. She was used to the cold shoulders for those of her race, identifiable by the thick and sweet timbre of their voices. At market, others might smile at you and extend a greeting, withdrawn when she opened her mouth and spoilt the charade of being a decent American. She'd even laughingly practiced with others, flattening her round, fruit-filled vowel basket until the hard, native tones of Massachusetts filled the ear, sounding as if the speaker was perpetually unpleased.

There were ill feelings against the Irish. They were second-class citizens only fit for the trades or the mills. Bridget herself especially hoped to avoid a station at one of the roaring machines she heard as she passed by. She'd never set foot in one of Mr. Borden's several textile mills, but even upon a walk past, the very walls seemed to tremble with the clack-clacking of the mechanical shuttles going to and fro on the same task a woman could render in silence, if not as rapidly.

One heard tales, too, of the bosses who took pretty girls aside and abused them, for the girls desperate to keep their jobs would never dare register a complaint.

And of course the machines themselves enjoyed tugging at a girl's skirts like an unwanted lover, crooking her backward for an insistent kiss, unraveling her threads until the others noticed and cut the power to liberate her. Fingers were lost to the machines' ardent courtship. Hair was scalped as if the Wampanoags were still fitfully trying to preserve their impossible holdings. Girls died in the mills if the pulled fabric wrapped around their necks and suffocated them. Hair was so very carefully pinned up, but pins failed. Machines loved braids, adored apron strings, swooned for the fringe upon shawls.

A place even in an unpleasant home like this suited Bridget far better . . . especially given she was not worked so hard with the bedrooms being cleaned by the occupants. She had the luxury to lie down and let the sun plaster the window and her counterpane until she slept. She could stand by the fence and bandy words with Mary Doolan. There was a fair amount of freedom in this household, despite its cold and haughty nature.

And really—what servant finds warmth from her masters anyway? Surely none ever sit and eat together, nor engage in more than the most cursory of conversations. She was fine here, so long as she didn't let Miss Lizzie bully her by lurking in the stairs to make sure she came home at a decent hour and not reeling with drink.

"The dancing keeps us trim, I find," Bridget finally managed to say, a carefully crafted reply that answered insult with insult, for Miss Lizzie was beginning to drift into the jowled regions of middle age, her waist thickening. In fact, she was to have a dressmaker come in the next week to prepare new gowns for her and Emma, purportedly to be in mode but also because the present gowns were too tight on her broadening midsection.

She turned her head to see the effect of this sly affront, but Lizzie was already gone. How long had she been thumping around the plates and flatware, when she had no audience to madden?

She looked through the window and saw her enter the barn, going to care for her pet pigeons. *Best that she have that task,* thought Bridget, *for with her spiteful personality she'll never have children of her own.*

CHAPTER 12

Brooke

JULY 12, 2016

Back at the apartment, Brooke logs on to check in with Miguel.

Went on a date. Got a little freaked out and told him I had a headache so I could leave.

I get it, he typed back. It spoke volumes. She and Miguel seemed incapable of romance. Their childhoods had screwed them up, stolen from them the possibility of healthy conversation with another, the easy-going flirtations she saw going on at a hundred tables in a hundred cafés, theaters, clubs, restaurants. She couldn't pull it off.

I robbed myself of a night of passion. He was cute, too.

Should've rolled the dice, chica. If nothing else, you blow off steam.

Like you do?

Now and then.

It would've been good to spend the night with Anthony. But he seemed too interested in her. When she stuck around long enough for men to start asking questions, then it was all over: "A group home? Were your parents abusing drugs? Abusing *you*? You don't know who your dad is?"

Occasionally she would find someone as messed up as she was, but she would always get scared. Their stories upset her, plunged her into despair that their joined life could never be normal. Her longest relationship had been ten months, with a man whose wrists bore scars. It had taken her a long time to ask about those, knowing how much she hated fielding questions herself. She assumed they were the marks of a long-ago suicide attempt. Instead, she learned his stepmother had held him down while his father used the knife on him to make it *appear* like a suicide.

He'd spent weeks in the hospital fighting for his life, and as his sobs choked through her apartment (six moves ago), she wasn't sure he was glad he'd survived. She was willing to keep the relationship going, but it seemed he resented having told her. He picked fights, stood her up a few times, forced her to conclude it wouldn't work. Like him, she had become very good at engineering the ends of relationships so that it appeared to be the other person's idea.

What would've happened if you'd gone home with him?

Miguel knows she can't invite a man to her home (the wrist-knifed man having been the exception, due to his longevity). Anthony's place, an attorney's home: what would it have been like? As lavish as the Carrs' lakeside home?

Well, duh, Miguel. What do you think would've happened?

Crap. You saw through my attempt to picture you in action.

You dog.

She sees the ellipsis appear that indicates he's typing. Then it disappears. He's deleted whatever he'd written.

What? she prods.

The ellipsis appears . . . and disappears.

We should try harder. Both of us, he types.

For a second, she thinks he means "try to be a couple," but then realizes he means both of them with other people.

Why?

What do you mean, "why"?! To have a shot at a happy life.

Are you seeing someone?

It's as if she can hear him inhale through the computer.

I started seeing someone.

Like, more than just sex?

Yeah.

She can almost hear the huskiness of his voice, remembered from those long-ago porch confessions.

That's great.

It's really new. Just giving it a shot this time instead of assuming I can't do it.

That's great. So great.

It's weird; it's like everyone else in the world can do it. I might be damaged goods but whatever. I want to try.

If you get married, I want to be your best woman.

Shut up! Jesus. I shouldn't have told you.

Miguel, no no no no. I wasn't kidding.

You're jinxing it by being so . . . you know what I mean. I can't even think that far ahead.

What's her name?

Big pause.

I don't want to jinx it.

Her mouse moves in rage to the top of the page where she X's out of Facebook.

She can't believe him. He thinks telling her . . . *her!* some other woman's name is going to ruin things. Like he's afraid she'll perform some jealous voodoo.

She goes to the kitchen to pour a glass of water from the tap. Her last apartment's one redeeming quality was that it had a dispenser in the fridge door. She'd loved that thing.

Why'd he assume she'd be upset? He kept typing and erasing. He didn't want to tell her.

She drinks the lukewarm water, her throat tight like she isn't swallowing correctly. She should get back on right now, pretend there was a power surge in her apartment. The longer she waits, the bigger a deal it becomes. And then it seems like she is jealous. Dammit, why didn't she go home with Anthony?

She sits down in front of the laptop again but finds she just can't log on.

The feeling in her chest grows. She's a problem. Miguel will have to explain her to his girlfriend: *See, I have this friend from way back, and we live chat every day because she keeps changing her name and this is the one place where she's always there, and I have to be her friend because she'll fall apart if I'm not, and I feel responsible for her just because we have this history together, but don't worry, she doesn't really mean anything to me. She's just a fragile thing I can't set down because if I do, she will break.*

Someday, he won't chat with her. A day will go by, two days. Because he'll be wrapped up in the other woman. And then someday it will seem strange and unfaithful to the real woman in his life to be so connected to Brooke. And he'll maybe even have to tell her formally: *I can't do this anymore.*

She'll have to muster everything in her to reply: *That's fine, Miguel. I totally get it. Go on and be happy.*

She makes microwave tea, staring at the chipped counter edge while it brews. How did everything suddenly get turned upside down? She can't lose Miguel; she has to swallow her pride and log back on. She'll tell him it's okay to back off their friendship but it still has to stand. She throws the tea bag into the trash; it lands with a light thwack at the bottom, one of the few things she's thrown away in this apartment.

She goes back to the laptop, sickly chamomile coating her tongue.

Miguel has already written to her, with a JPEG of a bouquet of red roses.

You are the most important person in my life, and a girlfriend won't change that, he had written.

I think I'm worried that it will.

She waits, but he's no longer online.

But it should change, she continues. *You deserve love and a chance for all the real things that come with it. Not just messaging with me. I don't want to be selfish. Miguel, please get married. Do that. Pull it off. And someday I'll be so goddamn proud to see the pictures of you two at the wedding.*

She knows he can't invite her, "best girl" or not. The same way she knows the nightly chats will become monthly ones. If that.

I'm not being sarcastic here. You're the only one of us who can do it. You're the . . .

She pauses.

. . . least damaged. LOL.

Will you stop with the marriage talk??!!!!!! He's suddenly there. *And honestly, mija, you're not as damaged as you think you are.*

I'm crumpled. The UPS truck ran me over.

Then collect the insurance and start over. Anything I'm capable of, you are, too.

Don't think so, but thanks.

Jesus, Mary, and Joseph! (An Irish guy started working here, and he says that all the time.)

The holy nuclear family, she types.

No group home for them.

She's elated. Miguel didn't give up on her, and they're back like they always were. *Listen, Miguel. Let me say this one time so you know it, and then I won't have to say it ever again. I totally release you when the time comes that your girlfriend doesn't like the idea of me.*

Any girlfriend who doesn't like the idea of you can appreciate my firm muscular ass as I walk out the door.

No, it's not like that. She is going to feel like I have a hold on you, and it'll cause trouble.

She already knows about you.

She does?

She has the terrible thought that maybe the girlfriend's sitting on Miguel's lap right now, watching him type.

Of course. You're a staple in my diet, mija. I'm not going to just drop you. I'll never do that.

But you can.

Stop staying that! I don't expect you to drop me. Why do you think I would?

One more time . . . slowly. You have a chance at this. I never will. I don't want to screw it up for you.

You don't have half the PTSD I do, girl. So why are you so permanently off the market?

You know all this. I have to keep moving.

Suppose you just stayed put and waited to see what would happen?

He's awful, making her think it, making her type it. *They'd catch up with me and kill me.*

A long pause. Ellipsis. Erase. Ellipsis.

Something I like about therapy, he types, *although it costs me many pesos, is that it makes me question all the assumptions I've made about my life. Like that I can't have a relationship other than just a sexual one.*

So you don't believe me about why I have to move.

I do, mija, I do. I believe you feel this.

You believe that I believe it, but you don't believe it.

This is difficult given my limited grasp of the English.

Ha ha. You think it's an unreasonable fear. They got my mother.

You told me she died in a car wreck.

There are a lot of ways to make something look like an accident.

Why were they after her?

I told you this years ago! They wanted to get me. They must've thought I was in the car.

"They" being the brothers?

Yeah.

But wasn't there a period of years between the death of that lady and your mom?

She can't handle the disbelief, the common-sense questions trying to frame understanding of a situation that was *not* common, that made *no* sense.

She'd told him everything on the group home porch, all the evidence—and it looks as if he's forgotten. If he didn't care enough to remember, then screw him.

She'd explained about the day a package had arrived at her house with her name on it. She almost never got packages in the mail. Her mother was the only one to give her presents, and she would never waste money shipping something that she could simply hand to her daughter.

Brooke had ripped the package open, intrigued. Inside was a simple dinner plate, white, used. It was spiderwebbed with gray lines, scuffmarks from forks and knives. "A DISH BEST" was written in Sharpie on its face.

"This is not a best dish," her mother had said. "It's all scraped."

They had turned to the box to see if there was more inside, but there was only newspaper to protect the plate.

"Why would anyone send you a *plate*?"

Brooke kicked the empty box. She'd been so excited to get a package, and it was an ugly gift. She couldn't even use it as a plate with the marker on it.

"Are you going to keep it?" her mother asked dubiously. Brooke watched her examine the box. "How'd they even get it mailed without a return address?"

"Who sent it, Mom?"

"I was going to ask you the same thing. Girls at school being mean?"

"No one even notices me."

The second plate had arrived a few days later. This one's Sharpie message read "SERVED."

"I don't like this *loco* gift," her mother said. "You sure nobody at school is giving you a hard time?"

She had tried to mentally filter through the students arranged in rows, in classrooms, on lunch-table benches. Walking down the hall, chatting to other people, no one giving her eye contact unless they bumped into her accidentally. "Sorry," came the breezy and quick apology, and then their conversation resumed.

"No one, Mom."

"Should we tell your principal?"

"Why?"

"I don't know. Maybe they're doing it to other kids." Her mother's beautiful accent, making "kids" into "keeds."

"It's stupid. Why would they do that?"

But someone *was* doing it. A third plate arrived. She had put them all next to each other on the kitchen counter, hating them and their inexplicable messages. She was ready to throw them away, but held onto them a little longer to wait and see if a fourth plate came.

When the police had come into the house to talk to her, to inform her that her mother had been killed, one of them had pointed and snorted at the plates. "Sorry. I'm so sorry," he said. He was ashamed at laughing in the household where he'd just delivered such terrible news.

"Why are you laughing?" she'd asked him.

"Clever craft idea," he said. "You made them?"

"No. What do you mean, they're clever?"

"You don't . . . ? Oh. It's a saying. 'Revenge is a dish best served cold.'"

Her blood had run as cold as the promised revenge. The third plate, it was true, had only "COLD" written on it. Together the dishes spelled out part of the saying.

She hadn't put it together then, hadn't understood the full meaning. She was confused. Her mother, her only known relative, was dead, and the police were making phone calls to try to place Brooke with someone before night fell. A female officer was on the way, they'd promised, as if their maleness made it inappropriate to hug her, to comfort her.

And just as the officer who had explained the saying opened his mouth, maybe to say more about the plates, another officer thrust a stuffed animal into her arms. It was a cheap Teddy bear with the kind of hair too sparse to hide the loose-weave fabric underneath. She thought it came from the convenience store around the corner.

"I just wanted you to have something," said the man. "I know you're a little old, but it's good to have something to hold onto." Tears shone in his eyes, so she hugged the bear. "I have a five-year-old," he added.

She wasn't thinking straight. She should've had them dust the plates for fingerprints, but instead she'd put them in the trash because it was trash night, and her mother expected her to roll the cart to the curb. And if she was going to leave the house for a few days, she had to take out the trash so it didn't smell up the house; there were raw chicken parts, fat she'd cut off the tenders before frying them the previous night.

The evidence that could've protected her and put the brothers behind bars, had she only thought about it: she herself rolled it to the curb so that the morning's trash truck would take it away forever.

You still there? Miguel types.

Sort of.

You should tell someone, maybe they can investigate it and get some closure for you.

Maybe.

You know the brothers' names; right? Have you tried to Google them?

I have to go. I'm sorry. I'm glad about your girlfriend.

Okay.

She logs off, deflated by his questions. "Get some closure" means "have someone tell you you're nuts and no one is after you."

The plates were real. They were proof that someone wanted revenge.

And the only thing she could've been accused of?

The death of Mrs. Carr.

CHAPTER 13

Brooke

JULY 4, 2002

Brooke stood in the Carrs' upstairs hallway, lit by an enormous semicircular window at the other end that took up an entire wall and displayed the tufted greenery of the estate's well-fed trees. She thought that if it was cold that night, they could stand at the window, all of them, to see the fireworks.

The hallway itself had significant footage. To the rich, even a room that consisted of doors to other, genuine rooms, with purposes and mission statements, deserved thick carpeting, a focal chandelier, and a lounge sofa halfway down its stretch, as if you might get over-come with exhaustion and need to rest before carrying on.

She waited and listened, wondering which of the rooms could be hers if she lived here someday.

Simple, flat doors wouldn't do for the Carrs. No, each one had inset panels, creating a small lip outlining them, on which dust could perch if Brooke's mom wasn't vigilant in her duties. Her mother must crouch and stand on tiptoe alternately before each of these doors, worshipping some strange monolith, her damp rag swiping at each inset to redefine it for the portal deity.

She had none of these thoughts because she was only nine, but she saw, and was silenced by, the evidence of wealth at every turn.

At the end of the hall, closest to that large window, was a set of double doors. She suddenly burned with desire that this be her room. She imagined a canopy bed inside, draped with pink transparent fabric that would billow in the wind as she threw open the windows to the lake, and there would be a miniature velvet sofa she'd pile high with the stuffed animals she'd always coveted at other kids' homes, fixing adoring gazes upon her. A white and gold vanity she could sit at to do her makeup—and in this fantasy, her mother would *let* her wear makeup.

It became so deliciously real that she put her hands on the two door handles, ready to accept her future as a spoiled and pampered child, when she heard rustling from within.

Heart pounding, she silently ran down the plush carpeting, plunking to her knees in the only hiding place possible, behind the lounge positioned to restore the elderly and ill during their punishing trip down the length of the hall.

The doors opened and her mother came out, along with Mr. Carr.

"Idiot," her mother said in a whisper that carried down to her daughter's ears. More like *ee-dee-ot* in her extended vowels. There was affection in her voice despite the terrible thing she was calling her boss. "You're going to get us caught."

"We were gone for all of ten minutes," Mr. Carr said, "and it was worth it." His arm withdrew from around her waist.

Brooke was sure they would see her as they came down the hall, so she pushed herself completely under the lounge. She watched their shoes go by, her cheek pressed to the shag. It smelled good, fresh and floral. Even the floor in this house was worth thrusting one's face into.

Mr. Carr wore huaraches and his ankles were pleasingly shaped and not too hairy. Her mother wore the gladiator sandals she'd bought especially for this day. She hadn't wanted Mrs. Carr to see her battered flip-flops, which had curled to conform to the contours of her feet.

The Carrs carelessly wore their shoes throughout the house, without the sign by the door Brooke saw at so many people's houses, requesting shoes to be taken off. The Carrs had someone to vacuum daily, so it didn't matter if dirt got tracked in; in fact, it was a good thing. It further justified the maid.

It occurred to Brooke she didn't need to stay hidden. This was her mother, after all. She might get scolded for startling her, but then she and Mr. Carr would flap their hands near their hearts and laugh, as if panic could be fanned out like a flame.

Brooke stayed under the lounge, however, so she could see that room, take ownership of the canopy bed and village of stuffed animals. After her mother and Mr. Carr had gone downstairs, she rose, padded down the hall, and entered.

Disappointment.

The bed *was* large but lacked four posters and gossamer. Rather than pink, the bedspread was a royal blue-and-white stripe. It wasn't a child's room. The furniture was sized for adults, covered with boring things like a clock and a charging station. An odd, close smell was here, but soon the open windows would suck that odor back out to the lake.

She wondered if the barbecue would be ready soon. If Mrs. Carr had been stoking the coals, maybe the meat was already on the grill.

She pulled the double doors closed behind her and checked each door on her way out, standing just inside each room to see every detail.

She wouldn't consider herself a snoop, but Mrs. Carr had said it was okay. The boys had their own rooms, themed by color.

The boys had homework desks and toy chests and bookshelves, all color-matched: royal blue for Abraham, maroon for Ezekiel. A piece of art above Ezekiel's bed spelled out his name in puffs of smoke from a steam train with a broad grin.

A guest room and a workout room accounted for the remaining doors. Brooke reluctantly supposed those could be made over for her and her mom. She descended the stairs and went back to the kitchen, thinking much more strongly about that promised barbecue.

In the kitchen, Mrs. Carr was squeezing lemons. Homemade lemonade was underway in a large glass pitcher. Next to it on the island was an empty, blood-streaked platter. Good: the meat was already on the grill. "Are you looking for your mother, sweetie?" she asked.

"No, I just saw her upstairs," said Brooke in surprise. "She was—" She stalled. Mrs. Carr would wonder why Brooke hadn't come down with her mother and know that she'd been helping herself to a self-guided tour.

Mrs. Carr frowned. "Is she up there now?"

"No, they came down together," Brooke said, adding defensively, "Just a few seconds ago. I had to use the bathroom."

Mrs. Carr turned away. Brooke looked out the window to see the boys still on the dock, throwing rocks into the water. She would've been willing to gather flat stones for them, good skipping stones, and stockpile them on the dock, but not after what they'd said to her.

"You hungry, sweetheart?" Mrs. Carr asked after a silence.

"Kind of."

"We have some yummy things for you today."

"That's nice." The two of them engaged in a strange and extended surveying of each other. To Brooke, the mother seemed alien with her pale, pale skin and hair so blond it was nearly white. But the look on Mrs. Carr's face was the same as she saw on her mother's: love.

"I always wanted a little girl."

"I wish I could live here," said Brooke without hesitation.

Mrs. Carr laughed. "The boys are boys. They tear through the house, and they destroy things, and they *never* shut *up*."

Brooke smiled but wasn't sure she was supposed to. Wasn't it rude to agree how awful the boys were? By the same token, Mrs. Carr was the hostess, and her mother had taught her to always agree with the person who's setting food in front of you.

"A girl, though. A girl would be in the kitchen with me, helping put frosting on the cookies."

"We could make cookies," said Brooke slowly. Was that the right thing to say? She felt out of her element in this kitchen the size of a restaurant's, the wide expanses of marble counter without appliances on them to explain their immense planes.

"You're so sweet, Felicita," she said, because that was Brooke's name back then. Her true name, the one her mother had given her: the one on her birth certificate and her Facebook profile.

"You are, too," said Brooke.

Mrs. Carr opened one of the cabinets.

"I'm just going to have a quick glass," she said. Brooke watched her brisk, knowledgeable movements as she plied the corkscrew and poured a glass of deep red wine that looked like elixir squeezed from rubies.

"Your mother is very beautiful," said Mrs. Carr, just before she tipped back her head and the entire glass of wine slowly, methodically disappeared.

Brooke tried not to stare. In movies, people sipped wine and walked around cocktail parties holding the same glass throughout many conversations. "Thank you."

"You're beautiful, too," said Mrs. Carr as she poured a second glass. "You'll be a stunner when you're grown up."

"You, too."

Mrs. Carr nearly choked, laughing as she wiped at the wine spilled on her cheeks and chin.

"I meant, you're beautiful, too. Not that you aren't grown up."

"I'm grown up; it's true. I've even developed wrinkles already. Can you see them?" Her face loomed in front of Brooke's.

"No," said Brooke honestly.

"You're being polite. That's so sweet. Your mom has raised you well, even if she's a single mom. I don't know if I could've done it."

Mrs. Carr turned and looked at the faraway boys on the dock. "Not that I did a great job even *with* a husband at my side."

When Mrs. Carr raised the bottle to pour a third glass, Brooke realized she wanted to stop her. She didn't know why; it was some gut-level insight beyond her years. People had always been telling her she'd had to grow up fast.

"Do you think the food is ready?" she asked Mrs. Carr.

Mrs. Carr still poured and drained the glass. "Burned to a crisp by now, I'd imagine," she said. "All that steak."

CHAPTER 14

Brooke

JULY 13, 2016

"How'd it go last night?" Maria sings out when Brooke arrives.

"It didn't," Brooke admits. "We got into a really weird conversation, and I bailed."

"That is the saddest thing I ever heard. What kind of conversation?"

"One where I didn't like what he had to say."

"About what?"

"Nothing."

"Oh, my God, you're crazy, girl! He's so good looking. If you don't want him, pass him to me."

"Your daughter's father isn't around?"

"Oh, no, he's long gone," says Maria.

"Sorry. That sucks. How old is your daughter?"

"She's nine."

The age Brooke had been when she and her mom had been invited to the Carrs for the Fourth of July. The day she'd learned her mom's job was something to be embarrassed about. She wonders if Maria's daughter is proud of her barista mother.

"What's her name?"

"Magdalena."

"That was my mom's name," says Brooke.

"Was?"

"Oh, yeah, she died a while back."

"What about your dad?"

"Never really knew much about him."

She glances at Maria, who's looking at Brooke intently. "That's what it is for Magdalena, too. Was it hard growing up that way? A lot of people ask questions?"

Brooke shrugs. "Sometimes I'd say he was dead. I didn't like to tell people I didn't even know his name."

"Shit, girl, maybe he's rich. And I know he for sure owes you something."

"I doubt he's rich."

"Maybe track him down just to be sure."

Brooke nods so she doesn't have to say "No."

"Find out his name so that way, when you curse him in your prayers, it will land on the right back," says Maria.

"I think you might have misunderstood how praying works."

"So what are you going to do when Mr. Weird Conversation comes in?"

"I don't know. I hope he doesn't."

Throughout her shift, she whips her head around every time the bell at the top of the door rings. Anthony never comes. He's avoiding her. She feels bad she ruined his favorite café for him.

But never fear, she thinks. *I'll be gone in a while anyway, and you can start coming again.*

After her nightly chat with Miguel, refreshingly back to normal with no mention of his love life's progression, Brooke picks up her library book about Richard Speck, the man who killed eight student nurses in one crazed night in 1966. She feels herself falling into the same state of fearful worry she always does, that she's preparing herself somehow, learning the tricks of the killer's mind so she can combat one later.

But her mind drifts back to the chat with Miguel. He's right. She should Google the Carr boys. She hasn't wanted to in the past, kind of like turning around when you're being followed and looking at the person. It would let them know that *she* knew, because it's clear they've looked at her computer.

Their surveillance started in the city Brooke had moved to after aging out of the system—someone had come into her apartment when she wasn't there. The signs were so subtle they might not have been noticed by anyone other than a maid's daughter, who was used to picking up an object, dusting under it, and then replacing it in exactly the same spot. Spend a few years tagging along with your mom on her weekend and evening jobs, and you become an expert in object placement. So when Brooke had come home to her apartment and seen that the mouse had shifted on its mousepad, she had instantly known that her space had been invaded.

But she hadn't been too alarmed; puzzled would have been a better adjective. Her studio apartment wasn't worth breaking into. She had no TV, let alone a large-screen one, no jewelry, no cash. Even the laptop someone must've sat in front of was not worth thieving. It was a remodeled older Dell that held a tenth of the memory that an average cell phone did.

She had thought, was it someone poorer than herself, maybe, who needed Internet access? She had glanced through the browser history, but if the intruder had been navigating on her system, they had covered their tracks.

So maybe it was a kid who liked the thrill of walking around someone's apartment, not knowing when she'd come home and catch him. "Creepy-crawling," it had been called in *Helter Skelter*, the first true crime book she'd read, about Charles Manson and his deranged family. The secretive gush of danger coursing through the brain as you move a stranger's furniture was a high for some people—or so she'd read.

Or . . . she herself had jogged the mouse by accident, not realizing it. In her rush to get out on time for her first-ever job, the one that might dictate her entire future if she were to be categorized as "lazy, late, not worth anything," might she have hit the flimsy desk with her hip? She was klutzy. Always had been. Her mom had even taken her to the doctor once to find out why she always ran into things.

But that episode became the first of many. A curtain pulled to the side, as if someone was checking for her arrival. A photograph set back on the shelf cantered just slightly past the angle she'd originally set it at. Because of these subtle changes, that was the last apartment that she'd rented under her real name, Felicita Hernandez.

Although she had worked hard to build a reputation as a good employee, she had dropped it all for the chance to start over in a different city. She prepaid months of rent under a new name to avoid particular paperwork, using the small proceeds from her mother's life insurance.

Since then she'd become many women, sometimes with a Spanish name, sometimes—as now—with an English-sounding name as if she was trying very hard to assimilate. "Brooke" had been a choice she liked, and she hoped she could keep it for a while. She loved its connotations: well-to-do, uppercrust, perhaps British rather than American. Someone who lived in a vine-covered cottage with expansive lawns that led down to . . . yes, it's apt, she must say it . . . a little babbling brook.

She took names from newspapers, movies. Once she'd decided on Philomena after she'd taken a walk through the older part of a cemetery, where death dates quickly followed birth dates, where children's markers were in sad abundance, their namesakes felled by diseases whose defense was now logged on stiff yellow immunization records required by every elementary school.

With each move, she felt sure she couldn't be traced. She told no one where she was going, other than Miguel. She changed her name, sometimes cut or colored her hair, and chose a city far enough away that she'd never run into someone from her old life.

She was now only twenty-three, but since leaving the group home when she was eighteen, she's lived in twelve cities, eight states, and too many apartments to even recall the floor plans, views from windows, neighbors.

She discouraged attention from the latter. Sometimes a single mom evidenced jubilation at seeing a nice, young woman move in down the hall: now she could have movie night with her girlfriends; now if she needed to step out for a missing dinner ingredient, she had only to knock. So Brooke had developed a coldness when encountering neighbors. She'd say, without smiling, "I'm gone a lot," just so they'd know she wasn't going to join them for a glass of wine, wasn't up for lingering at the mailboxes for chatting. The fewer people who knew her, the fewer to remember her. She was like a shadow slipping down the wall as the light changes. Her movements were not to be detected at the time of motion, only long after she'd moved.

But no matter how careful she was to remain detached, quiet, difficult to notice, somehow she was always pursued. It might take a few months, but there would always be a day—and her breathing deflated when she encountered it—when the salt shaker was on the other side of the pepper, when the medicine cabinet door wasn't completely closed. And then she'd begin planning her next name, next town, next job.

This was why she could never have a man in her life, other than someone to spend a night or two with. This was why she could mentally shrug that it didn't work out with Anthony. If she did fall in love, if she ever permitted herself that extreme indulgence, she'd be screwed because she could never stay.

She had hesitated to learn more about the people pursuing her, Abraham and Ezekiel Carr, because it would make it real. It's only surmise right now that they are the perpetrators—and sometimes she can even talk herself into believing none of it has happened and she's a victim of her own paranoia—but if she leaned into their lives, breathed into their identities, she'd be acknowledging that she knows them. And somehow, she fears, they would sense it and speed up their revenge.

But it's been too many years that she's been living under this shadow without investigating it.

She rubs her forehead with her palms and makes herself start typing.

An article about Mrs. Carr's death is the first hit: "Holiday Turns to Tragedy." She clicks through to read it. *Drowned . . . no one aware for quite some time . . . alcohol in her system . . . survived by her husband, Christopher, and two children, Abraham, age 13, and Ezekiel, age 8.*

Nothing there that she didn't know already. A picture of the family arranged on the stairs draws her attention, though, and she studies each face in turn. Mrs. Carr's face makes her sad. Such a gentle and sweet woman with her frazzled blonde curls. Mr. Carr is good-looking even if his hairstyle now looks dated. The boys are just as she remembers them, except that they're smiling at whoever took the picture.

With a jolt, Brooke realizes that person could've been her mother. "Oh, Magdalena, would you mind? Clean the toilet and then take a quick family photo for us?"

Brooke shakes her head at herself. Mrs. Carr would've never talked that way.

Brooke clicks back to the search results and scans them. One article makes her gasp and click on the link with one hand pressed against her mouth.

Abraham Carr, 21, found guilty in the murder of former classmate Wendy Allen.

Brooke reads in disbelief. The two had attended the private St. Joseph's High School, graduating in 2007. Sometime over the summer, the two had met up; he had followed Wendy to her apartment. At her door, they had been heard fighting, and he shot her. A neighbor had filmed him getting into his car; he was identified by his license plate and booked within hours. The trial had taken place a year later, and he had been sentenced to serve ten years for a second-degree charge.

So Abraham's a convicted murderer. He doesn't look much like himself in the disheveled mugshot. His face gives Brooke a chill, so she closes down the browser. Enough for one night. Even if she'd protested to Miguel, she had to admit that there was some part of her that did wonder if she was right about being followed all these years.

This confirms it, though.

Abraham had murdered. He wanted to murder her. He'd sent her the plates, tracked her city to city.

Wait a minute, though.

Cursing herself for closing everything down, Brooke gets back online and looks at the dates. Abraham had been incarcerated since 2008.

So he hadn't been breaking into her apartment. Was it Ezekiel?

She stands up, walks to the kitchenette to boil water for pasta. She'd been raised on quesadillas, arranged a hundred ways: three kinds of beans to choose from, and what else might we put inside, cheese for certain and perhaps some chicken or tough carne asada if it had been on sale. Sometimes her mother had prepared them with squash and zucchini inside, and it was always a treat to get both sour cream *and* guacamole. But now that she was cooking for herself, she ate a lot of pasta, penne with Alfredo from the jar, and salad. She wondered if her mother would like that, should they happen onto some *Twilight Zone* household where her mother would sit down to eat with her once more.

She salts the water and returns to her laptop, hitting the space bar to wake it up.

The only times Ezekiel Carr shows up are in articles relating to his mother's death and one quote a reporter had managed to get from him after his brother's sentencing, "Abe's been troubled ever since our mother died." And after that date, nothing.

It's almost impossible not to have a digital presence, but she and Ezekiel seem to have managed it just fine. Abraham, too, has had no hits since his incarceration, which is to be expected. But shouldn't Ezekiel appear on some "staff" page at some company, unless he, like her, is doing the low-key, part-time life. But that seems unlikely, given his background. He should've had his dean's list announcements run in the local paper, his move to VP of innovation publicized in his industry's trade paper . . . probably even his times for the 5K and 10K races the well-off seem to do.

She tries searching for him again, without quotation marks around his name, but that of course creates a sea of Biblical proportions and one that can't be parted with a staff raised in the air.

She returns to the kitchenette and pours a cup of farfalle into the boiling water. There's something else she should research while she's at it. Maybe it's time to find out who her father is, an idea she had always rejected aggressively.

It's such a long shot, but . . . maybe he could protect her. Perhaps after so many years of failing her and failing her mom, he'd be on fire to fix things for Brooke.

Her heart races as she considers what a difference it would make to not have to move. To not take the shit jobs and make her employer think she was truly helping the poverty-stricken refugees of Jalisco and Juarez. What if she could go back to school and have a real career?

She hasn't filed taxes since that first job out of the group home that was arranged for her, but she could use her insurance nest egg to hire an attorney and get back on track with her social security number. She still has the card in the cigar box her mother had kept important things in. Brooke has always supposed the cigar smoker was her father, but probably the wooden box had been passed to her as a discard from Mr. Carr or another employer.

The thought of finding her father exhilarates her at the same time that she knows how absurd it is that this man who has remained hidden for a quarter century will somehow save the day. Her mother had considered him a dirtbag; why should she question her judgment? You don't hunt down dirtbags. You hope they stay in whatever despicable existence they've carved out for themselves.

Plus, she has to face it, it may not be that he's been "hidden"; he may not even know she exists. Good luck arousing retributive action against the Carr brothers from a guy who thinks he's in no way involved.

She has no proof. What man is going to look at her birth certificate and say, "Oh, yeah, this must be me! And let me now correct the errors of my ways. When we're done, angel, you can call me cleanbag!"

Which makes her laugh a little to herself, ruefully, hating how the sound echoes in the basically empty space of her kitchen. It's the first time she's laughed in here. Her mother, the *maid*, was unable to clean the dirt off her dirtbag of a sexual partner.

She searches online desultorily, and her mood deflates. Her first name and her mother's, their surname: shared by millions of people.

And how does she account for her father as she searches online? "Paternity suspected?" "Unwitting sperm contributor?" "Possible rapist or one-night stand approximately nine months before August 12, 1993?"

She rises, drains the pasta, and mixes it in the Alfredo straight from the jar. The pasta heats it up enough. Sad to think this lukewarm dinner is acceptable to her because cooking is such an effort. The one person she's ever witnessed taking true pleasure in food preparation was Mrs. Carr before she'd opened that bottle of wine. She was like a TV mom, taking time to squeeze lemons instead of throwing flavored powder in a pitcher and adding water. She'd marinated those steaks and shrimp with an attention Magdalena had never given the quesadillas monotonously slapped together. It wasn't just about having the money for fine ingredients; it was a care genuinely taken.

Brooke eats, washes the simple array of bowls and ware she's dirtied. She goes into the bedroom to get the cigar box. The only thing she can think of is the address on the birth certificate given as her mother's at the time. The habit of moving wasn't one Brooke had invented. She had never lived in the house on her birth certificate. Correction: by the time she had been able to understand and memorize her address, it wasn't that one. She might've come home there as a newborn, but she doesn't remember.

She looks up the address and sees a one-story without a garage. What's surprising is that it *is* a house, a stand-alone, not an apartment. The street view shows it to be part of a shabby but decent neighborhood with sidewalks. Some of her former neighbors have even planted flowers at the bases of ornamental four-foot stretches of fence. It's a street she'd like to live on today. Why did her mother take her away from there?

She can't find a name connected with the house. She'll have to write a letter, an odd exercise last practiced by grandmothers. She starts one in the small notebook she uses for her shopping list.

Hello, I was born when my mother, Magdalena Rosa Hernandez, lived at your address. I was born in August of 1993. My name is

She breaks off. She'll have to write her real name, and she can then be traced to it. If this person writes back, they'll put Felicita on the envelope. She hasn't spent six years covering her tracks to give it all up for what seems to be a doomed mission anyway. She could say she's writing on behalf of Felicita. She tears out the page and starts again.

Hello, I'm writing on behalf of Felicita Hernandez who is trying to connect with her birth father. I'm her friend.

That was better. Someone would have to actually *read* the letter to draw a connection between Felicita and Brooke. She's paranoid, but perhaps not paranoid enough to worry about that.

She finishes the letter, stamps it, and immediately walks it out to the metal rabbit hutch that is the complex's mailbox and puts it in the outgoing mail slot. She knows she might not send it if she allows herself to think about it.

*D*ear Brooke,

Please tell Felicita I would love to see her. Thank you for your letter letting me know Magdalena has died. I had thought of her many times over the years and hoped she was well. I'm sorry she is gone but glad to hear she had many years of happiness with dear Felicita before she passed. Please tell your friend she was a darling little baby. I went through some old boxes to find this photo for her.

Brooke's heart beats so quickly she feels nauseous. There's a photo? She turns the envelope upside down and it drifts out onto her kitchen table. She stands up blindly, stumbles to the cupboard. She doesn't drink wine, not after seeing what it did to poor Mrs. Carr, but she has a handful of nips for moments like this. She opens the miniature Cuervo and downs it.

Sitting back down, she picks up the photo, surprised her hands aren't trembling.

It's her mother, young, smiling proudly, sitting on a brown plaid sofa Brooke hasn't seen before. She's holding up a baby, wrapped so securely only the tiny moon face is visible. The part that makes Brooke emotional is the man next to her mother, his arm slung around her. His other hand rests on the bundled baby. It's her father.

This is her father.

She shakes her head. Reeling. She's never seen him, not once. And she's never seen a picture of herself as a baby, either. Her mother's American plans hadn't involved the purchase of a camera.

So this was the family. By the sight of it, a happy one. Her mother's beautiful dark coloring, her nails painted a pretty magenta against the stark white of her baby's fleece bundle. Of *my* fleece bundle, she thinks.

And her father.

Her father was blond. Big white teeth in that satisfied and generous smile. He wasn't Mexican. Brooke had always assumed he was. No, he looked as white as they come. He even wore a white button-down shirt. So formal.

So, what does she do with this? What changed happy, proud Dad into a dirtbag? Didn't one fill out the paperwork before leaving the hospital? So maybe her mother had reconciled with him, but not bothered to add his name to the documentation after that?

Or . . . maybe this wasn't her father. Maybe it was a friend who had stepped in. And obviously, soon thereafter, stepped out.

She turns the photo over. In blue ballpoint, someone has written, "Magdalena, Felicita, and Burhardt, September 1993."

She'd been a month old then. The tequila makes acid in her stomach, just as she realizes the rest of the letter may contain answers. She resumes reading.

Felicita's father Burhardt Aalfs was from Belgium. He came over to go to high school, and I hosted him as a foreign exchange student.

Holy shit! He was a foreign exchange student. Her father was Belgian. *She* was Belgian! A Mexican-Belgian-American.

When they told me at church that this poor girl had come in from Mexico knowing not a soul, I took her in, too. I was like a foster mom to her but not in an official way. She was a year older than him so I guess I was naïve, but I didn't think there'd be anything between them. Then she turned up pregnant, surprise surprise!

I hope you can find a nice way to tell your friend the next part. He was mad at her mother and thought she'd done it on purpose. They did try to make it work, but he really wasn't ready. He was a high school junior. He barely spoke English, and Magdalena hardly spoke it either. He was scared to be a father at his age. He ran away back to Belgium when the baby was born, but he came back, and they were happy for a little while. It wasn't ideal. They'd have misunderstandings. Jealousies that young lovers have, but they didn't have the language skills to solve them. Maybe I'm being too detailed here but since your friend's mother is gone and apparently never told her these things, I feel a responsibility to help her understand that I think her parents really did love each other, but they were just too young.

Taking on a child was a lot to ask, although Felicita was an easy baby. When Burhardt's year was up, he went back to Belgium. They never married, although I tried to get them to. He left her with as much money as he could. I forced him to do that, and believe me, I made some international phone calls myself to make sure his parents understood the situation. For all I knew, when he called them he was talking about the school lunch menu. Even got a special plan with the phone company so I could talk freely and impress on them the responsibility he'd created here in the United States. Kind of a worst-case scenario for parents sending their kid off for a year abroad. But please don't let Felicita think of it that way. She was a blessing. I know Magdalena thought so.

A second nip goes down easily, not so fiery in the throat the second time around.

Anyway, they set Magdalena up financially, and she let him go back home. No idea what happened to him. The amount of money was sort of a parting gift.

Was *this* the basis of the life insurance payments her mother had kept up? Certianly it was not the type of expense one would expect of a maid barely getting by. Or was there a bank account somewhere holding all that money still? After her mother had died, a detective or someone from the placement agency had helped her go through the apartment. If her mom hadn't kept the bank statements, perhaps there was a cache no one knew about? Or maybe the helper had helped himself to it, considering it a reward for the punishing drudge work done every day for the disenfranchised and ungrateful?

Two extraordinary things revealed to her today: well, three, including the photo.

First she now knew her father's name . . . and he might be alive.

And second, her mother had once owned a significant sum of money.

The end of the letter gives no new information. Magdalena had decided to try her hand at living as an adult and moved out. She'd phoned now and then over the years. The last contact the woman had with Magdalena was when Felicita was being enrolled in kindergarten. She closes with well wishes for Felicita.

A postscript gives the phone number for the family in Belgium.

I wrote it in my diary in case there was ever any trouble for Magdalena. You made me read back through my diaries, not a pleasant task at my age! The number is probably useless, but you never know.

She holds the letter in shaking hands. She can hardly believe its contents. And now she has a new name to research. She's making strides in the last few weeks that she hasn't made in years. She's learned Abraham Carr was a murderer, she's seen a picture of her father, she's been given a telephone number and history of her father's brief involvement in her life.

And the rumor of money.

And most heart-stopping of all, a possible release from her furtive half-life. She tries to picture herself a year from now, free to tell everyone her name is Felicita: which means happy, which is the root of *felicitous*, which is a vocabulary word she might encounter if she went back to school, if she was pre-law, if she owned a home and got to paint the living room the vivid saffron she's always wanted but instead knew her landlord would have her head for, or at least every cent of her security deposit.

With her heart pounding, she types the strange name, referring back to the handwritten letter in front of her to spell it correctly. She puts Boolean quotation marks around the words and hits enter.

Burhardt Aalfs has a web presence, but it's all in French. Nonetheless, she clicks through, and there's a group shot of the members of a law firm (seriously?!) arranged in three rows in a conference room. Did her mother know this to be Burhardt's plan? Is that why she chose that career for her, a desperate echo of the lifestyle that should've been hers?

Burhardt's tall enough to be in the back row, so she can't see his hand to see if he married. His wife would surely not welcome this particular 5'4" blast from the past. Nor would his parents, if that telephone number even works. They'd paid their hush money long ago.

Did any of them ever think about her, wonder what became of her and her mother? Had the woman taken several photos, and maybe Burhardt took one home in his luggage with him? Or maybe he had a bunch of them: wealthy enough to come to the States for a year abroad, he probably had a nice camera in the era before smartphones. He probably took a ton of photos of the beautiful girl so luckily placed in his host home, as if for him! "The U.S. will give you a taste of

mediocre schooling, confusing culture, the arrogance of a former su-
perpower not aware of its slip and fall on the world stage, and . . . a
sexual partner just down the hallway! You, of course, should provide
your own condoms to avoid the disastrous consequences."

If he hadn't destroyed everything, somewhere there might be
an abundance of photos of her mom. And of her, too, adorable and
moon-faced.

She studies his face again. No one would pick him out of a police
lineup to be her father. No resemblance. Well . . . maybe the chin.
The shape of the jaw.

"Hello, Dad," she says to the screen. "Want to come back to the
States and pick up where we left off?"

CHAPTER 15

Gus

DECEMBER 17, 1889

Gus couldn't help overhearing the kerfuffle from down the hallway. He set his broom against the wall, ready to lend aid to the woman sobbing in the Sunday school classroom. He'd been listening as she tried to regain authority, but the boys sang out in their foreign tongue, drowning out the efforts. He began to walk toward the classroom, but coming from the other side was Reverend Buck, his face aggrieved. The minister ushered the woman out to the hallway so they could speak. She was in her thirties, her hair in a tight bun and her bangs crimped. She took care with her appearance, and she looked to be respectable if not one of those matrons who owned half of Fall River.

"They don't listen to me or mind my instructions," she told Reverend. Buck while Gus hovered nearby. She seemed to be trying not to hyperventilate, her breathing hitching with her sentiment. "They are so rude! They sass me to my face! It's unbearable, it's just not, just not—"

"I know," soothed Reverend Buck. "They haven't had the social training to understand how to treat their betters. I'm sure you are doing a marvelous job, and if their background were equal to your training, it would be a delight. But this only underscores the vital need for what you're doing for them."

Well, weren't that always the way? Feed a dog, and it bites you? Gus didn't approve much of the Chinamen with their queues falling down their backs: men with braids! Might as well put a bonnet on, tie the ribbons, and make it official.

He continued listening to the choked-up explanations the woman gave Reverend Buck. Here she was just trying to help them, and they were like little monkeys worrying at her skirts, impudent and thankless, making her cry. Poor thing. Nothing worse than a pack of urchins sassing you.

He heard the minister go into the classroom and thunder at the children. Silence followed, but Gus knew it would be of a temporary sort. As soon as the authoritative reverend left, the woman—Miss Borden, as he heard her called—would again be prey to the small monsters' insolence.

As Reverend Buck exited the classroom, Gus stepped forward.

"Reverend, you're needed in your office. But I'm of the opinion she'll be plagued again. Might I step in if'n I hear them giving her trouble?"

He saw at a glance the gratefulness that crossed her face as she stood uncertainly in the middle of her classroom.

"That's a good thought," said Reverend Buck. "And I'm sure Miss Borden would welcome the assistance."

"I would," she said.

"That's settled then. As you continue your work, Gus, you may keep an ear out."

Gus was slightly disappointed Reverend Buck didn't introduce them to each other, but knew it would be inappropriate. She was Miss Borden; he was called by his first name like a child.

Reverend Buck withdrew, and Gus lingered in the doorway of the classroom to assert his authority over the rows of boys—with their jet black hair, the charity cases learning English during the week when Sunday school wasn't held. Their clothing the bright, glossy silks that society ladies would kill to have several yards of for their own gowns, buckled with the strange embroidered frogs, their eyes the shape of almonds with an overhang of skin so distinctive to their race.

Miss Borden appeared flustered by his presence as she resumed the lesson, a bright red spreading across her face. She stumbled over her words. Was *he* getting her disconcerted, or was it just having any-one watching her lead a class? He supposed that he shined up pretty nice. Perhaps her blush was of the admiring sort.

He waited to smile until he'd left his post, so as not to embarrass her.

As the weeks passed, he grew to enjoy eavesdropping on her failed attempts at leadership and popping into the classroom like a vengeful savior, quelling the disruptive students with his big body and loud, sharp admonishments. Boy, did they take their seats and bow their heads when he came in shouting!

One day, he entered the room at the same time the boys did and sat down with them as if he were also a student. He wanted her to have one day of ease, one day of knowing she wouldn't have to raise her voice to them. Afterward, she thanked him, that same blush spreading across her face although the boys and their unruliness had already departed.

"It's my pleasure," he said. "You're doing them such a kindness, and it kills me to see them treat you like that."

"If I were better at talking at their level . . . "

"No, and don't you think that. It's them that's got to rise to your level."

She shook his hand then in gratitude and in farewell, and he liked the way her fingers quivered a bit in his grip. She'd never been tried, he could tell. Not bad looking, either, if you didn't mind the protruding eyes. Her figure was a bit on the solid side, but he liked that. Those sylphlike girls, you thought you might break them if you were to get upon them.

He couldn't court her; he'd learned she was Andrew Borden's daughter. He worked night shift at the mill on Ferry Street—his janitorial duties at the church being in exchange for his seat in his pew—and one never aspired to step out with the boss's daughter.

He watched her on Sundays in the pew she paid for, up on the left, sweat making her curls wet at the back of her neck. He marked the day she first noticed him there and gave a nod and discreet smile as she walked past him up the aisle. She reached out a hand to steady her hat, just like a nubile filly. He knew he'd made her do it.

How one progresses from sitting in a miniature chair in a Sunday school classroom policing boys to crushing a woman against the chalkboard with your kisses, he couldn't exactly say. She had always expressed her willingness with her blushes and her trembling hands, but he wasn't so bold as to cross the lines drawn for them by decent society.

It was a step forward that she took, when they were already standing too close in the empty classroom. Her skirts brushed against his pants leg, and he could smell her soap or maybe it was cologne, a cloying, false attar of roses.

She lifted her eyes to him, cheeks scarlet, and he saw that she wanted what her girlfriends giggled and whispered over, what she'd read about in certain forbidden novels, the mysterious coupling of man and woman, the trysting, the secrecy, the feeling of being special to someone.

He placed his hands on her shoulders, testing it, steadying himself or her, or perhaps both, and then he bent down and pressed his lips to hers.

She inhaled so sharply that he pulled back, startled. Her cheeks reddened further. "Don't stop," she said in a voice broken with emotion.

"All right," he said. "I thought . . . "

He tried again, and this time she didn't reel. She kissed him back, her breath heaving. Oh, she'd be a piece and a half could he ever get her to his room at the workers' dormitory. Grateful for every caress, undone by her own disbelief as he'd unbutton her, a fluid puddle of acquiescence in his thin, metal-framed bed.

But he couldn't, because she'd never recover. A virtuous woman can't embark on an affair, like some of the loose girls who could have a bit of fun and shrug it off.

She'd think it the destiny she'd long awaited, the slow gears of her life finally cranking up to speed, her ears deafened by the grind of iron upon itself.

He couldn't take her just to take her. He'd owe her something, an offer of marriage, and no one wanted him to give that to her. It would reflect terribly on Reverend Buck, scandalize the congregation. He'd lose his job—both of them, here at the church and at her father's mill. Andrew Borden would never accept him as a suitor for his daughter.

It was not that he thought all this as he kissed her the first time; it was just the fleeting moment of thinking "No," as his hands crept up her back, as a primal moan came from her prim throat and hummed in their connected mouths.

CHAPTER 16

Bridget

MAY 16, 1890

At breakfast, Mr. Borden looked strangely exhilarated, an energy radiating off his restless body. As Bridget brought in oatmeal and maple syrup in its white porcelain pourer, she saw him pick up his spoon, set it down. He moved it to his other hand and laid it sideways across his water glass, like the pulley pole over a well.

"I've decided to give in to her," he said to Mrs. Borden, sitting across the table already eating.

"I think it's best," she said. "And it will give us all some fresh air to breathe. Will Emma go?"

"She has no interest."

"So it's just the ladies from the Fruit and Flower Mission?"

"Yes."

"It may repair things," said Mrs. Borden, "end her bitterness over the Fourth Street house."

"And maybe you'll become her 'mother' again," said Mr. Borden. Bridget watched a wry smile come over his face. She longed to stay and hear more, but she had brought in and settled all the wares for the meal and to linger would mark her as a snoop.

"Bridget, what do you say to Miss Lizzie going off on a tour of Europe for four months?" asked Mr. Borden abruptly.

"Oh!" said Bridget. "Is that what you've been speaking of?"

"Yes. She's been campaigning quite heavily for the chance to go, with a group of her lady friends, and I believe it to be a fine idea."

"It will be quite expensive," murmured Mrs. Borden.

"It'll keep her quiet for a few years; won't it? It will be money well spent."

"When will she go, sir?"

"This summer."

Bridget gave a genuine smile, thinking of the respite from the woman's unpleasant company. "Well, she'll have a grand time."

"And we'll have a grand time as well," said Mr. Borden dryly.

"Oh, watch your tongue. She's probably skulking around the corner listening to every word we say," said Mrs. Borden.

"I'm paying for it; can't I enjoy the prospect of a calm summer?"

Bridget hid her laughter, returning to the kitchen in high spirits. 'Twould be like a holiday for her, just as Mr. Borden had said. And given how desperately hot these New England summers were, and the resulting barometric rise in irritability, summer was exactly the right time for Miss Lizzie to go.

Maggie had been premature in her giving up of this position. Bridget would have a fine summer tending to the small wants of the older Borden couple, while she freely took her nights at the *ceilidh* with Mary Doolan and the cart driver Aidan who had recently started dancing attendance on her.

She danced a jig step there by the kettle. All one had to do in this world was keep one's head down, stepping ever forward. Troubles sorted themselves out, they did, if one could only give them a back door and a breeze to push them through it.

CHAPTER 17

Bridget

MAY 18, 1890

Bridget climbed the stairs back up to the kitchen knowing she wore an odd look on her face. She hardly knew what to think. One didn't launder the family linens without noticing that one woman had stopped her flow.

She vacillated between horror and amusement. It could only be Miss Lizzie; Mrs. Borden was well past her childbearing years, and she didn't think Miss Emma capable of trifling. So, the woman so proud and so upright, who scolded Bridget for a few flirtatious words, had actually lain with a man and gotten herself into that particular kind of trouble.

But Bridget worried, too, that perhaps Lizzie hadn't invited the attentions. Had she been attacked? If so, why had no alarm gone up? She never saw a day when Miss Lizzie came home looking shattered; if anything, she had the cat's cream of satisfaction on her expression on those odd errands she didn't bother to explain to Mrs. Borden.

And she wondered if Mrs. Borden suspected, for recently she had begun posing questions as Miss Lizzie would leave: "Where are you off to?" whereas previously she had not kept track of her coming and going.

It could either be the ruination of Miss Lizzie Borden, her reputation and what little she possessed to hold up her chin in this town, or it could be her deliverance.

The object of her speculation was there in the kitchen when she stepped in. Miss Lizzie, sugaring strawberries, didn't notice her right away, so Bridget took the moment to look critically at the fabric ever so slightly starting to pull under the pressure of the buttons on the back of Miss Lizzie's dresses. A stomach slope so sweet and hopeful that on any married woman would be greeted with exclamations of delight.

"What is that cart man's name?" asked Miss Lizzie without turning around. She'd heard Bridget come into the kitchen after all. Ears like a cat.

"The cart man, Miss Lizzie?"

"The one you carry on with."

For all Miss Lizzie knew, he had offered to drive her somewhere one day many months ago. It was true, Bridget had gotten to know him a bit at the Nancy Spain's doings, and he showed fair interest in her. His name was Aidan, and he was respectable and well liked. He did perhaps wink a bit too freely, but she had confidence such a habit could be tamed by an upright woman. Miss Lizzie's characterization of their beginning, and very proper, friendship as "carrying on" was rich considering what Bridget had just learned about her.

"I don't carry on with anyone, Miss Lizzie," she said calmly.

"You're young, and you're handsome, and a man can turn your head very quickly."

Bridget paused. Was it possible that Miss Lizzie was warning her in a benevolent way? That if she had so easily become a fallen woman, she wanted to help Bridget avoid the same circumstance?

"Don't worry. I shall keep him in his place."

Miss Lizzie scoffed. "Maggie, I know the women of your class can fall into frailty. We are thinking of creating a special committee for the friendless girls who become *enceinte* out of wedlock."

"Become what?"

"It is the French word for having a child come."

She stared at Miss Lizzie, and her temper rose. "Why do you spend your advice on me, when you ought to turn it upon yourself?"

As soon as the words left her mouth, she knew it had been a terrible mistake. Lizzie's face reddened to a degree she had not seen before, the high pitch of an iron whose sides have taken on the glow of the fire.

"How dare you speak to me, you Irish bit, you mouthy piece of . . . !"

"Ah, you ask me, and you'll learn what I know, Miss Lizzie! And then you'll be dying for to clamp down my tongue!"

"What do you know?" seethed Miss Lizzie. She took two steps until her face was inches from Bridget's. In an instant, Bridget's temper deflated, and all she knew was the ice working its way down her spine, sending its frozen blood into each vein of her system. Miss Lizzie's eyes and her anger: Bridget could never win against these.

"I'm only talking out of turn," whispered Bridget.

"But what made you say that despicable thing? Your threat that you know something?"

"It was only to anger you as you angered me. How could I ever know anything, Miss Lizzie? I don't travel in your circles."

Miss Lizzie perhaps imagined the bucket downstairs was full of an indeterminate number of cloths, and that it was impossible to number them. Bridget would never tell her. She would keep her counsel. Oh, she'd be dying for to tell Mary Doolan, but she had been warned, and she knew her place.

"You must speak to me with more deference," said Miss Lizzie.

"You have entirely gotten out of your place. Just as Maggie did before you."

"I beg your pardon most humbly."

"Your position here depends upon the happiness of your betters."

"Well do I know that, Miss Lizzie." Bridget kept her eyes down because she felt the stirrings of resentment again, but did not dare risk Lizzie seeing it. Nothing forced her to stay here, she thought. She had left the Remingtons; she could leave the Bordens. A rush of joy followed this thought.

"You have been good here. But do not take liberties with Mrs. Borden's affection. You must uphold our family's good name."

She was still on that, Bridget thought. Convinced Bridget was spreading her legs for all and sundry.

"I will, at that."

"I am leaving for Europe. Did Father tell you?"

"Yes."

"Nineteen glorious weeks out from under this shabby bit of shade. I will revel in it."

Bridget nodded, still looking down at the kitchen floorboards.

"Mind yourself while I'm gone," said Lizzie.

"An unnecessary admonishment, and of course I will."

Lizzie paused, and Bridget ventured a look at her face to see that the spit and venom had left her. "Finish sugaring these and bring them to me," she commanded, pointing to the strawberries.

"Yes, miss."

Lizzie left, and Bridget regarded her thickened stomach as she went into the sitting room. She was a foolish woman to think she could get away with that for long. Perhaps Europe would be colder in the summer, and she could drape a shawl around her; Bridget didn't know.

But all those sweet innocent friends of hers would be in for a surprise as the many months elapsed.

CHAPTER 18

Anna Borden

NOVEMBER 11, 1890

Anna Borden looked around the church hall with satisfaction. All her dear friends were here, celebrating her group's return after months away in Europe. The tables had pressed white tablecloths and china lent for the occasion—the Grand Social—by Miss Eliza Johnson. The girls all wore white, and dahlias festooned the tables. What a dear group of friends she had!

Sitting opposite her was Miss Lizzie Borden, looking uncomfortable in her gown that seemed a bit tight. It had been difficult not to overeat in Europe when the pastries and marzipans were so different from the fare offered here. Lizzie had undoubtedly availed herself just as much as Anna did, and possibly more.

"Are you settling back in all right at home?" Anna asked.

Lizzie turned her large, glassy eyes onto Anna. "You recall the things I told you in our stateroom."

"Why, yes, of course I do." Anna was taken aback. This was the thing that never worked about Lizzie; she didn't know how to answer lightly. The proper response would have been, most ladies comprehended, "Thank you, and it is indeed time I finally unpacked my trunk!"

Instead, Lizzie wanted, in the midst of all the bright conversations unfolding around them, like a flock of brilliant-colored birds wheeling and drifting above the tables, to refer to the dark admissions she had made on the ship that her home life was unpleasant.

"I am not therefore 'settling in,'" said Lizzie.

A silence fell. Anna knew with great agony that she was required to elicit more information, offer condolences, and even perhaps to invite Lizzie to come to her home to spend a happy afternoon. But she held her tongue. She was done with Lizzie.

She was furious with the organizers for placing her opposite the woman, in fact. At her right was a beloved friend she'd far prefer to talk with, Lottie Cook, but Lottie was chirping away with the friend at *her* right, and so in turn was Ella Brigham at Anna's left, making herself unavailable. Anna had no one to attempt conversation with, other than Lizzie.

Anna took a bite of the cold chicken in aspic to gain time to formulate a safe response.

"When I think we could be back on the ship now," said Lizzie. "It was like a beautiful dream."

Gratefully, Anna seized the opportunity to talk of issues other than the character of Lizzie's home life. "Yes! Such lovely appointments on the *Scythia*. Handsome wood burnished to a shine, and although the staterooms were small, I thought the furnishings quite fine."

"I can't even conceive that we were there just a bit ago."

"Yes. I believe we have regained our land legs by now!" Anna laughed, but Lizzie did not join in. *What must one do to get a smile onto that ham hock of a face?* Anna thought. She craned her body around to display to Lottie that she was ready to talk, but Lottie was animatedly engaged.

"I would love to go again and truly see the sights," said Lizzie.

Anna looked down at her plate.

"Would you go again, do you think?" Lizzie asked.

"It was the trip of a lifetime," answered Anna slowly. "I don't foresee undertaking such a lengthy voyage again. I believe I will have to cherish the memories."

Lizzie merely nodded.

Anna folded the napkin in her lap. The band started up, and she could've shouted with joy at the transition it offered. She rose, giving a brief smile to Lizzie. "Enjoy the rest of the evening," she said. "I'd like to freshen up and then listen to the music."

"Wait for me!" called Lottie. "I'll go with you."

Grateful, Anna linked arms with her friend.

"I'll never forget our time in Europe," said Lizzie to them, still seated. At this angle, Anna could see the line where she frizzled her bangs.

"Nor will I," said Anna. She turned her back and practically danced away. Free!

Later, Anna and Lottie sat at a small round table. Anna draped her shawl across the only other chair, to signal it was reserved for someone, although it wasn't.

"Such a bad prospect, to be bored to tears at one's own fête," she said in a low voice to Lottie.

"I know! It was all I could do not to laugh. You kept trying to disengage, and I kept pretending to be deep in conversation so you couldn't pull *me* into that morass."

"You knew and didn't help?"

Lottie leaned back in her chair and laughed fully, showing the full array of her pretty teeth. Anna doubted Lizzie Borden's mouth had ever opened so wide.

"How did you ever get through half a year's journey with her?" asked Lottie.

Anna made a scoffing sound. She wasn't sure if she should tell and waited to see if Lottie would press.

"And amazement of all amazement, how did she even get issued an invitation to the Grand Tour?"

"She begged us," said Anna. "Oh, that's too uncharitable to say."

"No, go on." Lottie's eyes glistened with cruel interest.

"When we began speaking of our plans, she so thoroughly asserted her desire to be included that it became uncomfortable, and what could we do but say general things like, 'How nice it will be for you when it's your time to sail for Europe,' but she did not take the hint of these niceties. I never imagined she'd have the means to go, with her family fortune so untouchable, so I had thought there to be little harm in talking to Carrie about it while Lizzie was there."

"Did she outright invite herself?"

"She just made it so uneasy that it would've been a snub if we didn't ask her. I'll never forget, we were arranging the bouquets for the war widows, and I stuck myself with a thorn, and she ministered to me, so very concerned, overly so, and it seemed she was pressing herself into the light conversation with Carrie. I almost wonder, if I hadn't had her applying her handkerchief to my bleeding finger, if I might've found the fortitude to continue on with vague encouragements: 'Perhaps you and your sister Emma might book a trip someday.' Instead, she pressed and pressed so, and I had to say, 'If your father will let you go, why, you might come along with us.'"

"Which she seized upon and it would've been impossible to retract the offer."

"Exactly so."

Lottie suddenly made a surge toward the third chair, rearranging the draped shawl. "Our friend's been away so long," she said loudly and pointedly, pretending to crane her head and look for someone in the crowd.

Anna stiffened but didn't dare look. Eye contact with Lizzie would bring her over, whether she had a seat to sit in or not.

"She's gone now," said Lottie in a whisper. "I wonder how, and under what circumstances, she broached the idea to her father."

"She had her passport sent to our house, as if she was keeping it a secret."

"And thus pulling you into the scheme! How unkind. And did you feel obliged to invite Emma?"

Anna sat up straighter. "Oh, good lord, no. If Lizzie's the gloomy seat at the table, I imagine Emma would have us all sunk to the floor, lying there in despair. I fixed in my mind that if she wanted to come, she'd have to do the same scrape and push her sister had."

"But if Emma had gone, she would've shared a cabin with Lizzie and you wouldn't have had to."

"I suppose that's the one bright spot in all of this—Lizzie's coming kept our company at an even number. Although surely we could've enlisted another more socially graceful friend. You, for instance! I'm enraged you didn't go!"

"You've seen me on the yacht—well, that one time! A month at sea would've killed me."

"So, Nellie shared her cabin on the way there but refused outright for the return trip. Carrie and I drew lots."

"You didn't! Scandalous!"

"I know, the poor thing. She just isn't a pleasure to be around. Always downcast, with nothing to say. Carrie and I laughed our way to Liverpool, and I'm sure she and Nellie did the same back to New York, while Lizzie and I had stilted words, and I was pleased each night to turn down the lamp."

"So during all the travels she was a bleak shadow following the rest of you?"

"Well," said Anna. She paused, still unsure whether she should tell.

"What?"

"I'm not proud of myself."

"Tell me! You must!" Lottie's eyes positively glimmered in her hunt for good gossip.

"It can go no further than this table."

"But . . . "

"I'm serious. It will be her ruination. I know your love of tittle-tattle, but this is quite too severe. I'll tell, but you can never share it. Our friendship will end over it."

"I'm dying for you to spill it. I promise all the things. I'll never tell another living soul."

"All right." Anna looked around them, ensured no one was close enough to hear. "Lizzie was fine in the British Isles, but became ill as soon as we reached the Continent. She couldn't rouse herself from bed. And we made a fuss over her, but there didn't seem to be anything truly wrong. No fever; no phlegm. We had a doctor in to look at her. And we worried over what to do; we had our itinerary set, and the trains paid and the hotels . . . This is the worst of it: one night, she was in the room with Nellie—we were at a lovely hotel in Paris, the Hotel Bellevue et du Chariot d'Or—and it was indeed very late. She must've thought Nellie asleep, but she wasn't, and she rose up out of bed, just as healthy as you please, and she silently wandered their suite. Nellie thinks she even left for a while."

"She left into the night in Paris? With all those cutthroats and—"

Anna made a pained smile. "Possibly. Nellie's not sure. She thought she heard the door, but she drifted back to sleep. The point is, she was relieved to know Lizzie was well, and we could continue on, but in the morning, Lizzie was back in bed, claiming to be just as sick as before."

"So she was shamming?"

"I think she was ill in a sense. In the way that she didn't want to rise and spend the day with us. I sat next to her bedside. Carrie and Nellie were restless, and I felt responsible because I'd been the one who'd been bamboozled into inviting her. And then Lizzie herself offered that we could go on without her. She said she'd written to a distant cousin in Belgium who had agreed to take her in and care for her."

"That sounds . . . "

"I know. It doesn't ring true. *I'm* her distant cousin, in fact! Anyway, it seemed so odd that she wasn't previously planning to see this relative, but now felt comfortable enough to go convalesce in her home."

"I don't know what I would've done."

"It was getting dire. I was to meet up with Hannah Moffit and continue along to Sweden and Norway, and I didn't want to be stuck in Paris caring for a mere church acquaintance."

"What did you do?"

"I consulted with the girls privately. I returned and told Lizzie that it was indeed ideal for her to go to her cousin and that we would meet her back at the hotel in Liverpool before our return voyage."

"You left her?" Lottie appeared dumbfounded.

Anna's eyes filled with tears. "It was so odd a circumstance—she roundly insisted on leaving to see this distant cousin, and all of us were frankly fatigued by her company. It didn't take much consultation for us to grant her wish."

"What if . . . what if, instead of meeting her relation, she had a clandestine rendezvous with a lover? She might've never left Paris, the city of love, never left . . . " she lowered her voice, " . . . the hotel."

"I would laugh at your romantic notions but for the sheer ludicrousness. No man would ever choose Lizzie, and we saw that tonight."

"But her wealth . . . "

"She has no access to it! She had to wire for more money to come home, and I seriously wondered if Mr. Borden was going to leave her stranded in Europe. I was half-preparing to lend her the funds and had several stern discussions with myself privately about how a surfeit of kindness sometimes renders the giver a fool."

"So no lover for Lizzie. Why, then, do you think she wanted to leave the group?"

"I think she knew she didn't quite fit. With all the things we talk of, she had nothing to add. I believe, too, that our relentless gaiety wore on her. She was game at the beginning, and I do extend her pity, for I feel she genuinely wished to be a happier person. "

"So then, you went on to Italy and Greece, and she . . . ?"

"She went to the relative in Belgium, so she says. Unchaperoned in Europe, but at the advanced age of 32, she could safely ride a train, we trusted. She was met at the other end by her relative."

"If that story is true." Lottie placed her gloved hand atop one of Anna's. "Anna, dear, you have nothing to reproach yourself for. She petitioned to be left behind and was of such an unpleasant temperament that you all leapt upon the chance."

"It did feel, I confess, like the sun had come out from behind a cloud as we trained down to Rome." Anna laughed, but with her hand to her forehead, as if feeling for that elusive fever Lizzie had claimed.

Lottie gasped. "But . . . at dinner tonight, she lied, Anna. The gentleman on her left asked her about Italian sculpture, and she answered as readily as if she had clapped eyes on Michelangelo himself."

"Oh, she's claiming the entire voyage. She asked me to purchase souvenir photographs for her, and she's using these as proof of her having visited all these cities."

"No!"

"Indeed, she is gluing them into albums, she's told me, and copying out descriptions and literary references."

"How do you countenance such lies?"

"As difficult as she is to like, I feel sorry for her. Her life is nothing. I think perhaps the lowliest mill worker may have more joy in life than her. Whatever she did during those months—"

"*Months!*"

"—Even if it was just lolling around the Paris hotel room, it suited her better than being at home."

Lottie shuddered.

"She really is unhappy," Anna continued. "When we met again with her, she was bluer than ever before. She said the visit with her relative had not been a carefree one, and we could all believe that. She said no more, but only began whinging about the desire to not return home. I for one, and Carrie for another, had thoroughly enjoyed our traipsing, but were happy to go back and see the family . . . and you, of course, dear. It's always good to come home after a while away and this 'while' had been so lengthy I was overjoyed at the prospect of reunion. But Lizzie had no such desire. As I said, Nellie made me switch cabins, and during the crossing all I heard was how awful Mrs. Borden was to her, and how Mr. Borden no longer took her side."

"Did not Mrs. Moffat miss Lizzie? She was intended as your chaperone?"

"We told her what we'd been told, and she was satisfied, perhaps a little too easily."

"What might've befallen Lizzie over there," marveled Lottie. "She could've been kidnapped, taken into white slavery."

"You think they wouldn't return her within the fortnight?"

They laughed.

"I have learned my lesson," said Anna, "I will forever clamp my mouth when at my church work. None of this would've happened had I simply given her courtesy and not relaxed into open conversation with my sister in front of her."

"I'd love to see her paging through her album with someone, answering their queries."

"I know, it is scarcely credible that she has the boldness to do it! You must, of course, never tell anyone. It makes me look as awful as her."

"I will keep as silent as the tomb."

"You're a good friend. How I wish you would've been my companion instead of her!"

"I should've found a lover, I know it, and luxuriated with him in our pillow-bedecked bed," teased Lottie, "and wandered to Montmartre to be immortalized in some painting."

"And been stabbed by a jealous prostitute!" said Anna. "And left this life under the point of her stiletto!"

"At least it would've been exciting," said Lottie.

CHAPTER 19

Bridget

DECEMBER 3, 1890

"That's it, and no more!" said Bridget to herself. She watched out the window as Lizzie made her pompous way down Second Street, studiously ignoring Mrs. Kelly when she emerged onto the sidewalk at approximately the same time. Mrs. Kelly lifted her chin and pretended she had stopped to rearrange her reticule on her wrist, in order not to seem that she was ceding right to passage to the other woman bent on taking it.

Miss Lizzie had come home from Europe, prouder than ever. Her form was still blocky, but no longer swelled with child. Bridget had wondered mightily: did the child miscarry? Or leave her by intention?

There was no way she could stop herself from speculating who the father might be, and she had spent the last months doing just that. No man ever presented himself to the door as a suitor—but perhaps Lizzie had arranged for him to be in Europe with her? The ladies she accompanied would surely not let such inappropriate meetings take place. It was all a terrible mystery and worsened in Bridget's mind by moments like this when Miss Lizzie snubbed poor decent Mrs. Kelly, by far the more respectable woman for all that she was Irish.

As soon as Lizzie was out of sight, Bridget hastened to the back stairs, climbing before she could reason with herself to stop. She knocked on the bedroom door and opened it when Mrs. Borden called out a surprised "Come in!"

"Hello, Mrs. Borden," said Bridget.

"Oh, I thought you were one of the girls, come to our side of the house for once."

Bridget felt pity for the small hope fading from the woman's face. After all this time, she thought friendliness might reconstruct itself out of the barren, smote landscape of the daughters' scorn?

"No, 'tis only me. I've come to ask if I might talk with you for a bit."

"Well, shall we go down to the sitting room?"

"Aye."

With a smile, Mrs. Borden came out into the stairwell and preceded Bridget down the stairs. They passed through the kitchen with its chicken stew on a light boil: a meal Bridget relished the thought of *not* eating despite its wonderful aroma.

In the sitting room, Mrs. Borden sat down on the horsehair sofa. Bridget perched on the edge, hip firmly wedged against the ornate curled armrest, since Mrs. Borden's girth swallowed most of the space.

"Now then, what would you like to talk about?" asked Mrs. Borden.

"I'm turning in my resignation, and I wish to thank you for the year of kindness."

"Oh, no, Bridget!" Mrs. Borden's eyes were wide. "No, you cannot. Is there something that is troubling you?"

"You know what troubles me."

"And yet, you are so calm with her! It's a mark of your patience and good humor, Bridget, which we so value in your character."

"I've had enough," said Bridget flatly.

"Oh, please do reconsider, I beg of you. She can be trying, I don't deny, and I've been myself on the receiving end of such abuse at her hands that I completely and wholly comprehend the wish on your part. But we need you, Bridget, and you're wonderful."

"I won't stay; it's been too hard now that she's back from her trip."

"Bridget." Mrs. Borden re-settled herself and sighed. She smiled a resigned smile. "Will it help if I ask Mr. Borden for another bit to be added to your wages?"

"It's naught to do with money, and you know that, Mrs. Borden. I'm certain I may take a step down with my next position, but I need to remove myself from this atmosphere of unkind treatment. I hope you will be willing to give me a good character."

"I would, of course, but I hope I may yet convince you to stay with us. She's in a state, and she'll apologize to you as she always does . . . an apology I wish I myself might avail of . . . and then it will be bright again."

"It was wonderful when she was in Europe, and it made me think I might find employment where such an air of relief would always be existing for my lungs."

"Bridget, consider how much of your time is your own! We ask very little of you. None of the bedchambers are under your managing, and I often pitch in with sweeping or dusting. If you wish to stroll out of an afternoon, or return to your room for a rest, it is always permissible."

"That is true," said Bridget grudgingly. She knew at her previous houses, she was at the beck and call and whim of the mistresses who didn't like to see her idle a moment. They'd invent tasks simply to keep her feet moving.

"I know you've made a friendship with the Kelly girl, and you have wonderful conversations over the fence."

Bridget blushed, wondering how far their voices had carried when the windows were open in summer.

"There are many things to keep you here, and now I'll tell you of what valuable service you render us. You are of that calm disposition, despite your—" Mrs. Borden faltered to a halt, and Bridget imagined she had been on the verge of saying something about the hotheaded nature of the Irish. " . . . despite *her* ill treatment of you."

"She calls me Maggie. And Emma does, too, for all her seeming sweetness."

"They do, and I would ask them to cease except that my words carry no weight with them. I will ask Mr. Borden to do so. It's important to me that you stay. Your calmness is the foundation that keeps this house solid. Your predecessor—the Maggie whose name you are saddled with—she banged pots in anger, she fought back, her anger filled this household until headaches took up residence in my skull."

This was the first she had heard of Maggie's poor behavior, and Bridget paused to imagine her friend acting so childishly.

"You may not imagine it so, but your influence is one felt throughout this entire house! The girls do not acknowledge me any longer, and their father is so often gone. It is just me and them . . . and *you*."

To Bridget's horror, Mrs. Borden's eyes filled with tears.

"You make the house almost ordinary," Mrs. Borden continued, producing a handkerchief and wiping her eyes. "Your smile in the morning when I come downstairs; it's the best part of my day. You're more than civil; you're cordial. The battlefield that is my home gains a welcome harmony with your sway."

"I . . . never thought myself so central to the doings of the household," said Bridget.

"Oh, you are! So much so. Please, Bridget, stay on. I'll do whatever I can to entice you and make your days more pleasant. Perhaps Mr. Borden can be induced to talk to his daughters and ask them to treat you less harshly. And I know for certain he will fatten your wages. We need you."

Mrs. Borden's hand crept over to Bridget's lap, where her own hands sat dormant and obedient. She clasped Bridget's hand and that more than anything decided it. Whatever the mistress's opinion of the Irish, at least she felt true affection for Bridget. Mrs. Borden wiped again at her eyes and sniffled, awakening pity for her own worse circumstances. She might be the lady of the house, but her treatment was even poorer. And she didn't have youth on her side, or beauty, or the chance to go out and kick up her heels. All the good had passed from Mrs. Borden's life, and she hadn't even had her own child to join the sisterhood sired by her husband with another woman. She had nothing but the long days spent in a household of overwrought women, themselves of an age where dreams of romantic girlishness had burnt to a bitter crisp.

"Please don't cry, Mrs. Borden," said Bridget. "I'll continue on. I'll make the best of it."

"Oh, dear, good, Bridget, I am relieved!"

"I do wish Mr. Borden would talk to them, if he will do so."

"I'll surely ask!"

"And if the situation does not improve, I may yet come to you again. But I'm resolved to give it a try, now that I know my service here is truly welcomed."

"It is, it *is*!"

Mrs. Borden's face was a wreath of smiles, and past the pale and fleshy skin, Bridget could see the glimpses of a woman once attractive, if not for her visage, then for her mien. Bridget had not been there for the days Mr. Borden courted her, and some tongues might say he was only after a mother for his girls, but Fall River was full of many females, and he had picked her for this, for the kindly nature that shone now in her face.

"And take no notice of Lizzie," said Mrs. Borden almost defiantly, and Bridget couldn't help but turn her head to look at the front door to ensure the traitorous talk wasn't overheard by the same woman coming home. "Her ill will is a burden I bear, but I surmise it is a burden for her as well."

"Those are wise words, Mrs. Borden," said Bridget, "for a spiteful heart blackens and festers in the chest."

"I wish I might have done things differently," said Mrs. Borden with a tone Bridget hadn't heard in her voice before: one of longing. "But Emma turned her against me."

"How odd, when Emma seems the milder of the two."

"Lizzie is tempestuous, but Emma is the one who remembers her mother. And she has planted seeds such that affection for me is seen as disloyalty."

"Did you know the former Mrs. Borden?" Bridget couldn't believe she had the audacity to ask such a question, but Mrs. Borden was in her hands now, and there'd never be a more advantageous time to ask.

"I did, but only slightly. She seemed to have the volatile disposition of her younger daughter. I wonder if Lizzie might've felt the same emotions toward her that she does now to me, and if bacon would have spit faster in that pan!"

Bridget laughed, but she felt a pang for the woman who had donated her marriage to raising another woman's children, only to have them spurn her for her sacrifice.

"That pan needs a cover put on it," said Mrs. Borden, "and so it shall be. My first course of business when Mr. Borden arrives home is to speak to him. We cannot lose you, Bridget, and we shan't."

"Thank you," said Bridget. "I'll see to the dinner now." She rose and smiled down at Mrs. Borden.

"Won't you bring me my sewing basket? You're so much more agile."

Bridget delivered the basket and went back to the kitchen. She stared into the succulent stew, oil coming to the surface in amber circles, rounded glossy bits of chicken showing their sides and then diving back down to the bottom.

CHAPTER 20

Bridget

JUNE 24, 1891

Bridget was sweeping the front entry when Mrs. Borden came to her in a panic, out of breath and fluttering her hands near her corset, as if their ministrations could usher fresh air to the oppressed lungs.

"Bridget!" she cried. "Someone has been through our things and stolen my mother's watch."

Bridget balanced the broom against the banister and came to her mistress. "Are you all right, Mrs. Borden?"

"Oh, I'm all right but distraught. That was my mother's piece, a wedding gift to her."

"How awful!"

Mrs. Borden trembled, her hands shaking as she reached up to swipe away a tear. Bridget felt helpless to comfort her. If this were her own mother, she'd enfold her in her arms, but servants didn't embrace mistresses.

"The worst of it is thinking that someone was in our rooms," said Mrs. Borden.

"Was the watch the only thing taken?"

"No, some other trinkets of mine, and Mr. Borden's desk looked rifled but I was so frightened I didn't look closely. Will you go up with me?"

"I will, of course."

Mrs. Borden gave her a grateful look and took a deep, shuddering breath. She turned, and Bridget followed her, curbing her own steps as Mrs. Borden's girth made her move ponderously. She felt as if she was a nanny trailing a toddler who had not yet mastered walking.

They passed through the rooms, and Bridget looked with new eyes to see if anything had been stolen on the ground floor as well. All looked in order—but there was nothing of great value in the spare decorations of the sitting room.

Mrs. Borden stopped to check the side door to the outside. "Locked as usual," she said. "I don't know how he got in. Were there any tradesmen today?"

"No," said Bridget. "I locked the door again after bringing in the milk. There's many as can jimmy a lock easy as you and I turn it."

They took the back stairs, climbing with pauses for Mrs. Borden to catch her breath.

"I found our bedroom door left ajar," said Mrs. Borden. "I thought Mr. Borden was inside, although it would be strange for him to leave it open."

They approached the door and examined it. There was a single nail in the keyhole, bent. Mrs. Borden pulled it out and looked at it. "How strange. I can't imagine this would work to open a locked door."

Bridget wanted to laugh. A bent nail? It was like using a spoon to whip a horse.

Inside, there was no sign of unrest in the main room. It was only when they entered Mrs. Borden's dressing room that they saw her jewel box standing on the dresser with its top open. Bridget had not seen it before; it must typically be hidden away.

Nearby was Mr. Borden's small pigeonholed desk. Its slanted door lay open, and the papers inside appeared ruffled.

"I dare say something here was taken as well," said Mrs. Borden. "I don't know what he keeps in there."

"Should I fetch him?"

"Oh, would you? And we should call for the police as well."

"I can do both. Do you feel safe here?"

"I suppose I should find the girls," said Mrs. Borden.

"I wonder if their chambers have been disturbed," said Bridget. *And mine*, she thought silently, yet there was nothing a maid's garret might hold worth stealing, and the world knew it. Still, if an intruder continued up the steps, he could conceal himself in the morass of trunks and boxes in the attic to do even worse injury later.

"We ought to check. Oh, do go quickly and see."

The idea seemed to occur to both of them at the same time, based on the startled glance they shared: what if the girls had encountered the thief, and he had harmed them? They looked at the door that led to the women's chambers. "I could fly down and across—or we could knock," suggested Bridget.

Mrs. Borden hesitated and then seemed to resolve herself. She walked quickly to the door and knocked loudly.

"Emma! Lizzie!" she called. "Please open the door!"

Emma did so with a sour expression, standing in the doorway as if guarding the contents beyond her. "What is it?"

"We've been robbed! Are your rooms in order?"

Emma's face changed, and Bridget saw for an instant the genuine concern, that there was still caring in her despite her cold demeanor. "Yes, all is fine. What has happened here?" She came into the room and almost—but not quite—embraced her stepmother. She peered around the room, craning to see the disturbed desk around the corner.

Behind her, Lizzie also came into the room but made no attempt to examine the order of the room. "What was taken?" she asked.

"I don't know what they might have taken from your father's desk . . . cash? I'll send Bridget for him. But for me the true loss is that of my mother's watch. You know what I speak of, the golden timepiece with her initials on it. It's all I have of her."

"What a shame to lose such a piece," said Miss Lizzie.

"We of all people know how important a mother's memory is," said Miss Emma.

Mrs. Borden, ordinarily so calm in the face of the stepdaughters' insults, made a noise of angered exasperation. "At this moment, you choose to further abuse me? You are heartless."

Emma bowed her head.

"I've been your mother since you were a child. For twenty-six years, I've fed you, dried your tears, checked your schoolwork, while your own mother was cold in the grave. Her care of you may have been sweet in the early years, but I have been here more than double that time for you, Emma . . . and triple that for you, Lizzie!"

"Quintupled and higher," observed Lizzie with amusement in her voice. "How fine was the checking of the schoolwork when this simple math eludes you?"

"You don't even remember her, Lizzie!" cried Mrs. Borden. "You called me 'mother' for years, and I was that for you. And all of it cast aside because your father was kind enough to help out my sister in a terrible state of affairs."

"She isn't blood, and what he did for your family, he should do for us," said Lizzie.

"He did! He gave you the Ferry Street house, for all the pleasure it has brought you. You have tricked money out of him, you so cleverly think, that you then frittered away on . . . " Mrs. Borden couldn't gather together her words, so overwrought was she by the true telling of her anger.

"We didn't think of it as trickery, Mrs. Borden. It was our due."

"But it is to be your money someday anyway!"

"If he doesn't leave it all to your side."

"Lizzie, stop," Emma implored her sister. Bridget could see tears shining in her eyes.

"Don't you think I feel every 'Mrs. Borden' like a dagger in my heart? How did it all go so wrong, my dears? How have I ever offended to earn such cruelty at your hands?"

"It's simply the correct name for you," said Miss Lizzie. "I was a child when I called you 'mother.'"

"A child and then a young woman, and then an older woman! It is only your . . . *greed* that has changed the climate between us. And that is sheer folly. I loved you two like you were my own daughters."

Silence fell. Bridget's face was hot with shame for overhearing such private words, yet she couldn't leave the room without drawing undue attention to herself. Broad Mrs. Borden blocked the door, and she couldn't bear to make her move, as stalwart and brave as she was being. She had spoken earnestly, her face blushing red for such plain speaking.

"What have you to say to me?" she continued. "Can we not heal this horrible rift? What is money? It avails not. When we are all cold and in our graves, will not our petty grievances haunt us? It was only a shabby house, and my sister so destitute! Would you prefer she and her children slept on the street?"

Emma's eyes were full of tears. She stepped forward and clasped Mrs. Borden's hands. "Your words have thawed my heart," she said.

Bridget's hand crept to her mouth.

"Oh, Emma," said Mrs. Borden. The two regarded each other, tears running down their faces. Mrs. Borden pulled out a lace-edge handkerchief, embroidered with the initials of her maiden name, so ancient it was, and wiped at her eyes.

The mild sound of sniffling lengthened into a silence, until Bridget felt its awkwardness. She couldn't bear to look at Miss Lizzie's face, instead fastening her gaze on the hem of the younger sister's dress, speckled with street dust. This sweet conversation needed one more voice to chime in, to complete its satisfactory redemption.

Bridget watched the hem until the boots beneath turned in a lazy pivot, leading the owner back to the door between the two bedrooms. "I hope your watch can be recovered, Mrs. Borden," said Miss Lizzie.

After Bridget fetched Mr. Borden at the bank, he went upstairs to examine his desk and came down looking disgusted. "About eighty dollars and a bunch of horsecar tickets are missing," he said. "What foolishness."

"So bold for someone to make their way all the way up to the second floor, no jittery knave," said Mrs. Borden. "I wonder, will the police be able to get my watch back?"

"No need to involve them," said Mr. Borden.

"But they're coming," she said. "Bridget called for them on the way to you. They said they'd send an officer."

"Then have her go and tell them to stay where they are."

"But Andrew, they might find clues and resolve this. At the very least, a report should be made so they're on alert."

"This matter doesn't call for police interference."

The front doorbell rang, and Bridget could only suppose it was the officer. She darted past Mr. Borden.

"Don't bother running," he said grimly after her. She opened the door to see a sergeant in his bulbous helmet, offering her a quick smile.

"Might I speak with the gentleman of the house?" he asked, and she near to rolled her eyes. He was Irish, and this was just putting paper on the fire of Mr. Borden's aggravation.

"Come with me, sir," she said, gesturing him into the house.

"I don't want him!" Mr. Borden roared from further inside the house.

"Andrew, let us make a report," Mrs. Borden said.

"Mixed feelings in the house?" said the officer out of the side of his mouth to Bridget, and she stifled a laugh.

She ushered him to the Bordens, then made herself busy, grinning every time she heard Mr. Borden's voice rise. He was trying to get the officer to leave, but the bored Irishman was insistent on the proper carriage of justice.

After just ten minutes, she was called back in to escort the officer to the door.

"I don't want this in the papers," said Mr. Borden, as he nodded at Bridget to take him away. "It's a silly sort of crime, and I'm sure I know the culprit."

Bridget suppressed a gasp, her eyebrows rising.

"Oh, do you, then? And that's spelling your reluctance?" asked the officer, surprised. "Why didn't you say so? Give me his name, and I'll have a good talk with him and get your goods back."

"It's something I wish to handle myself."

"Are you certain? A good scare from a boy in blue can go a long way toward ensuring you won't have another young wretch going through your drawers again, sir." The officer smiled and rocked on his heels so his billy club lightly bobbed in its holster.

"It's entirely in my hands, and I thank you for your visit. There's no need for a report of any kind. We'll let this sink into the sand, shall we?"

"But Mr. Borden, I must record it. A burglary upon one of Fall River's leading citizens? It can't go unreported."

"May I pay you?"

Silence stretched, and Mr. Borden reached into his pocket. The officer shook his head, frowning. "You're serious indeed, then, so I'll not report it, but will take no money for the suppression of it."

"Thank you for keeping it all as quiet as possible."

"I don't understand it, but will comply."

Bridget watched Mrs. Borden's face. She looked puzzled.

"Andrew, might you have the officer alert the horsecars to look for those tickets? When someone tries to use them to board, they can be arrested. They were of a series, weren't they? The numbers will—"

"I say, it's of no consequence. I can deal with the situation on my own."

The officer made a noise of exasperation. "I've a mind to watch the tickets myself," he said, "to satisfy curiosity."

"I can assure you the tickets won't be used."

"All the same, sir."

"Bridget, won't you offer him some tea in the kitchen and let him continue on?"

Bridget bobbed a curtsey and a smile at the officer. "Please, do come this way," she said.

"Thank you, miss, but I'll be heading back to the station. I won't trouble you any further."

At the front door, he returned the polished bowl of a helmet to his head. Bridget closed the door behind him and then walked quietly back to the sitting room. She was on her way to the kitchen anyway, so she wasn't deliberately eavesdropping, but she did quiet her footsteps to perhaps learn more before her appearance was discovered.

"—install locks to stop her," Mr. Borden was saying. "And I'm not ashamed to do so."

"Upon the bedroom door?" asked Mrs. Borden, her voice sounding aghast.

"And why not?"

"Because we can't live in locked cells like prisoners. I don't want to!"

"She's gone so far down this bad road she can't see what she's doing.

I say a good lock will stop her in her tracks. And I'll keep the key right here on the mantelpiece so she can't take it without being seen."

"Andrew, it seems so queer." Her voice suddenly got quieter. "Do you think you can get the watch back?"

"I'll try," he said. "But with the vinegar in her, I'm sure it's a mangled mass of gears and glass by now."

Mrs. Borden gave a sob at that, and Bridget walked past the room to her duties in the kitchen, catching only a glimpse in her peripheral vision of Mrs. Borden wiping her eyes on her apron while her husband, gaunt, stood by awkwardly.

And thus the system began. Mr. Borden now locked his chambers. Bridget came in with fresh sheets the day she found him kneeling on the floor installing a new doorknob with a lock on the door exchanging between his and Mrs. Borden's chamber and Lizzie's—and thus Emma's—on the other side. She pressed her lips together and retreated before he even knew she had been there.

Bridget never heard the speech Mr. Borden gave his daughters, but soon all knew that the mantelpiece had a new decoration, the slender one-eyed key that permitted entrance to the bedroom midway up the kitchen stairs. Its placement on the shelf each morning became another marker of the hours, true and steady as the grandfather clock holding its silence in quarter-hour increments until emitting its booming say-so.

She did see Lizzie idly pick it up one day when its residency was new, with a look of raw scorn. "Not supposed to touch it, but look at me!" she had crowed to Emma, who had replied with a mild, "Oh, put it back, Lizzie, or you'll lose it, and then where will we all be?"

It became a new object to dust around.

Bridget soon worried about its slender ethereal nature. Would it slip to the ground and go unnoticed, slide into a dustbin, and be deposited into the depths of the privy? Then how would the Bordens gain access to their chamber—and whom might they blame for its loss?

She hated the new regimen of locking, double-checking, keying and securing, and Mr. Borden's ostentatious placement of the key on the mantel each morning, as if he tacitly schooled thieves in his sitting room how not to behave so scurrilously.

CHAPTER 21

Brooke

JULY 15, 2016

At the café, Anthony's already seated at a two-top when she arrives. Her heart quickens at the sight of him—he's there for *her*. In the next second, she realizes he may not be. This was always his café; maybe he's bent on keeping it even if it's uncomfortable for a bit. Maybe there's no other convenient place for him to get coffee. He's certainly not hovering around at the counter waiting for her. She'll pretend she hasn't seen him.

Unfortunately, Maria, thinking she's doing her a favor, greets her loudly by name.

"Hi," Brooke answers quietly. She can't resist casting a glance at Anthony, though, who is now rising from his seat. He comes to meet her at the counter. He doesn't smile, but he looks at her with a sort of attention that seems open.

"How's your headache?" he asks. "I've been wondering if you were all right."

He's continuing the fiction that there really was a headache. "It's better," she says.

"That's good. Our conversation got a little heavy the other night.

I was wondering if you'd give me another chance to shut up about things and we could try again."

Oh no, she thinks. *He's too persistent. He's not going to be happy with just a night or two.*

And then like a bell in her brain, the odd idea rings out: maybe she wouldn't be happy with just a few nights, either. If Miguel can pull it off, maybe she can. Maybe it's time to set her fear aside, all of it: find out more about the Carr brothers, track down her dad and, yes, let Anthony into her life. She owes it to both of them to give it a shot. She's high on having found Burhardt Aalfs. Maybe she's riding a pendulum that's swinging her to the other side of her own luck.

"It would help if I shut up, too."

"We can just point to things on the menu."

She laughs.

"Should we have a list of forbidden topics?" he asks. "Like, basically, anything to do with my career?"

"Good idea. We'll just talk about my world: scones and mops."

"Glad we have that settled. Should I come back around 5?"

"Sure."

"Okay, I've got to get to work. See you at the end of the day."

He winks at her, goes to retrieve his belongings at the table, and then he's gone.

"He's been waiting for you forever," says Maria after he leaves. "It's kind of sweet. He kept looking at his watch."

He likes her, Brooke thinks. Enough to come back. Maybe she should play this one differently. Instead of jumping into bed with him, maybe she should let a courtship unfold as if they were Victorians. A kiss after several meetings, a wayward hand permitted roaming privileges after several more . . .

She smiles to herself thinking she has nothing to lose. If he doesn't want to wait for the slow unfurling of a liaison, then that's fine. He can walk. It'd be a fascinating experiment to see what it was like to date as if you thought you'd continue seeing the person months down the road.

She'll give it a shot.

The burger place is busy and loud. Brooke appreciates how it upholds their conversation, makes them just another couple yelling at each other to be heard. The menu is a laminated parchment and the mustards are in separate glass jars on the table: the owner's mother's recipes, the labels say. Above each table is a clock displaying the current time in a different world city. They are sitting under Rome, which reads eight o'clock.

"If it's eight o'clock in Italy, what time is it in Belgium?" she asks Anthony.

"I imagine they're the same time zone," he says.

"Do you think that's p.m. or a.m.?"

He puts his chin on his hand and gives her a long droll look. "As small talk goes, this is certainly better than whether murderers should get off the hook. And you haven't run off yet, so I'm happy to conjecture about whether the Belgians are in bed or not."

She can't resist smiling. Dating—her version of it—has always included a sort of raw anger to it, as if they both know they'll end up in bed, so why charm when you can smolder. She likes his silliness. "I bet they're waking up," she says.

"Probably. With terrible bedhead."

"Get into the shower, Belgians, before anyone sees you!"

"I've never liked that Greenwich Mean Time," he says. "Why does it have to be mean? Couldn't it be neutral until we earn its trust?"

"And don't get me started on that standard time," says Brooke, playing along. "Why does it have to be standard? Sometimes time wants to be unusual."

"I agree."

She takes a long draw off her Shipyard Ale and before she can stop herself, she blurts, "Fate sat us under the Belgian clock. Something pretty wild happened to me last night."

"Yeah?"

What is she doing, she asks herself. Don't tell him any of this. You're a fool. And yet, something about his concentration, his eyes patient and trained on her like a spotlight, makes her tongue spill secrets.

"I grew up without a father in my life," she says, feeling how her words are swallowed by the loudness of the restaurant, making it easier to say them. "My mom raised me. I've never bothered to find him. I guess I never felt like I *could*. I didn't even . . . know his name." She stumbles on that last bit, realizing too late that it moves her from the category of "It's sad your dad bailed" to "Whoa, big stuff was wrong."

"That's a shame."

She blinks away momentary regret. This was the moment where he could've jumped in and said, "I didn't know my dad, either," or mentioned his parents' divorce, if that had been the case. So, no, he's the guy with the intact family, and she's going to besmirch him with her broken shards of one. He doesn't have an inkling of what her life was like.

"So last week I decided maybe it was time to change that. I wrote a letter to the address on my birth certificate, and—"

"Where's your mom in all this?"

"She died when I was thirteen, in a car accident."

He frowns. "I'm so sorry. And what happened to you?"

Tell a lie, she advises herself as she takes another long drink of her beer: courage in a bottle. *A relative took you in. There was a bright kitchen and lots of Christmas presents, and they gave me a puppy.* "I was placed in the foster care system."

"You lived with another family? Were you adopted?"

"I want to tell you about Belgium," she says. She feels a genuine smile pushing at her lips. "None of that other stuff matters."

"Of course it matters." He's looking at her intently, and she can tell what he's thinking. Damaged goods. Crazy in the head, crazy good in bed. She wishes she had never looked at the damn clock.

"It's a happy story," she says. "In the last twenty-four hours, I've seen two photographs of my father. And before yesterday, I had never seen any."

He frowns again, trying to make a sympathetic expression. It's too bad that concern and anger look so similar on some people's faces. "I can't even imagine," he says.

"Anthony!" she practically shouts. "It's a good thing! I saw my dad!"

"I can't immediately celebrate the discovery of a person who so immoderately failed to perform his duties."

"Did you talk like this before law school?"

"I appreciate language."

"I appreciate people who give a girl a high five when she asks for it."

The waitress comes between them, bending her ample form over the table to set down his "Prague bog" soup appetizer and her admittedly unadventurous salad.

When she withdraws, Brooke sees Anthony is holding up his hand, palm facing her. She reaches out and slaps it.

"Tell me so I can understand," he says.

She nods. "Okay. It's just that knowing what he looks like is a huge step forward for me. Mom is gone. I . . . don't have any other relatives that I know of. Mom left Mexico when she was pretty young, and I know people tried to track down family for me after she died. They weren't able to find anyone. I'm alone in the world—"

Too late, she realizes the stupidity of confessing this. If he's a serial killer, she just basically told him she'd be easy to nab, a freebie victim.

"But you have friends," he says. "People who are important to you."

"Yes," she says, unwilling to specify that there's only one of those, and she hasn't seen him in person for at least two years.

"Are you hoping to reconnect with your father?"

"Maybe."

"So you saw the photo . . . and he looks like you?"

She laughs, then it's the kind of nervous diaphragm-based laughter that she can't control for a few seconds.

"It turns out my dad is a yellow-haired guy from Belgium. I'm a mongrel. I always thought it was funny when people said, 'I'm German, Scottish, and Irish,' and I would just say, 'I'm Mexican.'"

"How'd your parents meet?"

"He was an exchange student."

"In Mexico?"

"No, they met in the U.S."

"So where is he now?" he asks.

"Back in Belgium."

"Dang, are we going to have to take an international road trip?" asks Anthony.

"We might have to," she mockingly agrees.

"I've got a ton of frequent flyer miles."

The expression on his face stuns her. She spears a grape tomato. "You aren't joking."

"No. I love travel more than anything else in the world. If you present me with a reason we should go to Belgium, I'm instantly on board."

"But we hardly know each other."

"Let's get up to speed quickly so that we can go."

His trust, his openness, take her breath away. He has enough money that a flight to Europe isn't daunting, and even though they barely know each other, his past relationships have apparently been so uncomplicated that he sees no danger in committing to a big trip with her.

Is this what it felt like for Miguel when he finally decided he could try really having a girlfriend? Was this how other people did it—after twenty minutes of sitting at a restaurant table, before the entrees had even arrived, they were making plans to get on a plane together?

"Sure," she says dubiously.

"Oh my God, you need to work on your believability factor," he says with a huge laugh. She likes its sound, low and rumbling. "We'll take Belgium off the table for now, and let's just focus on finding out more about your dad."

"You want to help?"

"Of course I want to help."

"That's really nice." Her hand reaches across the table and squeezes his for a second before releasing it.

"Well, what else are we going to talk about? Blood dripping off elbows?"

*M*iguel, *how is it going with your girlfriend?*

It's really good. A little scary how good.

I can't tell you how glad I am. I've been inspired by you.

Headache Guy or someone else?

Yeah, Headache Guy. I've decided to call him Anthony.

That has a better ring to it. And probably makes it easier for him to get jobs. Tell me all about him.

You didn't tell me about yours yet.

Ladies first.

No, chronological order first. Or are you still worried about jinxing it talking to the likes of me?

Aw shit, I still feel awful about that. It didn't come out the right way.

I know.

Her name is Angelica, and you actually know her.

???

From the group home. She was there only a few months and got adopted out. Cuter than the likes of me.

Stop saying "the likes of me." It's really self-deprecating and my therapist says we can't do that to ourselves. Don't talk about yourself in a way that you wouldn't accept from someone else.

You're really seeing a therapist? I thought you were kidding about that.

Don't you think I should? Anyway, Angelica's a few years younger, so she was easier to place than us hardened teens.

So she's what now?

She's twenty. You approve?

Yes. We don't need to add cradle robbing to your list of woes. Is she in school?

No. Working.

In the world of middle-class normalcy, Brooke thinks, a twenty-year-old would be a sophomore or junior in college, and twenty-three-year-old Miguel would've already graduated. But the lack of secondary schooling erased that power differential. They're both just working adults.

So you like each other?

A lot. And it means something that she was part of my life back then, even if she was only there for a little while. She gets what it was like.

Brooke tries hard but can't remember the girl. *Did she go to a nice family?*

Yes, she's still there. They have me over for dinner a few times a week.

That longevity is unusual, amazing. A pre-teen went into a home that was so untroubled she's still there in her early twenties? What good fortune. She must've hit on a family doing foster care for the right reasons, not just for the payments that stop when a kid turns eighteen. For a moment, she lets herself feel a niggling of jealousy.

That same family might've picked Brooke instead if she hadn't had the wretched suffix "teen" tacked on to the end of her "thir."

What if her mother had died a year earlier? Brooke would've been a more adoptable twelve-year-old, but she would've missed out on a year with her incredible mother. She would've missed the trip to Lake Havasu, the warm water buoyantly lifting mother and daughter, the sand that accepted them throwing themselves down on their towels, exhausted, happy. That one trip, she thinks with a hitch in her throat, was worth not being adopted.

She'd been placed once. Soon after she'd arrived at the group home, before Miguel came. A couple whose daughter had gone off to college felt an urge to fill her bedroom, perhaps to subsidize the older girl's tuition. It hadn't worked out. The mom had a collection of what she called Depression glass. Brooke couldn't believe the ridiculous name until the mother, offended, told her it had to do with the Great Depression, the period of history in which this glass had been fired.

The pieces sat atop a table in the living room, unprotected, and Brooke's off-kilter coltish clumsiness had led to her bumping the table. Two of the pieces, in Brooke's opinion placed stupidly close to the edge, had tumbled off and shattered. "Now the glass is really depressed," she remembers saying, but the woman hadn't found it funny. She'd been enraged.

And a few days later, Brooke found herself back at the group home. It seemed she was not worth the risk of more broken pieces. Never mind that *she* was broken, and the return trip told her exactly what her value to the world was. She wondered if the parents had adopted again, maybe even from the same group home, and the staff had kept it quiet so she wouldn't be hurt.

What if Angelica had gone to this couple? No, it wasn't possible. She didn't see how such a monetary-minded couple would continue to keep a child after the checks stopped, unless they'd grown fond of her despite their wishes in the intervening years.

What are Angelica's parents' name?

The Fishers. You want to see if it's too late for them to take you?

Relief. That was not the Depression glass family.

So, her family feeds you, she knows your humble background: What else?

We both like animé.

You do?

Yeah. I'm pretty into it.

I had no idea.

I mentioned it once and you didn't jump on it so I knew it wasn't your thing.

I probably didn't jump on it because I didn't really know what it was.

Oh, well, it doesn't matter. But she's really into it and we're going to a con in a few months.

She doesn't know Miguel that well at all. She feels the discomfort of her scaffolding shifting slightly under her feet. He liked animé enough to go spend a weekend with other enthusiasts, and she wasn't even completely sure what it was.

Mija? I've got to run. I want to hear all about Anthony tomorrow, okay?

Yes, go go go! Talk to you mañana.

She sits looking at the thread of their conversation on the screen. This one was as awkward as one two strangers might have. It seemed like maybe she had never really known Miguel at all.

CHAPTER 22

Brooke

JULY 21, 2016

They've had a few more dates, and she's relaxing more in Anthony's company, yet always somehow on the edge of her chair with crackling energy. He makes her feel as if she wants to say smart things, make him laugh, and more than anything . . . get that look in his eyes when silence falls between them.

He's looking at her that way now, as they sit in a wine bar at a high bistro table. She can't even remember what they had been talking about; intelligence has fled because his eyes are trained on her face.

He leans in.

She's lost in the way the dark frames of his glasses echo the black lines around his pupils. His eyes are intense, the saturated blue that feels like a bit of the sky drifted down to nestle in his gaze.

"What are you thinking about?" he asks softly.

"You know."

He smiles, a slow unfolding that makes her stomach clench and her toes curl inside her Roman sandals.

"Brooke," he says simply.

Her eyelids drift down. Her lips open, and she moves closer to him. She can see his mouth through her half-open eyes.

His hand comes to gently rest on her neck, his thumb moving back and forth under her jawline.

"Do you think it's time for me to shut up and kiss you?" he asks.

She grins languidly and looks back up at him. "I'd say you're way overdue," she murmurs.

His expression makes her whole body feel as if it's quivering, as if she's wavering on the edge of a cliff and it's time to fly.

His hand on her neck tugs her gently forward, and his lips descend onto hers, warm and supple. His breath gives her another fragrant sip of the chardonnay; she feels overwhelmed by the sweet, acrid taste.

His beard stubble lightly, razes her cheek as the kiss deepens; his hand moves to her shoulder and ever so slightly pushes her spaghetti strap to the side. She shivers; every inch of her skin tingles with sensation.

He pulls away just a millimeter, and it feels like being deprived of something so good she can hardly stand it.

"Given what I want to do to you, we better leave before we get kicked out," he says.

She slides off her bar stool, and as she picks up her purse, she thinks So *what about your plan to take it slow and be all Victorian about this?*

His arm goes around her shoulders as he throws down bills on the table. His eyes promise a night of pure attention focused on her and her body, and in the past this has been all she's ever wanted.

They exit the wine bar and night air cools her flesh. Headlights are on; the street is dark. Her eyes adjust to the new mood.

Speak up, she coaches herself.

"Let's go somewhere private. But I think we should also . . . " Her voice trails off.

He stops short, turns to face her. "You set the pace," he says firmly. "And if you're not comfortable leaving, let's go back inside."

"I *am* comfortable."

She's never had to test this; even with her first lover, she'd been nothing but "yes."

"Seriously. We don't do anything you're not 100 percent enthusiastic about."

"All right. Let's go to your place and pull out that enthusiasm meter."

He cracks up as he chirps open the car. "Is that a euphemism?"

She's taken to pulling out her laptop in bed after Anthony falls asleep. He sleeps hard and doesn't wake from her keyboard tapping. The last few weeks have been amazing. She feels starry eyed, her heartbeat accelerating when he looks at her for more than a second: all the things the radio songs have always promised. She's let him into her life, her apartment, and let him see her fragile heart.

He's bought her a few plants to liven up the space, something she'd never permitted herself. Hard to move plants when one doesn't have a car, so she's never bothered. It astonishes her how good the ficus leaves, lit by sun from the window behind, translucent and verdant, make her feel. A houseplant is an extraordinary thing, an accomplishment in a small pot.

Out on the windowsill in the kitchen march three identical cacti in their separate vessels. He's put a blooming geranium outside her front door, an indication of nonchalant trust in the world that makes her wish she could believe that way, too. She made a mental bet it'd be gone within two days, but it has been there for a week now, beaming a scarlet *bonhomie* at her every time she fumbles for the keys.

As she planned, they have gone through a courtship, taking their time in savoring slow kissing sessions and long talks . . . even talks about her past, which she has always shied away from. But there's still one topic that she hasn't shared: her mother's murder and her own shifting identity as she tries to stay one step ahead of the killers.

Over a period of weeks, she and Anthony have kissed until their lips were sore, until their cheeks were flame red with wanting. And one night they came together as lovers. There had been something life changing in the way they held gazes as their bodies moved. Whether she stays with Anthony or not, she knows sex will never be the same again. The bar is higher.

She wants more now. It's a lesson she's learning daily, that if you expect more, very often you get more.

Now, as he sleeps, she opens up her Ancestry.com account. She hasn't yet mustered the courage to call Burhardt's parents' number or email him via the law firm's contact page, but she's been enjoying tracing her Belgian heritage. She's gone back a few generational steps, seeing Burhardt's great-grandfather born in 1911, and there the chain stops.

Brooke isn't sure who the person who's been tracing these roots is, a female relative somewhere along that chain, but that woman has become frustrated at not going any further. *What is this address?* the woman fumes in a forum. *It's a commercial building. The house must've been torn down? But why can't I get a parental name?*

I did a little digging for you, someone on the forum had responded. *That was a 'hospital' at the turn of the century. A particular kind. Here in America in the early 1800s, this sort of facility would be called a 'home for friendless girls.' This link is in Dutch, so just turn on Google Translate. It will tell you everything you need to know.*

Brooke follows the link and learns that the hospital—*Tehuis voor Onbevriende Vrouwen*—was a place for women to give birth to their illegitimate babies. Brooke smiles ruefully at this news. Her mother wasn't the only crooked branch in this family tree. Burhardt's father, presumably horrified at his son's fathering a child on the other side of the blanket, was a distinct beneficiary of this style of parentage.

Brooke returns to the forum. *The hospital is no longer extant, of course, but I'm hopeful its records may be archived somewhere,* someone has chimed in. *I'll jump back on this in a few weeks after my son's wedding (no 'friendless girl' here, ha ha ha!) unless someone else wants to take it over?*

The post is dated two years ago. Apparently the wedding had killed all momentum.

Brooke looks over at Anthony, grateful again for his presence in her life. Like Miguel, she finds the prospect scary, but a good, top-of-the-roller-coaster kind of scary. She begins a search for *Tehuis voor Onbevriende Vrouwen.* She locates a hand-colored postcard of it for sale on eBay, showing its sturdy and benevolent facade of earth-toned brick. In the photograph, two matrons in black stand in front of the door, ready to whisk inside any pregnant guttersnipe who failed to secure a ring on her finger. Brooke adds the word *records* to her search and sees that there's been a certain amount of web activity by others eager to locate their friendless ancestors.

She reads the entries, sometimes using an instant translator if the post isn't in English or Spanish. A few hours later, she yawns. She's a terrible researcher because she's fascinated by everything. She's spent a whole hour following the story of another family simply because she got caught up in the suspense of the photo of a forlorn French girl in a white frock, a huge hair bow nearly eclipsing her head. It didn't get her any closer to her own lineage, but it had been as satisfying as a good novel. How did others manage to avoid falling into the rabbit hole of tracking other lives? What cold-blooded people were able to stop reading once they'd ascertained it wasn't relevant to their search? She felt pity for historians and the heartbreaking task of pulling oneself away from a compelling tale simply because it wasn't on the agenda.

She clicks on one last link, promising herself it will be the last for the night. And she straightens at what she sees, adjusts the pillow behind her head to prop herself up higher. Bingo!

It has been like a wild goose chase for five years, writes the excited poster, someone whose avatar is Susan B. Anthony in lithograph form. *I'm going to tag this as many ways as possible to help those coming up behind me. I wish I knew how to make this show up first when someone searches for Tehuis voor Onbevriende Vrouwen. But anyway, major drumroll . . . this is big news, people . . . I've located the archives!!!!!! They're not digitized and probably never will be, but if you write to the nice people at this library, they'll do their best to help out. I made a generous donation to sweeten their willingness and maybe you can, too. At any rate, thanks to this MAJOR BREAKTHROUGH I was able to finally find a parent for little Agnetha, and it feels like my birthday and Christmas all rolled into one!!!!!!*

Susan B. Anthony continues to enthuse with countless exclamation points, but Brooke scrolls down until she finds the email address so nicely left for all the ancestor seekers.

She types a quick email and presses send. Would her email arrive smack dab in the middle of someone's workday? Would she even receive a response within the next hour? Was it worth waiting up for?

No. Time to sleep. Let Belgium perform research on its own time, an unwatched pot agitated to the point it is ready to boil.

CHAPTER 23

Brooke

AUGUST 4, 2016

An email is waiting for her when she wakes up. She can hear Anthony in the shower. He'd hung a suit in her closet last night for this morning. His toothbrush has taken up a jaunty residence in her medicine cabinet, along with a razor and shaving cream. As someone who has very few possessions, she loves it that he trusts some of his to her keeping.

She had logged on just on the off chance, and there it is, a message from the library. She opens it.

Dear Madame, easy to find for you this record. We have been receiving so many requests we have moved the boxes closer to the stairs. They are not catalogued or organized, but I had good fortune to find yours so quickly. Here is PDF. Of course, no charge for this service, but donations to our foundation are always welcome.

Regards—

Brooke resolves to make a donation when Jane pays her this week. She opens the PDF.

Date: October 12, 1890

Name: not chosen
Gender: boy
Weight: 8 lbs, 12 oz.
Length: 19 inches
Health: good
Hair: Auburn
Father: Name not given
Mother: Lizbeth Borden

Brooke snorts. All she can think of is Lizzie Borden, the woman who showed up in a jump rope rhyme for the distinction of killing her parents with an axe. But this can't be *that* Lizzie Borden.

Brooke quickly types, "Thank you! This is wonderful. I will send a donation in a few days. Many, many thanks."

She types Lizbeth Borden into her search engine, eliminating "murder" and "axe" as search terms. The search brings up less than two hundred entries—but they are all about Lizzie Borden.

"Please don't tell me I'm descended from a murderer," she mutters to herself.

"You're not getting ready for work?" Anthony's back in the room, toweling off his hair, another white towel slung around his waist like an Egyptian kilt. Brooke takes two seconds to admire his abdominal muscles; he's been working out more since they started dating, he sheepishly admitted one night. She loved him for giving her that vulnerable admission.

"I will in a minute." She returns to her screen.

She focuses on the image of a tombstone marked LIZBETH, low to the ground, looking more like a doorstop than a monument. Pennies cover its face; it's a well-visited gravesite. In fact, as Brooke continues to read, she learns this grave and its notorious mistress have an actual *following*.

Lizbeth Borden was the name chosen by Lizzie Borden to start her new life, post-murders. Like Brooke, she had changed her name and changed her address.

And with that frisson of flat abjection that has greeted moments in her life like the arrival of the plates, like the officer knocking on her door when she was waiting for her mother to return home: she sees that today, the day she is learning the truth, is the anniversary of those long-ago murders on August 4, 1892.

CHAPTER 24

Brooke

AUGUST 4, 2016

"**W**hy are you looking up Lizzie Borden?" asks Anthony, leaning over her as she stares at her laptop screen. "'Lizzie Borden took an ax, gave her mother forty whacks. When she saw what she had done, she gave her father forty-one.'"

"That's awful, making a jump rope rhyme out of two people's deaths."

"Did you used to play ring around the rosie?"

"No, but I saw younger kids at the . . . I've seen other kids do it."

"That's supposed to be about the bubonic plague. Guess what it represents when you 'all fall down.' We're really a pretty morbid culture. Winnie the Pooh is about dysentery."

"What?"

"Kidding. Anyway, it's an interesting case, but I've got to run."

He kisses her but she hardly notices.

She can't tear herself away from the screen. All the true crime she's ever ingested has led her to this minute. Elation fills her body. It's *historical* true crime, a genre she's rarely read although she did have a months-long Jack the Ripper phase once. She knows all about killers, but not killers in corsets. Not women whose skirts drag the floor, who eat foods cooled only by ice, who use privies and chamber pots and ride in horse-drawn buggies.

As Anthony leaves, she hears him calling the law office and apologizing for running a little late. Reluctantly, she closes the laptop. She quickens her routine, too, deciding not to wash her hair in the shower since she doesn't have the twenty minutes to dry it. She winds it into a loose bun and secures it with a few clips. She grabs her bag to make her way to the café.

As soon as she walks in, Maria rushes at her, her face upset. "Where have you been? You don't have a phone?"

"I've never had one. Are you all right?"

"Magdalena is sick, and I had to bring her *here* because you don't have a way to be contacted!"

"I couldn't have come in any earlier anyway." She looks over at Magdalena, who's slumped at a table with her head lying on it.

"She's got a fever! Her forehead is like an oven."

"I'm sorry you're sick, Magdalena," Brooke calls over to her, but the girl makes no sign of having heard.

"Why didn't you just close down the café for an hour? And where's Jane?"

"She's out of town. If I closed the café, you'd never be able to open it because nobody trusts you with a key."

Brooke rears back. "I understand you're upset, but I've worked here all of, what, a few weeks? Why *should* I have a key?"

Maria takes a deep breath. "I'm sorry. I didn't mean it. I just get so . . . I can't handle it when she's sick like this."

"So take her! Go, go, go! Don't stand here scolding me!"

"All right. Tell the evening girl—I think it's Veronica—that when she leaves tonight, she should hit the lock on her way out and call Jane to tell her she did it. You're on your own." With that, Maria bustles over to her daughter, helps her rise to standing, and together they leave.

"Feel better soon!" Brooke calls. The only answer is the bell above the door ringing as the door closes.

There's no one here anyway, Brooke thinks. Maria held the fort for nothing.

Brooke walks around, puttering, straightening chairs, checking the sugar and cream station. She returns behind the counter, wishing she'd brought her laptop. She could use the free wifi to learn more about her infamous ancestor. From what she'd been able to read this morning, Lizzie's stepmother and father had been discovered hacked to death, separately, by hatchet rather than axe. Their deaths, a few hours apart, according to the fact that they'd breakfasted at the same time and Mr. Borden's stomach contents showed a far more advanced state of digestion.

Important for the laws of inheritance, Mrs. Borden had died first, meaning that everything went to Lizzie and her sister, Emma, rather than being distributed among the stepmother's sisters and heirs as well.

It seemed Mrs. Borden hadn't brought much to the marriage financially, while her husband, Andrew, was quite the well-off fellow, having owned several banks and mills. Since they had no offspring of their own, it seemed fitting (at least to Brooke's clinical, ten-minute, Wikipedia-based opinion) that Andrew's wealth should go to his blood kin from his first, deceased wife.

Unless, of course, he'd been killed for his money. Murder should never be rewarded. Andrew and his second wife, Abby, were elderly; any heir would be guaranteed their gains soonish. Perhap some impatience sprang from the "donation" Lizzie had made to the *Tehuis voor Onbevriende Vrouwen*.

The murder date was August 4, 1892, but the child had been born in 1890. What was the connection, if any? Festering anger?

An occluding despair?

Brooke found it interesting that Lizzie—which was her birth

name, not Elizabeth—had given her name as Lizbeth in Belgium, an identity she didn't adopt in Fall River, Massachusetts, until 1893. The new moniker arose after her acquittal, when she moved from the tight quarters where the murders had been committed, to a grand home in the expensive part of town. A house fancy enough to get its own name, as if it were an English estate: Maplecroft.

The causes of murder are often selfish, stupidly so, Brooke has learned over a lifetime of reading her sordid books. Frequently, the motive is money, as if one could enjoy one's lavish surroundings while visited relentlessly by the memory of feral grunts and moans and hands scrabbling for purchase, for defense.

The Borden crime scene photos are widely available on the Internet. It isn't right. Brooke hates the thought that pictures might've been taken of her mother's body in the car, just like Princess Diana, and that an archivist could look at them, and maybe in the future when it was judged that enough time had passed, her mother's photos would be downloadable. No one deserved to be looked at in that moment of complete, utter helplessness. It was a double offense, salt in the wound. Not enough to leave your life in terror and pain; now perfect strangers could examine your supine body and your powerless hands. Brooke would've never chosen to look at the Bordens' crime scene photographs, but they pop up with every Google search of her ancestor's name.

In Andrew Borden's case, Brooke finds the photo of him on the autopsy table, a folding wicker affair, incredibly upsetting. His head was so befouled by his own slashed-in face and skull that she couldn't even identify it as such in the grainy photograph. It took investigative work to realize what she was looking at. His pale chest, thin to the point of emaciation, and even with a womanly hourglass indent at the waist, and his muscle-less arms, were what led her to understand that, following the line of the chest up to the neck, that mass there *must* be his head. And then, yes, once she knew what it was, she could discern the beard in that rubble, and where his nose *would* be.

She ached for the shame this Victorian gentleman would suffer, not only for the exposure of his destroyed face, but perhaps equally so because of his naked chest with the sickening lines from the autopsy scalpel that went after his stomach. He didn't go out in public, Wikipedia reported, without his Prince Albert coat, even in the hottest weather. Perhaps even his wife barely saw him without a shirt; she had her own dressing room and at their age, Brooke wondered how much sexuality was still part of their lives. There had never been any issue from the marriage.

The Prince Albert coat had last been seen tucked under Mr. Borden's destroyed head. Some theorized that Lizzie had used it as a shield while murdering him and then folded it and placed it beneath him, where the blood spatters would merge with the more significant bloodstains.

Thinking about the Bordens makes the café seem too empty. The day's brightness appears to be fading, as if clouds are rolling in. Brooke can't help it; she descends into the bad feelings that have plagued much of her life, the knowledge that she will never see her mother again. For so many years there had been a remote sense that it was a mistake, or a terrible joke on her mother's part, or someone else had been in the car and the police had identified the wrong woman, while her mother was somewhere trying to return to her, valiantly climbing over things . . . rocks, high swells, volcanoes . . . trying to get back to her daughter.

The loss of a parent is a ruinous thing. If that woman in Massachusetts had grasped a hatchet and made it happen, there must have been something desperately wrong with her.

CHAPTER 25

Alice Russell

APRIL 7, 1892

Alice had to temper herself not to exclaim at the sad choices available to the Borden sisters. Hannah Gifford's fabrics, pre-culled for price, lay in swaths on the bed in the Bordens' spare room. She watched Lizzie—to whom it mattered most—pick them up one by one and extend them between her spread arms, like a maid on washing day seeking stains to treat.

Not that Alice was terribly wealthy herself, but her gowns were cut of a finer cloth than miserly Andrew Borden would permit for his girls.

"This is rather nice, don't you think?" asked Emma of Alice. She held up a length of pale cotton with a crimson sprig.

"It is that," agreed Alice.

"Are these all you have?" asked Lizzie.

"Yes," said Mrs. Gifford, seated at the sewing machine and looking through her kit for thread to match Emma's dimity.

"Surely you have silks?"

"Not at the cost we prearranged this time with your father, Miss

Lizzie," remarked the dressmaker mildly. "Now don't forget, we can make these quite nice with ribbons and pleats and good buttons. These are two penny each," she said, nodding at several cards of buttons Alice did find admirable, raking her fingers through them. "It's not just the cloth; we can do so much to make them agreeable. You've looked through Godey's, and I can copy any that you've seen."

Alice felt a pang for Lizzie, yet attractive and curbed by the funds her father would permit for this undertaking.

"Lizzie, what about this one?" she asked, pulling out a lilac-colored cotton with a pale blue stripe.

"It is the nicest of the lot," Lizzie allowed.

"And it will look most favorably with your lovely eyes." Alice considered it her duty to compliment her friend whenever she could, for Lord knew she never got kind words from her family. Even Emma, who should support her younger sister, still perhaps of marriageable age while her own time had passed, was reticent and ill favored to pass along the rose-water scented words that every young woman deserved to hear.

Alice knew Emma had resigned herself to a matronly life, just as Alice herself had. But while Alice, only one year younger, chose to stay vivacious, Emma's decision was evidenced by her slowed demeanor and failure to brightly engage in the meetings and committees that Alice and Lizzie indulged in.

Emma did not make effort at conversation, at wit, at making herself pleasant to be around. Lizzie at least made an attempt at these arts, such that Alice felt she benefited from her example. Thankfully, Lizzie did not stoop to the high-pitched falsity of so many of the society ladies featured in the newspapers, whose effervescent prattling Alice caught snatches of before and after church. Lizzie was not frivolous nor foolish; her skills were solid.

"It will make for a nice gown," Mrs. Gifford said.

"A serviceable one at the least," said Lizzie.

Alice and Mrs. Gifford glanced at each other. Then Alice chose to focus on the two sisters holding up the cloth and visualizing the future gowns.

"Is that the one then?" asked Mrs. Gifford of Lizzie. "Let me measure you and cut the cloth."

"Oh, do look away, Alice!" laughed Lizzie. "Since we've returned from Europe and its regimen of walking to see all the sites, I fear I've gained a bit of extra around the middle."

"Don't mind that. It's what a corset is for," said Mrs. Gifford stoutly. With her measuring ribbon, she took Miss Lizzie's numbers, jotting them on butcher paper with a pencil nub. "Let me calculate the yardage," she muttered, writing down figures.

She took the fabric in hand and was just about to cut, when Alice couldn't stop her outburst. "Oh, it *is* a shame, it is, that you don't have silk!"

Lizzie blushed, and Alice felt the reproach of her friend's humiliation.

"I'll spare some money for an early birthday gift," said Alice quickly. "And if Mr. Borden won't give more, what about Mrs. Borden? Surely she has her pin money, Lizzie!"

"You know she's a mean, good-for-nothing thing!" flared Lizzie.

Alice saw Mrs. Gifford sew her lips together, if she couldn't sew silks, in disapproval. Alice felt awful for she knew she had inflamed her friend.

"I don't believe you mean that," said Mrs. Gifford quietly.

Alice watched Lizzie regard her own reddened countenance in the mirror above the dresser. Oh, she had blundered. And all because her heart was good, and she wanted Lizzie to have all the luxuries her family could afford but wouldn't.

"I don't have much to do with her," said Lizzie. "I stay in my room most of the time."

Alice rose to embrace her. She didn't know it had gotten so awful.

"Those are cold words for your mother," observed Mrs. Gifford.

"She's not my mother!" said Lizzie with venom.

"Isn't she?" replied Mrs. Gifford. "Don't scorch me for it—but I believe you called her so all the other times I've visited to make dresses for you all."

Lizzie fought her way out of Alice's embrace. She stormed out of the room, and a few seconds later Alice heard her bedroom door slam. It was sad; there was no true escape in such a tiny, thin-walled home. She could yet hear Lizzie's angry stamping until she threw herself onto her bed, and the three remaining women heard the mattress accept her.

In the mirror, Alice surveyed the tableau of the three of them left behind in the wake of Lizzie's anger.

"Well," said Emma quietly. "Perhaps you'd best measure me next."

CHAPTER 26

Bridget

JUNE 17, 1892

Sobs that Bridget could hear from the kitchen. Guttural crying, ugly sounds. Bridget wiped her hands on her apron and listened a little longer. Did one race toward trouble like that or lock the doors against it?

She went to the window and peeked from behind the curtain. Miss Lizzie was outside, sunk to her knees just outside the barn door. Her hands rested on the ground before her, braced as if she were trying to crawl.

"Silly woman," Bridget thought, instantly ashamed of herself for the cold-hearted assessment of someone so obviously in pain. Yet it was true that Lizzie had histrionics over the most foolish things.

She took a deep breath and prepared her face with kindness to go outside. Mr. and Mrs. Borden wouldn't go to comfort her, although surely they could hear the sobs as well. The sister who would usually go to her was visiting at a friend's. Bridget walked to the unhooked screen door.

"Well, now there, Miss Lizzie, whatever can be the matter?" she called as she approached.

Out of the corner of her eyes, she saw the Kelly girl looking over the fence and shook her head slightly at her.

Miss Lizzie didn't answer. She settled back on her haunches, picked up something small and gray from the ground before her.

"Do not, do not!" Bridget almost called to her. It had been a dewy morning and her skirts would get mud from her sitting on the ground like a child. Bad enough Bridget would already have to scald and scrub the front. As she came closer, she saw that Miss Lizzie cradled a small pigeon. Its head was missing. Miss Lizzie ran a blood-smeared finger along its feathers like petting a cat. One could so rarely touch a bird with such lavished attentions. They were meant for skittered flight, not to lull in a woman's palm.

"Why—is it dead?" Bridget asked stupidly.

"Father murdered it and all of them," said Miss Lizzie in a low, awful voice. It was such a voice, indeed, a growl from some hell the woman had reserved inside her, half feral, wholly formed of all that was not Fall River, that Bridget took a step back.

"For God's sake, you will have the neighborhood crying fire for all your caterwauling," said Mr. Borden from the side stoop.

"You *killed* them, and I loved them," Lizzie said in that same disturbing tone.

"Boys were breaking into the barn to steal them," Andrew said.

"They came in to feed them and watch them," Bridget found herself saying, wincing the second after the words were out of her mouth. It was Andrew who paid her each week, not Lizzie. Embarrassed, she walked past Miss Lizzie and into the barn.

The coop had puzzled Bridget. If putting fowl in, why not chickens, so the table would have eggs? The barn had, until a year ago, been the domain of the horse, a gray nag of gentle disposition who'd been sold. Lizzie had loved the horse and petitioned most fervently for its keeping, but Mr. Borden had been set. There had been some tears. Besides affection for the beast, it provided her a certain amount of liberty. Miss Lizzie knew how to drive the buggy, and it did give her freedom to get out farther than she could on foot, without the dirty crowds on the streetcar.

She can't use those horsecar tickets anyway, Bridget thought. *They'd catch her if she used them.*

The sale of the horse had been a bitter morning. Miss Lizzie had even cried in front of the buyer so that the poor man had tried to withdraw, but Mr. Borden had been grimly relentless. He didn't want the horse anymore, and he didn't want to pay for its upkeep if he wasn't using it.

"You don't want me going out," Miss Lizzie had said bitterly to her father.

Once the horse was gone, Miss Lizzie had turned her attention to the pigeons. She had been tending them as if they were pets, a useless pursuit if Bridget ever saw one. But it gave her a task each day when the household required naught of her. She took pleasure in the garbled coos and preening of the birds.

Bridget had indeed seen neighbor boys enter the barn but had only smiled to herself at the adventuring spirit of lads. What harm could they wreak? Surely nothing so butcherous as what Mr. Borden had done.

As her eyes adjusted, she saw a pile of headless birds next to the coop with its door open. They formed a rough pyramid of limp souls, and at the bottom there was a circular red platform of their commingled blood, as if they rested on a crimson plate.

Did Mr. Borden mean for them to eat the birds? Bridget's mouth tightened at the idea. She'd never pluck these sorry attempts at squab, nor would she roast them. Pigeons were dirty birds. Miss Lizzie might've loved them as pets, but they were known to swarm with lice.

Feathers were everywhere, the ticker tape festoons that demonstrated the struggle that took place. Each pigeon saw the other pigeon die before it, and must've butted its head against its chicken-wire roof in desperation to fly.

Atop the coop sat the hatchet, encrusted with gore.

In this world, there are two types of people, Bridget remembered her mother saying, "Those who put away their tools, and those who leave them idle at the end of the task."

Mr. Borden had expected someone else to clean the hatchet and put it back down in the cellar, to gather up the lifeless bodies and . . . burn them? Throw them to neighborhood dogs to rough with?

And someone was meant to dash buckets of water on the floor to remove the blood, to sweep up the matted feathers and close the door of the coop. It was probably intended to be her job, Bridget thought angrily.

She went back outside, thinking, "I'll go straight back to the kitchen and Mr. Borden will see I have no intention of addressing myself to that chore."

She stopped short at the sight in front of her.

Miss Lizzie's hands were covered in blood, to the extent that Bridget thought for a moment she had donned crimson gloves.

She had more than the one bird with her; rather it looked to be about six that she must have brought outside in her arms. She sorted the birds, bodies away from heads, and lined them up like playing cards in solitaire. The bodies were settled so each gore-encrusted vacancy faced Bridget, and the rows of heads were positioned so the clouded eyes gazed over at their separated forms.

Lizzie wedged the heads into the grass to keep them upright. Bridget had the fearful impression that the pigeons had been buried in the yard and they were struggling to the surface to escape, only their heads emerging.

"Don't, Miss Lizzie. You'll get your hands . . . " Her voice trailed off as Lizzie looked up at her from her court of destroyed play things.

Miss Lizzie was smiling. "Each gets to pick its own body," she said. "We can never know now which is proper, so they get to decide." She smoothed the feathers around one bird's eyes and placed a kiss on its quieted beak, then held it above the sprawl of lined bodies. "Look at them. You cannot recognize yours, can you?"

Bridget stood stupefied at the vile child's game created out of the trauma for which Lizzie had been sobbing mere moments ago. Lizzie had made mockery of their puffed breasts, askew heads dished out on their own ladle of blood.

"How about this one?" Lizzie picked up a body and tried to adjoin it to the head in her other hand, clumsily, like a toddler with her wooden blocks. "We'll have to fetch Mrs. Gifford to sew them back on. Red thread. And she can stitch a tiny jet bead onto each ruined eye."

Bridget waited until Miss Lizzie's attention returned to the field of victims, then she swiftly ran back into the house. She skipped the kitchen and went straight up to her attic room, locking the door behind her. It wasn't far enough, though: through the lace curtains, she could see Miss Lizzie kneeling down below, still coaxing the pigeons into selecting another head.

She would leave this awful house. No amount of pay was worth being maid to madness, cleaning up the shattered portions of another woman's sanity. She would pack and tell Mrs. Borden the instant that she was done.

She bent to her purpose immediately, pulling out her trunk and opening its lid to accept her meager assortment of belongings. She knew she was making a commotion but didn't care.

Soon, she could hear movement below her in the Borden bedroom. "Just dare to come up and scold me," she muttered to herself.

She could tell by the labored steps, slow and heavy, that Mrs. Borden and not her husband approached the attic. Bridget inhaled and turned to face the open door.

"No, Bridget," said Mrs. Borden. "I know what you're doing, and you cannot leave us."

"I also cannot stay, so what am I to do?"

"This is dire, I know. She has lost her reason temporarily, but you are the only one who has been able to insert a certain serenity in her."

"She doesn't even like me!"

"She's fond of you more than you realize, or you'd be the victim of her tirades and rants. Bridget, I won't waste your time in words when I know that in this particular and devastating circumstance they won't persuade. However, I have high hopes that this will sway you." Mrs. Borden held out a fifty-dollar bill.

Time stood still as Bridget looked at the bill that represented three months of her salary.

"It's yours on top of your regular pay if you promise to stay another six months. And after that, we'll see how things sit and make sure you're happy."

Bridget wished fiercely that she might scorn the offer, but the last letter from Allihies had outlined worrisome conditions at home. Fifty dollars would make a huge difference for her parents and brothers and sisters. It would take a weight off her shoulders and theirs.

She hesitated, and Mrs. Borden produced another ten-dollar bill.

"We must have you," she said, and Bridget reached out for the money.

CHAPTER 27

The Intruder

AUGUST 8, 2016

So this is her new place.

He looks around at the shabby furnishings that came with the apartment, the pleather sofa with its dimming and peeling patches, the carpeting that needs a steam cleaning. In the kitchen, tired grout holds chipped tiles together. A worse apartment than the last. She must be running out of money and being more careful.

Stupid girl. She never hides her laptop.

He opens it and sees that, as usual, she's left her Facebook account logged in and running.

One click, and he's looking at her thread history with that man from her group home. It's early yet for her to be thinking of moving again, but he always looks.

To give himself some outside surveillance, he friends another profile he'd created for this purpose. He's done it a few times over the years, when it seems her circumference of possible living spaces has expanded. He doesn't worry too much.

He knows he'll always find her.

CHAPTER 28

Bridget

JUNE 18, 1892

Mary Doolan whistled her over, so Bridget set down her basket of damp clothes to be hung on the line and went to the fence.

"I saw some of it," breathed Mary, "and what I didn't see, I heard. She's mad as a hatter."

"Miss Lizzie is troubled," admitted Bridget.

"Troubled? Ah, lass, speak it plainly! And he's hardly any better, slicing away at her pets."

"I don't know, Mary. I don't think he realized how much she cared for them."

"Even if she didn't and only tended them, he owed her the courtesy of a warning."

"Yes."

"And so you'll be getting out of here, won't you?"

"Aye, that was my first intent."

"Thank the lord you're finally seeing the truth!"

"But the missus begged me to stay. She believes I provide a calming influence in the house."

Mary drew back with a look of disbelief. "Oh, surely not. She'll never get better and neither will he."

"I can't help but think the mess is all of her making."

"How can ye say that when your yard was a slaughterhouse? He's made her what she is!"

"Most families butcher their fowl, I guess."

"Aye, but that was not mere butchering!"

Bridget didn't reply but leaned away from Mary to glance back at the side of the house. Were ears listening at the windows?

"You've noted the ring on his finger? Not his wedding ring, but the other?"

"No," said Bridget. She never noticed things like that.

"It's a gift from Miss Lizzie back when she was youthful if not lovely. In her teens. She purchased it for his birthday as a token of her affection. And it's been fastened on his finger ever since."

"You attach significance to this?"

"Only to think that there was a time she truly esteemed him, and it has gone all sour. 'Twas Oona who told Mary Greene who told Maggie: there used to be smiles all around. Hugs, even. Oona didn't even want to leave but had to tend her sick father."

"Oona was maid here?"

"Aye. And during the time of Mary Greene, another of our country-women, that's when Miss Lizzie's mood changed. It must've been hard on her to see her school friends become popular and go on picnics and sleigh rides, while she sat out uninvited."

Bridget pondered the not-yet-bitter version of Miss Lizzie. It had probably taken years for the news to settle that she would not partake in the courtships and romances others did.

"She cried over the society pages once, Mary said."

A long series of maids had served the Bordens, getting a closer view of the family, perhaps, than friends did. The maid's presence was negligible, unvalued, and thus Miss Lizzie could be unguarded enough to weep in envy before Mary Greene and her tea tray.

"She gave you such a hard time over going to the *ceilidh*," Mary Doolan added, "for she couldn't stand to see you off for a night so hopeful and young."

"A maid never gets to marry anyway."

"Well, she does, but only to a mill worker who'll leave her with a home full of brats as he embraces his bottle."

They laughed and Bridget reached out to touch the weathered wood of the fence between them. "The sins of being lowborn," she said.

"Well, it's no laughing matter when you're stuck in a madhouse. Why don't you go stay with Maggie a bit as she offered? A nice lot of girls share the flat, and you can settle yourself for another position."

Bridget rubbed her thumb, rough with years of using lye, against the wood grain. "I might," she said. "'Tis a pity to leave poor Mrs. Borden to it."

"But she's made her own bed, hasn't she? And ye had naught to do with it."

Bridget nodded.

"She's paying ye extra, ain't she?" asked Mary bluntly. "But your skin is worth more."

"Times are hard for my mum and da," said Bridget haltingly. "Their last letter . . . well, ever since the mine closed, they've fought to scrape along. Even if I send every penny, they're still hungry."

"And how much can ye send them if ye're lying in the yard without your head?"

Bridget withdrew her hand so fast a splinter dug deep into her thumb.

"How could you say such a thing?" she cried.

"You need a bit of scare put in ye, Miss Sullivan, for ye can't see what's right in front of your nose!"

Bridget stumbled away, pulling the shard from her thumb. She left the laundry basket where it lay and ran inside to tend her wound.

She sucked at the side of her finger, angry at the splinter that would make her tasks painful for a few weeks. She went down the dark hall to the kitchen and stopped short at the sight of Miss Lizzie.

She stood near the southern window, one hand still holding back the curtain.

"I've asked my father for that ring back many times," she said calmly. "He won't return it. Says it would be the end of us."

Bridget remained stupefied and motionless as Miss Lizzie walked past her toward the sitting room. She appeared unfazed although it was clear she must've heard most of the conversation in the yard.

"Your friend has quite the mouth on her. She takes pleasure in gossip to compensate for her own wretched existence," she said at the door without turning. She held her head proudly, the auburn curls tightly pulled into an impeccable bun. "Of course, the opinions of an Irish servant mean very little to me."

CHAPTER 29

Bridget

JULY 9, 1892

For once, Miss Lizzie was in a gay mood. She and a group of her friends had decided to rent Dr. Handy's cottage in Marion, which included a promised sail on a yacht.

"The sea air is a miracle, Maggie. When you return, you smell the factory air of Fall River. We drown it out every day breathing it, but when you come home from away, you realize what a desperately awful thing it is."

That smell puts food on your plate, Bridget thought, ignoring her as she punched dough for bread. Whatever came out of the smokestack went right into Mr. Borden's purse.

"I can't wear my one silk for the salt spray would ruin it," Miss Lizzie mused aloud. She was leaning against the wall, and Bridget was wishing she would leave the kitchen. It'd been a month since Mr. Borden had killed the pigeons. Lizzie had spent the days following the incident in her room and then emerged again as if nothing had happened.

"Will Miss Emma go with you?" asked Bridget when the silence had become wearisome.

"Oh, no, she's going to the Brownells at Fairhaven. Sometimes the ocean air is so brisk you can even feel *cold* in the hottest August afternoon."

"That *is* a miracle."

"Do you find me attractive, Maggie? I know I don't look my best in this drudgery of a morning dress."

Bridget inhaled deeply, thinking of the promised six months she must stay here. The sixty dollars had been like manna from heaven for her family. It was worth it to walk a careful path around Miss Lizzie.

The morning dress she referred to was a disaster. Miss Lizzie was a touch slovenly in her mornings at home, persisting in wearing the Bedford cord that had gotten paint on it mere days after its making. Bridget had thought that day that all of Second Street could have heard Mr. Borden's roar when he realized he'd paid for a dress that could never be worn outside the home.

No one called at the house, so Miss Lizzie would never be caught in the dress. She did always improve her look before stepping out.

"Of course I do, Miss Lizzie," she said. *And what else can I answer?*

Bridget had always found those pale gray eyes unnerving, so large and protruding from the profile of Lizzie's face. She didn't know if a man would find her mistress beautiful, but he would find her respectable. It was only Miss Lizzie's temperament that had kept her a spinster, and after witnessing her madness Bridget thought it a good thing to spare any suitor from a lifetime of misery.

"I am attractive," said Miss Lizzie. "And I'm not the only one who thinks so."

With that, she flounced out of the room—as much as a woman of advanced years could flounce, thought Bridget.

CHAPTER 30

Bridget

JULY 18, 1892

Bridget got up early to make apple cider doughnuts for Miss Lizzie's birthday breakfast. This was a New England recipe she'd learned to embrace, the sweetness of the doughnut tempered by the cider's spike. She'd come to feel a certain pity for Miss Lizzie, whose life would never come to anything. It was a light bit of work to make something nice for her.

The family didn't make a large fuss over birthdays, but there would be a few gifts. She wondered if they would sit down all together for this special day. She put on the water for coffee and waited.

Andrew came down first, glanced at the doughnuts sitting on a dish towel to lose their grease, and said, "Those smell quite good."

"They're in honor of Miss Lizzie's birthday."

His eyes narrowed but he said nothing. Last year, there had been several letters for Miss Lizzie, the typical flower-bedecked cards that two or three friends signed together. No one had stopped by, but that was hardly unusual. This year, in spite of the mixed feelings Bridget had for her mistress, she hoped there'd be more affectionate output for the woman. And might this mysterious young man who found her attractive send her some sign of his regard?

Mrs. Borden came down a bit later, yawning.

"These doughnuts are for Lizzie's birthday," Mr. Borden said stiffly. "Did you get her a gift?"

"Not the way she's been treating me lately," said Mrs. Borden.

"Perhaps I'll make her a cash gift," said Mr. Borden. "It's all she wants anyway."

Miss Lizzie appeared in the doorway, resplendent in her bombazine silk, her most elegant gown. It was a mellow brown, the color of woodland, with darts to make the most of her stolid figure. The dressmaker had done a lovely job of it.

"Silk in August? Lizzie, you'll ruin it with sweat," said Mrs. Borden.

"But today's a day to dress up," said Miss Lizzie. "Maggie knows how to get stains out of silk."

Bridget clamped her mouth shut and said nothing.

"Happy birthday, Lizzie," said Mr. Borden.

"Thank you, dear father," said Miss Lizzie. She came to him to receive his kiss on her forehead. She walked right past Mrs. Borden into the dining room.

"The cheek of her," thought Bridget. She brought in the platter, and the bacon she'd fried to create the oil for the doughnuts.

"No eggs?" asked Miss Lizzie.

"I can make some on the instant," said Bridget. "How would you like them?"

"Fried lightly, and with some bread, please."

"Is Emma not coming down?" Mrs. Borden asked.

"She won't," said Miss Lizzie shortly, popping a doughnut into her mouth.

Bridget walked away quickly to not get involved in that dangerous silence. She busied herself with the eggs and cutting a generous slice off the loaf and buttering it liberally, as Miss Lizzie liked.

After the family had breakfasted, Mr. Borden rose and went to the front hall to get his coat. Bridget watched Miss Lizzie follow him.

"You're off for your day, I see," she said. "Since we may not dine together tonight, I'd be happy to accept your birthday blessings."

Without fanfare, Mr. Borden handed her a few bills. "Spend it wisely," he said.

"Thank you, Father," she said and bobbed him a curtsy before rushing past him to climb the stairs again. He unlocked the front door and went out without a word to any of them.

Bridget and Mrs. Borden caught each other's gaze. "It is getting so hard," said Mrs. Borden. "Nothing's right."

Bridget longed to offer her words of comfort. "Just think," she said, "Soon she'll go to Marion, and Emma to Fairhaven, and the three of us can get along famously."

CHAPTER 31

Bridget

JULY 20, 1892

Two days later, Bridget was in the kitchen stringing beans into a pan when she heard the voices in the sitting room beginning to rise. She shook her head to herself. Why were they all in the same room? Everyone did better when the sisters stayed upstairs when the parents were down.

"He's not of Borden quality," she heard Andrew say. His voice was high and furious.

"You married a Gray!" Lizzie snapped back.

"It's not seemly, and you won't marry him."

"I will! I have the money from the Ferry Street sale and the savings I have, and I'm going to go with him whether I have your blessing or not."

"I'll freeze your account!"

"You wouldn't dare, you mean, despicable old man! Why are you ruining my only chance of a true life?"

"A true life?" Bridget heard him scoff. "You can't marry such a low-born man."

"Our reputation is hardly one of grandeur and high living! If you could only see how others see us! We're the penny pinchers who won't bring in electricity and barely have running water."

"We're thrifty people, and that is decent and well advised. You little snip, don't you question the methods that have fed you and kept you dressed and warm all your life!"

"I love him, and I want to marry him!" screamed Lizzie.

"Find someone of your caliber!"

Bridget heard the crash as something was thrown against the mantel and broke. It sounded like china. One of the gewgaws Lizzie'd brought back from Europe, perhaps.

"I won't stand for this!" yelled an enraged Lizzie, and before Bridget could make her way to the pantry, Andrew came storming into the kitchen, glanced at her, and thumped his way up the stairs. In a moment, the door slammed closed.

But what of Mrs. Borden?

Bridget stood stock-still and listened.

"Lizzie, he's only doing what's best for you and the family. This man is not respectable; he's not a gentleman!" she heard Mrs. Borden say. Her voice wasn't gentle, but there was no anger in it either.

"You have nothing to say about this," said Miss Lizzie in that low voice that made Bridget's spine contract. "You aren't family; you aren't my mother although you've tried to be all these years. You're worthless and nothing to me."

Bridget's hand flew to her mouth when she heard the unmistakable sound of spittle pushed between teeth and lips. Miss Lizzie had spat on poor Mrs. Borden.

"Get out of my sitting room," said Miss Lizzie in that same horrid voice, and Mrs. Borden came into the kitchen then, her face drawn, her color pale. She had no fight left in her, Bridget could see, after so many years of battle.

Bridget went to her and with her dishcloth, silently wiped the wet spot on her chest. Mrs. Borden lowered her head to Bridget's shoulder and rested it there, like a child being comforted by her mother.

"She's all bluster and no bite," whispered Bridget.

But they both knew that wasn't true.

After Mrs. Borden went upstairs, Bridget ventured into the sitting room to see what had been broken. Miss Lizzie had gone back upstairs, and Bridget surveyed the small landscape of chips of porcelain. It had been a plate. She crouched with her whisk and chocked the pieces into her dustbin. She knew the noise could be heard upstairs and wondered if Miss Lizzie felt any guilt.

As she rose to standing, she saw that the plate had knocked a book off the tripod table near to the door to the front entry. It had landed like an off-kilter bird, its covers flayed open. She picked it up to replace it on the table, and a piece of paper fluttered out.

My very dear Lizzie,

I feel that there is a very fragile coating over my Heart now. It is the cleanest, brightest gold, and underneath it my Heart beats only for you. I know that should you grace me with your consent, the coating will burst and from that I shall Fashion you a Ring. My life will be Incomplete without your Presence in it. I died a hundred Deaths when you were Abroad. I await your Answer with great & anxious Hope.

The letter wasn't signed, but it was clear Miss Lizzie truly did have an iron in the fire. Was it the same man who had fathered her child two years ago?

So Miss Lizzie had a beau. Bridget couldn't help it. She smiled. There was relief to know Miss Lizzie hadn't gotten into that state in an injurious way.

The temper on that girl was monumental, and her hysteria troublesome, but perhaps a husband could put her into order. Knowing Miss Lizzie's steely resolve, Bridget had no doubt she would indeed do as she had threatened: take her money and set up in another city. Perhaps that would resolve all her unhappiness and restore her mind.

Bridget tucked the letter back into the book, smoothed the cover, and placed it back onto the table.

CHAPTER 32

Bridget

JULY 20, 1892

Dinner wasn't pleasant. Bridget tried with the pork roast one last time, addressing it with a dripping gravy to increase its appeal. The elder Bordens ate alone, and Miss Lizzie and Miss Emma ate afterward.

Miss Emma had been upstairs in her room during the whole fight, Bridget realized. Doubtless she had heard it all but not bothered to come down and intervene. Was there a shade of jealousy on her part that the younger sister might still achieve the feminine dream of marriage and children? Well, if so, she should shelve it and celebrate for her sister, Bridget thought, for if she continued kind and loving, Miss Lizzie might even find a place for her in the new household.

"We're going to New Bedford tomorrow," Miss Lizzie abruptly told Bridget.

"Who is?"

"Emma and I. We've had it. You'll have only that hateful couple upstairs to cook for in the next few days."

Bridget couldn't think quickly enough to fashion a response that wouldn't be insulting for the couple upstairs, should they overhear the conversation, so she nodded with a smile and withdrew to the kitchen.

She guessed that was the end of the Marion trip Miss Lizzie had been so excited about.

The next few days were peaceful, although Mr. Borden was more surly than usual. He barked gruff orders at Bridget, and she simply did as asked, knowing he'd calm down without Miss Lizzie there to incite him.

The heat continued, like a wet towel pressed against one's face. When Bridget went out marketing, all the vendors seized on her for a chance to talk, to divert themselves from the wretched reality of sweat dripping from their faces onto the produce.

"You've pear trees out back, then, do ye?" asked the Irish butcher. "Send me up a few, won't you? I'll give you the best cut here."

"Aye, that I will, and with me best regards," said Bridget, lapsing into a fuller brogue under his influence.

Bridget found herself with little to do. She didn't enjoy reading. More often than not, she leaned over the fence to talk with Mary Doolan. Another *ceilidh* was being planned, and this was what she pinned her hopes on. That, and for the weather to cool.

"You chat with that Kelly girl quite a bit, do you not?" asked Mrs. Borden one night at dinner.

"We talk of nothing, really," said Bridget, fearful Mr. Borden would think her to be gossiping.

"I know. I can hear every word from our window."

Bridget set down her platter gently so she wouldn't thump it. Perhaps she had a bit of Miss Lizzie's temper in her, too. "Do you wish that I might stop my conversing with her?"

"It sends the wrong message, that kind of idleness. I'll come up with a good task for you to do."

We did the spring cleaning in spring, Bridget was tempted to say but held her tongue. "I'll wait for that," she said.

Someone knocked at the front door, and Bridget answered it to find a messenger boy with a telegram. He was placidly eating a pear with his other hand, and she took the paper gingerly in case it was sticky.

She suspected he had availed himself from the trees out back but hadn't seen him through the windows. Ah, well. Lads always find the fruit, and it sweetens them.

She brought the telegram to Andrew and retreated to the kitchen to give him privacy to open it. But he and Abby discussed its contents without lowering their voices. Miss Lizzie was back in Fall River but had chosen to stay in a rooming house.

"That fool!" thundered Mr. Borden. "Is she trying to make the whole town know our business—that we've fought?"

"And alone? Emma's off to Fairhaven. Oh, it just doesn't sound right. It doesn't look right," fretted Mrs. Borden.

Bridget put water to boil and thought about the rooming house. Would Miss Lizzie indeed stay alone there, or would her beau join her? A secret, illicit dalliance in the rooms that always smelled of coal from the tiny stoves that heated them, grease on the wallpaper from the men so crude they leaned their chairs up against the wall to read the papers. Climbing the stairs with everyone peeking out, smirking. The stained ticking on the mattresses.

How terribly sordid.

But she couldn't help thinking, "Good for Miss Lizzie."

CHAPTER 33

Gus

JULY 26, 1892

She summoned him to the boarding house where they'd met before. Her message was so terse in its wording that he knew it was all over. He came to hear her out and comfort her.

The stairwell hung heavy with the smell of tobacco from all the various rooms, and while he climbed, he noticed grit at the corners where no one had bothered to broom.

As soon as he rapped, she flung open the door as if she'd heard him climbing the stairs and stood just on the other side awaiting his knock. She was red-eyed with tears, and her skin was puffy and blotched.

"Come in," she said, her voice winnowed by emotion. "I'm not at my best right now."

"I'll make you pretty soon enough." He always praised the blush across her face after they'd indulged in wantonness, the way her loosened hair softened her and made her, a right good girl for a soap advertisement.

"I don't feel like that now," she said.

He smiled and ran a hand over her curls. "Tell me everything."

They sat on the iron bedstead for there were no chairs in that stripped-down room. The springs made a discontented screech as they lowered onto its thin mattress.

"He won't consent to our marriage," she said flatly.

"Did you truly expect that he would?"

"I thought he might be glad for me."

"That bent hairpin?" scoffed Gus. "He ain't been glad since Lincoln was in office."

"My father loves me." Her eyes filled with tears again. "It's Mrs. Borden who turns him against me. She wants me stuck in that house like she is."

"Lizbeth," he said, knowing that the use of his pet name for her would soothe. "Don't matter what she want; we do as we like."

"We can't do as we like without money!" Her face was defiant, her voice loud.

"We can get along just fine."

"I won't skulk and live as a mill worker's wife in worse circumstances than at present."

"You got your money from that house business. That'll keep us for a while."

"And then what?"

The thought filled him with gloom, too. He'd wanted to live in that Ferry Street house with her and rent out the other side, but she thought it beneath her. She wanted a grand lifestyle, and he was never the suitor to give it to her.

She lay down on the yellowed pillow and made a strange sound, a howl of rage checked by sobs.

"Aw, don't, Lizbeth. We'll work it out. When two people are in love, they make it out just fine."

Lizbeth Borden had already stirred him to greater things than he'd ever thought possible. He'd burnished his language, borrowing from poets of the day, to write her love letters. Setting aside drink to begin a small savings account for her keep, he liked to think he was more cultured now after the things of Europe she'd informed him of. He scarce couldn't believe her fine penmanship in those albums; a talented wife he'd have indeed.

Her proud face: he loved it. She was beyond any woman who'd ever deigned to speak with him. Many of the fine volunteering ladies at the church would politely greet him, but conversing with him would've sickened their nature. She, though, welcomed his attentions and was so different from the snipe-mouthed girls of the mills—girls rough from the minute their heads hit the cradle. *She* was refined and of a world he'd like to inhabit. Yet it seemed Mr. Borden was standing at the gate and blocking it.

"My mother would want me to be happy, I feel it so strongly," she said.

"Of course she would." He lowered himself down, too, and stared up at the ceiling, browned by smoke.

"Emma says our mother loved the both of us more than breath."

Gus, too, had lost his mother at a young age. But he liked the woman his father took up with, a fair thing, young, a hard worker, and good with him and his siblings.

"I said so, too," she continued. "I told him my mother would want me to marry you and have some happiness."

He made no reply. Andrew Borden was an old-world snob. If Gus was earnest and bent his back to labor, why couldn't he marry Andrew's daughter? No more trips to Europe and silks for her gowns, but if Lizbeth was willing to step down, what concern was it of his?

"Give me your handkerchief," she demanded.

"Got none," he said, embarrassed. He'd not had the money to pay the laundress this week.

"Then fetch mine."

He rose and brought her carpetbag to her. Annoyed, she sat up and began rummaging through it. "I meant for you to *find* it and bring it to me." She wiped her eyes and blew her nose. "Emma will give me her money from the Ferry Street house."

"You asked her?"

"No, but she will. However, if we rent in the Highlands, that money will be gone in a matter of months."

"Oh, no, we can't live up there," he said, alarmed. "Money will drip through our fingers like water. And how would I walk to work each morning? It's a mile away!"

"You can rise early," she said calmly. "And we must live there."

"I can find us a good place closer to downstreet. A good, pretty home. Nothing to be ashamed of."

She threw the damp handkerchief to the floor. He picked it up, suspecting her concerns were deeper than she admitted. Marriage to him represented a social retreat, and all the ladies of the church would snigger. Why ever couldn't he have been high born? The world was so unfair.

He went to the window and looked down at the carriages below on the street. Men in their top hats and watches ostentatiously linked by gold chain; they exited buggies like they owned *every* buggy, walked through crowds as if they were secret princes enjoying a stroll among the commoners. He'd never felt that golden edge to his spine, and that was what she deserved. Maybe after all, he'd best leave her alone so some other gentleman could step in with more polished shoes.

He'd despoiled her, although since her trip to Europe two years ago she'd only allowed him to spend on her, not in her, as if someone there had counseled her on what was and wasn't permissible. She was "shopworn," but not publicly, and she could be a good liar. She could make a society man happy and convinced of her virginity. "What about the Swansea farm?" he asked abruptly.

This had been one of her latest ideas, that they might live by the sea if her father gave her the house. It had been a holiday house for the family and Lizbeth had happy memories of it. It had recently fallen vacant from the death of its tenant, and she had wondered what her father would do with it. Gus's earnings could keep them in food if released from the burden of rent.

"He has other plans for it."

Run away, they could run away, but he bit back the words because they never succeeded with her. She was a clever girl and could see ahead to the day he hurt his leg and couldn't work and they became destitute in some strange city. She was smart enough to want stability, and he admired that in her.

Down below, a gentleman handed a lady into a carriage, or rather, handed a hat into a carriage since that was all Gus could see of her from this vantage point, the large, round platter of felt and flowers and ribbons. He wanted to be able to give his future wife such a hat. He had bitten off more than he could chew. He should never have raised his gaze to hers, kept his subserviently lowered. His hands on a broom handle, he dared to treat her as an equal, and now he was beholden to her.

When the mill girls rolled in bed with him, it was no investment. They did it with him because they'd done it with others. Bodies skinny, lithe from labor, hands calloused, speech gruff: he wouldn't complain, though, he thought with a private smile.

But when he embarked on what became courtship with this extraordinary woman, it was wholly different. Just getting her undressed—her genteel layers of petticoats and stiff fabrics, so unlike the linsey-woolsey the mill girls could shed in an instant—was a feat. Her plump frame, pleasingly filled out, the little wattle under her chin: he loved it for what it suggested of her dining room table's offerings.

She had been eager to taste carnal fruits. No shy protestations; she outright *placed* his hands where she wanted them. They'd started with kisses, but he'd expected that to be the end of it. It was her passion that led him to take liberties, to ease a hand up her skirts, to unbutton buttons deeper than he should. He couldn't blame himself for what had arisen between them; it had been a mutual undertaking, and he had not taken her maidenhead so much as accepted it.

Her sobbing quieted, so he returned to the bed and sank down beside her, running a hand over her forehead and giving her a look of open adoration.

"We can live in humble conditions for a few years," he said. "He's elderly. He can't live long, and we'll inherit from him when that sad day comes."

"If he doesn't leave it all to her and her wretched relations!"

"He'll of course remember you and Emma in his will." He thought, though, of some of the battles she'd recounted. She herself had sowed incredible bitterness with her father. It was hardly surprising he wouldn't bless their union or hand over a valuable seaside property. And perhaps in a surge of spite, he had or would adjust his will to exclude the daughter who had become such a bane to his later years. "I am willing to throw my lot in with you, dear Lizbeth."

She pulled him to her for a sudden, fierce kiss. "Gus, you are everything to me," she said. "We may need to take extraordinary measures."

"Are you to hire someone to shake him down on the street? Seize his wallet and run?"

"Emma and I hate Mrs. Borden."

"I've heard, lass, I've heard!" he laughed.

She didn't smile. "Why didn't he stay a widower? Emma was mother to me after our true mother died. There was no need to bring Mrs. Borden into the family."

He was determined to lighten her mood. "He must've had a lust for her as I do for you."

She shuddered.

"We'll make a go of it," he said. "Emma will help out, and if he don't give a cent, we'll still thrive and thumb our nose at him while we do it."

"He'll fire you. He won't let us live happily. The moment he finds out you're his employee, we'll lose even that small salary."

"There are other mills in town."

She sighed, not a sweet feminine sound, but one of matronly discontent. She, destined to be the wife of a vagrant man fired from a mill and gone tail between his legs to the next.

"We need money," she said.

"We don't, not really. I can't promise you a mansion, but I'll set you up with something tidy and when money comes our way, we'll improve it."

"I won't have a servant, will I?"

He stopped himself before he guffawed, thank God. "It won't be what you deserve."

"I'll cook and clean like a common drudge."

He hung his head.

"Things will have to change, because we need money."

"I don't see how they can," he said honestly.

There was a long silence in which she sat up, folded her handkerchief, and set it on the bedside table.

"Don't you see, Gus?" she asked. "There's something we could do."

"What?"

"We could change things." She seemed to be waiting for him to understand, and he felt the same uncomfortable twinge he felt in the one-room schoolhouse of his youth, when called to stand in front and do ciphers in his head.

"What would we change, Lizbeth?"

She looked angry at his failure to grasp what she was on about.

"Just tell me!" he said.

"My father has a lot of enemies," she said. "He's cheated so many people in Fall River, dunned them to death. I wouldn't be surprised if someone cuts him down in the street someday."

"I would hope not," said Gus. "Seems like an awful way to go."

"He has so many enemies; it'd be hard to trace it back to any one person."

"Everyone wants him dead? I never got that sense, Lizbeth. Seems like he's tight but fair."

"He's hated throughout town."

"Well, he hasn't won my heart," Gus admitted.

"I get worried sometimes," she said. "Worried something will happen to not just him but all of us. Somebody might be mad enough to do it."

"Then quit that house and come be with me," said Gus. "You don't need his blessing. Reverend Buck'll marry us up, and we can get started on our lives."

"You don't see it," she said, and again he saw anger at his failure to comprehend what she was urging.

"See what? Just tell me, and I'll do it. I want us to be together."

He waited through the long silence in which it appeared she wanted him to read her mind.

"They could be attacked."

"Who . . . the . . . your father?"

"Yes," she said with a sibilant emphasis. He was the student who finally got the answer correct.

"But . . . what do you mean?"

A smile played on her lips, unpleasant and of an ilk he only rarely saw in his life, from the people who were "off."

"You mean . . . arrange for him to be . . . ?"

"And her."

"Oh no, Lizbeth, no. That ain't worth it. That ain't ever right. That's not . . . "

His voice trailed off as he realized that she was ablaze with silent fury.

The nice lady teaching English to little boys in the church basement was not what she had seemed to be. He sank into the depths of her colorless gaze.

He felt very cold suddenly, as if someone had poured well water all over his hot skin. The room seemed very small, hardly enough to contain her silvered rage. He was afraid to look away first.

He saw that she was capable of madness.

Miss Lizzie stayed in the rooming house four days and then returned to Second Street with little fanfare. She didn't greet her parents but went straight up the stairs to her room, closing the door behind her.

CHAPTER 34

Brooke

AUGUST 8, 2016

Nearing her front door, Brooke stops short, and Anthony bumps into her. "Shit," he says. "That's too bad."

The geranium he'd dared to place right by her front door is now tipped in a sea of its own potting soil. The earthenware pot is shattered.

"Wonder how that happened?" says Anthony. "Someone must've kicked it carrying in groceries, not seeing it. I thought I'd put it pretty close to the wall, though."

Brooke kneels to the small catastrophe. The pot had sat on a white plate to keep liquid from spilling out when she watered the flowers. The plate itself remains undamaged. She picks it up, half-expecting to see Sharpie marks on it. With relief, she sees it's clean. Anthony's right: some clumsy neighbor hadn't seen it and had kicked it over. You'd think, though, that maybe they'd try to set it back upright, clean the dirt. Maybe leave her a note. Maybe get her another plant.

"You okay?" asks Anthony.

She doesn't like how unsettled this makes her feel. She's been in this apartment only a month or so now. Have they already found her?

Has *he*? She mentally corrects herself. Abraham's in prison; Ezekiel's the only one who could be following her. She rises to standing with a red decapitated bloom in her palm.

Things had been going well. She was finding out things she never dreamed possible, about her heritage and the person who had once meant something to her mom. But she had been so arrogant. She'd forgotten she wasn't allowed to have a real life.

"I'm fine," she says automatically. She unlocks the door and stands for a minute, listening. Her apartment looks to be untouched, the living room and kitchenette anyway. A magazine lies still slung on the coffee table, her orange juice glass by the sink that she hadn't washed before leaving this morning.

"I can cover you," says Anthony.

She turns around and sees he's standing sideways behind her, his hands pressed into the shape of a gun at the ready. He imitates the silent motions of Navy SEALs planning who will go which way.

"You idiot," she says, and she hears in her voice only the slightest echo of that long-ago accent, that made something sensuous and affectionate out of the long E sounds.

"We're going in," says Anthony into a fake mouthpiece at his collar. "Operation Geranium in full swing."

"Come in and have a beer while we arrange the hostage negotiations," she says. She puts down her purse, and by the time she turns around, he's already sweeping up the dirt of the flower pot with the little dustpan she keeps under the sink. How funny he'd noticed that was there . . . or maybe assumed?

"Every time we're together, something or other has to be swept or mopped," he jokes. "It's like we're domestics who found love."

Her face flames as the word *love* sinks in.

It's on the tip of her tongue to tell him that her mother was a maid, but it's so stereotypical, the woman who comes up from Mexico and has a child out of wedlock while cleaning other people's houses.

He empties the dustpan into her trash. "Don't throw it away," she says. "We can replant it."

"I'll just buy you another," he shrugs.

"No, no, no." She goes to the trash and pulls it back out, the greens withered with the dirt. Out of context, it now appears that the plant was perhaps stepped on. She wants to look through her apartment, see if she can detect the subtle signs of someone having been here, but she realizes that Anthony has changed everything. He adjusts the coffee table to fit his long legs when he sits down. He picks up her magazine and looks at it briefly before setting it down somewhere else. Her museum-like precision in determining whether someone's been in her space: it's gone. She traded meticulousness for kisses.

As she turns on her laptop, she looks at its angles. It isn't a perfect ninety degree angle to the side of the kitchen counter anymore. But that could be Anthony instead of Ezekiel. That could be even *her*, in her new lackadaisical way of moving through her apartment. She likes the sprawl of legs on her coffee table, the fact that a cushion is being reshaped by his body. Maybe it was all an illusion anyway. Could Ezekiel have tracked her for so many years, through so many identities and towns?

She puts the geranium in a mixing bowl for now, filling it with water. There's not enough soil but hopefully it can survive in water overnight. She likes the look of the bare roots making mud in her cooking bowl. It's all earthy and messy. She's needed more mess in her life.

A few days later, with an offhand smile, Anthony hands her something.

Accustomed as she is to the bent covers and softened pages of library books, the volume impresses with its untouched, sturdy nature. It's made of maroon leather, its cover embossed in gold lettering. It's

Trial of Lizzie Borden, by Edmund Pearson.

"It's a loan from my firm's law library," says Anthony. "Part of a series no one reads. In fact, I doubt it's even been cracked."

Just holding such a book feels like a privilege. It's like a volume taken from a mansion's library, spine stamped with filigreed designs. Turned on its side, the book's compacted pages present a uniform brick of gold. There's even a slender woven ribbon that emerges from the spine, a built-in bookmark to be laid between the pages.

But more than the book's pageantry, Brooke is touched by the fact that he brought it home for her. Gifts have been rare for her since her mother died.

"That's really nice of you," she says.

"Just trying to get on your good side."

"So this is the actual trial transcript?"

"Most of it. It's edited down. But I flipped it open for a few moments, and it's a great read. You'll learn a lot about your ancestor."

"Like why she was in Belgium having a baby?"

"Maybe," says Anthony.

"Wikipedia didn't say anything about it at all. Do you think it's possible no one even knows?"

"You have fresh scholarship on the cold case file, perhaps," says Anthony. "For her to travel all the way to Europe to have a baby and leave it there, doesn't it seem like something she was keeping secret?"

"How does a Massachusetts woman in 1892 get to Europe and no one knows?"

"You've got a mystery to solve," he says. "I've got some other research to do tonight. Is it okay if I get to work?"

"Of course. Yeah," says Brooke. She feels like an anthropologist watching as he opens his briefcase and takes out an accordion file. He settles deeper in her sofa and starts making notes on pages as he reads. Brooke feels an unfamiliar ache arise and makes herself open her own laptop to distract herself. This is how so many families spend evenings. She's seen it on TV, had even lived it herself for the first decade or so of her life. The lamplight flooding their faces as they sit, the legs curled, the ease and unselfconsciousness. Anthony knows how to do it effortlessly. She will have to work at it.

Searching under "Lizzie Borden" and "Europe" yields the information that Lizzie took a Grand Tour in 1890. She and a few female cousins visited England, Ireland, Scotland, and many countries on the Continent. If Lizzie was swelling with child, the others on the trip surely knew it. How could that have been kept secret, such a shocking offense in that Victorian era?

Brooke knows from looking at photographs of Lizzie that she had an ample form. News reports occasionally blast out stories of girls hiding their pregnancies until prom night when they give birth in the bathroom, or women who didn't even know they were pregnant until they went into labor. Could Lizzie have cloaked a growing stomach?

Biting her lip, Brooke can't see it. The women were so tightly corseted, and it was summer when Lizzie took the trip to Europe, so she wouldn't have been wearing a shawl or outerwear. Was it possible Lizzie went off on her own while the others frolicked through museums and cathedrals, hunkering down in Belgium until her child was ready to be delivered, and then delivered up?

Lizzie was gone for nineteen weeks, says one source. A pregnancy is forty weeks, so she would've left Massachusetts when she was halfway through with her term. Brooke looks for photos of women at twenty weeks and sees that for some, the stomach only shows a paunch, while others look ready to drop.

She finds she can't stop scrolling through image after image of women standing sideways, phones aimed at the mirror, a handwritten sign on the counter reading "Twenty weeks." So much pride. These were seriously happy women.

Brooke glances over at Anthony and angles her body so he can't see her screen, should he look up. She's become so entrenched in her lifestyle of solitariness. She couldn't bring a child along into her troubles. The Carr brothers would wreck her child's life just as they think she wrecked theirs. That pool of light cast by the lamp on the table . . . it can shine on her. It can shine on Anthony for a while. That's all right. But it won't ever shine on a third person. She'll be long gone before that can happen. A year from now, other people will be sitting on this sofa.

With a mental face slap, she snaps out of her melodramatic thinking and starts leafing through the book. The introduction pulls her into this long-ago drama. The first illustration is the floor plan of the murder house, produced as evidence in the trial because of the oddities with locks and passageways. She sees that the upstairs has no central hallway; one has to walk through Lizzie's bedroom to reach the elder Bordens' room, but that door was kept locked. So Andrew Borden used the servant's back staircase to get to his room. The front door had multiple locks, like a serial killer Brooke remembered reading about once. That many locks meant keeping the world out . . . or keeping a victim in.

"Good read?" asks Anthony ten minutes later, and she smiles with a nod, not looking up. She doesn't want to stop. The day of the murders, the house had an interesting rotation of inhabitants. An out-of-town relative had shown up, John Morse, the brother of Andrew's first wife. He had breakfasted with Andrew and Abby before departing on errands along with Andrew. Lizzie came down to eat breakfast separately and spent her morning doing tasks of varying believability.

"She was supposedly ironing handkerchiefs on one of the hottest days there had been that summer," Brooke finally looks up to tell Anthony. "Could there be a stupider thing to claim? She said the iron wasn't hot enough, so she put it back on the stove to warm up while she went to the barn."

"Handkerchiefs were important back then," says Anthony. "You never knew when a bout of crying would hit you."

Brooke can't conceive of the misery of keeping a fire going in the stove in a world where air conditioning hasn't arrived yet. And to iron handkerchiefs? Was this one of those busywork things to fill the hours of a day when one didn't have Internet access or a job?

There was one other person besides Abby and Lizzie moving through the house on this morning: Bridget Sullivan, the Irish maid. Her choice of employers having been a poor one that doubtless informed her nightmares for the rest of her life.

Bridget'd gotten up, vomited perhaps from food poisoning, and performed a hideous task in the August sunshine, cleaning all the windows inside and out. What possessed Abby to request such a dire task?

Maybe Bridget had been stirred to murder by the careless request of a person who didn't have to make multiple trips to get water in her bucket, and use vinegar on her poor, chapped hands. Were the windows really *that bad*? They couldn't wait another few months until the days cooled? Abby had known Bridget had vomited and still sent her out to work with the strongly odorous cleaning product.

Bridget, loath to do her task, found some insubordinate pleasure in talking to the Kelly girl, another Irish servant, over the fence. They might've whiled away quite a bit of time. Then she went indoors to do the interior side of the glass.

She let in Mr. Borden when he came back from his tasks around town, the side door locked against him and his first attempt to enter the house, the front door strangely triple-locked. She saw him go into the sitting room with his newspaper.

Lizzie tried to get Bridget to go into town for a puzzling errand, buying fabric on sale. She told Bridget she'd seen the sale advertised. Nothing could've been less attractive to the nauseated maid. But Lizzie seemed impervious to the heat, ironing, envisioning bolts of fabrics and presumably the related dressmaking, at a time when the idea of fabric itself must've been abhorrently warm.

Bridget demurred on the fabric sale and instead went upstairs for a nap. She'd barely drifted off to sleep when Lizzie called up to her that Andrew was dead.

"Okay, you have to listen to this," Brooke says to Anthony. He looks up obligingly; he had given up on his paperwork and been looking at his phone. "Lizzie calls to the maid Bridget to tell her the father is dead. She asks her to go call for the doctor across the street. So, you find your bludgeoned father . . . and you don't *leave*? You don't run screaming out into the street?"

"She was in shock."

"The only person in the house: you send them *out*? Leaving you alone with whoever might've killed your dad? That right there spells guilt to me."

"It was an odd thing to do. But perhaps she was frozen."

"I think even in shock you'd pick up your damn skirts and be running down the street!"

"Some people have really strange reactions to traumatic situations."

"C'mon! Not even one scream? She's calling Bridget down from the bottom of the stairs as if she needs tea instead of a coroner."

Abruptly, Brooke turns her attention back to the book. She reads on, learning that Lizzie had stayed inside the screen door, waiting for Bridget to return with the doctor. Based on the floor plan, she could've been nabbed from behind by the killer coming downstairs, or up from the cellar. She was in the middle of a thoroughfare, essentially, and defenseless. She was in servants' territory, perhaps not such a familiar area of the home to her.

A thought strikes Brooke.

Lizzie's not even supposed to use the staircase that leads up to the Bordens' bedroom; she only uses the front staircase. It's just so odd.

"You're fascinated by this case," Anthony observes.

"There's a lot to it."

"With the added lurid pleasure of knowing you're related to a murderess."

Oof.

"Don't say that."

"Right, she was acquitted."

But that wasn't what she meant. She'd been offended—stupidly, she realized—by the idea, as if the long-ago crime could be visited at her door.

The Carr brothers thought she had murdered their mother. Nothing so sadistic as the sea of blows endured by the Bordens' skulls. A more ladylike method, really requiring no strength, no vitriol.

Brooke had already learned that many people thought Lizzie Borden had been acquitted simply because the jury didn't believe a woman capable of such carnage. They literally didn't think a woman possessed the physical strength to wield a hatchet. In 1892, women could not vote, nor could they participate in the legal process. Lizzie faced a jury of men, perplexed about how a nice decent woman who taught Sunday school and served on the Ladies' Fruit & Flower Mission could ever be thought to commit such deeds.

"Look at this," says Anthony, turning his phone's face to her. He's been reading up on Lizzie, too. He shows her a JPEG of Lizzie's warrant. "It's a preprinted form with male pronouns. They had to add 's' in front of 'he' to make it a 'she' on every line."

"Any wonder the jury didn't think a woman could do it!"

"So the elephant in the room," says Anthony. "I'm sure you came across it already."

Brooke frowns. "No idea what you mean."

"You know I love to travel," he says. "I told you I'd go to Belgium with you."

"I know, but I'm not sure it's worth thousands of dollars when I could start with just a phone call."

"True. But I meant a travel destination that's a lot closer."

"Fall River?" she asks.

"The B&B!" he practically shouts. "You must've seen it online!"

"Actually, no."

"Oh. And here I was thinking you were screwing up the courage to ask me to go with you."

She lets that one pass without comment.

"We could sleep in your ancestor's bed," he gloats. "How's that for connecting with your past?"

"I don't get it."

"The murder house is a bed and breakfast. You can stay in the guest room where Mrs. Borden's body was found, or Lizzie's room, or Emma's. Even up in the attic where the maid's room was. It's probably a cheesy proposition, but what a story we'd get out of it!"

Brooke feels sick to her stomach for a variety of reasons. One is that she's afraid she'll be the "story" he relishes telling other attorneys over drinks at conferences: "I once dated this girl who was a descendant of Lizzie Borden . . . remember her, the one who supposedly axed her parents? Well, she and I actually went and *stayed* at the house where the murders took place!" She'd be nothing but an anecdote, the ex who's fun to talk about. And if they end badly, he'll probably incorporate some joke about how he feels he got away with his life just before she channeled her ancestor and stood by the bed in the middle of the night, moonlight glinting off her knife.

The other source of nausea is one of judgment. How tone-deaf, how atrocious, that the house caters to people who want to sleep in the room where a poor old woman was bashed to death. There seemed to be a glamorizing of the crime, just as Jack the Ripper's deeds take on a certain mystique simply by drawing a veil of fog and gas lamps around the hideous reality of poverty-stricken prostitutes disemboweled and "written" on with a knife. The Vaseline on the lens was pea soup fog and the simple words *Victorian, London, Cheapside.*

Were crimes in the 1800s somehow more romantic, less sordid? She couldn't see tourists of the future booking a room at the JonBenet Ramsey house. So why did people think it was okay to torture the Borden ghosts with their gleeful interest in how they died?

"I'll *never* go," says Brooke.

"It's only a few hours away."

"It wouldn't matter if we could walk there." She gives him a look of contempt. "Do you really find the idea attractive?"

"That's not the right word. Maybe . . . compelling."

"If you had been killed in a barbaric way, would you want strangers tramping through your house in 150 years and looking at photos of your brain spilling out of your skull?"

"Probably not."

"So I'm not spending my money to reward the ghouls who set this place up as a hotel."

"Fine, my self-righteous friend," he says, wholly without anger. In fact, she thinks his smile is fueled by respect rather than mockery. "But just so we're clear, I'd totally pay for it so you aren't funding ghouls."

That night she sleeps alone. Anthony has an early meeting, and it's logistically easier for him to leave from home. Lying there, feeling bereft at the emptiness that had been customary only a few weeks ago, she begins the dangerous ritual of remembering her mother.

Her beauty, her brown arms firm with thin golden bracelets that slid up and down with a dull sort of chime. The humming. Too self-conscious to outright sing, Brooke's mother still filled the air with tunes, sometimes just a phrase from a radio song—all she could remember, over and over.

Her cheek, warm against Brooke's as she hugged her. Her perfume. Brooke had kept the small bottle, applying it to her own pulse points until it ran out.

Her mother was wonderful . . . and then, in an instant, gone. This loss was the root of everything Brooke was or would be. She would forever struggle to return to that warm, fragrant entity that bent her life around Brooke's and influenced everything she was.

All children are so, she thinks in the dark. The Borden sisters lost their mother even earlier: what a tragedy. Brooke had at least kept her mother until she was thirteen. Lizzie had been so young she didn't remember Sarah Morse Borden.

But Emma.

Emma would have remembered her fiercely. Nine years old at the time Sarah died, she would've felt the loss acutely. Reputedly she had promised Sarah to be a mother to her toddler sister. Sarah had known, then, she was going to die. Not like Brooke's mom stepping into the car for an errand that would take an hour at most until that hour became eternity. No, Sarah had seen the reaper at her bedside with his scythe sharp and patient. She must've said touching things to Emma. The household must've been tearful as she declined. And Andrew, bitter at the cards dealt him by being an 1800s man with the mortality rates so unfair compared to now. He must've said his goodbyes, too.

A funeral later, they were struggling. They had to have been. No maternal lamp of love. No one to tell the toddler to tamp down her furies, to exert the firm and love-guided influence that Lizzie had to grow up without. What does a nine-year-old know about raising children?

Andrew knew he had to find another wife. He picked Abby Durfee Gray from church. It was surely no love match, nothing more than a dull exchange of goods: *help me with the children, and I'll get you out of your parents' home so you don't have to be an old maid.* Food, shelter, even wealth, although it wouldn't be lavished on any of them. Except, perhaps, Lizzie for her trip abroad.

Abby had jewelry from her former life, and it was stolen. Everyone thinks Lizzie killed her. But Emma, silent Emma, away in Fairhaven at the time of the murders, was the more entrenched spinster (perhaps approaching Abby's age when she accepted Andrew's pew-driven advances?). She was the one who remembered her mother. She had never called Abby by that term of familiar affection, "mother," unlike Lizzie, who did so until petulance over money stole that word from her mouth, replacing it with the very formal "Mrs. Borden." Emma had always called her Abby.

What agonies in that small household when things didn't go the children's way . . . and it is always true that children feel the injustice of simple duties of life, balking at the everyday for inexplicable reasons. The weight of the world rests on some children's shoulders, and Emma felt it keenly.

In court, she said Lizzie had always been "cordial" with Abby, but she had not. The more hate-filled sister was not home the day of the murders. Was there any possibility that Lizzie, entrenched in the role dealt her by fate, had tried to please her elder sister, by restoring her to the proper mother substitute she'd promised the dead she'd be? And like a dutiful daughter, Lizzie had done it at a time when the proxy mother could not be suspected, a day's carriage ride away, a telegraph's distance away.

One of the authors Brooke found in the library, Victoria Lincoln, says a letter from Lizzie came to Emma's friends in Fairhaven the same day as the telegraph announcing that Mr. Borden was ill (a device of Dr. Bowen, who thought the real truth would be too shocking—he only needed her to come home, after all, to be properly told on home soil). That letter was destroyed. What regrettable words might it have contained? Lincoln thought the friends would be worried the letter could be misconstrued as evidence against Lizzie.

Seething sisters, bereaved sisters. Girls, then women, who felt acutely the injustice of their diverted happiness. Had Sarah Morse Borden not died, might they have become mothers in turn, clucking over their own broods, presenting Andrew with grandchildren, boys to run the mills and banks and bring prosperity and continuance to this family? Lizzie too busy with her housework and children to join so many committees. Maybe she would've never seen Europe, but she'd feel vital and in her bed would be a man who'd turn her in his arms and start another child.

Aunt Emma with her own parade of babies. Solemn faces outright cracked by smiles, because when parents live and children crawl onto their laps and demand stories and patty-cakes, a simple grace arises. It would've saved everything had Sarah lived. Abby would be merely the unmarried woman sitting a pew apart, watching all the doings, perhaps even with private relief that such rustling and handkerchief-blowing and hissed counseling of children during the sermon was not her fate.

Brooke sits up in bed, rubbing her face with both hands. She takes her laptop off her bedside table and logs on. Nothing from Miguel.

So it's already started. The loss of the nightly check-in. She'd hoped he'd have posted, saying *where are you,* and it had been a test of herself to withhold it, to give him that breathing room, that space. But he hadn't needed her permission. He was already off, breathing gustily.

All the air.

CHAPTER 35

Brooke

Throughout the next few days, Brooke thinks about Emma and continues to read about the case. She doesn't consider Emma the killer, but believes that Emma knew about the plan.

She has read that Lizzie stood at the kitchen stove the day after learning she was suspected for her parents' murders. A few days had passed since the crimes, ones in which Lizzie had been coddled and comforted by friends, and asked a lot of questions by the detectives. It wasn't until the mayor fumblingly told her not to go anywhere that she was given the news that she was suspected.

So, the next day, she stationed herself in Bridget's territory. She was somewhat hidden from the windows, on the other side of which were police officers milling about, watching for the potential return of the true killer, and keeping the hordes away from the property. According to the court testimony of family friend Alice Russell, Emma had said, "Why, Lizzie, what are you going to do with that dress?" This was followed by a very stilted discussion about burning the dress. As they spoke, Lizzie was tearing the shirtwaist and skirt and dropping the pieces into the kitchen stove.

That discussion was surely scripted, Brooke thinks.

Evidence must be gotten rid of if one is officially a suspect. There was blood on the dress, but Lizzie couldn't summarily destroy it. It had already been inventoried, talked about. Police had been inside the upstairs dress closet to look at it. It was a light blue dress of Bedford cord, *whatever that is*, Brooke thinks, wearily Googling it to learn it is a lightweight cotton.

The dress had to be destroyed in a way that wouldn't arouse suspicion. The Fall River police had quickly surveyed the gowns, but they were men uncomfortable with the task and perhaps unfamiliar with looking for irregularities in the field of a woman's patterned dress. The intimacy of handling a woman's clothing, perhaps exuding her scent, and doing so within the feminine realm of her closet: this represented a significant invasion in the Victorian era. Brooke had even placed a post-it note in the Pearson trial book where the defense attorney scolds the police for questioning Lizzie *in her bedroom*.

They performed their examination hastily—who could blame them?—and by lamplight. But now that Lizzie was suspected, the dress would be looked at again, more discerningly.

She and Emma must've devised this nonchalant conversation to be performed in Alice Russell's hearing, to casually dispatch the dress.

How "fortunate" it had paint on it, brownish drab paint, the color of dried blood. And no mistake—Lizzie chose it for her purpose in case she couldn't change in time afterward, in case the gossamer raincoat didn't cover everything.

No one burns evidence. The jury would believe that Lizzie was so completely innocent she could have the luxury of cluelessly destroying a dress that others would want to put under the microscope's lens. But Alice Russell, the dupe in this, would—the sisters expected—support the "reasonable" decision to burn the dress *then*, when there was question of its use in a murder, when there was hardly a push to clean the house and purge the closet. No other dresses or objects were burned, just the one dress said to be worn on the day of the murders.

The Borden sisters didn't keep a rag bag, the typical place to put fabrics to later be torn for cleaning scraps. Their only response to old clothing was apparently to feed it to the mouth of flames.

Yet Alice Russell, listening to the conversation from the nearby dining room with its door open, told Lizzie to step back from the windows. She knew it was suspicious behavior, but her first reaction was to protect Lizzie from the *appearance* of suspicious behavior. To her detriment, she did not actually stop the action, and the dress was indeed burned. Conscientious soul that she was, she fretted.

She knew it wasn't right. As she listened to the tearing of fabric a room away, did horror clutch her by the throat and lift her up to the ceiling? She had comforted Lizzie from within moments of the first body's discovery. She had slept in the house as a loyal friend since that moment. But now she reeled from what she'd seen and heard, a murderess so calmly destroying what the police would call evidence. She likely replayed in her mind everything she'd seen and dismissed. After soul searching, Alice told Emma and Lizzie she had lied to the prosecutor about the dress. She had been covering for Lizzie! All three agreed she should tell the truth.

To Brooke, this all seemed according to plan. The dress's disappearance had to be accounted for, and earnest Alice could say the sisters had discussed it as easily as whether to discard coffee grounds. The problem was, Alice knew it was a faulty pantomime.

She ended up a witness for the prosecution, and so much for that friendship.

Brooke eyes the pile of books on her bedside table, library finds and two from a used bookstore. She's becoming an amateur scholar of the case, and she begins to see that perhaps the people who stay overnight at the B&B aren't necessarily tasteless blood-lickers, but maybe people caught up in the case in a sincere way.

People who wanted to see that crazy floor plan for themselves, to climb the stairs and see if Lizzie could've failed to notice the corpse at eye level. There was nothing noble about the curiosity, to be sure, but so long as no Ouija boards came out, it seemed a harmless morbid fascination.

Maybe it would be a good thing to go, she thinks. A pilgrimage of sorts. She can't go to Mexico, has no idea where to look for the home of Magdalena Hernandez. But she can touch base with her DNA by a few hours' drive. She can even put pennies on her ancestor's grave, whatever that means. *A penny for your thoughts, long-dead woman, except maybe I don't want to know them.*

Why'd you do it?

And was it worth it?

Resigned but still reluctant, she tells Anthony he can check the online reservations. She half hopes the B&B is full for the night they can go, but there's availability.

"I'm not staying in the room Mrs. Borden died in," she says.

She doesn't believe in ghosts—wouldn't her mother have come to visit her endlessly if they existed?—but the thought of rolling over in bed, staring down at the floor and seeing that massive face-down body in touching distance is an unsavory one.

"I'm in total agreement on that," says Anthony.

They consider the elder Bordens' room, especially since it has its own bathroom, and of course Anthony wants her to sleep in Lizzie's room, but something about the maid's room in the third floor attic sounds the least awful to her. It's at a remove from the horrors of the second and ground floor. Plus, Bridget was like her mother: the maid caught up in the drama of something she never wanted.

CHAPTER 36

Brooke

AUGUST 13, 2016

*M*iguel, *crazy news here.*

I haven't heard from you in forever; where you been? Miguel responds immediately.

Where have you been? Brooke asks.

I logged on a couple times, didn't see anything from you.

Her fingers still on the keyboard. So not like him. Why would he wait for her to post something first? He's breaking a pattern they've had for years: whoever's on, posts. She hates the idea of him looking at his page, seeing nothing, and then not bothering to write anything to her, then has to admit to herself that she'd done exactly the same.

Well, she can play the game of self-preservation. *I've been really busy with genealogy. You never would've thought I'd do that, huh?*

You were on the goddamn Mayflower, *weren't you.*

The Mexican Mayflower, mijo. *The* Nina, *the* Pinta, *and the* Santa Maria.

I think we are getting our history lessons confused. These ships are from something else.

Oh, righhhhhhht. The genocidal slaughter ships!

That's the one!

Nothing so dramatic, and I don't get any membership into any lunch clubs with white-haired women, but I did find out I'm a Belgian-Mexican.

That sounds like some kind of donut.

Long story. Not very delicious. But you will be interested to hear this. I'm going to go stay at the Lizzie Borden Bed & Breakfast in Fall River the Saturday after next weekend.

She waits to see if he knows the name.

Don't go, mija! No HBO, and they put an axe instead of a mint on your pillow!!!!! This is very bad juju!

Okay, so you do know who she is. I'm going with Anthony.

Oh wow, road trip! Road trip to DOOM.

Shut up. It's going to be okay. Just a trip to learn more about . . . clearing throat . . . my ancestor.

What?!

Yes, I'm the illegitimate child's descendant.

Your ancestor is an axe murderer?

Wellllll it was a hatchet, and she was acquitted.

So you're going to hold a press conference and let the world know?

Right! Totally my plan.

[grin]

[eye roll]

You be careful on your road trip, mija, okay?

Of course.

Send me a postcard?

With lots of Xs and Os.

Okay. Talk to you soon.

She mouses up to X out of the screen when she notices the notification that a friend has been added to her account. The loose security in Facebook makes her crazy.

Facebook always does this. Hackers get in. Friends get added that aren't really friends. Not people but bots. Their faces are egg shapes, placeholders until they hatch and become human, never.

She clicks on this one, and it's void just as she thought. No friends for this friend, no education, work history, photographs. Just the single egg and the name Randy Shotglass.

She writes on his wall, "I'll crush you, eggshell."

She tries to open a live chat with him, just out of infuriated whim, and for a second she thinks it's going to work. Maybe not a bot, but really someone. She waits to see if he types.

You there?

Big silence, but she can't rid herself of the sickening notion that there *is* someone there.

No ellipsis appears, so if there is someone, he is sitting there without his fingers touching the keys.

I only have one friend on Facebook, and you're not it, she types. *How'd you even get in?*

No answer.

She wishes Anthony were here. The apartment seems vast suddenly. The kitchen is far away, as if someone could be in there feeding clothing to the stove and she wouldn't know it. Is it connected, the shattered geranium and the sudden friend?

Leave me alone, she types. *I've already suffered enough.*

She waits, and then unfriends Randy Shotglass. She feels it's a bad idea, like destroying evidence. If something happens to her, Anthony should know about Randy. Maybe the police could trace him, penetrate past the eggshell and find the rich and viscous yolk inside, the albumen of festering revenge, uncooked egg, that dish best served cold.

In the morning, she shoots an email to Facebook: "Over the years, sometimes a friend will show up in my list that I haven't approved. It happened again last night. His name was Randy Shotglass. I value my privacy, and I always keep my privacy settings so nobody should even be able to see my account name. How are these bots getting in? You should have stronger walls."

The official language of Belgium is actually three—Dutch, French, and German—and Brooke doesn't speak any of them. However, English is widely used as a foreign language, and she decides she'll have to take her chances.

She writes out what she wants to say so that she doesn't freeze and say something stupid. One night she holds out the paper for Anthony's approval, but he's deep in a file and doesn't notice, so she retracts it before he sees.

It's so foolish to be embarrassed; she's done nothing wrong. Maybe her grandparents will welcome hearing from her. Maybe they had tried to get hold of her in the past, but couldn't find her in the morass of red tape after she went into the foster care system, and certainly no one other than a Carr brother could ever track her through her myriad address changes since she aged out. She has to face the fact, though, that she may get hung up on.

She wants to make sure, though, that she's not hung up on because they don't understand it's her. So after she has her final draft of what she'll say to them, she runs it through a translation program for Dutch, which, based on the last name of Aalfs, she imagines they speak. She'll try it first in English and if they seem confused, she will switch to the Dutch paper, speaking the words phonetically as best she can.

"I am Felicita Hernandez," she has written. "My father is Burhardt Aalfs, your son, and my mother Magdalena Hernandez is dead. I am curious about my family." (The Dutch word for *curious* is *nieuwsgierig*, and, although she practices, she has no idea if she's even coming close to pronouncing it correctly.) "I do not want money. I am only looking for my father."

She has to laugh at how her language plaintively devolves into broken English, as if she is an exchange student herself.

It's simple, it's straightforward, and if she can get them to hear it and understand it, she will be confident that she has done everything possible to reconnect with her father. Who might not have been such a dirtbag, but just someone who didn't grasp what he'd done.

No. Wrong. He is a dirtbag. How do you not grasp having created a child? How do you hold that sweet little kid and then get on an airplane and forget for the next twenty-three years?

No, no, no, she can't go down this path. She wants to be upbeat when she calls that phone number. If she gives off any kind of vibe of vindictiveness or anger, they'll hang up on her. They love their little Burhardt, who was such a naughty boy over in America, but boys will be boys, and that hussy should've kept her legs together.

For the first time, she wonders if racism played any role in his doleful return to Europe. If Brooke's mother had been blonde and white skinned, would Burhardt's parents have joyfully booked a passage to the States to meet her and the instant grandchild? Would Brooke be trilingual now? Would she never have entered the group home, because even if her mother still died in the car crash and Burhardt with her, Brooke would have had Belgian grandparents to take her in? It is sad to think she would never have met Miguel, but her cheeks get hot just thinking about how easily the broken walls of her life could have been bricked up.

Enough, she tells herself.

She's researched the country codes and how to make an international call on the Tracphone she purchased especially for this call. It has 60 minutes on it, and then she'll discard it. She can't imagine they'll talk for that long, but she had passed up the half-hour card just in case that wasn't enough time.

So, here goes nothing, she thinks, and dials the number. The clicks and clunks as if a heavy metal object is being set down directly on a file cabinet make her think something is wrong.

And then there is a whirring sound, and she thinks, *That's it; it's ringing in Belgium!*

It continues for a brief time and then a voice comes on the line. She knows it isn't Burhardt's mother's voice. It's too modulated, professional, perhaps even robotic. It says a brief message, and then the line goes dead. No chance to leave a message. Brooke imagines what she heard was the phone company's message that this number is no longer in service.

 She will have to try the law firm next.

Or give up. That's always a possibility, she reminds herself. Some people don't want to be found.

CHAPTER 37

Lizzie

AUGUST 3, 1892

Lizzie sat up in her room, seething. Her uncle John had shown up out of nowhere, and so she was stuck upstairs to get away from him. She moved her curtains away from the window, but there was not a breeze to be had for luck or money.

Her thoughts were chaotic, sifting through them like flour through her fingers. She had gone out on errands this morning and had no success. There was never success.

The mumble of voices from downstairs, Uncle John's nasal twang. Ugly voice for an ugly man. Even Mrs. Borden hated him. They were talking about the Swansea house, the once happy homestead on the water.

You will not get your hands on that house, Lizzie thought.

They couldn't get to Swansea anymore, now that her father had sold the horse. She should've gone to Marion with her friends, with the wind whipping off the ocean that could caress the nape of her neck, underneath her heavy hair where all the stickiness tended to gather. But if she'd gone, she would've had to listen to all the stupid gossip, the girls wishing for men without stretching out their arms to take one. She had no use for such silly, formless girls. When you want something, you take it. Otherwise, it never comes to you.

The very idea of Gus made her want to straddle him and put her hands around his neck. She imagined the jut of his Adam's apple pushing against her palm, the muscles she could so easily constrict. Just enough to remind him to be a man.

She wished she could open the door and shove Uncle John out, using enough force that he might stumble and land on his face.

Her family had been vomiting. It was too bad that Bridget became ill, too. Bridget was all right, although she seemed to take Mrs. Borden's part. Sometimes Lizzie saw a glimmer of sympathy in the young maid's face, but mainly she was fooled by Mrs. Borden.

Vomit your guts out, she thought. *Let's see that fat roll of intestines lumber out of your throat.*

Lizzie had told everyone she was sick, but she wasn't.

Emma was still in New Bedford, about as much help as Gus. Why did it fall on Lizzie to do everything?

She wet a handkerchief in her basin and wiped her face. This heat was enough to make a woman scream to the street below.

Uncle John talked and talked, and he talked, and he talked. Her father couldn't get a word in edgewise. Mrs. Borden was too stupid to add anything to the conversation. *Mumble mumble* drifting up from the downstairs window, like a beehive sat in the sitting room with them.

Was her father going to sign the Swansea house over to her uncle? He had been selling everything recently, almost as if closing down his inventory. Almost as if preparing for death.

The thought terrified Lizzie, not because she couldn't bear to see him go, but because if he died before Mrs. Borden, her shiftless relations would get everything, and Lizzie and Emma would finally see what she was really made of, when she wasn't deceiving their father.

He wouldn't dare sign the home over to Mrs. Borden, not after what happened with the Fourth Street house. It was only last month that he'd bought back the other house from Lizzie and her sister after their attempts at being landlords had failed. If Uncle John needed a house, let him buy that one from them. After all, he'd lived in it before. All of them had, together with Aunt Lurana, stuffed into that little stuffy house.

Lizzie pulled up her skirts, lay the cool handkerchief on each calf in turn.

Her stomach cramped. Odor exuded from under her petticoat.

She had her monthlies.

Lizzie lay back on the bed, thinking. She had her monthlies, and she'd seen the notice in the newspaper that the Fall River Police Department was having its annual picnic tomorrow at Rocky Point Amusement Park in Rhode Island. A skeleton crew would be left to deal with any problems in Fall River while the others were playing games of chance and riding the electric trolley.

It was funny how things could line up just when you thought there could be no victory. No one knows the awful thoughts behind a placid face.

She brought up an image in her head that was so uproarious that she burst out laughing.

Lizzie in her gossamer, the blue-and-brown plaid waterproof coat. Lizzie presenting herself to Mrs. Borden in it.

Why, Lizzie, it's not raining, it's such a hot day and never will rain.

All buttoned up. A glossy surface, so easy to clean. And she had her monthlies. And the lads were riding the trolley.

And she was *angry*.

CHAPTER 38

Bridget

AUGUST 4, 1892

THE DAY

Bridget lay atop her quilt, sweating. She was exhausted from her earlier bout of nausea and cleaning all the home's windows. Through the open window, she heard the cart traffic from both Second and Third streets, and the rare wind rustling the hickory leaves. Birds were too hot to add much to the muggy malaise and donated only an occasional shrill whistle to the tune Fall River sang today.

She ran the back of her hand over her damp forehead, letting her eyes drift closed. She was almost asleep when the church bells began to ring the hour of eleven o'clock. Her eyes bolted open in startlement, only to close again before the bell finished tolling. It was too hot to do anything but let dreams etch a coolness onto her wits.

The air was heavy, and her lungs cloyed with it, making breathing a pleasant challenge when one's entire self was devoted only to its successful carriage. Her face slackened, and her hands, usually so busy, lay dormant on her chest, a replica of the knight in effigy on his tomb that Miss Lizzie had so enthused about after her European tour.

Like a wisp of smoke drifting in with her breath, dreams began to form, washing her brain with the visage of her mother—the broad, proud face with the easy smile—and the very woman climbed the ladder to the loft, her skirts twitching as she stepped, and at the hem of her gown Bridget saw a limn of blood, as if her mother had dragged her skirts through an abattoir.

In shock, she woke, but it was not the skirts bringing her back to the cramped attic room broadsided by sunlight, it was a voice at the bottom of the stairs.

Miss Lizzie was calling loudly but not screaming.

"Maggie, come down!"

"Feck and Gomorrah," muttered Bridget, astonished to hear such crass words emerge from her mouth—words she'd heard stewards utter on the steamer here or sometimes rough men emerging from the pub, but never her. "What is it now?"

Feeling the lurch of abruptly being snatched from the dream world—still trying to retain some vestige of her mother oddly stepping through such appall—she rolled to the side of the bed and stood, temporarily dizzy.

"What is the matter?" she called.

"Come down quick! Father's dead; somebody came in and killed him!"

Bridget straightened, threw open her door, and pummeled down the stairs, stumbling and missing one in her clumsiness. Miss Lizzie stood at the bottom, and she gave a reflexive smile to Bridget, which Bridget with horror felt herself return before she mastered herself.

"How is this, Miss Lizzie?"

"Father is dead. Someone killed him." Miss Lizzie's face knit into concern, but in a detached way Bridget noted there was unearthly calm radiating from her.

"For all the world, where is he?" Bridget cried.

"In the sitting room."

Propelled by instincts to verify such an atrocious report, Bridget brushed past her and took three steps into the sitting room before her mind could catch up.

The room was dark. The blinds were drawn, hiding the handiwork of Bridget's earlier ministrations at the windows not even an hour ago. The view of the side of the Kelly house, with its windows sometimes giving a glimpse of Mary Doolan at her duties, was covered.

Mr. Borden reclined on the sofa in a posture Bridget had seen a hundred times. He slumped sideways and his feet rested on the floor so as not to mar the horsehair sofa with whatever refuse another part of the horse may have left on his Congress boots.

But she couldn't get a good glimpse at his face. Why did Miss Lizzie think him dead rather than merely napping? She continued into the room, calling, "Mr. Borden?"

The high-strung chit was mistaken; surely Bridget saw the rise of his chest as he slept.

But she still couldn't see his face, taking a few steps closer to await the pale oval to appear in the darkened chamber.

But his hands—

His hands were there, accounted for, touching his stomach, gleaming against the dark of his vest. If she could see his hands, why couldn't she see his face?

Another step nearer, and she screamed.

She discerned the jut of his chin, but all above that was concave. His jaw was an open drawer holding a tinker's assortment of teeth and cartilage. His head had become a bowl in which dislocated teeth floated.

There was no rhyme or reason in that vestige of a face—no nose to anchor the symmetry of eyes, to hover over the lips. The elements that constituted his countenance had been rearranged like keys thrown into a jailer's jumble.

Eyebrows and cheeks were completely absent in that skinless

structure, and in abject, discouraged languor, Mr. Borden looked at his own undoing from one eye split in half and left dangling askew inches from where nature had first ordained its placement. The other eye was missing, lost in the clotted stew.

Bridget screamed again, but her body would not move.

"Bridget, go get Dr. Bowen!" said Miss Lizzie. Bridget looked at her, standing in the doorway.

The order broke her paralysis, and she dashed past Miss Lizzie out of the room. She let the screen door bang behind her as she picked up her skirts to run to Dr. Bowen's house across the street. She couldn't control the short bursts of shrieks that bubbled up from her throat, nor seem to close her mouth, in a rictus. Like a tormented dog, she showed her teeth.

A doctor? Bridget thought hectically. *More like an undertaker.* Yet perhaps Dr. Bowen *could* do something, supply the elixir of life back into those stolid lungs, and sew up the face so grievously disordered.

Dusty Second Street didn't know about the murder, but held up its carriage traffic for her, somehow slowing the potato cart down by Spring Street and the tossing bay's head at Borden Street. She stumbled over the curb on the other side. She pounded at Dr. Bowen's door, still holding her skirts up until she realized in her bewildered state she had hoisted them to knee length and abruptly let them go.

"Hello?" Mrs. Bowen appeared at the door, eyebrows raised at the vehemence of Bridget's knocking.

"Oh, please, I need the doctor to come with me."

"He's away now. Is Mrs. Borden's stomach worse?"

For a second, Bridget's mind went to forbidden territory, in which Mrs. Borden was endangered, but she remembered Lizzie had told her she left the house earlier. "It's Mr. Borden; he's been murdered. He's at the house . . . oh, what will I do? I'm to fetch Dr. Bowen!"

Mrs. Bowen's trembling hands went to the front of her gown.

"Dear girl, I will send for him!"

Without acknowledgment, Bridget ran back across Second Street, this time forgetting to raise her skirts at all. It didn't matter. What was mud at one's hem when a man's skull had been plundered like an egg?

She headed for the side door, then stopped short as it occurred to her to try for Dr. Kelly on the other side. He was a doctor—but he was Irish. It wouldn't do. And equally unlikely was Dr. Chagnon, the French-Canadian whose backyard abutted the Borden barn.

Stumbling along the side of the house where not so long ago she had balanced her ladder and cleaned the windows, she still felt the half shrieks shuddering through her body.

It was too awful to leave Miss Lizzie alone in the house with the monstrous thing Mr. Borden had become.

And—she thought as she mounted the three exterior steps—the killer might yet be in the house.

"Miss Lizzie!" she cried as she entered, but she needn't have raised her voice. She was right there in the entryway, waiting.

"Where's Dr. Bowen?" she frowned.

"He's away on another call. Mrs. Bowen will get him. Oh Miss Lizzie, let's away to the yard; it's not safe in here!"

"I'll hover here by the door; it's all right. Let me think . . . oh, it's so hard to think! Poor Father! I think you'd best get Miss Russell for me. I don't think I can stay here alone. You know where she lives?"

"Yes, miss."

"Oh, do go quickly!"

"Will ye not step outside? The murderer may yet lurk!"

"Just go, Maggie. I need Miss Russell."

She obeyed, grabbing her shawl and hat, relieved to leave the house, but puzzling at the calm replies Miss Lizzie gave.

Borden Street—named for her employer—was only a few blocks away, but Bridget was already ragged with running, her lungs making pained work in her chest. She battered at the door of the small home with its brown shutters.

"Why, Maggie, what is it?" said Miss Russell when she answered the door.

"You must come at once! Mr. Borden has been murdered, and Miss Lizzie requires you."

Miss Russell's mouth dropped open in a loud gasp. "Surely, I will come! Let me . . . give me a moment to change my dress."

Bridget stood at her closed door, appalled, as she waited. Her housedress wasn't as plain as all that. The door opened, Miss Russell seized her hat from the small stand visible in the hallway, and stepped outside.

Bridget wanted nothing more than to run, but with the sedate older woman at her side, she slowed her steps to a mere bustle as they half-trotted back toward the house.

"What happened to Mr. Borden?"

"I came downstairs at Miss Lizzie's calling and went into the sitting room where he lay on the sofa. His head . . . " she trailed off, unwilling to state the specifics of what she'd seen.

"Yes?"

"His head is not . . . it's not there," said Bridget.

"He's been beheaded?" Miss Russell stopped walking.

"No, no . . . he's been, I don't know to say, pounded in or beaten!"

"And he's for certain dead?"

"Oh, most certainly. In that state, if he were to rise, I'd . . . " Bridget left unspoken the thought that if Mr. Borden rose from that sofa with his head such a splatter of skull and blood, she'd kill him again herself.

"Oh, poor Lizzie! Poor Lizzie! She visited me last night, and she was afeared of such a thing! And here it has happened!"

"What do you mean?"

"She said her father had been rude to so many, that she was afraid someone might do something to him. She thought the house might burn down around all of your heads one night! But I've spoken out of turn, I'm so witless with worry . . . but it seems she was right, and he has paid the price for his discourtesy."

"Miss Lizzie said that? I can hardly countenance it . . . Mr. Borden ain't . . . "

"Even yesterday he sent Dr. Bowen away rudely when he solicitously came by to check on his stomach."

"He did, but it was only because he knew he'd get better. 'Twas only a little food poisoning, this heat making the milk sour before its time."

"Lizzie was upset; oh, I shouldn't be telling you this! She thought this was just the latest offense of many, and that he would be brought low for his insolence. It seems that day has come."

"I wonder at her," said Bridget. "He seems no more insolent than any other! And does rudeness warrant himself being done so?"

Miss Russell shuddered. "I've spoken what I shouldn't," she said. "It's only because I'm shaken."

Bridget pressed her lips into a seam, still able to feel the sting at being put in her place, even at such a moment. Miss Russell had been speaking to her as if she were an equal, and then took back the confidences told in the ardor of alarm.

Miss Russell started first for the front door, for they were back at the house, but Bridget pulled at her sleeve.

"The side door, I think," she said. "In the kitchen."

She didn't want to say it, but using the front door would put the corpse between them and Miss Lizzie: one or the other party would have to cross through the ill-fated sitting room to meet with the other.

Inside the kitchen was a strange scene; the next-door neighbor Mrs. Churchill was there, in near hysterics, yet Miss Lizzie stood motionless, tranquil if not happy. She rushed to embrace Miss Russell. "I'm so relieved! Thank you for coming!"

"How could I not?"

"It's been awful, Alice. He's in the sitting room."

"Bridget tells me he is dead."

"I believe so."

"And Mrs. Borden?"

"She went out this morning. She had a note that someone was sick."

"Who?"

"I don't know."

"And she hasn't returned? We should fetch her."

"Ah, yes, but I don't know where to fetch her from," said Lizzie. "Bridget, will you make us some tea to calm us?"

Bridget went to the scullery to fetch water, and as she came back, she heard a male voice amongst the ladies'. Dr. Bowen had finally arrived. She came into the kitchen just as he prepared to see Mr. Borden's body. She almost wanted to warn him not to go, that the sight would never leave his eyes, but he was a doctor and had seen such things afore, she reasoned.

He staggered when he returned, pale, clutching at the table edge. "We should cover him," he said. "It's wrong to leave him so."

Everyone turned to look at Bridget. "I should cover him?" she asked in a small voice.

"No, no, we wouldn't expect that. But will you get a sheet for me, a blanket or some such?"

Bridget nodded. "I can get summat from Mr. Borden's room upstairs." She took a few steps and stopped. "What if the killer remains upstairs?"

"I'll go with you," said Mrs. Churchill.

"Oh, I do thank you," said Lizzie. "I don't think my nerves could take the trip up the stairs."

"We'll need the key," said Bridget. "The chamber is locked, and the key is on the mantel in the sitting room."

Dr. Bowen inhaled loudly. "The bedchamber is *locked*?"

"Indeed it is, sir. Might you get us the key?"

To all of their amazement, he released a foul word.

"I'm sorry, sir," said Bridget.

"It's none of your doing, but I don't relish going back in there." He walked away and soon returned with the key. Bridget was certain he hadn't looked, for he couldn't have and walked with such confidence back to them.

She preceded Mrs. Churchill up the stairs. "Now, why is the bedroom locked, and the key in the sitting room?" she murmured as they climbed.

"It's the way of the household after last summer's break-in," said Bridget.

She was relieved that the door was indeed locked, meaning no one could be inside, and applied the key. She cast a glance upward to her own continuing staircase; not for all the gold in Ireland would she sleep there tonight. Inside the room, Mrs. Churchill cast a curious eye.

"And where would we find the linens?" She didn't wait for an answer and began opening drawers and cupboards. Bridget stood there, aghast. She was relieved for the woman's presence and would not have come to the room by herself, but she had never witnessed before the upper class's easy confidence that drawers were theirs for the opening, that the right of entry that would get a maid fired was entirely excusable for them. "Ah, here we are." She took out two white sheets and nodded at Bridget to go back down.

In the kitchen, Dr. Bowen and Lizzie were talking about Mrs. Borden. "I don't know but that she is killed, too, for I thought I heard her come in," Miss Lizzie was saying. "We should check upstairs."

Bridget's heart pounded. "When did you hear her return?"

"I'm sure I heard her. Someone, please, go look upstairs."

"But why would she be on that side of the house?" Bridget asked. Everyone stared at her. She was meant to be the silent servant, making tea and fetching linens without cowardice.

"What do you mean, that side of the house?"

"The upstairs does not connect through," said Miss Lizzie. "Bridget, won't you climb the front stairs and see if she is there?"

"Why would she be in your rooms?" she asked stupidly.

"She said she wanted to make up the guest room bed for my uncle," said Lizzie. "She went up with fresh pillowcases. Maggie, I am almost positive I heard her coming in. Won't you go upstairs to see?"

"Not alone, miss."

"I'll go with her again," said Mrs. Churchill. "Someone has to do it, and Dr. Bowen is reluctant. Let us go."

"And I'll cover Mr. Borden's body and then return home to telephone for the police," said Dr. Bowen.

"Fortunate indeed that you have that modern convenience," said Mrs. Churchill, "so you won't be gone too long."

"I will of course be quick about it. I'll wait until you two come back, though."

Bridget and Mrs. Churchill minced through the dining room, skirting their eyes away from the open door to the sitting room, where Dr. Bowen flapped a sheet and wafted it down over Mr. Borden's corpse, as if he were a slender mattress.

Bridget's mind was spinning. Miss Lizzie had said Mrs. Borden was out on the sick call, so when did she think she had heard her return? After she had discovered Mr. Borden's body or before? And why was no one wondering why she had not previously shown concern for Mrs. Borden?

"I have a terrible feeling for Mrs. Borden," said Bridget under her breath. They were nearing the top of the front staircase, and she could see the door to the guest room was open. As her eyes reached the level of the floor above them, she saw directly underneath the guest room bed to what lay on the floor on the other side.

It took her a moment to understand what she saw, even as Mrs. Churchill was screaming in her ear.

She had never seen Mrs. Borden reclined, and certainly not face down on the floor. Her body was a large and formidable presence that took up the entire space beneath the bed, as if a large pile of lumpy garments had been thrust there.

"Don't go further," said Mrs. Churchill. "She's for the doctor!" but Bridget plugged on, needing to confirm. She reached the landing and walked into the guest room. The sweet Mrs. Borden, who had talked her out of quitting, who had wanted her stepdaughters to love her, lay on the floor half under the bed, half in the space between the bed and the dresser. By craning, Bridget could see a halo of blood encircled her head, like she was a terribly drawn saint in a Renaissance painting.

Bridget clutched at her waist as she saw a braid lying nearby, completely severed, a byproduct of the assault that had opened up the woman's cranium. There was ignominy in how she had fallen, her hands helpless at her sides, her shoe soles upturned and small and vulnerable, the hobnailed shoes she wore only for work.

"She's in her housedress," said Mrs. Churchill from the doorway. "She never went out on any sick call. She'd never leave the house in that dress!"

Petty, petty. Bridget wanted to spit at her. Who cared what dress she wore, and how humbled her final appearance? Mrs. Borden had been a good woman and done the best she could in a hard household, just as Bridget had tried to do.

She understood why Dr. Bowen had wanted to cover Mr. Borden; it was unfair to regard these bodies from which the soul had fled, left to the miseries of flesh and asunder bone. She wished she had the second sheet in her hands right now, to cover Mrs. Borden.

"Poor dear lady," she said.

"I'm going back downstairs," said Mrs. Churchill, and Bridget left the foot of her mistress, where she had stood for just a few seconds in mute grieving. Dr. Bowen stood at the bottom of the staircase, face intense.

"Is there another one?" he asked.

"Yes," said Mrs. Churchill. "She is dead."

A swarm of activity encircled the house, as if it were a beehive whose bees had brought acquaintances, uncles, cousins, friends, all to descend and describe panicked circles. The police came, and passers-by, and people crowded into the kitchen and even pressed their faces to the windows from outside.

Mr. Borden's body was photographed where it lay, and then he was moved to a wicker autopsy table.

"What will they do with that?" Lizzie asked Dr. Bowen as the folding table arrived, large and brown and strange.

"They will put him on it, to ascertain his time of death," he said simply.

"And how will they do that?"

"It is their stock and trade, and they will do it correctly."

Lizzie nodded and asked no more, but Bridget, who was pressed into service as tea deliverer to the medical examiner, saw Mr. Borden's slender, pallid frame, stripped to the waist, and a gigantic cut made in his chest. She saw that the wicker permitted air to circulate . . . and blood to fall to the sheet below. She gagged at the sight; had Mr. Borden not been cut and brutalized enough already?

"Thank you," said the examiner, Dr. Dolan, as he took a placid swallow of her tea.

"Why must you *cut* him?" Bridget burst out. She hadn't meant to, but tears sprung to her eyes as the private man lay there vulnerable, exposed to so many eyes, and she felt shame for his scrawny frame.

"We need to weigh his stomach," he replied gently. "It will help us establish the time of death."

"But what of it?" she cried. "'Twas this morning, were it not?"

"We'll do the same with Mrs. Borden," he explained, his eyes sympathetic despite his chosen profession. His voice was soft but firm, reassuring. "It's important to know, for estate purposes, who preceded whom in death."

She wiped away her tears. All for money, for bitter, worthless money. She understood in an instant. If Mrs. Borden died first, all her share in Mr. Borden's wealth reverted back to him, and then upon his death, to his daughters. If, however, he preceded his wife in death, the estate would be split between his heirs and hers.

"But you will never do *this* to *her*, will ye?" she asked, gesturing to Mr. Borden, who, although the sheet was pulled up to his waist, was clearly naked.

"I'm sorry, but we will need to. She'll be treated with the utmost respect."

Bridget turned her back on him. Respect? When Mrs. Borden would be stripped in front of these men, a knife making incisions between her pendulant breasts? When she had no hair on her head like a new-shorn lamb, nothing left to decorate her plain face? How the living Mrs. Borden would have been shamed to have herself on display so! This autopsy was almost worse than the crime itself.

She walked back to the kitchen, furious, sobbing.

Miss Lizzie sat in a chair as Miss Russell wiped her forehead with a damp cloth and gave her soothing words.

Bridget had slept as Mr. Borden had napped. He had likely never felt the blows, never left the dreams in which he walked again with the vigor of youth, two wives by his side, and his daughters happy, factories giving productive smoke to a sunlit sky, and flawless textiles that any girl could afford from her dressmaker.

She had been pulled out of slumber by Lizzie's call from the bottom of the stairs, but he had never departed that unearthly country, had earned permanent citizenship there where faces reassembled and the dead again smiled.

"Miss Lizzie," she asked abruptly, and Miss Russell's ministrations stopped. "Where were you?"

CHAPTER 39
Alice Russell

AUGUST 4, 1892

Alice couldn't settle down to sleep. Or was it that she couldn't bear to turn down the lamp? She glanced at its kerosene level; it would last another few hours, but probably not until dawn as she might wish.

One side of the bed—the only bed available to her—sagged and sank, a mattress punished by Abby's girth, so Alice moved over to Andrew's side, but the lingering scent on his pillows of his hair oil made her creep back over to Abby's side. It was closer to the lamp anyway.

She opened up the newspaper she'd brought upstairs with her, easing the paper open slowly so as not to wake Lizzie in the next room, catching what small reprieve sleep could offer the brutally orphaned woman.

The door now stood open between this room and Lizzie's. While Lizzie had undone the nails on her side with a small claw hammer, she had said stiffly, "This is only the second time this door has been opened in five years."

Alice had then penetrated into a part of the house she'd never been in before. So odd to take the place in bed of the two people now lying in the dining room downstairs, shrouded in their own bed linens. Their things surrounded Alice; the loose coins on the dresser, Mrs. Borden's needlework with the needle safely tucked into the white field sprawled above the spray of forget-me-nots. She had undressed, placing her waist and skirt on a hook left empty, presumably taken normally by the housedress Abby had died in.

She turned a page, but she wasn't really reading, listening to the settlings of the house in a nightgown Emma had lent her. Tomorrow's paper would be full of the news she was now so close to. She stared at the advertisements, the mundane items one would want to buy at the reduced price if one wasn't remembering the panicked knocking at one's door by the maid frantic with fear, her chest heaving with the exertion of her run across town. Alice had been reading when Bridget came, and how she wished she had that volume with her now, the comfort of a story unwinding in a world quite different from this one.

She heard Lizzie's bed creak, and hoped she hadn't woken her. She stilled, listening to the bedclothes rustling in the next room. A solid creak from the bed as weight substantially moved. And then, Alice heard footsteps moving quietly from the bed.

She assumed Lizzie was going to use her chamber pot, so out of courtesy she tried not to listen. But the footsteps didn't stop.

Where was she going?

Alice had never liked her own sense of curiosity. Over the years, she had learned things by her questions that she wished she didn't know. And it had opened neighbors and acquaintances up to further-more *continue* to tell her things that after all, she didn't really like hearing about. Would that a person's mouth was a spigot one could turn on and off at one's pleasure. She knew much about Lizzie's relations with her father and stepmother, uncomfortable admissions Lizzie gave unsolicited, after she, Alice, had erroneously made herself agreeable to listening.

And now, curiosity bid her to wonder where Lizzie could be

treading in the dark of the night. Surely not downstairs, no. Not where the bodies lay rearranging themselves into stiffer, solidified versions of themselves, the spirit fled and the blood stopped.

But . . . where?

Alice pulled back her sheets and placed her bare foot onto the floor with its thin layer of carpet. It still retained warmth from the formidable heat of the day. She eased the door open and peered into Lizzie's room but couldn't see her. She could *hear* her, though, perhaps out in the hallway? Boards creaked under Lizzie's feet as she crept.

With a surge, Alice stood and grasped her lamp. She walked into Lizzie's room and saw the bed sheets tossed to the side. The door to the hall stood ajar, and as Alice went out, she saw Lizzie walking past the room in which Mrs. Borden had been found.

Alice watched her pause before the closed door. It was not possible to sleep in the house with that door open, and the police had closed it anyway. A thick puddle of blood remained after they took Mrs. Borden downstairs. The police had sliced a portion of the carpet she had laid on, to take as evidence.

Lizzie paused a moment and then continued forward.

She was approaching the clothes press at the end of the short hall. Alice watched her produce the key and enter. Alice presumed that Lizzie was unaware she was being watched, although Alice had made no attempt to disguise her steps.

Why?

Why was she going into the closet?

Alice didn't want to approach. She didn't want to hear the answers Lizzie might give to her questions. She didn't want to see the prevarication on that face. There was no good reason for her to go in there. They were all hot; no one needed another blanket. She didn't need a dress at this hour. Alice closed her mind to the idea that Lizzie might be . . . might be . . .

It was too awful. She couldn't bear to think it. The whole sordid shamefulness of the affair was making her think terrible things about her friend. She withdrew and went back to her bed.

She didn't bother to pick up the newspaper. From far away, she heard the key as Lizzie locked the closet door and returned, with quiet step, to her room. Alice closed her eyes as she felt, rather than saw, Lizzie pause in the doorway to her room. Alice slowed her breathing, opened her mouth to breathe louder.

Her heart was pounding. How she wished herself home in her calm and clean apartment, rather than this horrible house with strange things happening.

Lizzie stepped away, and Alice's eyes flew open. She listened as Lizzie crawled back into her bed.

She stared at the ceiling, wondering if she had the boldness to grab her clothing, dress and flee the house. But somewhere out there was the killer. She clung to that belief. Walking the dark streets of Fall River, a woman alone at night, was never a good idea and especially not now when a killer was on the loose with his dripping hatchet.

Perhaps an officer, one of the ones stationed outside watching the house, might escort her home?

She longed to go to the windows and see if one was out there patrolling, looking friendly, protective. But she didn't want Lizzie to hear her getting out of bed. So she lay there.

She lay another half hour until she heard Lizzie move again.

Surely not.

But it was true. Instead of following her this time, Alice listened to the path Lizzie took. Out to the hall, the key working in the lock, and into the dress closet.

Alice crooked her index finger and bit her knuckle, as hard as she could, to keep herself from crying out.

What was Lizzie doing, checking for something? Did she think the killer lingered in the dress closet, although Alice and the concerned church acquaintance Mrs. Holmes had watched the police explore the closet for a hidden assassin? And if she thought the killer there, why would she go by herself to check?

Or was she checking for something else? Her own clothing?

Alice did not have the bravery to dress herself and quit the house, but she could do one thing to make herself feel better. While Lizzie was still in the dress closet, Alice stood and silently eased the door closed. She knew Lizzie would see it when she returned and know that Alice had heard her up and abroad, but she didn't care. It was more important to carve out some small and reliable space for herself.

She did hear footsteps return to Lizzie's room and halt, seemingly at the sight of the closed door. She prayed Lizzie would think nothing of it, assume Alice had heard nothing suspicious.

She exhaled when she heard Lizzie's bedsprings creak—but still lay awake all night, listening to see if there would be a third visit to the dress closet, cloth moved, checked, hidden.

It had been an awful day, mourners coming to the house to express their horror, and of course many more looky-loos trying to get into the home. Police asked question after question while Lizzie and Emma, having hastily returned, answered and, when not speaking, sat vacantly with their eyes fixed on each other.

Alice felt keenly her duty as one of the women's closest friends to stay with them as a solid source of comfort. In the light of day, her fears during the night seemed unfounded. The family was fond of locked doors—Lizzie had only been ascertaining all was in order in the clothes press in the hallway, the same way Alice confirmed that windows and doors were locked multiple times before leaving the house, checking although she knew she'd already checked. Lizzie was also likely in a delirium from the draught Dr. Bowen had given her, Alice thought. She may have even been sleepwalking.

Lizzie's comportment today had nothing suspicious to it. She seemed what she was: confused and distraught. Alice cobbled together breakfast for the sisters since Bridget had abandoned her post, afraid of staying in the murder house. Their appetites were understandably scant. The doors to the dining room remained closed due to the burden on the cane tables inside, so they ate with plates perched on their knees in the parlor.

Bringing toasted bread and eggs to them, Alice walked quickly past the spray of darkening blood on the walls and door as she passed through the sitting room. The sofa had been removed for evidence, but no one had cleaned further. It was almost difficult to discern the blood in the fusty Victorian wallpaper, roses at a kilter in all states of development: the tiny buds, the opening blooms, and the fatuous overblown ones you knew a wind would knock twenty petals off of. She shuddered a bit at the outdated design. She knew she hardly could judge when she had come down so far in circumstance herself, but this family had the means to bring the house out of the current century and into the quickly pending one.

The day passed in a confusing barrage of coming and going, the locks in the home put to a frequency and volume they protested at. Lizzie and Emma remained stationed on their sofa in the parlor, until Lizzie claimed she felt unwell and went up to recline on the lounge in her bedroom. Emma stayed on the sofa like a hen unwilling to leave her egg to cool, brooding.

Alice dreaded the fading light in the windows, and in early August it was late in coming but still seemed too quick. She didn't want to spend the night in the house again. "May we prevail on you to stay again tonight?" Emma asked Alice as she stood and lit the lamp that had been waiting for this attention on the doily-bedecked sidetable. "You've been so kind, and it makes us feel so much less despondent to have your support."

"I wouldn't be anywhere but here," said Alice stoutly.

"Nothing to it but to go up then," said Lizzie. She gave Alice a brief smile.

This night, Alice wore her own nightgown. The sisters had paid for a boy to go fetch her belongings for her. She had her book again, and her toothbrush and powder.

She closed the door between her room and Lizzie's, calling softly, "Good night, girls," cringing as she closed it at how she had used such a motherly term. They weren't girls and hadn't been in very many decades.

She read until she yawned, feeling drowse overcome unease. She could sleep through this ugly night and arise with sun streaming through the curtains. But it was not to be.

A few hours into the evening, she heard the metallic scrape of the handle in the other room as Lizzie lifted her slop bucket. She was emptying it in the middle of the night? It must be full. Alice rose and brightened her lamp. She could light Lizzie's way if she was bent on going now.

She opened the door between the rooms without knocking, and Lizzie turned, startled. She held the bucket with two hands before her body, almost as if holding a sacred object up for adoration, as Alice understood Catholics did.

"Let me help you. It's too dark to go down without a lamp and you need both hands."

Lizzie looked as if she were to refuse but said, "Thank you." She looked tired. She turned back around and exited the room, making her way down the stairs with Alice close behind, holding the lamp aloft to increase the pool of light it offered.

Lizzie went very quickly, and Alice feared for the contents of the bucket. If it was full enough to empty after midnight, Lizzie might take a bit more care.

Lizzie walked without hesitation through the sitting room. The two doors to the dining room, flanking where the sofa had been, seemed of Greek tragedy to Alice. The door to the left leads to matricide, the one on the right to patricide, the two bodies resting in the dim of a theater whose lights are flicking low to make the audience bite its collective lip.

No one stood watch over the bodies. Emma and Lizzie had sat with them earlier, but well before bedtime the doors had been closed, and they had returned to the parlor, Alice with them, a stranger in their quiet, unusual grief.

Now, she could only imagine Mr. and Mrs. Borden's eyes open, staring at the ceiling, a cavern where their organs had been, like they were dolls savaged by dogs. She knew how their skulls had crumpled like potsherds of antiquity. As she and Lizzie passed the closed doors, she thought she might discern the beginning odor of death. Flies would be upon them soon. They needed to bury the couple. How awful, how unspeakably awful, to have ended this way.

Without waiting for assistance, Lizzie pushed open the door to the kitchen, dangerously holding her bucket with one hand. Alice followed her into the kitchen, regretting the proximity of the bucket to the place where food was prepared, and then down the staircase to the cellar.

Alice didn't like this one bit, going into the earth, into the complex of rooms: the vegetable keeper, the woodpile, the coal cellar.

"I'll go in here." Lizzie indicated the water closet with her eyes. Alice didn't offer her the lamp. She wouldn't have been able to stand there waiting for her in the sinister dark.

She saw a shadow at the window above her, at ground level outside. It was the shoes of a policeman, and then he bent down and stared in at her. She nearly shrieked. He pressed a hand to the glass to shade his eyes and see into the cellar. Of course. It was the light she held that had drawn his attention.

Their eyes met, and she began to tremble. What was she doing—what had she allied herself to? He remained crouched at the window. No gentleman would. It was clear two women were about their womanly business. How crude of him to watch. A hot flush crossed her face. She was glad that Lizzie was not actually holding the slop bucket for his prying gaze.

After a moment, she heard the flush, and Lizzie came out with her bucket. She didn't look at Alice, who tried to communicate with her eyes the presence of the policeman at the window. Lizzie walked to the laundry room, and Alice cried out to stop her.

"What is it?" Lizzie asked.

"The . . . don't go in there."

"Whyever not?"

Alice pointed. Could she not see? Alice came closer with the lamp so Lizzie could understand.

The clothing lay on the floor in the laundry room. Alice turned to look with hatred at the man in the window but at this range could not see him. Their brutal carelessness, their hackneyed lack of professionalism. They had left the Bordens' clothes here in a crumpled, bloody pile on the floor, as if the murdered couple were slatterns who discarded their clothes and danced off in squalor. No care taken to fold or place them to the side.

There was so *much* blood. The clothing appeared to be of a different material altogether, wood perhaps. Or a sculpture cast of iron, the sleeves frozen in their matted solidity. It hurt to see the faint gingham of Mrs. Borden's housegown, so utterly despoiled by the great black blotches that covered it.

The light flickered—Alice's hand holding the lantern was trembling so badly that it seemed a small lightning storm was taking place in the cellar.

But Lizzie stepped around the clothing, so insouciantly that it seemed her hem touched the ruined garments. Alice cried out, but Lizzie didn't pause. She walked to the washtub and bent to put something in the bucket that sat beneath it.

Alice understood then. Lizzie had her monthlies and was putting the napkins to soak until their proper laundering. She whirled around to see if the man still persisted in watching such an intimate activity.

As if it was broad daylight and the floor clear and her father alive, Lizzie walked swiftly back out. Alice switched hands on the lantern once they were at the top of the stairs, her arm was aching so. But they had so many more horrors to pass, such that Alice could barely breathe: the unseen bodies in the dining room, the spray of blood in the sitting room, the stairs that crept up to the floor upon which Mrs. Borden had died.

"Good night," said Lizzie only, when Alice quit her.

It wasn't until Alice was back in the unfamiliar bed that she realized how odd it was that Lizzie seemed to have used her slop bucket for two things: the fluids she had had to empty out into the water closet, and the napkins she had stowed under the wash tub.

CHAPTER 40

Bridget

AUGUST 5, 1892

Bridget thought it best to return to her duties; she felt obliged to honor the six months Mrs. Borden had dictated with her sixty dollars. She couldn't sleep in the house the previous night, and even Mary Doolan's offered quarters seemed too close, so she had stayed with another maid in a household that appeared very safe: Dr. Bowen's. The nice doctor, so visibly shaken by the day's discoveries, had made the offer himself, and his maid Bridie had taken Bridget up into her attic room. As Bridget lay tossing, Bridie had calmly talked with her in the dark, asking questions about their shared homeland, distracting her with talk of grikes in the Burren and how she spent her idle hours weaving St. Brigid's crosses.

The next day, she woke feeling cleansed of the previous day's cold horrors and realizing that households still needed running. Even when things came to a standstill, food must be prepared, laundry washed.

She entered by the side door, Alice Russell unhooking the screen door for her. "I'll cut some bread for the family," she said. "And get the fire going for coffee."

"We've breakfasted already," said Miss Russell kindly.

"All right. I'll think about lunch then."

The house was mayhem as she'd expected, men investigating, looking everywhere, asking questions. Bridget was glad she was conscientious and that few surfaces contained dust. She saw one officer's eyes light up as he spied her, and quickly she turned and made her way to the cellar. She would get potatoes for a stew.

She made her way down the dark steps, seeing the rectangles of light that emerged as she descended, the narrow infiltration of the ground-level windows. She could see the feet of many people outside, gawkers milling around wishing to hear a blood-curdling scream come from the house.

Lizzie had never screamed. Bridget had cried out at the sights she'd seen, and Mrs. Churchill had doubled her for emotion, but not the one who ought to have.

She reached the bottom. It was silent down here, the kingdom of roots and tubers and recumbent coal, all awaiting their uses. Upstairs, the scuffled feet on the floorboards above her, the endless questioning voices.

She went to stand under the sitting room. The ceiling was stained above her. Mr. Borden's blood in the shape of sinister flames, flickering between the floorboards. She put her hand to her mouth. It was nearly worse than seeing him upstairs. This was she alone with his life's blood, forgotten and unnoticed as it soaked the carpet and then funneled down to the cellar.

She looked down and instantly stepped back; the packed dirt floor held more blood.

It was horrible, wretched, the things that lay upstairs in their mordant hardening, like bread dough never punched down and put in the oven. Andrew and Abby were different indeed now. They were returning to the clay.

Instead of fetching potatoes, she went to the washroom. Their clothes were here. Such a large and blousy pile, because of Mrs. Borden's size, and then the somber clothes of Mr. Borden. They exuded a smell that was cloying and made tears prickle in Bridget's eyes. They didn't deserve this; never did they.

Her head spun with whoever could do such devil's work to older people, quieted people. They were nearly done with their time on Earth, and someone had ruthlessly hastened them anyway.

"I'm so sorry, Mrs. Borden," she whispered in a broken voice. She hated to think of that poor woman scuttling away from her attacker, her head split, too astonished to cry for help. It was God's blessing that, as they all thought, Mr. Borden had been asleep at the time he was attacked. But Mrs. Borden—she had known and seen, tried to crawl away under that bed, her body forsaking her.

Tears dried as Bridget felt instead the rush of anger and indignation. The lady had been kind to Bridget. No one deserved such a hellish and torturous death. Whatever foul person had brought low such a gentle and sweet woman deserved to hang. And Bridget wanted to help the police hang that person.

Helpless, furious, she could only follow her feet as they led her into the washroom, remembering the automatic steps of years. She went to the washtub, contemplated it, and saw the soaking pail beneath.

She lifted it. A smell arose from the unsettled water. The water looked thick, thickened with blood.

It was Miss Lizzie's time.

Holding her breath, she began to pull the menstrual cloths out to launder them, then paused. This was fully as many napkins as when Miss Emma was home, since the sisters always had their monthlies at the same time. But Miss Emma had been at Fairhaven until called home yesterday.

Miss Lizzie had had a very mighty flow indeed.

Bridget lifted another napkin out, crinkling her nose. The water sloshed with a viscous feel, clinging to the cloth.

Oh, no.

Bridget battled nausea as suspicion arose. Was she dipping her hands into Mrs. Borden's blood? Into his? She transferred the napkin to the tub of fresh water, then went to retrieve another of the bloody scraps.

This one was different.

It was not the scrap of old pink calico that the sisters had been using. No, someone had sewn new ones since last month.

Bridget dropped the cloth as if it were unholy, then ran up the stairs toward the grace of the yard—stopping halfway up as she heard all the commotion upstairs. She paused, looking down at her soiled hands.

She returned to the washroom and cleaned her hands. She spent what seemed like hours, hunting down the slimy jag when she dropped it, but she knew they would never feel clean again. No soap could ever undo this.

How to account for it?

How to account for it?

There was an explanation that didn't involve what happened to the Bordens. It was this: that Lizzie had seen a need for new napkins and sewn them.

But the other explanation was very wrong. That Lizzie knew she'd need to clean up blood, and how better to hide it than with menstrual cloths?

Women know when their monthlies are coming. A little dot marked in the calendar, counted ahead. The cycle doesn't always run like clockwork, but it *is* a clock. An egg drops, just as surely as the hen gives her solidified version in the roost. A week anticipated in dread, with certain events to be avoided—like a week at the seashore with one's friends, because how dreadful to contend with the napkins and soaking bucket oneself, without a maid obliged to make them magically clean and dry again.

A woman would wish her friends to choose a week when she

was free of that unpleasant circumstance that might stain her skirts. And this was perhaps why Miss Lizzie did not go to Marion, Bridget thought, mind spinning. She lathered up the soap to wash her hands yet again, trying not to think about how the other side of that thought could be true, that perhaps Miss Lizzie chose to stay home *because* . . .

So much had happened of an unsavory ilk: the desultory birthday, the forbidding of Lizzie's marriage, the sale of the horse and the slaughter of the pigeons . . . and Bridget was certain Miss Lizzie must still feel the sting of that life that had grown inside her, whether it had been squelched or not. It had been a distressing few years for the younger sister. And then the heat that one could not escape from, even at night when no wind rose and the air stayed sultry, and Miss Lizzie going through her monthly courses when sometimes the pain would bend her double, and the stink and mess of it . . . .

There was never any defense for such a deed. No way to ever justify it before God. Bridget remained standing there, wiping her hands and wishing she had never come to this house. Why hadn't she heeded Maggie's warnings and fled? She could be in a nice house in the Highlands now, hands sharp with the acrid smell of lemons she'd be cutting for lemonade they'd permit her to chip ice for. She could practically see the segmented rounds floating in the lemonade, the glass pitcher, light hitting it, the clarity and beauty of that bitter drink rendered sweet.

She climbed the stairs and walked past the men, trying to look determined, not catching anyone's eyes. She walked through the ruined sitting room to the front entry, then up those steps that had made Miss Lizzie laugh.

All the doors were closed up here. She could hear quiet murmuring in Miss Lizzie's room and imagined Alice Russell was in there comforting the two sisters. Perhaps the Holmes woman was in there too.

She looked down at her hands, clean, but reddened from years of work and lye, against the crisp white field of her apron. She wanted to see for herself. She walked to the clothes press, wanting to look at Miss Lizzie's waterproof. How easy it would be to wipe blood off such a surface.

You might appear as a demented woman to your victim, expecting rain inside on such an insistently hot day. You might don the sea captain's yellow rubber hat and slicker. You could wear your boots and put a corn cob pipe between your teeth. It could make you laugh to think of it.

It could make you laugh on the stairs to think of it.

The clothes press was locked, of course. Everything was locked in the Borden household.

CHAPTER 41

Brooke

AUGUST 27, 2016

Fall River doesn't appear to be as downtrodden as the reports had promised. Like in so many New England towns, Main Street shows shuttered shops, the trickle-down of the Walmart they'd passed on the interstate, but the streets are clean and infrastructure seems intact. She and Anthony drive over the Quequechan River and curve around to the side.

"I won't ask you to pronounce that river's name," says Anthony.

"Totally relieved. Thank you."

"But where's the Fall River the city's named for?"

She smiles. "The river goes down a series of waterfalls, or once did, to fuel the mills. That's the 'fall.'"

"So why isn't it called Falls River, in the plural?"

"You'll have to take that up with the city council."

"Don't think I won't."

They drive past the B&B on the first try, the house small and unprepossessing in a downtown block that hardly seems residential. There's a church on the corner where they make their U-turn.

Brooke wonders if that's the church Lizzie had made everyone attend until Andrew left in bitterness over a deacon—a tax assessor—raising his property taxes. Would that he had been angry enough to move house, rather than move churches! It might've been the difference that spared his and Abby's lives.

Maybe Lizzie and Emma (perhaps even Abby?) would've been successful in petitioning for a home in the Highlands neighborhood, although Andrew would have balked because he liked to do his rent collecting on foot since the horse had been sold. A house in the Highlands would require replacing that nag. But timing is everything; if the horse hadn't yet been sold, and the tax assessor made him angry enough, maybe *he* would have been master of Maplecroft. Maybe he grudgingly would find he enjoyed using a nicer, central staircase rather than the servant's, appreciated being plumbed for gas and having a toilet and running water on each floor. Sometimes all that the grim people need is to have nice things thrust into their hands.

The trip down there had been a marvel for Brooke. So this was what a road trip felt like: coffee in the twin cup holders, Anthony's sheepish stop at Dunkin Donuts for a chocolate creme-filled ("before they sell out"), the thoroughly enjoyable bickering over his radio presets, mild panic at the toll booths as she fumbled for coins for him, the way he handed her his phone and said, "You be navigator." Although the phone did that itself, interrupting them in her steely but refined voice. "Does she yell at you if you go the wrong way?" Brooke had wanted to know. She could tell Anthony was somewhat charmed, somewhat disdainful of her failure to own a phone.

"She goes into silent sulk mode like my mom because you did it *wrong.*"

She had laughed and continued looking through the windshield, eager for all the sights. It's not like she doesn't ever ride in cars, but the idea of a true trip, two hours in the car with him, makes her feel like the dog she sees a few cars ahead, full of so much excitement he's leaning his head and chest out the window, open mouthed, wind blowing his fur back like a hairdryer.

After the U-turn, they go slower as they approach the forest green home. A simple hanging sign by the front door reads, "Lizzie Borden Bed & Breakfast" in the same gold lettering as on the spine of the Pearson trial book. Anthony takes the driveway to the left of the house, the historical drive where the horse took the buggy to the barn. There's a parking lot now behind the house, enough to hold six or so cars.

At their left, the barn is a reproduction, and its ground floor is a gift shop. She and Anthony park and wander inside to see the wares.

"This is why I didn't want to come," she hisses in his ear.

The choices are appalling. A Lizzie Borden bobblehead, spattered with blood and holding an axe, glares with wide-open, creepy eyes. Above the cash register, a hanging axe dangles extended iron blood drops: it's a wind chime. Perhaps worst of all, coffee mugs show the crime scene photos, Mrs. Borden beside the bed on one side of the cup, Mr. Borden forever merged with his lounge on the other. Just the thing to start your day with, she thinks angrily. *Good morning, sunshine, would you like to stare at male misery or female misery today as you get your coffee on?*

She walks straight back out into the parking lot, looking up at the backside of the Borden house. Up there near the eaves is the maid Bridget Sullivan's window, the place where they'll stay tonight.

Check-in is at 4:00, and it's only 3:40. They leave their luggage in the car and decide to walk around the house and its environs to kill the twenty minutes. They amble up to the side stoop where a woman sits on the bottom step smoking. She's in her mid-thirties, wearing a flowing peasant skirt and a black T-shirt. Brooke suspects she is one of the staff at the house.

This is the screen door behind which Lizzie stood, waiting for Bridget to return with Dr. Bowen or Alice Russell, or anyone to make her feel not alone in her home where her father lay dead. Mrs. Churchill next door (Brooke notices the house is gone, just gone) had looked out her window, watched Bridget run across the street for Dr. Bowen, and had seen Lizzie at the door and called out to her.

This was how close the houses were to each other: Mrs. Churchill could stand in her own kitchen and carry on a conversation with Lizzie in her house. How had anyone managed to kill two people without screams erupting, without the thumps of collapse being heard and noted?

Brooke knew that the screen door led to the base of the servant's staircase, and then down a short hallway to the kitchen. Was this how one entered the B&B? Through the servant's door? Fitting for me, Brooke thinks wryly, but Anthony the attorney should enter through the front door.

The woman moves her cigarette downwind from them, a nice gesture although smoke winds back to them anyway. "Are you overnight guests?" she asks.

"Yes, but we know we're early," says Anthony.

"That's fine. Let me put this out and show you in." The woman begins to stand, but Brooke stops her.

"No, stay and finish your cigarette. What's your name?"

"I'm Amelia." She shakes hands with them, and Brooke considers bumming a cigarette, just to make her feel validated. But would that elicit great horror from Anthony?

"Which room are you in?" asks Amelia.

"Bridget's," says Brooke.

"Is that a good choice?" asks Anthony.

"Well, it's not a room where a lot of activity happens supernaturally, you know what I mean? Maybe that's not what you want anyway.

But down the hall from you, the Hosea Knowlton Room is the most haunted."

Brooke looks at Anthony. She had selected the third floor in part to stay away from the angry ghosts she doesn't believe in but still would prefer to avoid.

"That casts a pall on things," says Anthony.

"A pall?" says a man coming up to them with a duffel bag on his shoulders, probably another overnight guest.

Anthony and his vocabulary, thinks Brooke.

"A dark covering," says Anthony.

"That's how we get pallbearer," adds Amelia, surprising Brooke. "The pall is the blanket they put over a coffin."

"Do we sleep under palls tonight then?" the man asks. "Hi. I'm Jackson." He holds out his hand to shake Brooke's, and she feels a frisson of electricity when she fully looks at his face. He's handsome, with a strong face and dirty blond hair long enough to tuck behind his ears. He turns to shake Anthony's hand, and she can't help but compare them: Anthony so clearly formal, an attorney even on the weekend, his hair closely clipped and his clothes immaculate, and Jackson looking like an artist, maybe, his wrinkled linen shirt untucked and a bead on a rawhide necklace around his neck.

He shakes hands with Amelia. "Which room are you in?" Amelia inquires over her shoulder as she opens the door. "We can go in now."

"The one you were just talking about," Jackson says.

They step into the back hallway of the Borden house, passing the stairwell that leads up to Abby and Andrew's bedroom, and further, to Bridget's, and that leads down into the cellar. The hall opens up into a kitchen where the cupboard pulls are wooden pears. Brooke gets the gentle in-joke. One of Lizzie's alibis for Andrew's murder was that she was outside eating pears, in the orchard that is now essentially the parking lot.

A few more people arrive as Amelia checks a printout on a clipboard and has everyone sign. She hands the clipboard to Anthony, but with a knowing smile, he hands it to Brooke. He's good at details like this: knowing that she'd want to sign the register for the home where her ancestor lived.

"All right, so you're free to go through the house on your own," says Amelia. "You can drop your stuff in your room and just leave your door open if you don't mind so people can look. The house isn't open to the public now, so it's all yours. I'll lead you through an official tour at 8 p.m. It's much more detailed and full than the tour the day visitors get; it lasts two hours and we'll go into the cellar which they don't get to do. Insider info! Let me know if you have any questions."

"Where's our room?" asks a middle-aged man wearing a Boston Red Sox cap. He's carrying a huge camera bag and a tripod. Next to him and looking aggrieved is his wife. They must have hit traffic, Brooke thinks.

"You're in what room?" asks Amelia.

"The John Morse Room."

"You go straight through there," Amelia points to another hallway, "then up the stairs, first door on the left."

They reserved the only bedroom in the house where a body was found, and they're not even familiar enough with the case to know where it is? It strikes Brooke that there is some responsibility involved in booking that room. What if friends organized a night here and didn't tell someone they'd be in that room? That's why there's a real estate law about disclosing violent death in a home. No one wants to sleep where the dead might be coming awake.

Before the disgruntled couple can truly get underway, there is a knocking at the front door, and Amelia bustles away to answer it, just like Bridget.

Brooke watches her walk through the sitting room, a shotgun approach to the front door. The sitting room is the other place a body was found, and without thinking she follows Amelia, stopping with a shock at the sofa.

It's one of those old-fashioned Victorian affairs with an asymmetrical sloped back, made of maroon velvet. It sits against florid wallpaper, and the rug is a different, contrasting floral design. It contributes to the oppressive, fusty, overly busy design that probably made Lizzie just as hair-trigger angry as the August heat had.

Brooke has seen the sofa in the crime scene photos, but doubts it can be the same one. How could anyone get blood and brain matter out of velvet? Still, it gives her a chill to see how ordinary its placement in the sitting room is. Just a sofa against a wall. She feels no sense of "energy" here, no otherworldly mutterings of grievances from the past.

She turns her attention to the front door, where another couple is entering. They look to be teenagers, two girls with brown hair that they've straightened, wearing shorts and shirts with Pokemon characters on them. They look way too wholesome to be staying in a murder house.

"Your mom or dad with you?" asks Amelia.

"Mom's getting a reading from the outside."

"Mmm, okay. You guys in the Emma and Lizzie suite?"

"Yeah, I think so."

"I'll show you up."

Feeling like a tagalong, Brooke listens to this conversation and stands at the bottom of the stairs, watching the clump of visitors follow Amelia upstairs.

"Ready to go up?" asks Anthony.

"Let's take our stairs," she says. "The maid's stairs."

They retrace their steps back to the kitchen, peeping into the parlor and the dining room on the way through. Now Brooke can see how easy it would be for Alice Russell to be in the dining room, listening in on the discussion as Lizzie burned her dress. There's a vintage, hulking stove in the kitchen. Again, Brooke wonders how much of the furnishings are original. The kitchen also has modern appliances, but hidden. Jackson's still in the kitchen and with a flourish opens a set of cupboards to show the refrigerator hidden inside.

"Clever," he says. There's a modern stove and a phone plugged in on the countertop, but enough of the older looking furnishings—a work table, a giant silver kettle—to establish a feel of how it might've been for Bridget.

"Up we go?" invites Jackson, and Brooke stiffens, thinking, *just because your room is also up there doesn't mean we're all doing this together*, but then she realizes that is *exactly* what it means. In a few hours, they'll take Amelia's tour and in the meantime they can visit each other's rooms.

They're all here because they have an intense interest in this strange story, except perhaps the camera-toting guy who is here for some other reason, like building his portfolio of haunted houses without bothering to research them first.

Both men step aside to let her go, and she squares her shoulders, thinking as she climbs, this is where Lizzie might've called Bridget from, and then she turns the corner and there's the door to Andrew and Abby's room, and there are already people in there, bustling around.

"Hi, we're Donna and A.J.," a woman says when she sees Brooke. "We're on our honeymoon!"

"I'm Brooke," she says, feeling like she should attach some other descriptor like Donna did. *I'm related to Lizzie Borden!* or *My boyfriend made me come!*

"Come on in and look," says Donna. The room is smallish, nothing like the master suite even the most modest of homes seems to have now. Anthony and Jackson introduce themselves and politely look around.

"I'm going to head up," says Brooke.

"Oooh, can we come? The maid's room?" asks Donna.

"Absolutely," says Anthony.

It's interesting to enter one's hotel room with a troop of strangers, but then again this isn't a normal hotel. No key is required, and as Brooke enters, she swivels to look at the interior of the door. There's just a pop lock. It would be an incredible irony if a serial killer picked this house to visit. He could rampage through the rooms, and everyone would think the screams were just atmospheric.

The ceiling slants down, following the pitch of the roof above. There's one window, and Brooke goes to it to see the nearby homes and the sun starting to go down. Is that Dr. Chagnon's house, spurned by Lizzie because he was French? It looks old enough to be. She thinks of Bridget in this room, exhausted from a day's labor, stripping down and trying to catch a breeze at the window. Attics are always hot in summer, cold in winter, the "you can't win" room of any home. There's a light wallpaper covering the walls, fussy, but not to the headache-inducing degree of the sitting room downstairs. Brooke puts her bag down around the corner where the closet creates a little alcove. She'll keep her purse with the laptop inside it with her, but there's nothing worth stealing in her bag.

"Look at this," murmurs Anthony as he sets his bag down next to hers. Propped up against a wooden trunk is a framed newspaper advertisement. It's for the dress goods sale at Sargent's, the one Lizzie had urged Bridget to go to. As flimsy as one can get for a way to clear the house for a crime spree. *Here, Bridget, I see they're selling woolen mittens, five cents a pair. Perfect to think ahead for winter. Or perhaps you'd like to go cross-town, taking the streetcar because it's* that *far away, to get an inflatable dachsund?*

They explore the third story, all of them, the Hosea Knowlton Room named for the prosecutor who tried everything he could to get a jury to see that Lizzie must've done it, and the Andrew Jennings

Room for the old family attorney who defended her, succeeding by pointing out her status as a woman.

The last bedroom on this floor contains no luggage; maybe the room didn't get taken. It's nondescript Victorian, more of the same. Somehow it isn't interesting because it hadn't been a bedroom in 1892.

If no one takes this room, the attic floor will be just her, Anthony, and Jackson. They'll share a common bathroom (which used to be a spare bedroom, occasionally used by John Morse if the dressmaker was occupying the second floor guest room). It's a long, narrow, in-hospitable staircase down to the Bordens' room.

After the intensity of the house and the informal poking around in the rooms, Brooke and Anthony leave on foot to go out for dinner. "Falls River," as Anthony is now calling it, is known for its early Portuguese community, and he wants to try their cuisine.

It's a good brisk walk in the cooling evening and a relief to be out from under the house's clouded influence. For some reason, Brooke can't imagine eating in the house. It's a bed & breakfast, and breakfast will be served—supposedly the same meal the Bordens ate that fateful morning: johnnycakes, donuts. Apparently Lizzie slept in and ate a few cookies. Famously, the first round of eaters, Abby, Andrew, and John Morse, ate a mutton stew warmed over from the roast that the family had been working on for a week.

In an era of no refrigeration, a block of ice kept meats cold. Sort of. Food poisoning was much more a fatal disease in the 1800s. People lost their lives for something so easily combated today. If the food looks off, microwave the crap out of it, and it should be okay. Or don't let it go bad in the first place: freeze it.

The whole family had had a bout of food poisoning two days before the murders. Abby Borden had been so sick that she formulated a different opinion. It wasn't the mutton's fault. She had made that kitty-corner visit to Dr. Bowen and found him in. She told him that she feared someone was trying to poison the family.

How odd to suspect poisoning, and die by hatchet two days later.

Perhaps it was coincidences like this that made the jury acquit Lizzie. Because Mrs. Borden hadn't said, *I think Lizzie is trying to poison us.* She had said *someone.*

And yet, there was a druggist who said he had seen Lizzie trying to buy prussic acid, a deadly poison, the day before the murders. She had told the druggist she wanted it to clean a sealskin cape. So believable, tending to one's furs in the height of August. And using acid to clean fur is the first cleaning method to spring to mind.

When Brooke had come across this mention in her Pearson book, she had read it aloud to Anthony. It was incredible to her that the court said that there wasn't a clear enough connection between the murders and the supposed purchase of poison . . . and they had suppressed the evidence. The prosecutor had even said he had multiple accounts of Lizzie trying to buy poison in different drugstores. Yet after a conference at the bench, the druggist was not permitted to testify.

"How is this possible?" she had asked Anthony.

"There is something quite odd about it," he had said, reading over her shoulder. "What would you give to be a fly on the wall overhearing that whispered conference?"

A lot. How incredibly wrongheaded of the judges to see no connection! Brooke saw one, especially if you added in that food poisoning.

"So, you want to kill your parents, and your first thought is poison because that's easy and doesn't require much out of you besides the ability to sprinkle some in people's food," she had said. "You try to buy poison, but no one lets you. Instead, you concoct a little homemade something and see how that goes."

And that would have been the "food poisoning" two days before the murders.

"Lizzie wakes up, sees that her parents are still kicking. So she continues to try to buy real poison. The morning of the murders, Bridget is still vomiting. So then Lizzie thinks, okay, I've got to do something more decisive."

Brooke's stomach lurches at the thought of Lizzie watching her parents over the course of three days, waiting to see if they'd succumb, frustrated that they didn't. The slow treachery somehow seems worse, in a way, than the heated, passionate bludgeoning . . . although where is the heat and passion when two hours elapse between the murders?

And it hurts to think of poor Bridget Sullivan vomiting, too. What had she ever done? Or did she have to be poisoned, too, to cover Lizzie's tracks, all or nothing if food poisoning is being claimed? And Lizzie would've claimed she'd been sick, too; no one could contradict her on that point.

There aren't many people out on a Saturday night, but when she and Anthony hit the Portuguese area, the restaurants are filled to bursting, and incredible smells waft out onto the street. Maybe the Bordens needed a Portuguese maid rather than an Irish one who unimaginatively flogged the mutton so that it stretched from meal to meal, because no one could bear to eat much of it and make it go away.

They enter the warm, aromatic restaurant and are lucky to be seated at a small table while several families wait for a larger one. Brooke's glad to see sangria on the menu and orders a pitcher for them to share. Everything looks good: beautiful fresh seafood, Littleneck clams, bouillabaisse, a beef so tenderly marinated she knows she will be gorging herself.

"Happy?" asks Anthony after they take their first sips of the sweetened, fruit-clustered wine.

His look is so affectionate it nearly takes her breath away.

She nods, not trusting her voice. Is this what it is? Is this what you feel when you fall in love?

"Some lovers have Paris," he says. "But we will always have Falls River."

She bursts out laughing. "It is indeed a special place to commemorate the slaying of people we don't even know."

"I bet Abby was a fun gal to spend Saturday night with," he says.

"Aw, don't be mean."

"Have you ever thought about what dreadful luck they had to be born when they were? Maybe it was their era that spelled their unhappiness, not them. Maybe Abby would've gone to Zumba and done mani-pedis and loosened up if she didn't have to wear a corset and sweat her way through every wretched summer."

Brooke nods. "I've actually thought about that. Like, what if the Borden sisters could've gotten their own apartment and moved out? Gained a little independence? Their dad gave them a duplex, but they could use it only as a rental property because having two unchaperoned sisters on their own would have been a horrible scandal."

An appetizer arrives, and they dig in, glad to be thriving in the twenty-first century, wearing deodorant and accustomed to flush toilets, antibiotics, refrigeration—and electricity to dispel the darkest of the darks.

"Look. It's that guy from the house. I think he's alone," says Anthony, and before she can stop him, his arm goes up, and he waves him over.

She turns her head and watches Jackson smile in recognition. He comes over to their table.

"Join us," says Anthony, and Brooke is disappointed. She liked being the two of them and wanted to see that look light up Anthony's face again. He won't do it if there's another man there.

"If you're sure," Jackson says. He takes a seat next to Anthony, so that he faces Brooke. "Looking forward to tonight's tour?"

"Of course," she says. "Everything will be made clear, right? We get all the insider information?" She smiles to herself, struck by the fact that *she* has the ultimate insider info, that when Lizzie shipped off to Europe, she had a bun in the oven, and her sous-chef was a secret.

Brooke doesn't know how or when she'll share the news. Apparently the Dutch woman didn't catch the import of the mother's name listed on the form. As of this minute, only she and Anthony know.

Jackson orders his own dish, and Brooke pours him a glass out of the communal pitcher. After a bit, she has to concede that it is good to have him with them after all; he's got a wry sense of humor that makes the dinner fly by. She likes his voice, it's deep but not a bass, just with an interesting sort of . . . what Anthony would call *timbre*.

When Anthony gets up to go to the bathroom, Jackson gives her a quiet look.

"What?" she says.

"You seem so nice."

"How am I supposed to take that?"

"As a compliment, I guess."

"Why wouldn't I be nice?"

He doesn't respond, and she feels a deep flush begin at her cheekbones and swallow her face.

She looks down at her plate until Anthony returns. She knows something about Jackson, can see it in the ever-so-slightly hunched posture, his quick movements. He's like her. He doesn't have the lax trust in the goodness of life that someone like Anthony wears as carelessly as a coat. Something happened to Jackson once. Something that made it a marvel that someone would be nice to him, call him over to eat with them.

"Why are you at the Lizzie Borden house?" she asks him abruptly. "You're here alone."

"It's kind of hard to explain."

"Try me."

"No, really, it would freak you out."

"You're studying her murder methods," she guesses.

He laughs. "No, I don't like murderers. I especially don't like murderers who get away with it."

"So you think she did it."

"Almost definitely. Don't you?"

"Not sure. I've been reading up on the case a lot, and there are so many things that point to her guilt."

"What do you think?" Jackson addresses Anthony.

"The fact that Lizzie was in the house during a period in which not one but two murders were conducted, several hours apart: I think she did it. It doesn't make sense that a murderer would've skirted around her and Bridget in broad daylight. The father could've been out all day, and the murderer is hanging out in a closet biding his time? It's too much."

"Well put," says Jackson.

Anthony starts in on an enthusiastic forensics discussion about the hatchet head discovered in the basement with dust on both sides, as if someone had ham-handedly tried to make a cleaned-up weapon appear that it had never been taken out of its dusty cellar toolbox.

Brooke notices two things as they talk. One is that Jackson doesn't seem to be knowledgeable about the details of the case. How odd, then, that he's booked a room in a house of such esoteric interest. It's one thing if a friend books you ignorantly, but to decide to go alone? The other thing she notices is that Jackson very effectively changed the subject when she'd asked him why he was there.

A second pitcher later, Brooke looks at her watch and realizes they only have fifteen minutes to get back for the eight o'clock tour. Anthony throws down a hundred dollar bill, and Brooke feels a pang at how casually he does it. She's never held such a bill in her hands.

"I've got to use a card," says Jackson. "But you go on ahead. I don't want to hold you back."

"It's okay; we can wait," Brooke says, but Anthony squeezes her arm. Although he was willing to share dinner with this guy, he doesn't want to miss the tour on his behalf.

"No, go on ahead. I'll probably catch up with you before you make it back anyway. I love running on a stomach full of liquor," says Jackson dryly.

They step back out into the warm August night, walking up the gentle hill out of the Portuguese area to the flats where the Borden house sits. A moon has risen behind the house, and Anthony tries to capture it on his phone, but it's a pale imitation. The lights blaze in the bed & breakfast. Lizzie, who was notorious for hosting parties after her move to Maplecroft, would have been so happy to see the silhouettes in the yellow windows tonight, people interested in *her*.

With a lurch of disgust, Brooke thinks that each of the people in there would love to get a chance to talk to Lizzie if they could only master time travel. And if she is a murderer, she doesn't deserve the kindness, the attention. If she really plunged a metal blade so hard it cut her father's eyeball in half, she would not be a good person to talk to.

By instinct, they go to the side stoop again instead of the front door. Perhaps there is a genetic predisposition to go to the servant's entrance, thinks Brooke. Maybe on her mother's side, there is a long line of women cleaning others' houses.

Inside the kitchen everyone is gathered, standing around eating snickerdoodles and chatting with Amelia. Brooke refuses the offered cookie plate; she's sloshing full of sangria still and doesn't want to push her luck. In a few more minutes, Jackson enters.

"Sorry if I'm late," he says to Amelia.

"You're not," she says, pointing on the clock on the wall. "But if you were Mrs. Churchill next door in 1892, you'd be very confused about time, and the whole town would be talking about the failure of your timepiece to properly operate. So I'll get started there. Feel free to interrupt me anytime you have a question. I'll just talk and move us from room to room." She pauses. "Timing was everything for the case. Andrew Borden came home at 10:40 a.m., and by 11:10 Bridget

Sullivan, the maid upstairs, was being called down by Lizzie because her father was dead. Everyone was questioned, to establish the window of time for the death. Next door, Mrs. Kelly had seen him on the front porch, confirming his 10:40 arrival. Several bankers downtown had seen him between 9:30 and 10:00, and a shopkeeper said he left his store just before 10:30. A police officer even walked his route later with a timepiece, to see if it was possible for him to have made the stops he made and still get home by the hour mentioned. Any idea why anyone cared so much?"

Brooke looks at Anthony. She's sure he probably has a theory.

"Because there was only about ten minutes for the crime to be committed?" ventures Jackson.

"Exactly so!" says Amelia. "If the crime was done in so very short a time, how can we account for anyone doing it other than someone who was already in the house?"

Anthony nods thoughtfully. Brooke looks around at everyone's face. She adores this level of specificity, thinking about Mr. Borden making his stops (the post office, she knows, and the bank). But she can see that perhaps the others are here for blood spray rather than clock ticks.

Amelia leads them through the dress burning that happened several days after the murders, standing where it is believed Lizzie stood. "And Emma was down the pantry here," she points, "That's a staff area, sorry. No one can go down there, but you can see it's a narrow pantry, and situated at the very end, thanks to the odd decision of Mr. Borden, was the sink. So Emma's down there washing dishes, and Alice Russell's over in the dining room, and Lizzie's shredding the dress and feeding it to the stove. Let's go into the dining room."

They move slowly, clumpily, a big mass of people in a small space. The dining room has a glass case with replicas of the Borden skulls bearing the hatchet marks, produced as evidence in the trial.

On the sideboard is a framed photo of Eli Bence, the druggist who wanted to tell the jury that Lizzie had been trying to buy prussic acid the very day before the murders.

"We dismiss that story—which otherwise would be the undoing of her innocence—because there had been a sort of sting in Fall River to catch druggists selling poison without a prescription. Apparently there was a police officer's wife who looked a lot like Lizzie," says Amelia.

Brooke groans inside. She doesn't want Eli Bence explained away. It's disappointing in an odd way. But then it does explain the hushed conference with the attorneys and the judges, and the lame excuse given for not letting Bence testify.

"Now, at the time that Mrs. Borden was lying upstairs in the guest room, already killed, Lizzie said she was here in the dining room ironing—oh, and also outside eating pears, and also upstairs in the barn loft, looking out the window eating pears. She had a whole bunch of alibis," says Amelia. "But let's say she was in the house. I'm about the size of Mrs. Borden who was 180 pounds . . . maybe I'm a little less, but in the thereabouts. So if she was killed and fell to the floor, you would hear this."

Amelia jumps up and comes down hard on the floor, creating a booming thud that makes Brooke shriek. She blushes as everyone smiles at her. She's the girl who screams in movie theaters, and now they all know it.

"See?" says Amelia. "It makes a big noise. If you were Lizzie in the very next room, as she claimed, there's no way you wouldn't hear that. But she said she heard nothing. Maybe that's why she amended her story to have been in the barn."

Amelia takes them through the sitting room, showing them a key on the mantelpiece and telling the story of the robbery. "That's not the original sofa," she says. "The real one sat in a warehouse for a number of years, along with lots of other furniture, because the Borden sisters rented this house out when they moved cross town to Maplecroft. It's unknown where it eventually got to. But we studied photographs to make this as authentic as possible to what was originally here."

Brooke notes that the door to the dining room contains hinges closer to the sofa than the corner, discounting the theory that Lizzie could have stood in the other room and craned her arm around to hit the sleeping Andrew without getting blood on anything other than her lower limb. But it would have been impossible to stretch across the open door, using it as a shield.

They go into the entry way and turn to regard the staircase. "I'm going to do something for you that the jury members did," says Amelia. "They were brought here to climb the stairs and see if it was possible to *not* see the body of Mrs. Borden under the bed as one climbs to eye level with it. So I'm going to go lie down—like I said, I'm her body type and approximate weight. So you can see for yourself. Just one of the many sacrifices I make for my tour. Come up one at a time."

Amelia goes upstairs, and the group forms itself into a line to climb the stairs and see. Brooke glances over at Jackson and sees he looks nauseous. "You don't have to do it," she whispers.

"I'm not going to," he says. "I'm just going to go up there without looking."

She privately agrees with him that this is just too . . . something. And yet, she has been so curious about this particular detail herself. Lizzie laughing on the staircase: Was she literally looking at her stepmother's corpse as she did so?

Everyone has spaced themselves about three stairs apart. When it is Brooke's turn she gasps at the sight of Amelia under the bed. She is a true and obvious form. It *would* catch your eye, Brooke thinks. You would wonder what that shape in the periphery was. Lizzie would've had to be dashing down the stairs to miss it, but Bridget said she was standing there. She had to have seen it. And since she didn't admit to seeing it, then she must have created it.

Brooke joins the group crowded into the guest room, which had sometimes been used as a sewing room where the Bedford cord had been sewn. Amelia continues to lie on the floor for the benefit of those still on the stairs, and so Brooke gets another vantage point of the corpse. "Don't Instagram this, okay?" Amelia says to those already in the room.

In the crime scene photo, Mrs. Borden was lying in a straight line, perfectly centered between the bed and the dresser. But her body had been moved for the photographer, Amelia informs them. "She had originally been found half under the bed, crawling toward the wall. It's thought she was trying to escape the blows."

Brooke winces, and her heart drops. Why are they all here? Why are they standing clustered in this room, looking down at the proxy body? A sickness. Brooke thinks again about her mom's body in that car, how it must have been draped over the steering wheel, arms flung, her hair—that beautiful mahogany hair with the natural wave—clotted with blood.

Death is the great humiliator. Just as Andrew Borden would've suffered for the exposure of his girlish body, Mrs. Borden would've died a thousand deaths (instead of just the one, brutal as it was) to know her bulk lying on the floor would be talked of, photographed. Most touching of all to Brooke were the hobnails visible on the bottom of her rough boots. She was photographed in a housedress of such plainness that the prosecutor questioned Lizzie on the believability of whether Abby would go out in the street dressed that way. One of Lizzie's explanations for not wondering about her stepmother's whereabouts was that Abby had received a note to go see a sick friend, and Lizzie assumed she had gone. "But would she wear such a dress out?" the prosecutor had asked. With great disdain, Lizzie had replied, "Oh, she wouldn't care."

But she would have. Brooke feels she would have. It was only a small dig Lizzie allowed herself when her hatred didn't subside upon Abby's death.

The list grows worse: Abby's hair appears shorn in the photographs, as humbled as a cancer fighter, because as the hatchet cut through bone, it also cut through hair. The fact emerged that this woman of thinning hair needed to wear a switch, a sad necessity to plump her bun. The switch was found near her body and taken in as evidence.

"You can see that hair extension in the Fall River Historical Society exhibit," says Amelia. "As well as the bloody pillowcase from this room. Mrs. Borden was in the act of putting on new pillowcases when the killer attacked her."

Brooke has seen a photograph of the back of Mrs. Borden's head, shaved by the coroner to better examine the hatchet marks. The marks show in different directions, erratic. If Mrs. Borden was crawling under the bed, Lizzie probably had to change her stance, straddling the body to try to get at her.

"Was she not screaming?" Anthony asks. "Why didn't Bridget hear her?"

Amelia pushes herself up to standing and sighs. "We don't know. Bridget was outside washing the windows. They had been closed for her to do that job. But the glass isn't so thick. I guess Mrs. Borden just didn't get enough out before she lost the ability to speak."

"Maybe she didn't know how angry Lizzie was," suggests Jackson. "She saw her approach and maybe she thought she was coming to help with the pillowcases."

"Maybe," says Amelia. "Although Lizzie was not known to be very helpful. But I agree with you that Abby didn't think to start running. She was trapped by this bed and her own weight. The killer delivered the first blow facing her, and she fell to the floor, and then probably scrambled only a few minutes before the next blows killed her."

Brooke bites her lip. So that means Lizzie kept striking well after Mrs. Borden had stopped moving. There was such *rage*.

She can't help but think about the aftermath. She knows from reading that Bridget and Mrs. Churchill came upstairs to see if they could find Mrs. Borden. Bridget had been afraid to go up alone, so Mrs. Churchill had gone with her. But who brought the body down? Did it take several men to get that ungainly body down the steep stairs? Did Lizzie watch?

Her body was taken into the dining room with Mr. Borden's, placed on a folding autopsy table. And then to receive her cuts, by scalpel rather than by hatchet, she was stripped. Stripped of whatever femininity she possessed, the fragile fortress of a dress she probably hated.

The original Jack Sprat and his wife, their weight discussed openly in court. One of the books Brooke read drips with disgust for Mrs. Borden's poundage; she is not spoken of moving without it being described as "waddling."

The mood in the room has changed. The honeymoon couple looks at pains to be spending their romantic night in such a place of sadness. Jackson is visibly upset, and even Anthony is playing with his phone like he'd like to be anywhere else. "And this was your idea!" she thinks.

They move next door to Lizzie's bedroom, or what had originally been Emma's. "When Lizzie came home from her Grand Tour of Europe," says Amelia, "she had so many souvenirs she'd purchased that there wasn't room to display them in her room. So Emma offered for her to have the larger room."

They peek into the smaller room, only accessible through the larger. It's almost like a walk-in closet with a bed. Brooke thinks about the repercussions of having the larger room. Not only does it make one feel more important in the world, but it gives one the freedom to leave at night without being detected.

Hmm . . .

Lizzie had gotten pregnant somehow. Did she pull a teenager's trick of sneaking out at night? Easy enough to do when your parents use an entirely different staircase. So did that mean she continued seeing someone *after* coming back from Europe? How on Earth did a Victorian woman pull off an affair of this sort—she can't show her ankles in public, but somehow she manages to find a space to get naked and have sex?

"You can see the nail holes in the door between this room and Andrew and Abby's room. Lizzie pounded nails here to keep the door completely closed."

"I can sense that she was protecting herself," says a woman. With a jolt, Brooke realizes she hadn't seen her before. Based on the fact that she's standing near the two teens, she figures that this is their mother. "I'm getting a strong read here."

Anthony glances over at Brooke and frowns.

"I'm a psychic," the woman.

"Ah, we get you guys here!" says Amelia. "Yes, well, two different psychologists have been on the tour and told me that this is an example of textbook molestation, the nailing shut of the bedroom door."

"So Andrew . . . ?" says one of the daughters.

"That's one of the theories," says Amelia. "Make sure to look through Lizzie's room before we go on into Andrew and Abby's room."

Although the tour is wonderfully detailed, Brooke notices the dress closet at the top of the stairs doesn't get mentioned. It's been converted into a bathroom. Whatever secrets it held are now tiled over.

Amelia talks about the false robbery in Andrew and Abby's room; the dressing room where the thefts occurred is also now a bathroom. The B&B proprietors have performed the renovations that Lizzie and her sister would've wished for.

On the third floor, Amelia leads them through the rooms. There is a scratching noise that emanates late at night from the closet in the Andrew Jennings Room, she says. Brooke's glad they didn't book that one.

It's odd to stand with everyone in the Bridget Sullivan room, hoping no one steps on their overnight bags. Amelia tells the group about Bridget's actions the morning of the murders, and a bit about how the family called her Maggie. There are two photographs on the wall of Bridget as an old woman, including one of her standing next to her husband. After moving to the Midwest, it seems life permitted her to get dour and plump.

"The last stop on our tour is the specialty," says Amelia. "Only folks who stay overnight get to go 'downcellar,' as Lizzie and her contemporaries would've called it. Ready for three steep flights?"

They tromp down the narrow wooden steps to the cellar. It's a vast space, musty and low ceilinged.

"Here you can see the outlines of where the water closet once was," says Amelia. Brooke closes her eyes briefly to try to imagine Lizzie and Alice, illumined by a lantern, cautiously making their way down the steps, skirts rustling.

"This was the only flush toilet in the house," she continues. "You may wonder at the judgment involved in placing it in a dank, cold basement. In case you're wondering, the other options were a pit seat in the barn and of course the chamber pots under the beds."

Brooke recalls Bridget's testimony that she had seen Mr. Borden dump his "night soil" outside. He hadn't cared to make the two-story descent in the night to make everything flush away.

"The police investigated down here, looking for a murder weapon. And they might've found it." Amelia points to a shelf halfway up the wall facing the remnants of the water closet. "There was a box of old tools here, including a handleless hatchet. What's odd is that all the tools in the box were dusty and untouched, but the hatchet head had a very strange coating that looked like ashes. As if someone had recently cleaned it, realized it looked too shiny, and tried to make it grimy again."

"Sounds like that's the weapon," says Donna, the honeymooner. "She could've easily broken off the wooden handle and burned it in the stove."

"But you said they *might've* found it," says her husband.

"Right. It wasn't firmly established as the weapon—and remember, mostly everybody thought the real, crazed villain must've taken off still holding it. Forensic testing found no blood on the hatchet."

"But you said it looked recently cleaned."

"Talk to the jury," says Amelia.

"How do you 'easily' break off a hatchet handle?" asks the psychic mother.

"Adrenaline?" says Amelia. "There was a vise in the barn, where Lizzie sometimes claimed she was."

"In case she was seen coming out of the barn that morning, like the ice cream peddler said," says Brooke, surprising herself by piping up.

"That's right. Someone knows her Bordenalia," Amelia says with a smile. "There were so many scattered reports that morning. Someone was seen knocking at the front door who was *not* Andrew Borden. Someone saw a bloodied man sitting on a stump, crying, saying, 'Poor Mrs. Borden.' Everyone wants to supply that key bit of information when there's been a murder."

Brooke looks at the clutter around her. Boxes and old furniture, props for the plays put on in the home. A "bloodied" sheet hangs with period costumes from a rack. Some of the boxes hold gift shop inventory; Brooke pokes Anthony and points at cartons marked "Bobblehead Red" and "Bobblehead Blue."

The cellar is divided into areas: the coal room, the place where wood was stacked, the vegetable cooling spot. Amelia shows them a spray of bullet holes in one wall, and they all conjecture about its significance. She leads them to the laundry area with its stone tub mounted in a small niche. Under it, Brooke knows, was the soaking bucket for menstrual napkins.

For the paranormal enthusiasts, Amelia directs them through a cell phone activity: somehow, images taken of the laundry tub always yield a ghostly face hovering over it. Flashes go off in the small, dark space, and Brooke, who has no phone, instead looks at the walls. What was it like in 1892 for Bridget to stoop at the washing, her hands in cold water, and the air thick with the scent of the nearby coal and wood? She'd have to lug the heavy, sodden linens back up the stairs and outside to hang them on the line, dripping on her all the while. Her life seemed like one of misery even if the murders had never taken place.

The psychic mom nudges Brooke to look at her cell phone face, and it does appear that there's some sort of smoky visage in the wash-tub's alcove. Brooke raises her eyebrows to look impressed, and the woman smiles with satisfaction. Brooke doesn't buy it, though: it's the way the flash responds to the concave surfaces of the tub and the inset.

"Okay, back upstairs," says Amelia. "You lived through it. That's our tour."

Brooke looks at her watch; the tour really did take two hours. Amelia has made it fly by. Up in the kitchen, the psychic offers to do readings in the parlor and gets a few takers.

"There is a Ouija board in the parlor," says Amelia. "I just ask that if you call someone up, you close down the session and make them go away. We always have to deal with the aftermath the next day."

"Where do you sleep?" asks Jackson.

"I go home. If you need anything, like I said, there's the phone," Amelia gestures to it, on the counter. "Just call 911."

"So . . . we're alone in the house?"

Amelia grins, enjoying the ripple of slight horror the idea has caused. "The owner lives in the space on the second story of the barn," she says, "communing with pigeon ghosts to get their take on what happened."

There *is* relief to know someone is close by who is responsible for all this. "Thanks for a great tour," says Brooke. "That was really amazing." And it was: she has done enough reading on the subject to know that Amelia is truly an expert.

Amelia gets hugs and a few tips; Anthony gives her a twenty for both he and Brooke. Brooke declines a cookie when the plate comes to her, still full from dinner, but everyone else happily takes one, perhaps thinking of it as an emotional palate cleanser after all the talk of blood and gore.

After Amelia departs, everyone seems eager to do their own investigating. The Red Sox man tells everyone he's got two cameras going all night, one focused on the death sofa, and one that will record next to their bed in the John Morse Room where Abby was found. Brooke looks uncertainly at Anthony. She'd never told the group about her secret knowledge of Lizzie's illegitimate child. It never seemed to be the right time. And now she's ready to go to bed.

Jackson catches her eye and seems to understand her reluctance to join in the "festivities."

"I'll be leaving the lamp on all night," he says. "So don't be ashamed if you want to do the same thing."

He begins climbing the servant stairs, and after a few seconds, Brooke and Anthony follow him. Once they reach the attic, Brooke says, "Good night," and Jackson responds with a "We'll see."

She goes into her room with Anthony to get her cosmetics bag, then enters the bathroom shared by the upstairs rooms, aware that the two men can hear her running the water, brushing her teeth. This was once another bedroom under the eaves, she knows. After the murders, John Morse slept here because the guest room was a crime scene with a blood-dampened carpet. There are interesting floor-level cupboards here, original to the house, Amelia had said. Brooke can't help but open each one. Looking for clues? Thinking she'll find Lizzie's diary and understand who fathered her child? They are strangely shaped, and she wonders what they once stored. They are large enough for children to play hide-and-seek in.

She returns to the mirror and looks at herself. Brooke, Felicita, and a dozen other names . . . . She has reinvented herself so many times. And now she likes who she is. She might have to freeze it. Stop the transformation and just remain.

It's an odd feeling.

What if she were to stop running? The worst that could happen is that they come for her. And maybe she could talk them out of it. Tell them it was an accident with Mrs. Carr, that even if she had wished she could inherit their lives, she hadn't made it happen.

She doesn't want Anthony to get caught in the cross fire. He's like John Morse, showing up right before murder goes down. But there has to be a way to seize her own life back.

She needs to tell Miguel.

Anthony's already asleep when she goes back into their room. So much for being terrorized in the haunted house. She crawls into bed and pulls out her laptop, stiffening in shock when she hears noise outside their door, until she realizes it's just Jackson opening the bathroom door.

Rather than writing on her wall, Miguel has left her a message. She opens it, but it's not from him. It's from Facebook.

Thank you for your recent inquiry. We have researched the issue and found that the friend added on August 24 was added by you. Is there anyone else who has access to your account? We recommend immediately changing your password.

She's been hacked?

No. She's suspected all along someone had access to her computer. It's part of why she never wanted to Google the Carr boys, so her search history wouldn't let them know she was aware of their pursuit.

She always thought her Facebook account was safe, though, because of her password.

But what if, all these years, they've had access?

What if they saw each post on her timeline, when she thought she was secretively telling Miguel her new address?

Rage courses through her veins at her own stupidity. She has *told* them where she went each time she moved. She might as well have taken out a TV ad to give them her new address.

She stares at the screen, thinking hard. Sometimes she forgets to close down Facebook, leaves the computer running—if someone was physically at her laptop, he could add himself as a friend to keep watching remotely until she notices and unfriends.

It's real.

Her fears are not built of paranoia. She's someone's prey in a very long game.

It hurts to change her password. She's had it since she went into foster care and had access to a computer for the first time in her life. It's her mother's name and the age she was when she died. It hurts, but she changes it just to be safe. She'll have to shut down the computer each time she uses it. And the next move she makes, she won't tell Miguel. There will be no trail to find her, and this time she'll go farther.

She looks at Anthony in the glow of the lamp, slumbering without a care in a house where so much evil existed. He won't come with her. He's an attorney in a law firm; he can't just pick up and leave.

She never cries, so she stares at the ceiling, quiet with her bleak thoughts, just as Bridget must have done so many times.

CHAPTER 42

Brooke

AUGUST 28, 2016

It's after midnight when she decides she wants one of those cookies after all. She eases open the door to not wake up Anthony and creeps into the hallway.

She doesn't believe in ghosts, but she does feel the disquieting nature of the house. A pervasive sadness for the lives that were never happy here. For the waste of bodies that were mobile, tongues that talked and could express wishes. Why don't people do what they want to do when they're alive? It's a question she realizes she should be asking herself.

Why didn't Lizzie keep her baby, even if she had to live in shame in some other town, or reinvent herself as a newly widowed mother? She could've rented a flat in another town with a different name. She could've brought Emma along. "My husband died, and my dear sister and I, and my new baby, we are going to make a new life for ourselves here in your very nice and nonjudgmental town—not that you'd judge me for I'm entirely convincing in my role as a wife. Look, I even bought a cheap diamond ring to fortify the lie. Or maybe I shoplifted it. You decide."

With a pang, Brooke realizes that maybe the father of the child would've come along. Maybe instead of being a widow, Lizzie could be a wife. They could just put rings on if the minister wouldn't marry them with her belly out to there, and take up life as a married couple with their baby.

Who *was* the father? Nothing Amelia said tonight harked to any beau of Lizzie's. Was it someone she had met through church work? Maybe one of the Chinese laundrymen common in that era? Now, that would be a scandal. If you're too bigoted to call for a French doctor when your father's dead, how do you carry on a torrid affair with a Chinese immigrant? Maybe it was Mr. Buck the minister himself, or someone she came across in the church basement after hours, leaving her Fruit & Flower Mission meeting while he was leaving the deacons meeting? They met cute and started talking, and it got serious?

Could it have been one of the lads they'd join up with in Marion? A boating boy? A young man with a yacht? Someone her father had never approved of? She hadn't been able to give that boy her ring so in irony she gave it to her father?

Brooke has a flashlight with her, a palm-sized one from a dollar store. She shines it on the stairs as she descends. Bridget must've come down in the dark all the time, to get the stove started on winter mornings. Maybe she had memorized how many steps lay between the landings and didn't need the kerosene lamp.

Brooke shudders when she thinks of the utter darkness of that home in 1892 without electricity. How did Alice Russell *sleep* when she had no way to instantly create light, when there were two corpses in the dining room below her? And what about Emma, knowing her sister was capable of such deeds; did she worry that if she angered her sister, she'd be next?

When she reaches the kitchen, she finds Jackson there, bending over the coffeemaker. She tries to stomp loudly as she enters, so as not to scare him since his back is turned to her.

He whirls around and then softens when he sees it's her.

"You scared me."

"But the good news is, I'm not holding a weapon."

"Right. I'm making decaf, do you want some?"

"Sure," she says. "I started craving the snickerdoodle I rejected earlier. I just couldn't wrap my head around its name."

"I know. It's hard to be dignified and say 'yes' to a snickerdoodle." He opens up the Tupperware container and holds it out to her. She takes a cookie and sits down at the table. He sits down, too, and they listen to the coffeemaker drip and warble.

Looking at him in the stark fluorescent light, it occurs to her again that his face is familiar, kind.

"What do you think of all this?" he asks.

She shrugs. "I didn't want to come, but Anthony urged me to. It's actually not as cheesy as I was worried it would be."

"Why did he want you to come?"

"I've been trying to figure out a good time to tell Amelia. I have a sort of connection to Lizzie Borden."

He raises his eyebrows but doesn't ask more. Maybe he thinks she means through cousins, or through the thousands of other Bordens in Fall River.

"And you?" she asks.

"I'll tell you later," he says.

She smiles and looks down. There won't be a later. In the morning they'll eat breakfast and leave.

"I can tell you're a survivor," she says quietly.

"What?" His head jerks up, and his eyes blaze into hers.

"I can tell because I am, too. There's something different about those of us who've been through the fire."

He puts his elbow on the table and leans his chin into his palm. "I'd be very glad to hear what you have to say about this."

"I lost my mom and went into foster care when I was thirteen. I never knew my dad."

He doesn't say "I'm sorry," the first thing people say when she has managed to get this information out. She waits for his response.

"I lost my mom, too. I was young. My dad was around but might as well not have been."

She nods. "I knew it," she said.

"He was our little remote control man in the house, like a foreign exchange student who didn't care to try speaking our language."

She blinks at his uncanny evocation of the foreign exchange student. "That's awful," she says. She bites back the instinctive addition *but at least he was there.*

"My mother had been the softening agent in the house. She was a truly sweet soul."

"I'm so sorry for your loss," says Brooke. "How old were you?"

"Eight."

She gives him a wry smile. "Sucks, doesn't it? And top of everything, my story's a strange one. My mom was a maid for a really wealthy family. They invited us to their house for the Fourth of July."

He gets up to fill his cup now that the carafe has been filled by the machine. When he sits down, he sips his coffee without looking at her.

"The mom of the family died that night. She drowned off the pier we'd been watching fireworks from."

She waits for him to ask what the connection is between the two mothers, the two deaths. After a bit, she stumbles on. "No one noticed. The fireworks show ended, and she just wasn't with us."

She pushes the half-eaten cookie away from her on its napkin. "They brought out floodlights and found her. It was just awful. And I was just a kid. I was nine, and I wondered . . . "

She trails off. "Why the hell am I even talking about this? I should go upstairs and see if I can sleep."

"No, tell me what you wondered."

He sets his coffee cup down on the table and leans forward to look at her, *really* look. It's the kind of attention her mom once gave her, thorough and vast.

"Someone's been following me for years," she says. "I think someone blamed me for her death."

"Why?"

"All I can think of, is that someone thought I pushed her. And I didn't. I didn't push her. But I was so involved in watching those fireworks. I was like out of my mind with how cool they were. And I wonder . . . I used to be really clumsy. My mom even brought me to the doctor once to ask why I was so klutzy. And so I think, 'did I accidentally knock into her, and I didn't even realize it?'"

Jackson stands up, a strangely intense look on his face. "How could you not know if you knocked into her?"

"Because of the fireworks. Because I was just a kid."

"You would've felt it. You would've heard the splash."

"I don't think so. The fireworks were so loud."

"So you think you just . . . accidentally flailed out and knocked a grown woman into the water."

"Why else would someone be following me?"

"Listen, you aren't to blame," he says. "You wouldn't have been strong enough."

A dim *deja vu* rears its head, and of course it's Lizzie Borden . . . the jury and all of Fall River saying she wasn't strong enough to make that hatchet do what it did.

"I didn't think I did it," she says slowly. "But someone thinks I did."

"No," he says, shaking his head. "You're paranoid, and understandably so. You've been in foster care, and you've been just as messed up as me." His eyes glitter, and she wonders if there are tears in them. Why on earth would there be? "I know you didn't do that. You're a good person."

"A good person," she says. "Right. Doing a totally tasteful tour of a murder house."

He almost laughs, but it's more like a percussive exhale. "You should let that go," he says. "I bet that woman . . . got into the water a different way."

"How?"

"Who knows?" he says. "But it makes me sad thinking you've been carrying this guilt all this time."

"In some ways, it feels like it happened yesterday. But I wonder about the boys sometimes. What if I robbed them of their mom?"

"No," he says.

"You want to sit back down?" It feels weird with him standing there.

"I don't," he says. "I don't. I'm going to go up to bed. I'm so . . . "

"So . . . ?"

"So tired of talking about murder."

She nods and sits there listening to him climb the two flights of stairs. She waits until she hears his door open and close in the attic, then she herself goes up.

Anthony doesn't wake when she comes in. She pulls the curtains closed, taking note of the almost-full moon over Dr. Chagnon's, over the roof of the barn that isn't truly a barn, that stands where the barn stood, where Lizzie stood in the barn, like an old nursery rhyme, where the farmer's wife cuts with a carving knife, and the crooked fence stile keeps everything warped, like a woman's body straightened for the post-mortem photograph, run, run as fast as you can, you can't catch me, and the witch gets pitched straight into the oven like a bloodstained dress.

CHAPTER 43

Brooke

AUGUST 28, 2016

In the morning, they all gather for the promised second half of "bed & breakfast." Two new people are in the kitchen making johnnycakes and scrambled eggs; they look like teens employed from the neighborhood.

Brooke and the others sit down at the large official dining table and a second card table in the corner to handle the overflow. Brooke is anxious to get some coffee into her to combat her logy malaise. The house is air-conditioned, but she can feel the muggy heat pressing in at the windows. As soon as they step outside, they'll sag.

"Anyone see or hear anything last night?" asks the Red Sox man who stayed in the John Morse room.

Everyone smiles and shakes their heads.

"What about you? You were in the only room that saw real action," says Donna, the honeymooner.

"Nothing. Didn't even feel a chill. I set up my camera here to do a time-lapse video over the course of the night and I'll be looking through that footage later on my laptop if anyone wants to join me."

Polite murmurs of interest, but no one asks the particulars of when or where he'll be setting up the viewing.

"I did have a nightmare, though," says his wife. "About the closet. The one upstairs."

Everyone looks at Jackson, because his room adjoined the room with the haunted closet. "What was your nightmare?" he asks.

"A child in there in the dark alone. When I opened the closet door to let her out, she just looked at me blankly."

"What did the child look like?" asks the psychic mom. "I too had some visions of a young girl."

"She was naked. I don't know, nine years old?"

Brooke can't help it, she thinks of herself. She was nine when Mrs. Carr drowned.

"Well, that could have been Emma when their mother died."

"No, she was twelve," Brooke corrects her.

"Could the child in your dream have been twelve?" persists the psychic.

"Maybe. We don't have kids, and it's hard to guess ages."

"I'm sure it was her," says the psychic. "I too had a strong feeling about Emma last night."

Brooke wonders how the readings in the parlor last night went. If there was such a thing as ghosts, they were surely befuddled and made more miserable by the endless parade of different people coming into their home, sleeping in their beds, constantly trying to contact them. It would feel like being in a crowded train station with the cars coming and going, and announcements blaring and the doors always opening, expelling people and more people.

Around the table, the breakfasters look dissatisfied, as if the night hadn't given what they'd expected. And what was that? Rustlings down the hallway? A muffled scream? The replay of the thud as Mrs. Borden went down? Maybe they thought as they brushed their teeth, a glimmer behind them would be the malevolent, tousled-hair Lizzie checking her reflection to see if she'd gotten blood on her face, blood in her hair. Perhaps they wished a massive shape would rise from the floor next to the bed and try to exact a sort of revenge, or that from downstairs they would hear the sofa springs squeak as Andrew rose with his ragged remnant of a head, lurching toward vengeance. A nightmare seemed a poor substitute.

"I think Emma committed the murders," announces the psychic.

"She was in Fairhaven," Anthony reminds her.

"I think she pressured Lizzie into doing it."

Anthony tries hard to suppress an eye roll, and Brooke therefore tries hard to suppress her laugh at his suppression. "Then that would mean Lizzie did it."

"I think *Lizzie* pressured *Bridget* into doing it," says Donna.

"Is it even possible to make someone do that? I mean, to like, use an axe and just . . . whale away on them?" asks the older of the two teens.

"Some people just can't commit murder," says Jackson. "They're filled with the same rage that enables others to kill, but they just can't pull the trigger."

"It takes a certain kind of person to kill," says Anthony.

The eggs are awful, and the johnnycakes dry. Suddenly, Brooke is so ready to go she's almost unable to sit still in her chair. How lucky she is that she can shake off the morose claustrophobia of the house and move on. Lizzie didn't have that luxury.

"Let's go," she says to Anthony. "I'll go get our bags while you finish eating."

"I'll come up, too. I'm done anyway."

As she rises, she locks eyes with Jackson. "It was nice to meet you."

"You, too," he says.

That split second arises where she wonders if he's going to want to exchange phone numbers, and then she'll have to explain that she doesn't carry a phone, and then the moment is gone, and he's simply smiling a goodbye smile. She's used to those.

"Take care."

She turns and addresses everyone, since after all this was a strangely communal activity. Like the most morbid summer camp ever. "Nice to meet you all," she calls out, and Anthony does a hand wave aimed at the room.

"Remember, don't 'axe' your mother any questions," says Donna, and a few people chuckle.

Jackson shoots Brooke an understanding look. Mother jokes aren't funny when you don't have one.

CHAPTER 44

Brooke

JULY 4, 2002

Mr. Carr was mad. The steaks were inedible, and the shrimp had actually caught on fire, the presoaked skewers dried out enough to combust. It had put a stench into the air at the outside barbecue area, a curved concrete base with built-in tile seating.

Mrs. Carr didn't seem to notice his anger. She laughed at her culinary negligence and told him, "Call for pizza."

"No one's going to deliver on the Fourth of July," he snapped.

"But they're Italian," she said. "They don't care about the Fourth."

She turned to Brooke's mom. "You wouldn't be celebrating today if we hadn't had you over, right?"

Brooke could see her mom wanted to be able to say, "Of course we celebrate. I'm an American citizen," but Mrs. Carr was right—they didn't do anything for the Fourth. It had actually been part of the Carr Family Caucasian Outreach Program to educate the Mexicans, she thought bitterly.

"You're not into four, but you love *cinco*. Am I right?" Mrs. Carr was delighted with her own bilingual joke. "Chris had a *Cinco de Mayo* party at the office last year, and they all wore sombreros."

"I'm hungry," Abraham complained.

"There are plenty of other things to eat," said Mrs. Carr. "A really nice German potato salad and a green salad and a Jello salad."

"So many salads!" said Brooke's mom.

"Don't you dare criticize my meal!" said Mrs. Carr. Brooke, who had been holding out hope that Mrs. Carr would return to being the sweet person she'd been before the wine got opened, walked away from her, over to stand next to her mother.

"I didn't mean that at all. I'm so sorry!" said Brooke's mom. "It was a stupid joke, that every dish ended in 'salad.'"

"We brought you into this family," said Mrs. Carr. "I trusted you."

"Lillian, what is going on?" said Mr. Carr. "Why don't you sit down, and I'll work on getting something we can all eat."

"You can't have what I have," said Mrs. Carr, staring directly at Brooke's mom. "Maybe you have him for an hour here and there, but at the end of the day, where's your ring, where's your promise that he owes anything to you?"

Mr. Carr bodily ushered his wife back into the house. Halfway there, she burst into loud, ugly sobs.

"What's wrong with her?" Ezekiel asked his older brother in the new quiet.

Abraham didn't answer.

"We will go now, mija," said Brooke's mother to her.

"But I'm hungry," said Brooke. "They said they were getting pizza."

"We'll get something on the road," her mother promised.

The boys said nothing to them as they walked away. Brooke looked out over the water, sparkling in an expanse so purely blue it looked like a magazine ad.

"So we don't get to see the fireworks?"

Although she hated the boys, she had really wanted to see the fireworks.

"I'm so sorry, sweetheart."

"It's okay."

It was a holiday they usually didn't celebrate. Colored explosions in the sky, reflected off the glass calm of the lake, sounded great, though, and she thought she'd never get another chance. They headed to her mom's car, purchased fifth hand or sixth hand, her mom had joked. A collision from before he bought it had dented the back door so much that it no longer opened. It looked out of place on the Carrs' beautifully paved driveway, like a crushed tin can.

Just as they were almost to it, Brooke's mom swore softly in Spanish.

"What is it?" asked Brooke.

The despair on her mother's face was frightening. "I left my purse inside. I can't drive without my keys."

CHAPTER 45

Bridget

AUGUST 5, 1892

Alice Russell pressed Bridget to sleep at the home that night. "We'll all feel so much better having you here," she said. "And if you start the fire in the morning, it saves me having to do so."

"I'll try, miss," said Bridget. Her mind was still reeling about the washtub downstairs. Throughout the morning, she kept wiping her hands on her apron, although they were dry.

At one point, Officer Medley drew her down to the cellar to ask her about the napkins, for she'd left them there in the pail in their squalor.

He had the kind of frank eyes she'd always appreciated. When he looked at her, he was truly listening and not thinking about how a lower-class woman would have nothing to add to his investigation. He had a walrus's mustache and a strong no-nonsense build.

"Can you tell me about these?" he asked.

"They're our laundry," she said.

"But . . . the blood. What can you tell me about that?"

They were standing before the washtub, the Bordens' clothing close by. She noticed he had skirted them with respect as they walked in, gesturing for her, too, to walk around them.

"It's her time," said Bridget. She feared she was blushing.

"Her time of the month?"

"Yes, sir."

"And how long has this pail been here?"

Bridget narrowed her eyes, thinking. It was a good question. "I did the washing on Tuesday, sir, and this pail was not there then or I would've washed the lot."

"So, two days ago her time had not yet started."

Bridget nodded. "Or she might've kept them in her slop pail until bringing them down yesterday or even this morning."

"And that is your custom, that they soak here until you launder them."

"Yes, sir."

"That is what Lizzie told me as well, and Dr. Bowen confirmed." He waited.

"Is that all then?" she asked.

"Let me ask if you believe this is nothing more than that . . . sort of blood."

She was unable to raise her eyes to his. Her heart began a swifter rhythm in her chest. "And what else would it be?"

"We are in a house of murder, Miss Sullivan."

She hardly knew what to say. The same suspicions that had rocked her that morning were so much more fearful coming from him. She had put the thoughts out of her mind . . . and he wanted to bring them up into the open air and examine them like a stained bed sheet hung on the line.

"I don't know," she faltered.

He nodded, watching her face. She had the uncomfortable feeling he saw through her.

"I went out to the barn," he said abruptly. "Miss Lizzie has said she was up there in the hayloft eating pears. And looking for lead for a sinker."

"A sinker?" Bridget repeated.

"For going fishing."

"But she—" Bridget stopped herself. "She may well have meant to join the ladies at Marion. But I thought that she had canceled that trip."

"Does your mistress typically fish?"

Bridget took a deep breath. They were alone in the cellar, just he with his penetrating eyes and her with all her moiling thoughts. The bucket of blood there before them, the clothes so wretchedly tossed to the floor nearby.

"I've never known her to fish, sir, since I've joined this household."

"She hasn't fished since you arrived, when?"

"I started here three years ago, in 1889."

"Has she spoken of fishing in the past?"

"No, sir."

"And rather than borrow someone's line, she thought to create her own lure."

Silence.

"So she climbed to the barn loft. You've been up there?"

"Not recently, sir."

"No. It's stifling hot. No one would want to. And yet she voluntarily went up to look for lead to make a sinker for a fishing line she didn't need."

"I don't know."

"And she somehow managed to climb the ladder with three pears in her hands, and chose that dusty, suffocating place to stand there and eat them."

"She didn't tell me that."

"It might be nice to come inside and eat a pear," he continued. "So if it dripped, you'd have water handy. You wouldn't be sticky."

"There is a spigot in the barn," Bridget said.

"But she was up in the hayloft, she claims, so she sought the sinker, ate the pears, came down the ladder with sticky hands full of pear cores. And *then* washed her hands."

"If that is as it is."

"It isn't," he said earnestly. "You might carry pears up the ladder in your skirts, but no lady of my acquaintance would roll the sticky cores into her dress. I don't think it possible for her to climb down with them in her hands, a distasteful job if she did do it. And I can tell you that the cores are not on the floor up there."

"Did she throw them out the window?"

"No, miss. I walked around outside under the window and found no abandoned pears."

"This is strange indeed," said Bridget in a thin voice.

"Miss Sullivan, I was in the barn not ten minutes ago. I climbed the ladder. There is a layer of dust on that floor."

"I'm not surprised. Since May no one has been in that barn." She sags, thinking of the rows of pigeons on the grass outside. The heads with their sightless beaded eyes, Miss Lizzie playing with them and talking to them.

"I believe you are right that since May *no one* has been in that barn," he said with emphasis.

"Including Miss Lizzie?"

"Undoubtedly. Miss Sullivan, I saw no sign of movement in that dust. Her skirts would've created a trail, or her boots. But it was un-touched. I reached out and pressed my palm to the floor of the loft, and saw quite clearly my own handprint."

Bridget began to tremble. It was impossible to think it.

"There is acrimony in this household, I have heard," he said quietly.

"I don't know that word, sir."

"Bitterness."

Above their heads, a loud, brusque dragging noise. They were doing something upstairs, moving the bodies, moving furniture, preparing for autopsy, perhaps, or looking for clues.

"You are one of the few who knows the true patterns of this house," he said. "Its disappointments, its harsh words."

She recalls Mr. Borden pausing on the landing of the back stairs with her trunk, asking her not to carry gossip.

How could she tell this man of the life here so upsetting she'd tried three times to turn in her notice, and only stayed because poor Mrs. Borden begged her? How could she talk of the pale silver eyes that followed her wherever she went, feeling like the yawn of a grave that has not yet been dug? The serving of two meals since the sisters wouldn't eat with their elders, the separate stairs, the coldness and then the heat of intermittent arguments so stocked with spite she could shudder?

"It is not cordial," she managed to say.

He half-laughed, a bit of a manly sputter a woman is never capable of. "I know you have much to say, Miss Sullivan. And I want to hear every bit of it."

She was unused to speaking of feelings. There was really no way to describe the climate of indifference mixed with scorn. How did one explain the dislike between parties who rarely spoke to each other? Nothing tangible to describe.

"I hardly know what to say," she said.

"Has she ever seemed so angry you thought she could kill them?"

She cringed. What a desperately awful and bald thing to say. "No."

"You seem a little uncertain of that."

She could tell him of the coldness, but it was a terrifying thing, to cast suspicion on Miss Lizzie. She wasn't even sure that she'd correctly assessed the odd relationships in the home. Mr. Borden had told her never to talk of their doings. Would he want her to now? She hesitated, caught between her anger at how the Bordens had ended so despicably treated, and the unpleasant responsibility of being the woman whose loose words might cause a world of trouble.

Suddenly she was cross with the officer. She didn't like this discussion, didn't like being cornered in the cellar when she was after all an undefended woman even if she was only a maid. She disliked her vulnerability in a way that filled her with her own brand of fury, though probably less lethal than Lizzie's.

"I'll do only this, and then I must get upstairs and start the stew," she said firmly. "You've all been looking for a weapon, high and low. I know of the tools, the box of hatchet heads. It's here."

She went to the high shelf in the part of the cellar nearest the water closet. She pulled down the wooden box and put it in his hands. "Is one of these suitable for you?" she asked.

As she handed it over, she saw, half-buried, a hatchet head with a strange clog of dirt on it. Not the considerable and even layer of dust that had settled on the others.

It seemed Miss Lizzie could not combat dust, not even with the finest maid. It would spell her guilt, settled or unsettled.

"It looks like someone has tried to make it look as if it never left the box," said Officer Medley. "Thank you for this."

Bridget did spend one last night in her bedroom at the top of the house. Next door to her was John Morse, no longer able to sleep in the crime scene of the guest room. He had slept in the other attic room in the past when the dressmaker was in attendance; Bridget had never liked it, but he didn't interfere with her.

She slept not a wink, thinking Miss Lizzie would know what she had said to the officer, and that she had handed over the box in the cellar.

Miss Lizzie could be capable of vengeance. The kind of vengeance that led a woman to kneel at her keyhole and watch the top of her stairs all night long.

"This is the last of it," she thought. "Sixty dollars or no, I'm turning my back on this house forever."

CHAPTER 46

Alice

AUGUST 6, 1892

The next day, Alice again struggled with her sensations in the bright light of morning. She was so carelessly suspicious of her friend! What a diabolical thing she was considering her capable of, when she was the victim in all this, the woman made an orphan by cataclysmic sprays of blood.

It was the day of the funeral. Nearly a hundred mourners pressed into the small rooms to pay their respects. The sisters, with the guidance of Mr. Winward the undertaker, had chosen the flowers that adorned the coffins. Alice was glad to see this service, glad to think the bodies could go into the ground and everyone could begin to mend and heal.

Alice chose not to go to the cemetery, staying with Mrs. Holmes and the undertaker's assistants at the house. She did not envy them their duties, but someone had to do them. Bodies needed gentle hands to ease them into the next world.

She prepared tea, thinking wryly that she might ask Emma for the now-absent Bridget's wages, and brought it to the dining room. As she paused in the doorway, she overheard one man quite clearly say, "They will keep the heads."

As he swiveled his to see Alice, he visibly started.

"I'm sorry, miss," he said.

"What . . . whatever do you mean?" she asked. Once again her curiosity was getting the better of her, because both men looked incredibly uneasy at her question.

"It will come out soon enough," he said. "They need the . . . they need evidence. And so at the cemetery they will . . . "

"Don't tell her," advised the other man. "Mr. Winward will inform the sisters."

"Inform them of what? I insist you tell me. I am their closest friend and was intimate with Mr. and Mrs. Borden."

"They have been asked to remove the heads for evidence."

Alice fell back, nearly letting go her tray. The first man stepped forward to take it from her hands. She sank into a chair. "Of all the horrible, horrible, useless things! Why? It is so unfair, and these sweet souls have been through so much already."

"The hatchet marks on the skulls, miss."

"But they have photographed those to death!"

The man shrugged.

"So they are to decapitate Mr. and Mrs. Borden?"

"I believe so. They will render them down to the skulls."

At that, Alice got up and ran into the kitchen. She knew what they meant by "render." It was what was done to animal carcasses in the factories: boiling down the body to strip the fat, the skin, the tissue, the muscle.

She cried into her hands at the kitchen table. She could hear the men stirring, but neither came to offer her comfort. After a bit, she heard the clink of china. They were pouring the tea she'd prepared.

That night, Mayor Coughlin came to the house. It was an honor for the sisters, Alice saw, and Lizzie even smiled when he announced himself at the door. He sat down in the parlor with Mr. Morse and Emma and Lizzie, and Alice sat in a chair in the corner to not intrude. It seemed to Alice that Lizzie thought him there to console them and express his sympathies. But his conversation took an odd turn.

"Might I ask you all to remain in the house for the next few days? Just as a measure to . . . " his voice trailed off. "I think it best for all concerned."

"That is a strange request," said Miss Lizzie. "You do not want us to leave the house?"

"Just for a few days, that's all. You can have anything delivered that you want; I know anyone here in town would be eager to help."

Lizzie stiffened in her chair. "It seems that you are suspicious," she said. "Is anyone in this house suspected?"

A silence that could have been doled out to all the heathens of the far-flung parts of the world took place. John Morse gave a heavy sigh. Alice couldn't help glancing at Emma, but then returned to stare at Lizzie.

"I want to know the truth," said Lizzie.

"I regret to tell you this. It is most unfortunate indeed to have to say it. But, yes, you are suspected."

"Well, I am ready to go now." She stood up, as if she thought handcuffs would be produced on the instant.

"We haven't wanted to tell you," said Emma. "We tried to keep it from you as long as we could."

Alice looked down at her lap. Who was the "we?" Apparently Emma and her uncle, because no one had told Alice the world was thinking of Lizzie in that way. In the way that she, frighteningly, was trying to suppress within herself.

"Thursday's newspaper was the last I've read," said Lizzie. "I thought you had been having the paper held because of the upsetting news about Father. I didn't think the news might be about *me*."

"I am so sorry," Emma murmured.

Mayor Coughlin went on to ask Lizzie questions about her whereabouts after her father had come home. Alice clenched her hands into fists as she heard the tale trotted out again about climbing to the barn loft to find sinkers. It just wasn't credible. She looked at the faces of all gathered there. Emma's concern, John Morse's inscrutable face, the mayor who simply sat nodding.

"Well, I think I must go now. If you are bothered by the crowds in the street, do tell the marshal, or have an officer inform him if he is not here. We want you to feel protected," said the mayor. Like a true politician, he was ending on a good note, as if he had been here simply to reassure the family, and not to warn them not to flee.

"Thank you for your kindness," said Emma.

After Alice showed him out, the glum group sat in the parlor without speaking. Lizzie stared at the door into the sitting room as if awaiting her father's instructions from there.

"You have known?" she asked Emma finally.

"The questions we have been asked, Lizzie; they have been of a nature that led me to think so."

"And no one thinks *you* did it."

"I was in Fairhaven. How could I possibly?"

"I have been suspected," said Mr. Morse. "I have had every step of my morning retraced and confirmed."

"Did they talk to Bridget?" Lizzie asked. She looked directly at Alice for some reason.

"Of course they did," said Emma. "They've interviewed us all, exhaustively. I don't know how many times I've answered the same questions. It is tiresome. I think they are trying to catch us in a slip."

"They think you know I'm guilty."

"Lizzie, how can that be so when you are innocent?"

"They ask me over and over, and I can't keep a thought straight for they are so dogged," said Lizzie. "All I know is when Mother— when Mrs. Borden got that note, I didn't think anything more of her or where she might be, and Father came home, and I helped him settle on the sofa, and then I went out to the—"

"It's all right, Lizzie. We've heard you tell it a hundred times," interrupted Mr. Morse.

"You certainly came out of nowhere," said Lizzie, and Alice chilled at the tone in her voice.

"I had the terrible misfortune of arriving the day before my beloved sister's widower was murdered."

"It was *your* room Mrs. Borden was killed in."

Alice got up abruptly. She hardly knew how she'd return home in this dark, but one of the officers out there would arrange her an escort. A thought had entered her throat and expanded there, and she could hardly breathe around its terrible shape.

If Lizzie had killed Mrs. Borden, had she chosen to do it in the guest chamber Mr. Morse slept in to cast mistrust onto him?

The clog in her throat widened as Lizzie stood in the parlor doorway. Alice's hand was on the front doorknob, but the locks were still locked.

"Might we lean upon you yet again?" Lizzie asked. "You are the glue holding us together right now. I fear we are so fragile without your guidance."

Alice hesitated. She could not speak around the object in her throat.

"I see you are reluctant," said Miss Lizzie. "But you are of such comfort. Please do stay."

Emma came to join Lizzie, and Alice looked from face to face, comparing the lost look of Emma's eyes to the stone-colored confidence of Lizzie's.

"Lizzie's right. We need you."

Unable to speak, Alice turned her gaze back to the locks. Which one made the door open?

"Let's retire now. Come with us. Good night, Uncle John," Emma called over her shoulder.

He didn't reply, but Alice heard the sofa squeak as he rose to his feet.

Lizzie hooked her arm in Alice's and subtly pulled her toward the stairs.

From behind them, Emma said, "I will ask you to stay in my old room."

Alice reached out for the banister with her other hand to steady herself. These self-centered girls. She thought she knew them, and she didn't. Emma was the heiress now, and she was to take her proper place in the master bedroom.

The comfort of a friend who was devoting her days and nights to them didn't matter as much as her right to the larger bedroom.

"I think that I might not be able to . . . to stay here, dear girls." Her dark thoughts, her suspicions, so terrified her in the dark that she couldn't bear it. At least in the elder Bordens' bedroom, there was a firmly fastened door, and a staircase leading out and down, away from trouble, away from the strange missions in the night, inexplicable to Alice.

Stopping, Lizzie looked keenly at Alice. Alice sucked in her breath at that plain face that lately seemed to indicate that more resided behind its bland expressions. Much more.

"I shall not forgive you if you do not stay."

The shape in her throat expanded to fill her head and her chest. Alice nodded.

"You are our rock," pronounced Emma.

CHAPTER 47

Alice

AUGUST 7, 1892

The next morning, Alice got breakfast for everyone, acting agreeably, doing all she could to be her old self, the one that had trusted and believed in the girls.

"I need you to fetch Bridget for me," Lizzie asked. "I believe she is staying over to Dr. Bowen's."

Alice frowned. "Whatever do you need with her?"

"I want to settle up."

"That is honorable," murmured Emma. "We mustn't forget her in the midst of all our troubles."

"Bridget's been a solid one," commented Mr. Morse.

"Might I simply bring her wages to her?" asked Alice.

"I'd love a word with her, too," said Lizzie. "Won't you?"

Those eyes. She turned them on Alice, and Alice could well imagine the burning intensity Mrs. Borden might've seen in her last moments. "Yes, Lizzie. I'll get her for you. And then I need to go home for a bit."

"Of course," said Emma. "You have things to tend to, and we've been so wrong to keep you."

"It hasn't been a trouble," said Alice. "You are my . . . " Somehow her mouth couldn't form the words she'd intended, "dear friends."

"Return to us after a time; we need you so," said Lizzie.

Abruptly, Alice rose and gave them both a nod. She left through the side door, and an officer helped her push through the throngs of people to reach the sidewalk.

"Who're you?" a man in a battered felt hat asked her when she thought she was out of the thick of it. He swayed, as if a bit of drink had stirred his interest in the Borden home.

She didn't deign to answer. Such rough men, such a horrible side of the populace coming out to see old Mr. Borden undone.

"You her sister?" he called after her, as she made her determined way across the street. She reached Dr. Bowen's front door and knocked. Mrs. Bowen answered, and Alice delivered the message that Lizzie hoped to talk with Bridget. There was a strange moment when both women looked into each other's eyes.

"They all say . . . " faltered Mrs. Bowen.

"I know what they say," said Alice.

"It is so awful."

"It is beyond awful," agreed Alice. With the best semblance of a smile she could muster, she took her leave.

She turned to look back at the house, surrounded by onlookers like the big top of a circus. How she wished she had nothing to do with it.

She returned home, locking the door behind her. She sank into her rocking chair, exhausted.

The world had shifted and changed, and Alice wondered if she was meant to share her misgivings with the officers who kept asking her questions.

She was a timid woman, and it was scarcely believable to her all that she'd done since Thursday. She had slept in a household with two murdered bodies . . . and as her mind changed and her understanding grew greater, she came to think she had slept in a household mere feet away from the murderer.

Terrible, terrible, terrible, terrible. The rocking chair sang this song to her as she pushed herself backward and forward.

You have an obligation, she thought.

Poor Mrs. Borden and poor Mr. Borden.

You have an obligation to them.

But what do I tell, she fretted? There isn't anything to tell; it's all just feelings.

Lizzie had checked the dress closet. She had brought menstrual cloths to the basement and didn't care a jot about her parents' clothing on the floor. This was not evidence policemen care about, just a woman's feelings.

After an hour, she woke with a start. She'd fallen into dreams after three nights of disrupted sleep. And she was resolved. She was going to go to the house and find an officer and tell him what she thought. Perhaps she'd ask to speak directly to the marshal.

Back at Second Street, she entered by the side door, thinking Lizzie would be in the parlor and she could avoid being seen. But Lizzie was in the kitchen, and she could hear Emma down the scullery hall calling something back to her sister. Bridget was indeed gone for good if the girls were washing their own dishes.

Alice had to pretend she was there in her old role, to console the sisters.

Lizzie did not greet Alice although she glanced at her. She stood before the kitchen stove and loudly announced to Emma, "I think I shall burn this old dress."

Alice blinked. From down by the sink came Emma's voice. "You might as well; it is so badly soiled."

Alice looked at the dress, folded over Lizzie's arm. It was the blue Bedford cord, made for her only three months ago. Soon after it was made, Lizzie had rubbed against a freshly painted wall upstairs and gotten paint on it, but that had not stopped her from wearing it indoors. It was a good work dress.

In disbelief, she watched Lizzie tear the skirt into strips.

Trembling, Alice left the room, stepped in the sitting room. Stared at the blood spatter still on the door to the dining room. No one had cleaned it. Bridget was gone. No one would wash it off.

She put her head in her hands, in despair. How could this be *happening*? She should get an officer. They were all over the outside, they could easily see inside, step inside at any moment.

Alice walked swiftly back to the kitchen. Some strain of protectiveness still compelled her. "I wouldn't let anyone see you do that."

Lizzie moved, tucking her body to the side of the stove so if anyone looked in the window she might not be seen. Incredibly, she reached into the cupboard to the side of the stove and pulled out more fabric. The Bedford cord's waist. She had *stowed* it in there! She was burning her dress! She was calmly and firmly destroying evidence.

And Emma kept washing dishes in the scullery, as if this was the most natural thing for Lizzie to be doing, the very day after she'd been informed she was a suspect for the murders.

It is enough now, thought Alice. *I must take action.*

CHAPTER 48

Bridget

AUGUST 7, 1892

She'll never tell a soul. She'll never tell a soul.

Miss Lizzie had taken her aside, so Emma and Mr. Morse couldn't hear. She had put so much money into her hands that Bridget tried to give it back.

"No, miss, this is more than my wages. I'm done with it, and it's all right; what I've been paid I can manage with."

"I have one last errand for you," said Miss Lizzie.

"Ah no. I'm done with all that now."

"There's more coming to you should you help me out. Your mother is yet in Ireland, and you pine for her. I can help you get back to her."

Bridget started shaking her head, and shook it for the entirety of Miss Lizzie's following speech.

"There's not much I ask of you, just to run this note downstreet for me. And to remember whenever you are asked the difficult inquiries, to remember that we had a bit of kindness here for you, didn't we?"

"I'm in agonies, miss; I can't be running your messages any longer."

"One last time. There is so much in it for you. You might take the same ship I did! Kiss your mother one more time on that careworn cheek."

It was like she was quoting lines from the poetry section of those literary magazines she read. And there was a certain intensity around her pronouncing the word "mother."

Firmly, Miss Lizzie pressed a folded note into her hand.

"No," Bridget said. "I won't. You can't ask me, Miss Lizzie."

"Just bring it and ask for his response. It will take you ten minutes."

Even not knowing the contents of the note, Bridget knew she couldn't deliver it.

"I'll make it worth your while," said Miss Lizzie.

And what she spoke of, in adamant whispers, did indeed persuade Bridget to push through the crowds gathered all around the Borden home, speculating about the wild-eyed murderer who'd plunged in and out of the home, leaving two corpses in his wake. He was Portuguese, she heard whispered as she walked through. He was a man whom Mr. Borden had cheated out of rents. He was from Swansea. He was a deranged relative.

She walked through, head down.

It was a few streets away from the destination that she opened the note and read it. She knew she'd despise herself for the rest of her life if she didn't. Bridget could never stand suspicion and either wanted to let it go or fortify it. And then she closed it back up, walked to the door in question and rapped smartly.

When the man opened it, she thrust the paper at him. "It's from Miss Lizzie Borden and I'm to wait for an answer," she said.

He looked terrified. "I can't," he said.

"Can't what, sir?"

"She isn't . . . she's . . . dear God, she's . . . "

Bridget waited, still holding onto the note.

"She's a monster," he said.

He took a step backward, and with an expression somewhat apologetic, but better described as terrorized, he closed the door in her face.

She ripped the note into shreds as she walked back to Second Street.

CHAPTER 49

Bridget

AUGUST 8, 1892

Bridget had not bothered to report back to Miss Lizzie nor bring her the shreds of her torn-up note. No answer was an answer. Miss Lizzie had to know he wouldn't take her now.

She went straight back to the Bowen home, accepting the tea Bridie brewed her, then went upstairs. She couldn't stay here forever, not without working. If she didn't find something soon, she'd send a letter to her cousins and ask for shelter.

Her back ached with all the questions she'd answered, from officer after officer. Even the attorneys sought her out for interviews, and her head whirled with all that she could say. Worse, her head ached with all her thinking.

That night, she suffered yet another interrogation. Although Bridie had not pressed her for details of the goings-on across the street, Mary Doolan was here now and hungry for news.

She and Bridie perched in the attic like crows upon the narrow iron bedstead. Bridget hated it. She wanted time to mull over her showing Officer Medley the dusty tools without even being asked. She was a right turncoat, and no doubt about it. But then she thought Mrs. Borden would like the killer brought to justice, even if the truth was scandalous and horrible.

Bridget wanted to review her exchange with Officer Medley in the cellar, his recounting of the visit to the barn loft. Had Lizzie lied? And if so, where had she been? Where were her discarded pear cores? Where even was the *line* she intended to hook the sinkers to? The strangest falsehoods, and Bridget wanted to ponder them—but the lasses would give her no peace.

"How did you ever go back there and sleep?" asked Bridie.

"It was my job and I meant to keep it."

Neither noticed her use of the past tense.

"Did I not tell ye?" asked Mary. "The pigeons were the end of it, yet ye stayed on! No amount of money could keep me there, even if my family were skin and bones and weeping for bread."

"I hear they may arrest her," said Bridie. "And then who will be your employer?" It was as if Emma didn't even cross her mind.

"She did it, sure as a cat steals cream. Maggie was over in the morning when you were out, and she's outright convinced. She thinks they better hurry up and arrest her before she up and leaves town with all her father's money," said Mary.

They both looked at her expectantly.

"Pshaw," said Bridget after a pause. The mention of Maggie made her uneasy. It had been her name, off and on, for several years. And the original Maggie had warned her, tried to tell her, as did Mary Doolan. Bridget had not listened to either of them.

"But I thought you were going back to resume your position. You couldn't stand to stay there, could you?"

"It's too upsetting, and wouldn't you be upset, too?"

"I suppose so at that."

"They should bury them and let them be," said Bridie. "Keeping them there, cutting open their stomachs . . . it's as monstrous as what the murderer did to them, practically."

"They have to do the autopsies," said Mary. "There may be clues."

"However can you tell a killer based on that?" Bridie said. "Unless if the murder weapon was left inside the body. It's ridiculous. What kind of clues can you mean?"

"Well," said Mary. "You might be able to tell the dimensions of the weapon by looking at the wounds. They shaved her head, didn't they?"

Bridget didn't reply.

"So they can measure the cuts and see what size hatchet might have done the thing," said Mary.

"I hope it was quick for her," said Bridie. "She was a nice woman, didn't deserve any of that that come to her."

"She got dozens of blows!"

"She might not have been alive for all of them," said Bridie. "Let's hope the first dispatched her with merciful speed, and the killer went on without realizing he could stop."

"You say 'he'? So you don't think it could be Miss Lizzie? If you could only talk to Maggie! She's set on Lizzie as the one. The police ought to talk to her; they should."

"Miss Lizzie's proud, and she's cut her chin at your mistress on the street. I've seen her do it! But I can't fathom her doing such a deed as this . . . two times, no less! She don't have the nerves it takes to sit out that hour until Mr. Borden came home!"

"How does she seem, Bridget?" asked Mary, although the conversation seemed to move right along without Bridget's input at all.

"She's always thinking forward," said Bridget. "Who to have for undertaker, what arrangements to make."

"When you came to our door Thursday, I couldn't believe the news," said Bridie. "And when we started understanding whatever had happened, we were in such distress. But Mrs. Churchill said Miss

Lizzie was standing at the screen door, as calm as you please, and just called out to her, 'Why don't you come over?'"

"Nerves of steel, that one," said Mary.

"What will ye do now?" asked Bridie.

"Find other work."

"You won't stay with her?"

"I can't stay in that house again."

"My friend knows of a position cleaning for the jail keeper at New Bedford if you're all right with that."

"I am indeed," said Bridget. She didn't care if her employer dealt with criminals, so long as they didn't follow her home. And there were bars and cells to keep that from happening.

"You're smart to move on, for they'll arrest her soon," Mary said again. "They'll have to. Fall River's clamoring for it."

"And you'll have to talk to the police and the lawyers," Bridie said.

"I have already and will do more when asked."

"I don't envy you the sights you've seen," said Mary. "At any rate, I've got to return. Another early day in the morning for me."

It seemed Bridget might carve out another life for herself in which she might sleep into the mornings that make maids rise. Maybe the dreams could slowly exert an influence and obscure the images that haunted her mind, draw a misty veil over the horrific scenes.

Mary departed, and Bridget watched her safe passage across the street from the window. At the side door, Mary turned and waved up at the window. Bridget lifted her hand in return. Mary had tried to warn her. She might've avoided all this, and some other maid would still feel the blood on her hands. Or maybe . . . somehow . . . if that one detail, Bridget's staying in the home, had been adjusted, perhaps the outcome might've been different. Another maid might've cheered Lizzie. Someone else could've helped her the day her father slaughtered the pigeons, been kinder to her. Taken her side so that

Mrs. Borden could live, not the victor, but still alive.

Bridget climbed into bed with Bridie. In her mind's eye, she could still see the glow from the Borden house across the street.

"Can we leave the lamp burning?" she asked.

CHAPTER 50

Bridget

After the inquest and the preliminary hearing, Bridget had had her fill of endless questions from posturing men. It seemed impossible that they could find fifty ways to make the same query, but they did. Still, when the trial at Superior Court began—the one that would hang Miss Lizzie or set her free—Bridget found that she wanted to again sit through the interminable interrogations.

Beforehand, the lawyers had probed her until to her discomfiture, she was cast as a witness for the prosecution. Andrew Jennings, the Borden family attorney, had interviewed her several times and written down her words with a fast and florid hand. He frowned more and more as she couldn't quite say the things that he wanted. Finally, he told her he couldn't use her.

And then Hosea Knowlton, the cocky prosecutor, had nodded and tried to hide a smile as she couldn't quite bring herself to lie. But many a helpful thing for Lizzie had been broadcast simply through omission. Bridget had been promised Ireland.

More profoundly, because of the inquest she had heard tell of the trip Lizzie took to Mr. Bence's drugstore. Sleepless nights came after that revelation; along with Mr. and Mrs. Borden, she too had vomited. She remembered her nausea that day as she sank to her knees, forehead pressed to the hot grass in between heaving. That was the doing of Miss Lizzie? Bridget herself might've been a body on a wicker autopsy table?

It was thanks to the grace of God, she believed, that she still breathed. It was best to do as the woman wished.

Thinking to protect herself, she hired her own lawyer, a Mr. Cummings. She hoped this would show Lizzie she didn't throw in her lot with Mr. Knowlton. It was frightening not to be allied with Lizzie's cause. Mr. Cummings did indeed provide a buffer for her and made her feel better about the treacherous ice her feet stood upon.

She was keen to see how Miss Lizzie might answer to the lawyers when a long array of judges—three of them!—sat listening to every word. Even a former governor was involved, as one of Miss Lizzie's defense attorneys.

The first day of trial was swallowed by selecting the jurors. Bridget watched as Miss Lizzie challenged more than a dozen of them for no good reason she could see, and her attorney challenged even more. These men would decide Miss Lizzie's fate, and the smirks on some faces perhaps prompted her rejection. How nice for Miss Lizzie to be able to spurn men for once, Bridget thought with a bit of spite.

On the second day, attorney for the commonwealth Mr. Moody gave a lengthy summary of the facts of the case. Bridget could not bear to look at Miss Lizzie, pressing her folded Japanese fan to her mouth, when he spoke about the trip to the drugstore and the attempt to buy prussic acid the very day before the murders. He outlined the minutia of that terrible day's unfolding, and Miss Lizzie's unaffected walk upstairs to her room past the two corpses, and the perhaps damning fact that "without a suggestion from anyone" she had taken off her dress and instead put on a pink wrapper.

He showed the courtroom Miss Lizzie's shoes, stockings, dress, and skirt. Bridget did not like seeing a man holding up such personal items. The stockings still held the shape of Miss Lizzie's calves and instep; it was as if Miss Lizzie herself was lifting her skirts to show the world her legs.

When finished, Mr. Moody tossed the dress onto the prosecution table. Upon landing, it swept aside tissue paper covering the contents of a bag on the table. Under the tissue suddenly appeared the skulls of Mr. and Mrs. Borden, biding their time to be displayed and discussed.

Bridget would not look at those macabre emblems and instead cast a glance at Miss Lizzie, who opened her fan to cover her face and, seconds later, slumped against the police matron sitting next to her who cried out in surprise. With a rapid slide, Miss Lizzie dropped to the floor unconscious.

Bridget couldn't help but think of Mrs. Borden hitting the floor from a standing position. Miss Lizzie made no such house-trembling thump as her stepmother must've while Bridget was out washing her windows.

As Miss Lizzie was assisted with smelling salts, Bridget saw her mottled face, red and blue. She had not faked her swoon. Her eyes met Bridget's, and Bridget began to feel the old stirrings of pity. Her life had had no joy, and she was not right in her mind. What would become of Miss Lizzie?

The next day, there was a parade of witnesses, some of them men Bridget had never seen or only seen in passing that morning of the murders: fellows who measured things, photographed things, hid in closets to see if the murderer could've laid in wait, Uncle Morse who ignored the crowds surrounding the house and ate a pear in the back-yard before committing to entering, bankers and a hatter who had seen Mr. Borden on his last jaunt through Fall River.

Bridget was called to testify later in the day. Using some of the money Lizzie had given her, she'd had a new dress made, so she at least looked decent, yet she dreaded again telling the details of that day. Many speculated she had something to do with the murders, and she felt their suspicion radiating throughout the hot courtroom. She wished she, too, held a fan to dispell the close air.

That air felt even hotter, as if she were bending over the kitchen stove, when her brogue interfered with being understood. "Dr. Bowen wanted a sheet for covering Mr. Borden," she told Mr. Moody, the prosecuting attorney on Mr. Knowlton's team, "so I asked him to get the keys off the shelf in the sitting room."

"I'm sorry, 'the case off the shelf'?" asked Mr. Moody.

"Aye."

"What case?"

"No, sir, the keys."

The courtroom had outright laughed at her. The citizens of Fall River had never liked the Irish, and here was evidence.

Miss Lizzie smiled encouragingly at her. *Smile back*, Bridget told herself. *Keep yourself safe for your mother.*

Bridget went through a further barrage of questions until, thankfully, proceedings were interrupted to hear Mrs. Kelly's testimony. She had such a young child at home' that she couldn't be away for more than a few hours. With that respite, Bridget was able to answer the remaining questions without embarrassment.

Afterward, Miss Russell came to her in the courthouse hallway. Her face was serious, and she took care to step very closely to Bridget to address her with a hushed voice. "We have quite the duty to perform, do we not? They may call you back tomorrow."

Miss Russell was also a witness for the prosecution. Her friendship with the Borden sisters was over with a vicious finality.

"All we must do is tell the truth."

"But you . . . " Miss Russell looked about her. No one seemed to be paying attention to them. "You told the jurors that the relations were congenial, and you never saw any quarreling."

"And so I did not."

Miss Russell surveyed her, and as Bridget looked back frankly, she watched Miss Russell's eyes narrow.

"What are you afraid of?" asked Miss Russell softly. "You think she will . . . ?"

"I'm not afeared of a thing," said Bridget. "Except the man that done it, and I hope they catch him."

The next day, perhaps influenced by Miss Russell's words, Bridget couldn't resist a little defiance when she was cross-examined by none other than Governor Robinson. Something about his round glasses and equally rounded forehead made Bridget able to discount his stately manner and powerful past.

"I omitted yesterday to ask you about where you came downstairs, as Miss Lizzie had called you, as you were upstairs right after eleven o'clock."

He paused and Bridget perhaps saucily replied to the nonsensical question, "Yes, sir."

"You came downstairs and found her standing at the wooden door leaning up against that?"

"Yes, sir."

"Now what was she doing?"

"She wasn't doing nothing."

"Was she excited?"

"She seemed excited to me more than I ever seen her before, but not crying," she said.

"What do you say?"

"Yes, sir; she seemed excited to me more than I ever saw her before."

"Was she crying?" Governor Robinson leaned closer and gave her a coaxing smile.

"No, sir."

He frowned. "Are you right about that?"

"Yes, sir, I am."

"Have you ever said differently about it?"

"No, sir, I never said no different."

"But you testified at the inquest . . ." He paused and walked to his table to gather up a few papers. "Now let me read and ask you if you didn't say this. You were asked by Mr. Knowlton, 'Was she crying?' and you responded, 'Yes, sir, she was crying.'"

"Well, that must be wrong. I couldn't say that."

"That must be wrong?"

"Yes, sir. I didn't say that, for I couldn't."

"So your memory is better today than it was then."

"I don't care what my memory is, I didn't see the girl crying." She could have bitten her tongue when "the girl" slipped out. That was not respectful. That was how doctors and attorneys referred to servants.

"You don't care anything about it?" His face registered a light anger. It was important for the jurors to believe that Miss Lizzie had been in tears that morning, rather than the impassive, cold woman who had issued orders and seemed unmoved.

"No, sir."

"You don't care about your memory?"

"Yes, I care about that."

"Well, you want to be right, don't you, Miss Sullivan?"

"I swear I didn't see her crying."

He asked her a few more times, varying the wording, until he gave up and released her. She walked back to her seat feeling a quizzical silence behind her. Everyone was wondering, had Miss Lizzie sobbed? And why would Bridget change her tale? As she sat down, she tried to think what she had told Mr. Knowlton a year ago at the inquest. Back then, the money was still fresh. And back then, she had not heard about the trip to the drugstore.

On the seventh day of the trial, Governor Robinson confirmed his status as someone Bridget would dully hate for the rest of her life. When Officer Hyde testified about looking through the window to see poor Alice Russell trembling in the cellar, afraid to go close to the pile of bloodied clothing on the washroom floor, the governor pretended to be a palsied woman, imitating her shaking. The jurors, damn them, laughed.

"She had a kerosene lamp, didn't she?" Robinson asked. "Did it smoke, then, when she shook it so?"

"I never noticed," said Officer Hyde quietly, comprehending he was being made sport of.

"It didn't shake the chimney off the lamp?"

The jury laughed again. Bridget seethed. She would like to see how brave Governor Robinson would be in a dark night's cellar with two corpses hacked to ruin just upstairs.

After Officer Hyde sat down, the court resettled in anticipation of the next witness, Dr. William Dolan, whose tale would surely be gory and satisfy the hungry housewives crowding the benches. It was thought his testimony would be too upsetting to the prisoner, so Miss Lizzie was escorted into an adjoining room to hear, but not watch, the questioning.

Dr. Dolan was a man who might be considered handsome if he didn't always lift his head while talking, like an alert mastiff. He had light brown hair, a mustache, and an inquisitive face. After a brief listing of his medical qualifications, he spoke about the morning of August 4 in plain terms, unafraid to talk about the undigested contents of the Bordens' intestines. Bridget felt her fingernails scraping at the wood of her chair.

He discussed the bloodstained clothing that Miss Russell had quaked at, and which Bridget had last seen on the cellar floor. It had been buried in the backyard and dug up again a week later: some items brought to the marshal, and others reburied. Mrs. Borden's ugly work dress had been treated like an archeological treasure.

It was so odd to see things she recognized in this sterile courtroom: a bit of the sitting room's flower-patterned carpet, cut into a rectangle, held up for jurors to see. Dr. Dolan pointed to two large pools of blood on the carpet, and Bridget shivered. A second piece was the upstairs carpet in the guest room, lighter in color, but still besmirched with dried blood.

Bridget startled when she heard her name; she had given Dr. Dolan a sample of the day's milk and the previous day's, which had been tested for poison. She barely remembered that, but she had dippered the milk and given him two jars to take away.

Testimony continued, too fast for Bridget who was lost in disturbed revery about the chaos of that morning. The guest room bed had been moved before photographs were taken, Dr. Dolan was saying, and Mrs. Borden's hands had been moved. They had pulled her out from under the bed and moved her arms under her chest, rather than stretched out as if reaching for some nonexistent assistance.

Bridget's breathing quickened, remembering standing on the stairs, seeing her mistress so undone, and then racing up to stand at her feet. The motionless heft of Mrs. Borden, and Mrs. Churchill's breathy screams . . . it was a nightmare and she had lived it.

Dr. Dolan held up the pillow sham. Bridget had laundered it and its mates many times. She could nearly feel the fabric beneath her fingers as he enumerated its blood spots. He and Mr. Knowlton lightly bickered over whether it was inside out and took a pencil to write "top" on it to indicate its placement on the bed. That small detail bothered her. Writing on the pillow sham was yet another injury to the dead mistress.

The men held up more exhibits, a chip from the marble dresser top, and Lizzie's clothes. A blue dress, a waist, and a white underskirt.

A small hole had been cut in the petticoat for another doctor to look at the scrap under his microscope: a minute blood drop that Lizzie had said was from her monthlies.

And then the molded skulls were presented, the ones that a mere glimpse of had made Miss Lizzie faint.

Created from the true skulls, the casts showed vacant black holes where bone ought to have been. The prosecution had wanted to illustrate the intense fury behind the blows. In Mr. Borden's case, the sharp-boned jaw led to one eye socket merging into the vacancy that in life would have been his ear and side of his head. Mrs. Borden's skull from the back looked like an ostrich egg from which the young chick had destructively battered its way out.

However, Bridget could see that the prosecution's plan had backfired. The jury more than ever was convinced of Lizzie's innocence. How could the demure woman who had sat fanning herself in her chair through so much of the trial have caused such a torrent of violence? It was unthinkable. This was the work of a man.

Mr. Knowlton was so comfortable with Mr. Borden's skull that he put it on the rail in front of the stenographer's table to allow Dr. Dolan to better point out its features. Bridget nearly stood up at that, her heart aching so for the disregard for the rest of the body that once accompanied that head. There should be another way to do this, like a drawing, perhaps.

With seeming relish, the doctor went through a litany of wretched particulars. From the courtyard outside came a long shrill eruption of barking. Two dogs were fighting, and their savage snarls and yaps made the doctor pause. A sparrow alighted on the windowsill and trilled loudly. It seemed all nature was against his testimony.

He had the gall to admit that he had authorized the heads to be taken without informing Miss Lizzie or Miss Emma, and that the bodies had been interred without them knowing the true circumstances.

His insufferable listing of the individual hatchet blows included counting of inches assigned to the wounds, a despicable math.

Two inches, four inches, a cutting surface of five inches, perhaps more. Bridget stopped listening for a bit. She wondered what Miss Lizzie was thinking, sequestered in the nearby room. Could she visualize the wounds as they were talked of, as Bridget herself was resisting?

The second autopsy at Oak Grove Cemetery had revealed a previously undetected blow to Mrs. Borden's back, Dr. Dolan said. In order to demonstrate to jurors where it had been, the defense attorney Adams let Dr. Dolan draw in chalk on the back of his dark coat. "I hope that I shall not be numbered as an exhibit," Adams joked.

A detail came up that Bridget had heard before but not grasped the significance of. Mrs. Borden had one wound on her left forehead. The only wound on the front of her face, and as Dr. Dolan said, "Assailant and assaulted faced each other."

Mrs. Borden had seen her attacker, seen the hatchet raised in the air. She had been aware that it would be her felling. Bridget closed her eyes to keep the tears from spilling and sent up a fervent prayer that Mrs. Borden's time dancing with her killer had been brief. She had been brutally hit again and again, while Bridget rubbed vinegar into the windows and dashed dippers of water against them. She might've helped, but she was stolidly doing her work or, worse, at the fence chatting away with Mary Doolan.

For the first time, Bridget felt intense regret at her own inadvertent role. She had no responsibility, had done nothing to make this happen, but had conditions been different she might have rescued that poor woman.

The day was not over yet, to Bridget's disbelief. There were more agonies to undergo. Dr. Dolan passed out to the jurors photographs taken of Mr. and Mrs. Borden on the day of their deaths. People craned to get a glimpse. One juror, Mr. Hodges, a blacksmith from Taunton, was overcome at the images and began the sweat that brought his neighbor to fan him. He was given a glass of water, and Bridget watched his face as he was unable to school his emotions.

She wished he would look at her. She felt they might be the only two people who felt such wild sensations of pity and horror on behalf of the elderly couple. The court took a five-minute break so that he could retire to the jury room for a moment's respite. As they did so, Bridget took the chance to leave early. She saw Alice Russell's face as she walked past. She, too, looked sickened.

On the ninth day of the trial, the druggist Eli Bence was not permitted to testify. A long conference at the bench seemed impassioned, and Bridget wondered fiercely what they were saying. What he had to say was vital to the case, she felt. One doesn't try to purchase poison the day before a murder in one's home without it being connected. Mrs. Borden herself had told Dr. Bowen she thought someone was trying to poison her and Mr. Borden. How Bridget longed to sidle up next to these men in their black suits and white beards, whispering and gesticulating with the three judges. A servant can always overhear a conversation in a home, but she was at a loss here. Her movements could not be furtive and unseen. Mr. Bence sat patiently waiting for the outcome, his gaze leveled at Miss Lizzie as if trying to confirm for himself that she had really been the woman in his drugstore that day.

Bridget felt a return of bile in her throat. She had vomited, too, a day later than the Bordens. She might've been a third, inconvenient death nestled between the other two—intended or accidental. She sat fighting the nausea, and then felt a headache take up residence, as if it recognized the old signals and played along.

She avoided looking at Miss Lizzie. The headache battered along the inside of her skull. *A four-inch blow,* she thought. *That one was two*

and a half inches, from the side of the hatchet. That one hit in the same place.
And that one, too. And that one, too.

W hen the jury withdrew at the close of the case, on the thirteenth day, Bridget watched her old mistress carefully. She sat under a veiled hat so her face was difficult to see. Bridget had been stunned that one of the three judges, Mr. Dewey, had so clearly directed the jury to return a verdict of innocent. It seemed the jurors would have to go against him to find her guilty. But they seemed the type of men who had only ever known genteel ladies. A woman who was angry enough to wield a hatchet didn't seem possible in their world. They had listened carefully to every word of testimony, but Bridget also saw the playfulness in them, the leaning over to scribble a funny note on another's note-paper, the laughing when questioning became light—which in Bridget's opinion, it never did. Never throughout the entire proceedings did she forget the poor folks who had bled into carpet and bled into sofa, taken from their lives too soon.

While the jury deliberated, Bridget stared at her hands in her lap. Just as she was thinking she might go out and stretch her legs in the hallway, the door opened and the men filed back in. She knew the instant she saw them.

Their faces were open, relaxed, confident. They were not men who had sentenced a woman to hang.

In fact, after the anxious time wasting of the jury roll call and the tradition of having the defendant rise and hold up her right hand, the foreman interrupted the clerk mid-sentence to blurt out his news: "Not guilty!"

There was an outburst of clapping, and Bridget found herself putting her hands to that use, too.

Miss Lizzie sank into her seat, hiding her face.

Bridget glanced over at Miss Russell, whose blank expression could not be read.

It is over, thought Bridget. *And now I resume my life.*

Miss Lizzie spent that night with friends and returned to Second Street the next day. Emma had been living there alone for a year with the residue of madness. Bridget didn't envy her that bleak year. Whoever took Bridget's place in the attic bedroom must not be afraid of ghosts.

Bridget hired a carriage to go to Fall River and pay her last respects to the former residents of the house. With a few words to Lizzie, she'd be off to Ireland and a different life.

She stood in front of the drab home, wondering if she should go to her side door or ring at the front. She was not a servant of this household, but she also knew she'd burn with anger if Miss Lizzie looked askance at her for daring to use the front entry. She decided to take the chance.

She rang and a maid let her in with a few quiet words. She, too, was Irish. She brought Bridget into the parlor where Miss Lizzie sat with Miss Emma. They were sitting there silently, and Bridget saw tears in Miss Emma's eyes. Miss Emma got up abruptly when she saw Bridget and brushed past her without acknowledging her.

"Sit, Bridget," said Miss Lizzie.

Bridget did so, choosing the chair by the piano rather than to sit on the same sofa with her.

"So odd to be back here, isn't it?" said Miss Lizzie.

"Aye."

"You said many things in court."

"I answered the questions as best I could, miss."

"It was a surprise to me that you were part of Mr. Knowlton's parade of despicable witnesses."

"I had to testify," said Bridget, "and I couldn't choose which side to be on. They placed me."

"You did as well as you could, I suppose."

Bridget nodded. And then that terrible thing happened that she had always hated of her employer: the long stare from those silvered eyes. The lips coiling into lines of some restrained emotion.

Bridget looked down, unable to bear the gaze.

"You want a reward of some sort," said Miss Lizzie.

Angered, Bridget looked up. "Not a reward, miss. Don't you dare cast it that way. You told me you would—"

"And so I did. I believe there is an envelope with your name on it in my chamber upstairs."

"All right," said Bridget.

"You may retrieve it."

Bridget rose to her feet. She couldn't deny the cat-surveying-mouse quality of Miss Lizzie's expression. She slowly walked out into the front entry, looked up at the long staircase. The last time she had climbed it, Mrs. Borden lay upstairs on the floor.

She wasn't sure where Emma had gone. Hadn't heard whether she went upstairs or to the back of the house. She looked around for her, listening. She could hear the new maid set a pot on the stove in the distant kitchen.

"It's on my dresser," said Miss Lizzie from behind her.

Bridget whirled around. Miss Lizzie was at her heels, having silently left the sofa.

"Why do you not get it for me?" Bridget managed.

"You always did the fetching," said Miss Lizzie.

She could smell the rosewater on her, so close did they stand. Bridget took a step backward.

"Don't you want it?" asked Miss Lizzie.

Bridget swallowed. She took a second step backward, and her back hit the banister.

"You gave my family good service and deserve your final pay."

"Miss Lizzie," whispered Bridget, lapsing into her tongue. "I willna climb the steps."

"'Willna?' I have always loved the Irish in your voice. I know you are surprised to hear that. You think I ridiculed it."

"Please. Won't you get it for me?" pleaded Bridget.

"It's the matter of a moment for you to get it," said Miss Lizzie. Her eyes shone with the sidelights from the door crossing her irises.

Suddenly, Bridget gathered her courage. She whirled around, picked up her shirts and practically ran up the stairs. She refused to turn her head when she came into view of the guest room and continued pummeling up the remainder of the steps, loudly. If Miss Emma or the maid heard her, so much the better.

She entered Miss Lizzie's room, dashed to the dresser, and seized the envelope marked "Miss Sullivan."

The scent of rosewater was much stronger in here.

As she turned around, Miss Lizzie blocked the doorway.

"This chapter in our lives is now closed," Miss Lizzie said.

Bridget staggered a bit, her heart so quick in her chest it pained her. It almost seemed she could taste the blood the organ was rushing through her.

"Forever," said Miss Lizzie.

She waited.

"Nod, Bridget. Tell me you understand it is closed forever."

Bridget nodded.

"And now, you must go very far away. You will want Ireland, of course, to see your dozens of siblings."

An insult, but Bridget nodded.

"And if you return to the States, you must not come back to Fall River. I'm going to stay here. Emma and I will purchase the kind of home we ought to have had all along. But I don't want you here."

"No, miss," said Bridget.

"So this will be our final goodbye, then."

The pewter eyes, the fearless stare, the body grown heavy with its steady diet of no remorse.

"Miss Lizzie, step aside and let me go, and I promise you'll never see hide nor hair of me again."

With a smile, Miss Lizzie took two steps sideways until she was closer to the room where Mrs. Borden had died. Bridget said a quick mental prayer, inhaled as hard as she could, and rushed past her.

Her feet making a rapid drumming on the stairs, Bridget threw herself down, nearly tripping on the skirts she hadn't bothered to gather up. She clutched at the banister, and the envelope fluttered down to reach the ground floor before her. She reached the safety of the bottom, turned with the curve of the banister to pick up the envelope. Kneeling, she looked warily up at the stairs, but Lizzie hadn't followed her.

She faced the door and its regiment of triple locks, her hands again remembering the motions that had once been automatic. The spring lock, the bolt, and the key to be turned. *One, two, three.*

As she opened the door, clean air hitting her hot face, she heard the sound from the stairs behind her.

The laugh.

Bridget was so shaken she didn't bother to visit next door with Mary Doolan as she'd planned. Inside the carriage, she opened up the envelope. It wasn't as much money as she'd been promised. There was a short note in Miss Lizzie's hand:

You did well, but might've done better. Mr. Jennings was disappointed in you.

CHAPTER 51

Brooke

AUGUST 28, 2016

They have one last stop before they head back. Brooke wants to see Lizzie's gravestone, and since they'll be in the area, they can drive past Maplecroft, too.

Maplecroft isn't really so grand, she thinks, as they pause outside studying it. Whereas the Second Street house was two stories plus an attic, this home is a full three stories, with two chimneys and pitched dormers, several porches and a witch's hat tower. It's not so close to the street and has a large side yard of green. The neighborhood is the biggest difference, though. Although Second Street was definitely downtown, this home is in an area of grand mansions and a slower pace. No one would conduct business here. Mr. Borden could walk and walk and never find a bank.

A top step in the stone stairs leading to the front door has been carved with the word Maplecroft, as if it is a strangely elongated and shortened tombstone. "I'm sure the neighbors thought *that* was classy," remarks Anthony.

Without thinking about it, Brooke leans over and kisses him. Pulls back and inhales the good smell of him, runs her hand through his hair. Sitting there in the car is so mundane, so wonderfully everyday. Something she's never had. It breaks her heart that she'll have to go now. She probably shouldn't even go back to her apartment. Maybe . . . maybe she'll have him go in with her so she can collect up her stuff, and maybe she'll ask to stay at his place one last night before she leaves. Can she get away with bringing her Rubbermaid tub with her or will he question it? Will he think the opposite . . . not that she's leaving, but that she wants to move in with him?

How nice that would be.

But it's for some other woman to do.

"What was that for?" he asks.

"Just because I noticed you were over there."

He kisses her back, and pretty soon they're at the point where a police officer would be warranted to knock on the window and ask them to cut it out. She pulls away and grins as she pushes his hands away.

"What? I don't get some hot murder-mansion action?"

"You fell asleep on me last night," she reminds him.

"I never thought these words would emit from my mouth, but do you want to head to the cemetery?"

"That's a rhetorical question, right?"

It takes a little doing on the confusing streets, but they finally find the monumental gates to the cemetery. They park outside and walk in. "Oh, my God," says Brooke. "I can't believe it."

She points to the yellow arrows painted on the ground. What else can they be? They're guiding tourists to the Borden gravesite. They follow their lead, walking past many other departed souls who were somehow not worthy of an arrow.

"It's kind of unbelievable how much this case resonates with people," says Anthony.

"I think it's because she was acquitted," says Brooke. "If she'd served her time, I don't think anyone would care. It's that elusive element of 'she got away with it' that makes people so fascinated."

"Probably."

As they approach the grave, she sees that others are already there. The Red Sox man and his wife from the B&B, as well as a few people she doesn't recognize. She hopes to see Jackson here, her fellow denizen of the underworld of "not good family."

"Hello again!" calls the Red Sox wife. "Did you see Maplecroft too?"

"Yes," says Brooke.

"Quite the upgrade, eh?" says Anthony. Brooke laughs so he doesn't see. He's the only non-Canadian who could get away with "eh." All of a sudden, she's noticing all these little details about him that you'd have to know someone to notice.

He's going to be sad when I go, she thinks.

And I'm going to be a basket case.

As they pick their way through the graves, they notice the pennies left on the markers—is it meant to be ironic, since Andrew was a penny-pincher? Are they rewarding the Bordens posthumously with lots of pennies?

They stand looking at the necropolis stretching far into the distance. How many of these people lived as long as they wanted to? How many appreciated their lives to the degree that Brooke would, if she could ever stop running?

"Don't take this the wrong way," says Anthony, "But I think I'm done with Falls River."

He gives her a wry look, and suddenly all she wants is to be sitting at the café with him. What if she told him everything—told him about the Facebook friend who was really her worst enemy, someone who wanted to avenge her for a death that Jackson makes her question whether she's even responsible for at all?

He's a criminal attorney. He knows about police protection. He could help her. And then she wouldn't have to slip away like she was never there.

Maybe it wasn't up to her long-lost father to help her. Maybe she could help herself, with Anthony's know-how.

"Let's talk in the car," she says.

CHAPTER 52

Brooke

JULY 4, 2002

Mr. Carr was a great liar. He said things that made Mrs. Carr laugh shakily. "I shouldn't drink," she said by way of apology to Brooke's mom.

"It's all right," said Brooke's mom. "You should see me when I've got a few margaritas in me."

"That's why they call it the demon liquor," said Mr. Carr. "It makes wives make irrational accusations." He gave Mrs. Carr a kiss on the lips and Brooke, who was holding her mom's hand, felt the tight squeeze that came through that grip.

They'd come in to get her purse and even in that short amount of time, Mr. Carr had made great headway gaslighting his wife.

"I feel so foolish," said Mrs. Carr. "You're our *maid*. Of course he wouldn't . . . " She drifted off, drunk enough to have begun the sentence but sobering up enough to realize she shouldn't finish it.

"No harm done. Really."

"I'm going to make some egg salad sandwiches." For a second it looked like Mrs. Carr was going to start crying again. But she was laughing, a weird wine-fueled snicker. "Salad again!"

"That sounds fine," said Mr. Carr. "We'll eat that, and then Magdalena and her daughter can head home."

"No," said Brooke, surprising herself with her assertiveness. "I want to see the fireworks."

The adults all looked at her in dismay. They knew the get-together had to end, and the fireworks wouldn't start until dark, hours away. "Mija, I think it's best we go. I'll make it up to you, I promise."

Brooke started to cry. In later years, she would look back at this moment and hate herself. It was the last time, in fact, she did cry. How different would the night have gone, and all the nights following it, if Brooke hadn't cried, if she and her mom had gotten into the car and driven home to do whatever thing would substitute for fireworks: a full-sized Milky Way bar? A promise to go to a matinee on the weekend?

But the adults had relented in the face of a child disappointed she didn't get to see the fireworks celebrating the independence of the Great and Almost Unattainable United States of America.

Hours later, they had all trooped down to the dock. Brooke's mom had brought sweatshirts for both of them, knowing the night air would be cool on the water. Mrs. Carr looked completely sober by then, but her eyes still seemed red as if she was tearing up regularly.

"I can't believe we're spending the Fourth of July with our *maid*," Abraham said.

"Hush, honey," said Mrs. Carr automatically.

Brooke had stood on that deck, leaning against her mother, as the sky convulsed and erupted. So many colors. It dazzled Brooke's eyes. She watched until her neck ached from craning, and then she watched the fireworks reflected in the lake water instead. Her mom couldn't afford a car whose back door opened, but she overheard Mr. Carr say this wealthy community spent tens of thousands on the display. All for something so ephemeral that you couldn't get a souvenir from it, in the sky and then erased.

She looked over at Ezekiel, closest to her, his head bent back to look at the show, neck lengthened like a swan's. His pale profile against the darkness.

The fireworks went on and on until she felt a dizziness, swayed on her feet, pushed out her arms until her mother straightened her and hugged her from behind so she could lean backward and not have to hold herself up.

Each firework changed her life in some way, awakening her to what she couldn't have, to what others took for granted. The sky was magnificent in a way she would remember forever, even if the majestic noise, loud as gunshots in her ears, veiled the splash when Mrs. Carr entered the water.

Brooke could understand it. Mrs. Carr wanted to swim with the colors, be part of that spray that burst like a flower aggressively blooming, angrily outshooting its potential, screwing the sky over, leaving nothing but smoke behind.

CHAPTER 53

Brooke

AUGUST 28, 2016

She and Anthony drive past Maplecroft again on the way out, and from a block away, they can see Jackson standing on the sidewalk looking at the upper story of the house. A plane above them releases a sonic boom, and for a second Brooke goes somewhere else staring at his profile.

Fireworks.

His neck extended, face turned skyward, eyes plastered on the heavens. Joy, short-lived joy, at the spectacle unfolding in the firmament.

She's seen him before in just such an attitude with the blasts still quaking in their skins. That elfin little boy face transformed to be the artsy man face.

Jackson is Ezekiel.

She hits Anthony's hand on the steering wheel, hitting it in a cadence of panic. "Keep driving!" she hisses. "Go, go, go!"

"You don't want to look at—"

"*No!*"

Obligingly, he steps on the gas, and she sinks down below the level of the window as he drives another few blocks, barely pausing at stop signs and barreling along. After a few minutes, she pulls back upright.

"What the hell was that?" he asks her evenly.

"Get on the freeway first, and then I'll tell you."

No one in real life is ever on the lam, only in the movies. The changing of names, the moving every nine months or so and starting afresh, the shadow life she's been living . . . it's too much for straight-laced Anthony to understand. He's more Carr than Hernandez. But she's got to try. She owes him that much.

She had been planning to move on anyway; she can at least leave him with an explanation, even if it's completely unbelievable that the man they met and interacted with is actually the grown version of the boy who thinks she killed his mother.

She recites the facts as the freeway exits pass on the right, each one putting distance between them and Ezekiel.

"You told me you had never been a victim of a crime," says Anthony.

She's flooded first with relief that he seems to believe her wild tale, but then it sinks in what he's pointing out. "I'm sorry I lied. My life has been so . . . strange. I've never really known how to even . . . well, not that I wanted to, anyway."

He nods. "And a first date was hardly the time to get into it." He pauses, and she watches his knuckles turn white on the steering wheel because he's gripping it so hard. "I'm shaking my head at how uncomfortable that discussion must've been for you."

"It's okay."

"God! I'm an idiot." She listens to his loud inhales. "It's so scary to think I might've missed out on you."

She can't help it; a sound that is half disbelief and half laughter escapes her. He's not going to run the other direction.

"I'm so glad you told me," he says quietly. "Thank you for trusting me."

"I can't think of anything better I've ever done."

"I'm sorry about your mom. And I'm sorry you've spent most of your adult life being frightened. That stops today. *Now.* "

"Thank you." She can hardly say more. She laid down her troubles, and he will help her. She's not alone anymore. "Thank you for believing me. I know some people wouldn't. And I have one more thing to tell you. Brooke's not even my real name. It's Felicita."

"Your name doesn't matter. I'll call you whatever you want to be called."

Exhilarated, she feels she can tell more, the parts that seem too coincidental, too much of a stretch to be believed. "Abraham, the older brother . . . he didn't just kill my mom. He's serving time for shooting a high school friend or at least someone he knew."

"Wait a minute." His voice is low and intense.

He turns and looks at her, his mouth wide open. She sees the crenulated tops of each bottom molar.

"His brother is Abraham *Carr*?"

"Yeah."

"Brooke, that's . . . he's my client. I got him out early on parole. For good behavior."

"Oh, my God."

"His brother . . . this is crazy, I tried to track down his brother to write a letter to support the early release. His brother's name is now Jackson."

Brooke nods furiously. "Yes, that's him! We just spent the god-damn night with him!"

"He wouldn't write it. He actually . . ."

"What?"

Anthony appears to be too upset to speak. He wrenches the car to take the exit they have almost passed. He careens down the ramp then pulls over onto the side of the road as soon as there's space.

"I feel awful, so . . . this is my fault, Brooke. The brother tried to tell me Abraham shouldn't be released. And I thought it was just a brother being vindictive. I didn't listen to him."

Brooke tries to piece it all together, while Anthony stares at her wild-eyed.

"So he's out of prison now?" she says.

"Yes. Because of *me*."

The afternoon has settled blue into the air by the time they get back, shadows long in the parking lot as Anthony follows her without a word. She keys into her apartment and listens. She scans the living room, senses on high alert.

"Forget your stuff," says Anthony. "This doesn't feel right. Let's go."

He's right; something feels off. She immediately turns to the door. She'd love to have her mother's photograph. She should've brought it with her to the B&B. She'll get it another time, after they've called the police.

But it's too late.

Sound rushing down the hallway from her bedroom, a man running. "Don't move," he snarls. "Shut the door."

Abraham has changed. New lines added on either side of his mouth and eyes. Age is always adjusting faces. He now looks like his dad, in a way that Jackson doesn't. Something about the eyes.

The gun is so small she doesn't see it immediately. He's holding it close to his chest, not like a gunman in the movies extending it at arm's length. "I said, shut the door."

Anthony eases it closed behind her, but she doesn't hear the click of its being firmly thrust home.

"Sit down on the ground."

"Abraham," Anthony starts to say, but he gets cut off.

"Sit down."

Helplessly, Brooke sinks to her knees. Anthony does the same next to her.

"You're her attorney?"

"No. I'm her . . . we're dating."

Abraham laughs. "You're screwing her. Small world."

"Abraham, you're violating parole but as long as you set the gun down, I won't—"

"It's been a long time you've been moving here and moving there," he says directly to Brooke. "Maybe the best revenge is how scared you've been."

She nods. Nods vigorously, too much, overmuch, like the Lizzie Borden bobblehead in the gift shop.

"I'm a good sleuth. A tracker."

"Your brother doesn't think I did it," she blurts out.

He cocks his head to the side.

"He doesn't think I was strong enough to knock your mom into the water." How awful that sounds. How tritely described. A woman disappeared from her family and her vital life, and Brooke says it as if she simply hip-checked her.

Incredibly, he laughs. "I never thought *you* did it."

"You didn't?"

"No. It was your mom. She wanted my mom's life. She screwed my dad, and she wanted to move right into our house."

"*No*," says Brooke, shocked. "No, no, no, no, no, no."

"Oh, I think so."

"No. That was *not* my mom." She wishes he would put the gun down, because it's hard to think and talk and breathe knowing there's a bullet resting down that narrow black channel. "She might've . . . I think you're right that she slept with your dad. That part is true. But she would've never killed your mom."

"She did. She pushed her in so she could have my dad. But my dad was honorable in the end. He didn't take her."

"No, you have to listen to me. My mom was hugging me the whole time. Maybe I flailed my arm out; I was dizzy. I thought maybe I did, and maybe that I accidentally hit your mom. But my mom was with me all during that . . . the fireworks."

He just looks at her. She almost thinks she sees a door opening in his eyes.

"My mom never went back to work for your family. I don't think she even saw your dad again. How is *that* trying to take your mom's place?"

"She did come by," says Abraham. "The next night."

"No. I was with her. We watched some . . . God, what did we watch? We watched something on TV. She was crying."

"And then she put you to bed and snuck out to our house."

"No. She would've never left me alone."

"I think she did."

"No." She's shaking her head. Her mother was not a negligent mom, the sort to leave a child in bed and go out into the night.

"She came to our house that night, and she and my father talked. And he told her he didn't want her anymore."

"I wish you really knew my mom."

"I did. She was in my house every day for years. She might've spent more time at my house than at your apartment."

"So you know she was a good person."

"Why does a good person screw a happily married man? I've been wanting to do this for so long," he says. "Your mom ruined my life, my brother's life, my dad's life. Even, I think, your life."

She thinks, furiously, quickly, what can she say to him? How can she talk him out of killing her? This is that one last clarified moment where she can reach out to the cocky little boy who was destroyed when his mother died. She pored over all those books, all those years, exactly for this situation. For knowing what to say when the killer's gun has a bead on her forehead.

Or else this is where it ends for her. She and Anthony will be the face-down bodies in the crime-scene photographs, pathetic in their helplessness.

"I think your dad and my mom liked each other," she says, stumbling, appalled at how raw her voice sounds. It's like her throat has been scraped dry with a scalpel.

"He didn't like *her*. He liked her pussy."

If she's going to die, she'll die defending her mother. "My mom was incredibly beautiful, and she had a way about her that men liked. Your mother was a very, very nice woman, and she was nice to me."

"Don't talk about my mother."

"Your dad wanted my mom, and he got her. She would've never seduced her employer. She wasn't like that. The only way they would've wound up together is if he made the first move."

"My dad was a great man."

She's finally able to block out the gun. She looks above it, to Abraham's sad and wild eyes. "Your brother said he was like a foreign exchange student after your mom died. Like he didn't bother to try to talk to you."

"He blamed himself for what your mom did."

"There's something I have to tell you," says Brooke. "That afternoon, I saw my mom coming out of a bedroom with your dad. I was too young to understand what it meant."

The gun continues to stare at her with its one vacant eye.

"When I was in the kitchen with your mom, I think I . . . Well, I said something about it. About them coming downstairs together. So I think I might've . . . " her voice trails off.

"You're the one who told her."

"But without realizing it. Because I was nine."

"*You're the one who told her!*"

"I was just a kid. One year older than your brother." She hears a pleading tone enter her voice and knows she needs to quell it. To earn his respect, to stop him from killing her and Anthony, she needs to be strong and persuasive.

"There's something else about that day that's so important," she says. "What if . . . "

She doesn't dare break eye contact with him although she can feel Anthony rustling next to her. She ignores him.

What she's about to say will either get them both killed or save their skins.

There's no going back.

Her words are her only weapons, and she has to aim them right at the heart of this damaged man.

She takes a deep breath. " . . . What if your mom fell in? She had been drinking so heavily; you remember that. You *remember*. I thought she'd sobered up, but maybe she didn't. Maybe she snuck a few more drinks. And it was so chaotic, so noisy. You put your head back to look at the fireworks, and you get disoriented. I was dizzy. My mom had to hold me up."

Brooke accepts that this night may end with her eating a bullet, but she won't die until Abraham understands.

"I wish more than anything that I could go back in time and stop her from opening that bottle," she adds.

A long silence yawns. Brooke furiously tries to think of something to say, anything, to keep contact between them. She wants desperately to glance at Anthony and get reassurance, but she doesn't dare look away from Abraham's troubled gaze.

"You were with her when she was drinking," says Abraham before she can manage to find any more words. Brooke nods.

"I can't believe she drank in front of you." Casually, as if he's forgotten he's holding a gun, he scratches his forehead. "She was a secret drinker."

"But there was so much wine in the kitchen."

"That was for show. Her real stash, hard stuff, was in the hall closet upstairs."

"So she was already unhappy," says Brooke.

He looks at her for a long moment, and her heart contracts.

Shit. She said the wrong thing! She pushed him over the edge. But before she can stumble with new words, replacement words, his face crumples like a tissue being balled up.

He puts both hands to his face because he's crying.

He kneels down on one knee.

"She loved you so much," she says rapidly, without thinking. "She talked about you in the kitchen. She told me how much fun you were, you and your brother, and how much she—"

"She was unhappy," says Abraham. "She found comfort in a bottle."

"A lot of people do."

"Such a fucking cliché."

"Not a cliché," she says firmly, almost angrily. "Your mom's sadness was legitimate, and if a drink helped her feel better, who can judge her?"

"Our family has a history, you know." He wipes his nose on his sleeve, which makes the gun wheel around. He notices it, and sets it down on the floor next to him. Brooke can't stop herself from gasping.

He set down the gun.

"Insanity, suicide. On my mom's side."

"Do you think she . . . ?"

"I didn't want to think that. I never wanted to. I didn't fucking want to."

He breaks into fresh sobs, and as he covers his face, Brooke silently slides the gun farther away from him, toward Anthony. In her peripheral vision, she sees Anthony pick up the gun and then stand up beside her.

She wishes she could feel jubilation. She did the thing she practiced for. She talked the killer down. She saved her own life. But all she can feel is tears prickling in her eyes.

"It was easier to think it was my mom," she says.

"I fixated on that for years."

Brooke can hear Anthony's phone emitting small electronic sounds: he's dialing. Melancholy floods into her as she realizes he's probably calling the police. Abraham will go back to prison to mourn his mother.

"But . . . you sent *me* the plates," she fumbles. "And you wanted me to die."

"I wanted you to go first," he says in a voice she can barely hear.

"Why?"

He doesn't answer, and her mind races until she finds the answer. He wanted to torture her mother. No parent should ever outlive their child and nothing could have made her mother suffer more than seeing Brooke die.

And he must've felt that that revenge would still be valid even if Magdalena was already dead. *Hurt the mother by hurting the child.*

With that realization, all her sympathy evaporates.

Brooke lived through her mother's murder. She lived through the years of thinking she was going to be next. She unwittingly took it on so her mother didn't have to. A flicker of pride starts in her stomach, and she stands up next to Anthony.

She is the strongest person she knows.

And now she's been set free.

CHAPTER 54

Brooke

FOUR MONTHS LATER, DECEMBER 14, 2016

Brooke orders a decaf mocha, and when she tries to pay for it, Maria shoos her away. "I got this one. You babysat my girl last night; I buy you coffee today."

She notices Jane watching the transaction with great interest. Probably concerned Maria will stiff her on the drink, but Maria, grinning broadly, makes a big production of pulling out her purse. "Go sit down; I'll bring it to you," she says.

Brooke goes to the table where Jackson, Miguel, Angelica, and Anthony are waiting for her.

"About time," says Anthony. He gives her a long, lazy look, and she bends into his kiss.

"No, we're not doing that here," says Jackson. "Break it up."

She eyes him carefully. She'll never fully trust him, but she believes that he's been trying to save her life all these years. He'd broken into her various apartments, tracked her, added himself as a Facebook Friend to watch her from afar, all in the service of keeping a jump ahead of her for the day that Abraham got released from prison.

He could've done it a different way, but that's what he did. He knew Abraham was capable of killing her, had killed her mother. She considered returning to the name Felicita, because she *can,* finally, but she loves the fresh start Brooke gave her. She'll always miss her mother's voice saying Felicita in the four crisp syllables. Maybe someday she can pass the name on to a child, since Maria already used her mother's name. She's teasingly suggested that Jackson return to *his* original name, too.

Miguel and his fiancée Angelica are up visiting for a few days. They've come to Boston for an anime con and are staying with her. The first night, she caught Anthony speaking Spanish with them. He had been hiding his fluency, not wanting to embarrass Brooke about the day Maria and she talked openly about him, but he had grinningly made his confession in rapid-fire Spanish, interspersed with so many avowals of love and admiration that she had to laugh and forgive him.

She's turned to historical fiction and stopped reading true crime. The stories are too ugly, and they're not a representation of most people. The murderers in those stories are deviants, misfits. They aren't the people she's surrounding herself with now.

She and Jackson would never get closure on what happened to Lillian Carr. They'd talked about it a few times. "We don't have footage to run and get a definitive answer," she'd said.

The idea that Mrs. Carr had fallen in seems the most valid. Brooke couldn't believe her mother capable of murder, and if she so fervently wanted to take Mrs. Carr's place, she wouldn't have retreated from Mr. Carr the way she did. Jackson doesn't know anything about what Abraham spoke of, that her mother had come back the night after the accident. Maybe she had, Brooke conceded, but not to usurp Mrs. Carr's place, but to grieve with Mr. Carr.

It's also possible Mrs. Carr, disconsolate and drunk, chose to enter the water herself, brokenhearted by the news that Brooke had carelessly delivered. Brooke has to forgive herself—and her mother—for that.

She's working on a tentative relationship with her father. She'd emailed him through the law firm, and he'd answered the same day. He'd been too ashamed to look for her, and it was his wish come true that she has forgiven him enough to seek him out.

The missing pile of payoff money her father's parents had given her mother: it was applied to the life insurance payments over the years, yes, and the typical costs a growing child requires . . . but she's realized there had been one lump sum payment that had been staring her in the face every night for years as she logged on to her laptop: the trip to Lake Havasu. Maids don't take vacations, but her mother had given her a grand one.

All is well, except for the missing—Magdalena and Lillian, who never got to see their children as adults. It was both horrible and a relief to have her suspicions confirmed, that her mother had been killed intentionally. All because Brooke had cried. All because of goddamn fireworks. She'll always hate the Fourth of July and drink her stomach into rotgut on that one day every year. It'll be how she honors her mother. A fitting tribute for a flawed woman.

Angelica never asked that Brooke and Miguel stop their online chatting, but it's been an organic movement that the chats happen every few days, rather than every day. Instead of feeling bereft, Brooke feels exhilarated that her own life is so flush with things to do with Anthony, with the friends she's made, that she doesn't miss that nightly check-in.

It makes all the difference knowing she's staying. She was able to start driving a wedge into the sometimes-stony edifice of her co-worker, Maria, until she trusted Brooke to babysit Magdalena. She feels incredible kinship with the teen in part because she has her mother's name. And even though Brooke's enrolled at the local community college to think bigger thoughts about her future, she finds that she likes her job, loves chatting with the customers who want a connection along with their coffee. There are a lot of lonely people in the world. She's no longer one of them.

Anthony holds her hand under the table, and she runs her fingers over the warm knuckles. If it doesn't work out with him, she'll be sad, but will recover. She's learned so much, and she could go on to try this again. The real life, the real love, the letting someone in.

It's the ultimate act of bravery, presenting your heart, dense, saturated, vulnerable, to another. Our pasts haunt us, but at some point you must unfasten the locks, wrench the knob, and step the hell outside. Leave the haunted houses to the ghosts.

Bridget

MARCH 16, 1948

The intervening half century hadn't treated Bridget so well. It's like the murders had stolen her breath, too, somehow. One didn't pick up and just carry on after something like that.

Bridget had taken on many jobs since then. She had worked briefly as maid to the keeper at the New Bedford jail, where Miss Lizzie would've been kept if she'd been a man. Soon enough, she left New England, hoping to shake off her reputation as the "murderer's maid" by heading west, into the great blank prairie where a woman could reinvent herself. It was a gamble. She went to the train station and bought a ticket to Chicago, and then stood in front of the frightening bank of destinations on the board, closed her eyes and pointed with her gloved finger.

Why not?

She'd lost touch with Aidan the cart driver in the year awaiting trial, and he'd made no effort to find her. He'd fled just as easily as Lizzie's beau had. No one wanted the stigma of association with that particular crime. He was off somewhere winking at other maids, carrying their trunks for them.

And so the steam train brought her to Montana with much grinding and rocking and smoke clouding that beautiful blue, crossing the prairie with its landscape so vastly different from Allihies, the small settlements, the sod houses stationed in the middle of nowhere like a toy left on the floor when the children run to their dinner.

She'd met and married John Sullivan, a happy circumstance that didn't require her to change her last name. He worked in the smelter and that was fine for her; she was used to air aggrieved by factories. She had continued working as a maid but never again as a live-in. She kept John in her bed and slept securely.

John had died ten years ago, and now she at eighty-two was blind and coming to the end of her life. Their marriage had never brought children.

Should she right a wrong? Should she say what she knew? All the players were dead. She knew from a newspaper report that Miss Lizzie and Miss Emma had both died in 1927. Twenty years ago.

She'd kept away from rumors and gossip, just as she'd promised Mr. Borden. She'd been a fastidious secret keeper. No one could fault her. But now as her life wound to an end, in that blackness that she felt indicated to her that she should insert light, should tell truths, she called for a friend to come visit her.

A deathbed confession is so dramatic. Oh, she hated to stir the pot. She could imagine the headlines! "Murderer's Maid Finally Cleans the Slate." "Lizzie Borden's Maid Confirms the Deed Was Done by the Daughter." "Falsely Acquitted . . . and the Maid Knew All Along."

That last part was agonizing.

Would she be judged for not telling? For accepting a bit of cash to speed her back to Ireland to see her own mother—beloved and appreciated—one last time? For understanding that the murders were complex, that the reasons were tricky, that Lizzie wasn't innocent but that the cruelty in that household would be hard for an outsider to even comprehend? For feeling sympathy for those motherless girls who didn't know to raise themselves, and therefore did so faultily?

A day later, her friend sat on the edge of the bed and squeezed her hand. Both their hands so old now, the skin practically sloughing off the bone, in such a hurry to be gone off the body, to disintegrate, to decompose what had been so long ago put together.

"I'm here, Bridget," her friend had said, and Bridget had smiled to hear that voice. Lovely tones mellowed by time, work, two wars. How long had her friend continued at the labor of water, suds, dirt and dust? Had that endless battle finally completed as she retired to old age and let others fight entropy?

The world can never be scrubbed clean, Bridget learned. It is just a momentary illusion until soil regains footing.

"How I've missed you, Mary Doolan," she said.

"And I you. I'm told you have something to tell me?"

"I did," said Bridget. "But I'm happy to report I'm feeling so much better now. Shaking off the gloom."

"Indeed, my friend, right glad I am to hear that. But would you want to unburden yourself?"

Bridget inhaled, thought of the newspapers and the ink that rubs off on fingers, newsboys on every corner crying the headlines. She wanted to be dead and gone before all that happened.

"You've made a long trip, dear friend, and I regret your trouble in coming."

"'Twas no trouble, 'twas an adventure."

They laugh at the idea of adventures at their age. She knows the journey must've been arduous for Mary.

"I had something to say."

"I thought you did."

"But I find myself unable to say it now."

"It might do you good."

Unbidden, Bridget thinks of Mrs. Borden as clearly as if she stood in front of her and vision had been restored to Bridget's eyes. Deflated and sad as she begged Bridget to stay. Talking of the murders would stir up everything that would've been abhorrent to the woman. It would be like exhuming her, showing the world her brutalized head one more time, undressing her and putting only a bloodied sheet between her and a doctor's eyes.

Bridget couldn't do it to her. Let the guilty make their own penance, she thought. God alone knew how to seal these wounds and comfort the afflicted. It was not her job. Hers had only been to cook and clean.

"I'll tell you another time, Mary."

Author's Note

HERE BE SPOILERS

I never like it when historical novelists take great liberties, and yet I find I've done exactly that. Some part of me feels the story is fair game, because I do (with some reservations) believe in Lizzie Borden's guilt.

If the jurors of 1893 cut her that much slack, it doesn't matter if a twenty-first-century author adjusts and amplifies her story. Lizzie got her "out" while she was alive. In a few pages, you will find a brief summary of the things that persuade me of this.

A few other things to mention:

Baby Alice

There was a sister in between Emma and Lizzie named Alice. She lived for two years before dying of hydrocephalus (water on the brain). Lizzie was born two years after she died, and Emma would have been five when Alice was born, old enough to remember the infant. Emma must've delighted in helping her mother care for the baby, and Alice's death must've been the first brutal lesson for Emma that people we care about can be whisked away—and that their loss leaves very large holes in the souls of those left behind. I chose not to talk about Alice in the novel to omit confusion with Alice Russell, but felt her brief existence was important and should be mentioned.

The children in the well

There is an ancillary story that my editor asked me to remove because it was so upsetting that it distracted from the novel.

Long before Lizzie's family moved to the Second Street house, Lizzie's great-uncle Lawdwick Borden lived next door in what later became the Kelly house (and interestingly, Alice Russell lived there, too, before the Kellys). In 1848, Lawdwick's second wife drowned her baby and her two-year-old in the well in the cellar. She had a four-year-old, too, but apparently she ran and got away. The mother then killed herself with her husband's straight razor. At the time of Lizzie's trial, the surviving child was a mother herself and hopefully much better at it.

It is said that the murdered children haunt the Borden house, rolling marbles and sitting on the bed.

The story is important to the Lizzie Borden narrative because Lizzie surely knew of it, and it's an example of kin killing kin. Equally important, it illustrates that not all those who live under the name "mother" are good to their children.

In the deleted scene, my character Jackson questions why the child ghosts plague the house next door to where they lived and died—and why that particular chamber, the Hosea Knowlton Room. It doesn't make sense for a lot of reasons, including the fact that there *was* no room there at the time of the earlier murders; it was open attic space. The chamber was created specifically as a B&B guestroom.

When I visited the B&B, staying in Bridget Sullivan's room, I was accompanied by an old college friend, brilliant poet Alexandria Peary. She was truly disturbed, even hours later, by the well story. She hadn't heard it until our tour guide told us. I had long ago read about and digested the tale's horrors, so I fared better. I had also undergone mental immunity training by listening to the Violent Femmes' "Country Death Song" many times in the '80s. It is indeed an awful story and can even overshadow the darkness of Andrew and Abby's slaughter.

In 1848 when the children's murders occured, neither Lizzie nor Emma Borden was born yet. Their family took ownership of the Second Street house in 1872.

Murder tourism

When I realized there was a B&B created out of the Borden home, I felt great disdain. I explore this a little in the novel—what makes this sordid and tragic dual-murder house "fun" or a travel destination? I feel similarly about how Jack the Ripper has been glamorized, gaining a sheen of Victorian romance simply by being so firmly in the past. It's as if the murders happened to people who weren't really real. My instincts rebel at murder tourism, and if the elder Bordens still stick around in some guise, they must be tormented that their painful deaths are an object of fascination for strangers.

However, my beloved editor Lisa McGuinness (who suggested the concept of a modern-day narrative for this book) told me I had to go spend the night. Secretly, I wanted to, so this dictate was obeyed. And I'm so glad I went; sense of place is so important, and I'm sure the novel would have exponentially more errors than it does now if I hadn't gone.

Our tour guide, Colleen Johnson, was absolutely respectful of the Bordens and careful not to speak loosely of the facts. It's true that, like her fictional stand-in, she wouldn't discuss her personal views of the case until we stepped outside. Her knowledge was vast, and she took great care in treating the murders as something weighty.

I do have to report that I find some items in the gift shop to be reprehensible.

The incest theory

During the trial, Lizzie's uncle Hiram Harrington said some oblique things about Lizzie's bond with her father. Andrew was also known to wear a ring given to him by Lizzie. I battled with whether to include an incestuous relationship in the novel's historical chapters. If true, it makes a strong and even justifiable motivation for murder. However, I felt responsibility for Andrew's reputation. We simply can't know whether it was true, and if it wasn't, I don't want to be the person who adds insult to injury by associating a murder victim with such a loathsome, unforgiveable act. It is true that there are holes from the door being nailed shut between Lizzie's bedroom and the one occupied by her father and stepmother, and that the bed had been positioned to block it as well.

Pigeons

I substantially changed the pigeon-slaughter tale. The pigeons had been brought into the house, suggesting they were meant to be eaten, and their necks had been wrung by Andrew. A few, however, had their heads separated from their bodies, and Lizzie conjectured that a hatchet had been used on them. The only reason this story arose was when attorneys asked her for an explanation why there might be blood on the hatchet head. She likely wouldn't have even told the story if not asked such a direct question. Her answer is nonsensical: if her father was wringing the birds' necks, why would he also use a hatchet? His hands would be strong enough to strangle any bird . . . and if he had a hatchet at his disposal, why wouldn't he use it on all of them? I'm guessing his gusto in his task led to some heads ripping right off, and the hatchet stayed in its dusty basement box while this task was performed.

Andrew did kill the pigeons but in an era when many men did their own butchering or unceremoniously drowned their barn cat's unwanted litters. He gave the excuse that the neighbor boys had been going into the barn and bothering the birds; he may have been unaware of how much they meant to his daughter.

I chose for purposes of dramatic embellishment to have Andrew use his hatchet on all the pigeons, and for the bloodbath to take place in the barn.

Throughout the novel, there are other such small adjustments made to increase dramatic tension, such as combined characters and invented extensions of real-life situations; Bordenphiles will enjoy locating them. It's a funny thing to struggle to get everything historically accurate and then just decide to guiltlessly bend other details, but that's what I've done. (Here's one: Lizzie prevented Bridget from seeing Mr. Borden's body the morning of the murders). Tweet at me if you want to ask whether certain things really happened or not (@ErikaMailman or #MurderersMaid).

Cat killer

There are numerous stories about Lizzie murdering pet cats, including one report from her own family (Abby's niece, Mrs. Potter) which would tend to imbue some credibility, but

I went with my gut on this one. Killing animals seems to be a hallmark of young serial killers, and I don't believe Lizzie fits that profile. She loved animals and kept beloved dogs, even giving them carved tombstones after their deaths, and financially supported animal rescue organizations, including Fall River's Animal Rescue League in her will's largest bequest ($30,000 in 1927 dollars).

Prussic acid

I went back and forth on whether to include a scene showing Lizzie's attempt to purchase prussic acid. I had always found this to be a persuasive indication of her guilt, until the B&B tour where I first heard that there may have been a police sting with an officer's wife who resembled Lizzie. I'm sure scholars have already dug into police files and studied newspaper reports to see if there was indeed an upsurge in pharmacist arrests in the summer of 1892. I wonder why the sting would still need to be secret by the time of Lizzie's trial a year later . . . wouldn't they have caught everyone they meant to catch? Especially since the stakes were so high—a capital murder case—you would think the police department would let the court know. And perhaps they did, and that's what the quiet conference at the bench was about. I decided to vaguely reference Lizzie having no success in her "errands" and include Bridget's learning about the possible drugstore trip—and worrying about it— from the inquest.

Lizzie's clothing

The contents of that clothes press have been hashed to death. And yet, there's more to be said. Lizzie went dress shopping for several hours while in New Bedford just days before the murders:

looking for enough fabric to drape over an existing garment? Akin to the gossamer's job? If her dressmaker Mrs. Raymond (whom I've conflated with cloakmaker Mrs. Gifford) came each spring to stay for several days and sew dresses, why was Lizzie buying fabric in the summer when she was set for a whole calendar year? Lizzie is said to have dressed impeccably, and a quick glance through the existing photographs of her seems to support that. It may pain her and me to have a scene where a dressmaker brings fabrics to Lizzie that are less than *au courant*.

More to the story

There is so much more about this case that is fascinating: Lizzie's shoplifting habit (even after the murders); her friendship with actress Nance O'Neil; the fact that her sister abruptly left Maplecroft after years living there, and we don't believe they saw each other alive again—what was that fight about? I hope this novel spurred or deepened your interest in this absorbing case; in the following pages you will find a bibliography of books and online sites to continue your exploration.

A final word

If the Bordens can sense my words: I'm sorry for your lot in life. Hopefully you are off somewhere enjoying tranquility in a manner we can't fathom, and the thousands of people who tread your floorboards don't register with you.

Miss Lizzie, if you had nothing to do with these murders, I most sincerely beg your pardon.

REASONS WHY I BELIEVE
LIZZIE BORDEN TO BE GUILTY

In Atul Gawande's book *Complications: A Surgeon's Notes on an Imperfect Science*, he writes, "There is an old saying taught in medical school: if you hear hoofbeats in Texas, think horses not zebras." This case seems like a "hoofbeats" case to me. Lizzie was in the house at the time of the first murder and claimed not to hear anything although it would be impossible not to hear Mrs. Borden hitting the floor. While her father was being killed, she had three different alibis to cover her not being aware of that murder, either.

Lizzie's failure to flee strikes me as the action of someone who knew she was in no danger. She evidenced no fear for her own safety after locating her father's corpse, and rather than running into the streets in terror for her own life, she summoned her servant and then *sent her out of the house.* Why would she request a doctor rather than the police? Why wouldn't Lizzie herself run to Alice Russell's? The fact that she lingered in the house alone, hovering just inside the screen door, means that she didn't believe anyone was still lying in wait in the home.

The burning of the dress paints her as ridiculously guilty (or stupid beyond what could be possible). The day after she learned she was a suspect, she fed the dress to the stove. What was the urgency? Was she making way in the clothes press for another dress to take its hook? Was she just so suddenly *overcome* by the paint splotches she had lived with for months that she couldn't bear for the gown to remain in her life one more day? It is clear to me that she was destroying evidence. An officer testified that when they examined the clothes press on the day of the murders, they did a very hasty search—they were looking for a hidden murderer, not a bloodied dress. Alice saw Lizzie take the dress from the cupboard in the kitchen to burn it; perhaps no one bothered to search the maid's domain, and a kitchen cupboard was a very smart place to hide a stained dress after retrieving it from the clothes press. City Marshall Hilliard himself admitted under oath that he did not search every room in the house, including the clothes press and the giant storeroom part of the attic.

❦ If a purported murderer was trying to obliterate the Bordens, as it would seem with the fact that husband and wife were killed hours apart, why was Lizzie not attacked?

❦ Her story about the note Mrs. Borden had been given to visit a sick friend seems like a quickly manufactured lie to explain why Mrs. Borden's whereabouts were unknown. Lizzie had lived with a cooling corpse for two hours and had to figure out what to do with her. She might've cried alarm when Mr. Borden came to the front door, but instead laughed on the stairs in view of the body. Her saying later, "I don't know but that she is killed, too, for I thought I heard her come in," must've come as a great surprise to all the comforting friends gathered around her, because up to that point she had not mentioned any sort of concern for her stepmother.

❦ If the poison-buying episode can't be dismissed as a police sting, then this possibly more than any of the other reasons above spells guilt to me. Buying poison to clean a fur coat in the middle of a heat wave? Makes zero sense. Experts said at the inquest that they had never heard of prussic acid being used for this purpose. And who is concerned about fur in August? Especially linked with the "food poisoning," it seems Lizzie was experimenting with different methods of killing her relations.

 Finally, read the court transcripts. They are stocked with her lies and sometimes instant contradictions. Some say her being propped up with morphine explains her clouded testimony, but she was also lucid enough to be sharp with her questioner at times.

A BRIEF BIBLIOGRAPHY

Kent, David. *The Lizzie Borden Sourcebook*. Branden Books, 1992.

Lincoln, Victoria. *A Private Disgrace*. Seraphim Press, 2012.

Martins, Michael, and Dennis Binette. *Parallel Lives*. Fall River Historical Society, 2011.

Pearson, Edwin, ed. *Trial of Lizzie Borden*. Notable Trials Library, Gryphon Editions, 1989.

Porter, Edmund H. *Fall River Tragedy, The*. Out of print but available digitally.

Sullivan, Robert. *Goodbye Lizzie Borden*. The Stephen Greene Press, 1990.

Online:

Lizzie Borden Society Forum, www.lizzieandrewborden.com

Tattered Fabric blog, phayemuss.wordpress.com

Warps and Wefts blog, lizziebordenwarpsandwefts.com

ACKNOWLEDGMENTS

First and foremost, thanks are due to my husband and children for living with the person whose face is sometimes vacant because her mind is in 1892 Massachusetts. It was a dark and absorbing place to go, and I'm grateful to you all for letting me sneak away sometimes.

Thanks to Lisa McGuinness, editor and friend extraordinaire, who took Lizzie on and had so many wonderful, key suggestions along the way.

Christa, thank you for considering joining me at Lizzie's house, and I appreciate the fact that your calling me to Goose Rocks Beach for our very, very special time together made the side trip to Fall River possible. Thank you for reading and giving stellar advice and support!

Alexandria Peary, I believe it's a rare friend whom you can see only a handful of times over decades, yet answers your text about spending the night in a murder home with instant enthusiasm. I'm glad you were able to brew coffee by yourself in Bridget's kitchen . . . er, after I joined you.

Colleen Johnson, there could be no better tour guide at the Lizzie Borden Bed & Breakfast. I'm deeply grateful for your fielding my multiple questions after the visit with such kindness and generosity of spirit!

Saskia Charbonneau and Pamela J. Woolley cheerfully helped out with Belgian questions. Beta readers (and fellow authors) Mark Wiederanders, Jennifer Laam, and Becca Lawton gave wonderful feedback.

Thanks to Harry Widdows for transcribing the court transcripts and putting them online as downloadable PDFs. What a gift for researchers.

Thanks to Lee-ann Wilber, the B&B proprietor, for creating a space that permits such deep delving into the case and for answering my questions.

I'm also grateful to bloggers such as Faye Musselman and Shelly Dziedzic and forum posters who have, in some cases, devoted their life's work to ferreting out the truth about this mysterious case. Countless times these incredible sites provided a quick fact-check for me or answered a deeper question. Faye in particular was an incredible resource, sharing generously of her decades of accrued sources and wisdom. Thank you so much—I have enjoyed our interactions.

View of Second Street and Borden home from the *Boston Daily Globe*, August 11, 1892.

Crime scene illustrations from the *Fall River Herald*, August 9, 1892.

Commonwealth of Massachusetts.

Bristol ss. To the Sheriff of the County of Bristol, or his Deputy, or any District Police Officer of the Commonwealth, or any Constable of the City of Fall River, and the Keeper of the Jail in Taunton or New Bedford, in said County, GREETING:

WHEREAS, *Lizzie A. Borden*

L. s. of Fall River, in the County of Bristol, laborer, has this day been brought into the Second District Court of Bristol, in the City of Fall River, in the County of Bristol, by virtue of a Warrant issued against him upon complaint of *Rufus B. Hilliard*

of Fall River, in the County of Bristol, City Marshal _____ he therein upon oath

in and upon one Andrew J. Borden, feloniously, willfully and of her malice aforethought, did make an assault; And that the said Lizzie A. Borden then and there with a certain weapon, to wit, a Hatchet, the said Andrew J. Borden, in and upon the head of the said Andrew J. Borden, then and there feloniously, willfully and of her malice aforethought, did strike, giving unto the said Andrew J. Borden then and there with the Hatchet aforesaid, by the stroke aforesaid, in and upon the head of the said Andrew J. Borden, one mortal wound; of which said mortal wound, the said Andrew J. Borden then and there instantly died.

And so the complainant aforesaid, upon his oath aforesaid, further complains and says that the said Lizzie A. Borden, the said Andrew J. Borden in manner and form aforesaid, then and there feloniously willfully and of her malice aforethought did kill and murder

term of said Superior Court, to which the same may be continued, if not previously surrendered and discharged, and so from term to term, until the final decree, sentence or order of the Court thereon, and shall abide such final sentence, order or decree of the Court and not depart without leave, then this Recognizance shall be void.

With which said order the said _____

now before said Second District Court of Bristol refuses to comply.

You the said Sheriffs, District Police Officer and Constables are therefore hereby required to take the said *Lizzie A. Borden* _____ and her deliver into the custody of the keeper of our said Jail in said County, together with an attested copy of this Warrant. And you, the said keeper, in the name of the Commonwealth aforesaid, are hereby commanded to receive the said *Lizzie A. Borden* _____ into your custody in our said Jail, and her there safely to keep, until he shall comply with said order, or be otherwise discharged in due course of law. Hereof fail not, at your peril.

Lizzie Borden's arrest warrant, 1892.

Dr. Draper fits the axe in the skull of Mr. Borden, from the
Boston Daily Globe, June 21, 1893.

Lizzie Borden challenges a juror, from the *Providence Daily
Journal*, June 6, 1893.

Lizzie Borden circa 1893, after her acquittal.

Look for these other historically intriguing
novels published by

bonhomie 🍐 press

Catarina's Ring

From *New York Times* best-selling author Lisa
McGuinness, *Catarina's Ring* interweaves the story
of Catarina Pensebene, a 19th century Italian woman
who immigrates to the United States as a mail order
bride, and her American granddaughter Juliette Brice.
When Juliette flies to Italy for a cooking class, she
meets a man who may change her life and connect
her to her ancestor.

ISBN: 978-0-9905370-2-1

Dream House

Named by Amazon as one of the Best Books
of 2015. When Gina cleans out her childhood home
after her parent's death, she discovers a collection of
historically significant letters is missing, supporting
a decades-old suspicion that they have been stolen.
Lush with sensory detail and emotional complexity,
Dream House is about family and an architect's
journey to understand the crippling hold one
house has on her.

ISBN: 978-0-9905370-4-5

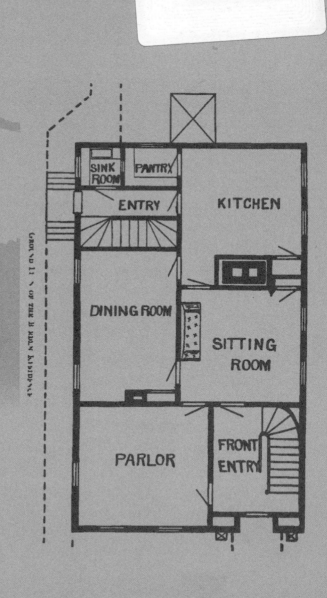

SINK
ROOM

PANTRY

ENTRY

KITCHEN

DINING ROOM

SITTING
ROOM

PARLOR

FRONT
ENTRY